WTL   04/17

This book should be returned/renewed by the
latest date shown above. Overdue items incur
charges which prevent self-service renewals.
Please contact the library.

Wandsworth Libraries
24 hour Renewal Hotline
01159 293388
www.wandsworth.gov.uk

Wandsworth

Paul Stanbridge

FORBIDDEN LINE

GALLEY BEGGAR PRESS

First published in 2016
by Galley Beggar Press Limited
37 Dover Street, Norwich NR2 3LG

Paperback ISBN: 978-1-910296-71-4
Black-cover edition ISBN: 978-1-910296-75-2

Typesetting and text design by Tetragon, London
Printed and bound in Great Britain by Clays Ltd, St Ives plc

In memory of my brother Mark, 1979–2015

PROLOGUE

Varied and numerous are the effects of lightning strike upon the person.

Among the more extraordinary we must include Martin Luther's sudden decision, in rejection of the marriage arranged by his father, to join the Augustinian hermits at an Erfurt monastery following that electrical fulmination, on the second day of July 1505, which threw him to the ground in the woods close to Stotternheim.

(Lightning, it is said, lies at the origin of all life. Lashing primordial rock through volcanic gas, the initial abiogenetic spark, synthesising in one small transgressive leap across the line dividing the inorganic from what-may-be: the possibility of all life on earth. By curious chance, the Indo-European cultures make correct identification as a result: their thunder god the king of all gods.)

Consider then this low hill, on a midnight, beside the dark hulk of the decommissioned water tower, at the heart of an East Anglian town, here: an upward streamer, a pretty capillary of purple fire, reaching up from the head of him. From the swagging belly of the cloud a jagged line of light cast down through the storm, angling this way and that, branching off into lesser channels, zagging over the rain-soaked town, following the path best prepared for it by the ionizing air; this stepped leader choosing at the final moment not the lightning rod of the tower but the streamer – the man – until the two meet in a kiss of opposites, and the great cloud discharges itself deep into the earth through him, and the air around the jagged channel superheated to the temperature of the sun explodes in celebration.

Varied and numerous are the effects of lightning strike upon the person, none perhaps so unusual as the sudden acquisition, by the man struck, of such a power of memory as might be capable of the formation of entire cultures, though he lie as good as dead in the street this night.

I

THEN CAME THE RISING OF THE SUN seeking out the edges of things. Redeeming the town of its nightstorm: the mazy light. The grey dawn stirring into retreat, cat-like withdrawing round the many corners of the town; day-made angles emerging. The town draped over the hill, and the sun building shadows in its streets. The buildings making shape in the clarifying air. The hill and the wet lowland meadow beyond and the river dividing it. The shadows forming, creeping down the buildings; the streets now still, and the river running its course. The streetlights switching off; the windings of the town declaring the day.

There, emerging out of the dawn-grey light, visible for miles around, the shallow apex of the water tower; high within it, two men.

From that morning on, the hermit tends to his unconscious patient. Unwrapping the linen cloth, he cleans and reapplies unguents to the wounds, binds on fresh bandages and boils the old in a great copper kettle. Pale the body he washes as if an alabaster Christ, or the Christ Himself, for he values the life of the patient inordinately. In whispers he tells of what they will achieve, though he has yet to learn his name. Urging his patient on to recovery through three days and nights he administers a light broth to his unmoving lips. Words of his grand orations drift through the large iron chamber in which he makes his home, no less fragmentary than the shards of experience which the patient's unconscious mind places before itself; each of these latter tumbling, turning through free space, as if the ur-matter of an unmade personality; similar, one to another, only in the aimlessness and sourcelessness of their drifting predicament – the lightning strike re-making him.

The third night. The patient wakes into a delirium of smashed memories, of auditory and optical hallucinations. Phantom shocks travel down his limbs to his peripheries, where they fizz and sputter and eventually spend themselves. Like clouds before the sun, memories come and go. At times there is her face and nothing else, the green eyes, beautiful in the way an ocelot's face is beautiful; or else not her, but instead a pale yellow corn field rustling all around him in waves and the sense of love somewhere amorphous inside and waiting to be brought out by some as yet unmet particular. A child and adult at once, he dwells in all times concurrent. He travels through innumerable moments, and feels repeated again and again the great vertiginous rush of being born into himself, a surging up into the present moment, though not yet into consciousness. Delirious moans echo all night from his mouth through the dark space as the hermit his carer works at the desk under lamplight, parsing the great discourses of the West until they collapse, the words falling down soundless as autumn leaves.

It was on the morning of the fourth day that Isaiah Olm came out of his fever. The fear within subsided, and dawn brought gradually a soft grey light into the strange room through the small aperture above his head.

He opened his eyes: an iron chamber, perhaps forty feet in length and breadth, with a spiral stairwell opening up at its centre like a navel. The only light came through the jagged hole in the ceiling close to one of the walls above his head; the walls themselves not so much walls as a ribcage: great sheets of iron, attached with huge domed rivets one to another, and at each junction, every few feet, triangular iron ties running from the ceiling down to the floor. The metal sent reverberations popping and creaking through the broad shallow chamber as it heated gradually in the growing morning. He attempted to move, but could not.

Isaiah closed his eyes and let his head fall back. The beads of sweat standing on his forehead quivered; the wet hair at the nape of his neck he felt vividly cold. Every sense experience was involuted with pain – as if pain was the sole index of livingness.

From some unseen place in the dull far reaches of the cell he heard some-one mutter to himself, the voice familiar though unplaceable. Indistinct words reverberated through the chamber and drained down the stairwell.

Again, Isaiah forced open his eyes. The ancient paint lay thick around every joint and sheet and rivet, or else flaked off in great rusted crusts to reveal the strata of many repeated paintings. A bed of sorts lay rumpled towards the centre of the cell. Deep into his flank – a jab of pain.

Again, mutterings came from the dark side of the room; something fell, and great acoustic disturbance ensued, running round the cell, amplified by the vast metal soundbox he appeared to be in.

Again, Isaiah attempted to move. He managed to turn his head a little as the crashing continued unabated, and look into the gloom. Upon the triangular metal ties which supported the walls of the chamber had been contrived a makeshift system of shelving; this ran all along the walls, some of it an advanced state of collapse, though managing still to bear up an assembly of every imaginable object: vessels of infinite variety as to shape and size; instruments both mechanical and musical; books of every dimension, as well, perhaps, as of every subject; assorted haberdashery, bibelots, trinkets, knick-knacks, bric-a-brac and what-have-you, all of manifest inutility; scraps of broken machinery which thrust teeth and claws into the air as if through the portal of some bestial mausoleum; offcuts of metals, plastics, rubbers, woods, fabrics; canisters of gas and liquid, many leaking, and forming with the substances contained putrefied cumuli of filthy spume; pipes and cables coiled sinuously into precariously nesting mounds of disorder; tools of menacing design and proportion. The light of the morning flowed through the ragged hole in the roof, though could not penetrate to the far reaches of the cell, such were its proportions and the intricate tangle of matter within. Dust coated thickly every surface upwardly aspectant.

There came a shout from the far reaches of the cell, and the commotion finally ended.

A slithering sound, and slow steps towards Isaiah, until:

This figure emerged out of the farther darkness:

Donald J. Waswill.

He carried a pocket knife in one hand and dragged a frayed duffel bag over the ribbed iron floor in the other. A thin old man, still muttering to himself; Isaiah looked him up, and looked him down. Was it a man?

—So you are awake! he said to Isaiah. I wonder if you know my face.

He brought this part of his body close to the eyes of his patient for inspection.

Isaiah answered with a barely perceptible shake of his head. What lines it had upon it! Ancient, and narrow like a knackered old ass's; a long face of the driest paper, or of leather, as to the books and their covers which he lived amongst as hermit. The eyes an extraordinary yellow.

—But your voice, said Isaiah. The sounds——

—It is as the blackbird's, is it not?

Not knowing what to say to this, Isaiah said nothing at all.

—Anyway, said Don. I will introduce myself to you. I am Don Waswill. And before I even know your name, I can tell what you are thinking: you are thinking that there is no possibility that this bag is big enough to hold all that we need to carry.

He held the shabby duffel bag up for inspection. Isaiah lay there immobile, hearing every word this man said play back in his mind in a scrambled mass of repetitions. What had happened? Can a mind become so disorganised as to disengage from time? Concentrating with effort, he wondered which was the judicious and which the injudicious word of reply. In the end, he said simply his name.

—But people call me Is. Where am I?

—Ha! replied Don, and, throwing the duffel bag on to the floor, he sat on a low stool beside Is's makeshift bed and began cleaning the blade of his pocketknife.

Is listened as the old man's exclamation echoed in the interior of his listening mind. Time was all rucked up, grit in the gears, something very wrong. For a distraction he looked around the room again. Where *was* he? What kind of a place had such walls, floor, ceiling. It was the belly of an iron whale! He turned back to this Don, who cleaned and sharpened and cleaned again his pocket knife with whetstone, oil and rag, smiling or frowning at the inward weather of his thoughts. A reposeful silence filled the room, save for the occasional clang of the expanding iron and the faint hush of passing traffic which found its way over the Roman wall of the town, up through the gently rustling trees, and into the hole high in the roof, full of sibilants like the push and drag of a distant sea over shingle.

—You kept calling out *Ruth* last night, said Don. What is Ruth?

At the mention of her name, the habitual bright openness of Is's face turned in upon itself, shrank back, fled like a frighted mollusc, and then ingloriously expired, as if in a cloud of its own ink. O sorrow.

Don wiped a streak of black oil on to his rag and tested the edge of his knife with a thumb.

—What is Ruth? he repeated.

A great sigh emanated from his patient's mouth as the question echoed through the crystalline chambers of his now-vivid memory. O time.

—She is – was – my wife.

—Ah, said Don.

—She kicked me out.

—When? asked Don, hastily adding afterwards: (Not that the past has any reality to it).

—The day I——

He faultered.

——the last day I remember. The day of the storm. She says I'm not a man.

—Ha! said Don again, this time with genuine joy. Ruth, or perhaps Ruthless.

—She is both.

—Well, you needn't worry about any of that any more, said Don, inspecting the curve of his knife's blade first one way then the other against the silhouetting light of the improvised window above.

—But what about my children? If I become a man, perhaps she will take me back.

Don gave late echo to the earlier sigh of his patient.

—I am ill-equipped to advise you on the subject of women. Rumour has it that the touch of a woman is akin to the chrism, though I have long been an heretic of love both conjugal and passionate, as will my excommunication here to this solitude you find me in attest.

Don cast his eyes about the lowly den as if in confirmation of his words – words which piled up in the convalescent's mind like pebbles hushed up against the shore by a gentle wave. There was most certainly something gone wrong in his brain.

—I wonder, Don continued with mischief in his eyes, how it is that you plan on becoming more of a man. You would need to know what constituted a man in the first place.

Isaiah shrugged with only the muscles of his face.

—Aren't there an infinite number of ways of obliging her? You could be indolent, hateful, cowardly, spiteful, warring, drunk. Where is the model for a man in this day? In any day? Isn't the whole history of man suffering from a surfeit of, well, *men*. But don't talk to me of history, that disgusting imposter. Perhaps Wife Ruthless meant that you should be *less* of a man, and thereby more of a *mensch*.

—I've never really known what she meant about anything, said Is.

—Such is the nature of words, said Don, as well as of marriage. But not for much longer! Fame beckons! And there will be time enough to discover how to be less or more of a man, whichever way your fancy takes you, for we shall be some weeks at our task (not that weeks have any real existence). We must prepare ourselves!

—Prepare?

—For our adventuring!

Is looked at the man before him in perplexity, who had risen and picked up the duffel bag again.

—I want to go home, said Is, and he struggled and failed to move.

Don looked imperiously down at his patient.

—You have nowhere to go, no time to be there, and, owing to your injuries, no means of transit. You should cease struggling, for it will benefit you naught, unless you enjoy pain.

—I want to go home, said Is again, and he struggled and failed again.

—You have no home, said Don in a violent outburst, dropping the heavy whetstone which he had used as an instrument of gesticulative emphasis on to the iron floor and causing a thunderous boom to travel round the chamber. Is stopped immediately: the admonitory words travelled also round the chamber of his mind. When would this distortion to time clear?

—Your place is at my side, adventuring with me, to the salvation of Being! said Don. It is decided that you will attend me, and be my servant, unto our very great glory. The lightning has proclaimed it!

Is looked into the striated face of his host – which peered aloofly down upon him, suffused, as it seemed, with some obscure notion of its possessor's unique grace – and began crying. Don again dropped the duffel bag and leapt to Is's side.

—What in the name of St. Isidore of Seville is happening to your eyes! he said. They are melting!

—You are mad, said Is, whose tears flowed unabated.

—I will appear mad to you, and so I will be accounted by everyone else from the point of view of the rat-hole of our civilization, an insult to rats as it happens. But I am not the one with the melty eyes!

As Don fussed about him, Is allowed the tears to flow down his cheeks; and in fact even if he had wanted to, he could not have stopped them, so complete was his grief, and so completely was he unable to move. Don settled beside the man he would call his friend, reached out to the rivulet upon his cheek, and touched it. A droplet formed upon the tip of his finger; he tasted.

—Salt!

—Please tell me where I am, said Is in a voice so plaintive that Don took pity on him, though not without the following preamble, as necessary as it is informative.

—Neither duration of Time nor extension in Space have any real existence, and so your question is nonsensical. But as you were not to know that, and as there is salt coming out of your eyes, and as you are an injured thing, I will formulate a reply according to common parlance: you are in the tank of a water tower.

Is's tears ceased.

—Jumbo? he said.

—If by Jumbo you mean Colchester's decommissioned water tower, then that is precisely where most people would take you to be (though I can only reiterate that they would be in error, for the reasons outlined earlier).

Is stared up at the iron ribs of the room without listening to Don. Jumbo! He was actually within its tank! The building he had looked at across the town of his birth every day; every day witnessing the shallow apex of its coppergreen roof atop the red brick arches – a lovely meeting of colours – appearing to move about the town as he made passage through it, as if a ship moving across an expanse of sea, nearer, then farther, then nearer again, continually rotating its planes into new orders; but no, not a ship, more of a harbour, for this, the water tower, was the image that intoned home to his sentimental heart.

—Jumbo, he said again.

—It is not a bad place to make one's home, said Don.

Indeed it was not. Is felt calmed by the notion that he was up in the sky above the town inside Jumbo; the pain that resided in every joint of his body lessened a little.

—Have your eyes stopped melting now? said Don.

Is nodded.

—Then I hope you don't mind if we discuss what needs discussing: packing.

Once more he reached down and picked up the enormous duffel bag.

—Packing? said Is.

—Packing for our adventure. Even though there is no such thing as the future, it pays to be prepared. And as my servant, you will feel the want of the necessary equipment more than me.

—Servant?

—Yes, servant. But protest not; I saved your life. And you'll be ten times the man that even Aristotle was when we've achieved our aim, and Wife Ruthless will curl up on your lap like a cat.

Is made visible articulation of scepticism through the use of the muscles of his face.

—You are welcome to go grovelling back to Wife Ruthless in your current state, said Don. Though even if she takes pity on you she'll undoubtedly spurn you before the next time the moon comes laughing round to you for having pleaded pity in the first place. Serve me, attain fame, and then you should have the pick of all the Ruths of the world.

Again the weight of that word hit Is deep in the chest. The line of his thought was beleaguered with images, words, textures, colours. Ah, Ruth. Worse by far than the pain at his side, whichever chemical it is which confers sorrow to the human heart again spurted deep into his tender interior.

—How much more or less of a man do I need to be? said Is.

—I cannot know. It is only upon concluding our adventuring that all things shall become knowable in the twinkling of an eye. Understand this: if you serve me, you will be ameliorated, and thereby cease to be the abortive specimen of mankind which you – along with everyone else – currently are. Wife Ruthless will witness your transformation, and she would be a fool indeed not to turn to you as if you were the sun.

—But Ruth hates the sun.

—And she a sunflower, Isaiah! Did not the inward folds of my rhetoric imply the heliotrope? Good Christ, it seems everything must be spelled out to you.

—Spelling wouldn't help; I can't read.

Don looked deep into Is's eyes.

—You, he said, are a miracle of perfect ignorance. It is this which makes you indispensable; the lightning chose well. Now say you will attend and serve me – the busy bee has no time for sorrow.

Is looked back into the yellow eyes of the peculiar man before him. It was true that he had no home – the echo from the door she had slammed ran down the street like a thunderclap. Faces appeared in the windows of the terrace to observe him in his shame. Love was, love was – no different to this physical suffering, except in its exquisiteness.

—I will do it, he said.

The yellow eyes flashed with pleasure.

—But why me? said Is.

His newly acquired master stood up and began moving about the chamber, gathering items from its recesses and throwing them into the duffel bag he dragged behind him.

—Tell me why it has to be me? repeated Is.

Don continued to move about the room.

—Tell me!

Don stopped fussing at his desk, leaned heavily on it with both hands, and turned.

—I cannot tell you.

A blank look on the servant's face. I cannot tell you. I cannot tell you. I cannot tell you. These repetitions were a nuisance, that was for certain.

—Why not?

Don scratched the grey whiskers of one gaunt jowl.

—This is no good at all, he muttered to himself. I cannot keep breaking my oath.

—What oath? asked Is. Or I won't come.

Silence filled the iron chamber as Don engaged in internal contention. He turned back to his desk and the shelves above it where thirteen large books of identical proportion and design stood in a line. He raised a hand and let it travel down their spines.

—You are a devious one, Isaiah. Know that this is the very final time I will break my oath: the solemn covenant between myself and my blessed Science, and the compact between my bride Time and I that forevermore I foreswear the notion that past and future have any reality. But before I go on and tell you this I wish to establish a covenant or compact between ourselves that you will serve me unto the ends of the earth.

—Okay, said Is.

Don looked at the wall for a time and mumbled sceptically to himself. Eventually, he relented.

—For many, many years, he began, I have lived and worked in the tank of this water tower at a single enterprise, and have sustained myself with rainwater and by catching the birds of the air for my food with snares. In just two weeks more I shall have been working on my *Encyclopaedia* for precisely Twenty-One years, which concludes its period of writing, this being the hallowed number at the very heart of my project. The book, when completed, will furnish the reader with the necessary knowledge to reject all falsity and live in truth. I will then put into action its teachings to the end that all Being shall be redeemed!

—It is absolutely true, continued Don, that there is no such thing as the past or the future, and that the myth of Cause and Effect which underlies all human reasoning, discourse and science is the greatest delusion in the history of the universe (though it is equally true that history cannot and does not have any real existence). Humanity has enslaved himself within the furrow of his reasoning, and now finds himself squeezed and squeezed by these self-imposed limits, though he enjoys being thus swaddled, for it makes him feel safe, and he calls it by the name Progress. By contrast, the true nature of the interaction of all entities in the universe is founded upon Chance. There is no preceding and proceeding; there is no chain, golden or otherwise. O Chance, thou very great Thing! And so at the conclusion of the writing of my great *Encyclopaedia*, whose progress has been mediated by Chance over a period of Twenty-One years of unerring work, we shall depart, and Chance shall attend us like some tutelary spirit, directing us to the means by which all Being may be redeemed!

Is looked with weary-eyed perplexity at Don following the completion of this speech.

—Now here's where you come in, Don continued. By long meditation I have trained the mechanics of my eye and the chemistry of my visual cortex to process the percepts it gathers from the phenomena of the world at a speed far in excess of the capability of the starling or house-fly. This capability allowed me to witness from the walkway at the top of this water tower the number of times a cloud passed its electrical contents through you to the earth.

—Lightning! said Is.

—Know that a single bolt of lightning is the visible manifestation of numerous electrical discharges, and that you were struck not twice, but twice Twenty-One times.

—Twenty-one?

—Isaiah, I would ask that you refer to the hallowed number as Twenty-One rather than twenty-one in future.

—Yes.

—And call me sir. It is fitting.

—Okay. Why Twenty-One, sir?

—Because it is the length in centimetres of the spectral line of the hyperfine transition of hydrogen, of course! It is an irrefutable fact that the number Twenty-One is in some way the key to the restitution of all Being. You were struck by lightning twice Twenty-One times, though this enormous water tower with solid copper lightning conductor running its full length, from the pachydermous wind vane at its tip, deep down into the water table below, stood beside you. What are the chances of that happening? But Chance it was that chose you for me! In addition to this, I have become aware in but a few brief interlocutions with you that your ignorance is so entire that you are as similar as an adult of our time can be to mankind before he invented the means of constructing his infernal written record, and thereby that abortive offspring History.

Now, as I already mentioned, it will be precisely Twenty-One years since I first realised the significance of the hyperfine transition of hydrogen for the restitution of Being in fifteen days (not that I believe that days have any real existence; 'day' being merely a convenient way of referring to one rotation of the earth upon its axis – which, itself, is in actual fact an impossibility, owing to the non-existence of numerous non-entities to which the common mind bows its too-malleable credence). And so, in short, fifteen days time is when we shall depart. Until then, you should rest while I continue working, and we'll be primed and prepared when the 'day' comes.

—Will I be okay then, sir?

—You will mend, said Don. There is some severe burning to your wrist where the lightning vaporized your watch – witness the dangers of a belief in the reality of linear time! – and a nasty hole in your side. But I have been administering an unguent of pork fat, thornapple, elder and primrose twice daily to your burns. Soon you will be healed. And very soon afterwards, you will have the very great honour of carrying the work itself, my *Encyclopaedia of Being, Synthesised in Accordance with the Eternal Verities Delineated by the Spectral Line of the Hyperfine Transition of Hydrogen*.

Here, Don gestured in a proud sweep before his bookshelf at the thirteen large volumes arranged there.

—Yours?

—That's right. These thirteen books began their existence as the 1928–33 edition, with Supplement, of the *New English Dictionary on Historical Principles*, a most pernicious work in its definitions, though it be a valuable storehouse of historical forms. As everything which is wrong with the world can be reduced to what is wrong with *words*, I have taken the 440,000 words within these volumes and merely corrected each entry with an encyclopaedic account based on the eternal lesson offered by the hyperfine transition of hydrogen. In short, my work is written tinily in the margins of these books. You should guard them well when you are their custodian.

All of a sudden the whole iron chamber became filled with the impossibly loud sound of a ringing bell. It clanged in a panic, and then settled into a gentle peal; a faint whooping sound came from without.

—Ha! said Don, and he went from his desk over to the wall beyond, where he stilled the bell – pulling slack the cord threaded through its cannons – and then drew it down, to the end that as if by magic there was delivered through a pipe in the roof tethered by its foot a fat and healthy wood pigeon. Its wings woofed hollowly at the air, stilled, and then woofed again in quick grey thrusts with the panic of the bird.

—Luncheon! said Don.

And the word rang through Is's mind to infinite iteration.

2

Over the next two weeks, these men talked on any and every subject which happened upon them in the room. Is regained his health, and was soon able to stand, and walk, both necessary attributes in a servant. He also attempted to bring up the issue of his memory, that he seemed following the lightning strike to be able to remember – moreover, unable to forget – any words which issued from his master's mouth. But no sooner did he begin than his master gave him such a wild look, and muttered such vigorous oaths against the idea of memory, that he soon gave up. Almost just as soon, Is became used to the tail of repetitions which followed every speech his master gave into his ear. At night he retrieved them, rolled them over, looked at the strangenesses they held, like those rare stones whose edges appear inobdurate, as if flesh, which on certain days when the air is clear and bright seem to emit a light which reason says they cannot contain.

The days – which really do exist – passed by, tracked by the oblong of illumination cast by the sun through the open window hatch in the roof, which travelled in a broad arc down one wall in the morning, gradually across the floor, altering its proportions as it went, the angles scissoring, and then up the opposite wall in the evening, where it matured into a red-gold and expired into night. Don, when he was not writing his masterwork, occupied himself in constructing a chest to contain and protect it. Very soon there arrived the appropriate day for their departure, and although the *Encyclopaedia* was not yet finished, Don believed that the time was auspicious, and that the hyperfine transition of hydrogen was directing him to conclude his work on the road, so to speak.

—When I first saved your life, said Don to Is, and you were moaning wretchedly about Wife Ruthless in your delirium, I manufactured you a suit of rabbit pelts, shoes of the same, and a hat of hazel twigs over which I contrived to stretch the bladder of a pig as an asylum from rain. All were strictly measured to fit your corporeal lineaments. I have kept this a secret because I have heard that it is characteristic of humans to delight in surprises. Anyway, I now reveal your tunic to you – how do you like it?

Don held up the coarse assemblage of dead animal pelts.

—Needlework was not something you thought to teach yourself over the past Twenty-One years then, sir.

—The autodidact, said Don, gesticulating grandly through the hot air of the iron chamber at his collection of books and the rag-bag of objects, is swept along by the twin streams of his enthusiasm and the scope of the materials available to him. It is not such a bad attempt. But cease doubting, good squire; the moment has come to dress you in your lapine habiliment!

—Here, he said, handing Is the pelts.

—Why do I have to wear a bunch of dead rabbits? What's wrong with my clothes, or just clothes in general? You're wearing normal clothes – or they look like they used to be normal clothes – so why can't I?

Don's clothes, it was true, consisted of a pair of suit trousers, a shirt, and some shoes. But they were so old and worn and dirty that it was difficult to see how a human form could even have climbed into them. Stains besmirched his shirtfront like mosses upon a rock. When he raised his arms, great tide marks of salts and minerals became visible about the pits of his arms, lightening in rings to the centre, like the crust around a hydrothermal vent. The true and original hue of the garment was impossible to discern with even the least accuracy.

—When a friend or family member marries, said Don, do you not dress according to convention in your suit and shirt and tie? Well, you are attending a marriage here – or you will be at the conclusion of our adventuring – and so it is only right to be dressed properly. The aisle that leads to the altar of Being is a long one! I have for myself a wonderful smock of badger and roe deer, and further garnishings befitting a bridegroom, which I will require your help in dressing in.

—But I thought you said you didn't meddle with women.

—Indeed I do not. My bride shall be Time herself, eldest and most beautiful daughter of Being.

—That's the stupidest thing I've ever heard, said Is. You can't marry time, it's not a thing like a person. And even if you could, she'd be sure to run off.

—You had better watch the words you allow to tumble out of that mouth of yours, said Don. Or I might find myself obliged to kick it off your face with my boot.

—You mean your badgerish slipper, said Is eyeing the footwear Don held in his hand.

—Be quiet Isaiah, and put the rabbits on.

Is pulled the garment over his head, and settled fussily into it.

—It's actually quite comfortable, he said in surprise. Maybe a little bit tickly. Have you got a mirror?

—One might say that a true mirror is precisely that which I seek to lift up before the world, in order to shame it into re-beginning. There is one leaning against the philology section.

Is padded across the room, and not knowing what philology is, rather identified this part of Don's library by the presence of the mirror than the other way round. Peculiar it was to see that face again – one's face never as familiar as it should be, when one really looks at it. But the rabbit suit – it was not so bad.

Very soon, Don joined his servant, standing at his side before the mirror in his own suit of deceased mammals. They cast their eyes over themselves and one another with wonder and delight.

—I believe we are ready! said Don with ample excitement. Excepting one final revelation.

He scuttled off into the debris of a dark corner of the water tank and very soon afterwards re-emerged with a bashful smile of pride on his face and a home-made chest in his arms.

—It is a noble receptacle, is it not? he said as he placed it with difficulty back on the floor before his servant.

Is looked down at the coarsely assembled assortment of sticks.

—It looks more like a bonfire waiting to be lit than a piece of furniture, he said.

—You can have no conception of what constitutes beauty and proportion as it pertains to the science of furniture design then, said Don. Because this chest is most certainly an aesthetic success. And I am glad that I decided to build it in oak – a tree whose multiple significances include reference to Zeus, the god of lightning – because the bearing of it upon your back will be a double piece of penitence for scorning its appearance, for it is by no means a featherweight. You may thank me.

—Thank you, sir. But if I am carrying the chest and your books, what are you carrying?

—Though it be less visible, the size and weight of the work my mind is engaged upon dwarfs that which it has produced over the past Twenty-One years, and which will form your physical burden. Diligently apportioned labour shall redound to our fame as it perforce enables our successful adventuring.

And to this, Is could muster no reply.

The servant loaded the chest with his master's *Encyclopaedia of Being* and sundry other reference works, and hauled it down the one-hundred-and-fifty-seven spiralled steps of the water tower. Full of hope and anticipation, or so we might presume from their countenances, our heroic pair set off into the morning, which lay before them over the fields of Essex as gloriously as a morning could for such a day of adventuring. And we would be remiss indeed not to follow them – *read on!*

Barely had they left the shadow of the formidable structure of the quadrapedal water tower than Is, already drenched in sweat, dropped the chest he carried down on to the ground and refused to move another step without taking a rest.

—As you please, good servant, said Don. Your respite from the burden of my *opera* will serve as a parenthetical gap in the day within which I can ponder the greatness of our task, and savour the sweet taste of its coming success. However, the Roman wall which we have not quite yet reached serves as a very great reminder of the obstacles which lie ahead.

—I don't see any roaming wall, sir, said Is. And the very idea of it doesn't sit well with me.

—You have not before noticed the dilapidated old ring of brick and flint which encloses the town you call home, then?

—Is that what it is, a wall?

—I might wonder what else you thought it could be.

—Well, I hadn't really thought about it at all. To me, it's always been a kind of great fossilized serpent that got stuck in the ground by his coils. Is it made by men then?

—It is, a plague on them! The Romans are the first stage by which the truth has been gradually obfuscated from the interior of our nation's mind. All writing, as far as England is concerned, originates in them.

—And that's a bad thing?

—It is the worst, lying at the source of all History. Before the Romans came here and enslaved the nation, this town was the great Camulodunon, foremost Iron Age town of England. (And note well the imaginative inadequacies of the Romans, whose Latinization of the town's name could only bear to alter three letters – to Camulodonum). The great Trinovantes tribe of Britons, speaking in their pure Prettanike tongue, ruled here, until the Romans deceived them and took their land, invading with artillery and elephants – none so beauteous as our good water tower, of course. Anyway, before the Romans there was no writing, and no history. A Golden Age of Albion! But why am I telling you this? Your value to me resides in your ignorance of such sophistries as history.

Concluding this oration, Don paused for a time, closing his eyes and feeling with pleasure the sunshine alight upon his grey and haggard face.

—I tell you what, faithful Isaiah, he continued. I think we'd better get a list together of all the words in the English language which find their origin (not that I believe in origins) in pre-Roman Celtic languages. This will enable us to converse with the populace in their lost tongue, and perhaps bring out some ancient unremembered character, which will serve as the first battle won in our long campaign. But Skeat! I will need my Skeat!

—What is your Skeat? said Is.

—It is a he: the author of the noble work *An Etymological Dictionary of the English Language*. We must return to the tower and retrieve this fine work.

—You'd better be joking, sir, because there's no way I'm carrying this bloody great chest up those steps again.

—Very well, sit on the chest and guard it, and I'll go and get my Skeat.

—Hang on a minute, how big is this Skeat character? I mean weight-wise.

—Middling. You won't notice him – it will be as if my great *Encyclopaedia of Being* had just had its lunch.

—And I'll bet that book of yours will keep eating and eating and never shitting and I'll be carrying a whole building of books unless we get out of range of that tower of yours.

—You mean a library, said Don. That is what a building full of books is called, so damn them. Wait here!

—I will, said Is. But bring down my boots too – these slippers are no good for manual labour.

Don reluctantly nodded assent, and turned, and Is watched his rickety gait carry him quickly across the vacant car park. He passed like an old greyhound between the bent bars of the railings, through the tall straggly weeds, and through the doorway of his old home. Sooner than Is's gently wandering mind could do much more than notice a big tree which stood nearby, Don was back, carrying an old book and his servant's boots.

—Right, Isaiah, said Don throwing the boots into his servant's lap and holding the book aloft. Let's take this, and get one of my lovely new notebooks out of the chest, and then we can start reading and writing.

—You're going to have to do both those things alone, sir, said Is, owing to my not being able to either read or write. I'll lift the lid, but if I could just put my arsebones back on it when it's shut again, that would be ideal.

—Do what you like, Isaiah. But here we go.

Over the course of the next several hours, while Is perfected the tying of his old worn-out boots, picked his nose, dreamed sorrowful dreams of his lost home, and generally let the time pass, Don flicked his way through the whole of the Reverend Walter W. Skeat's *An Etymological Dictionary of the English Language* and noted in his notebook in an appropriately small and spindly hand: 'List of those words of the English language with Celtic roots (not that the author believes in roots)', underlining it with a flourish (and those readers who dislike lists might as well pass on to the following page).

LIST OF THOSE WORDS OF THE
ENGLISH LANGUAGE WITH CELTIC ROOTS
(NOT THAT THE AUTHOR BELIEVES IN ROOTS)

Babe (infant), bald, bannock (a flat cake), bard, basket, bat (a short cudgel, not the flying mammal), bicker, block (of wood, etc.), boast (*v.* and *n.*), bodkin, bog (piece of soft ground), boisterous, bother, bot(t)s (small worms found in the intestines of horses), brag, bran, branks, brat, brawl, brill, brock (badger), brogues, broil, buck (to wash linen), bug/bugbear/bugaboo (terrifying spectre), bump, cabin, cairn, cart, char (a kind of fish rather than burned wood), cob (round lump, and 'to beat'), cobble, coble (small fishing boat), cock (not the male bird, but 'to stick up abruptly'), cockle, cog (a tooth on the rim of a wheel, and 'to trick, delude'), coil (noise, bustle, confusion), combe (hollow in a hillside), coot, cradle, crag, crock, cudgel, culdee (one of a monkish fraternity), curd, cut, dagger, dandruff, darn, dirk (poniard or dagger), down (hill), drab (a sluttish woman), drudge, druid, dudgeon (resentment), dun, dune, earnest (a pledge or security), frampold (quarrelsome), gavelkind (a type of tenure), glen, glib (a lock of hair), gown, griddle, grounds (dregs), gull (the bird and a dupe), gyves (fetters), hassock, hog, jag (a ragged protuberance), jog (to push slightly), kex (hemlock, a hollow stem), kibe (a chilblain), kick, knack (dexterity, trick), knag (a knot in wood), knick-knack, knob, knock, knuckle, lad, lag, lass, loop, lubber (clumsy fellow), mattock, merry, mirth, mug, nap (of cloth), nape, noggin (small cup), nook, pack, pall, pang, pat (a small lump of butter), peak, pert (forward, saucy), pet, pick, piggin (small wooden vessel), pike, pillion, pink (the colour, as well as to prick or stab), pitch, plod, poke (a bag or pouch, and to push), pollock, pony, pool, posset, pot, potch (to thrust or poke), pother (bustle, confusion), potter, pour, pout, pretty, prong, prop, puck (goblin, sprite), pucker, puddle, pug, put, quaff, quibble, quip, quirk (a quick turn, a subtle question), racket (of noise), riband, rub, shamrock, shoo, skein, skip, slab (viscous, slimy), slough (a hollow place filled with mud), snag, spate (flood), spree (a merry frolic), stab, tache (fastening), tack (a small nail), tether, twig (to understand), welt (narrow strip of leather round a shoe), wheal (a mine), whikt (gorse).

When Don had concluded these notes, he closed both books, urged Is up off the lid of the chest, and placed them where they were safe in its interior.

—Well Isaiah, I think you'll agree that just that short muster of lovely words tells us in an instant that the language of this land was infinitely superior two thousand years ago. Though it does seem that they were not at all fond of their children, and were in the habit of showing off. Also, it must have rained a lot, for there was a great deal of mud in amongst that collection of words. Anyway, this is all undoubtedly valuable data for my *Encyclopaedia*.

—I'm not sure this encyclopaedia of yours——

—Please refer to it in future as my *Encyclopaedia*, said Don. It may not have been published, but since when has publication conferred undisputed value upon a work?

—I'll do as you say, sir. But let me finish: this *Encyclopaedia* of yours, as I was saying – does it all make as little sense as what you've just written? I'm asking because, if a 'pat' is a small lump of butter, and 'butter' isn't Celtic – it not being on the list at all, unless I dozed off – then how did these Celtic fellows make something that wasn't there, small? Surely not being there is as small as it gets? And I'd find it difficult to believe that anyone can make something out of nothing?

—You incomparable idiot, Isaiah. The word 'butter' has its roots in Old English *butere*, corresponding with Old Frisian and Old Hungarian *butera* and West Germanic and Latin *butyrum*. This does not mean that the Celts did not have butter, merely that the Latinate word 'butter' conquered the Celtic word for the fatty substance obtained from cream by churning, just as did the Romans conquer the Celts, and the Saxons move in afterwards, and so on, unto this ragged pile of cultural waste we find ourselves inhabiting now. O lost truth!

Here Don paused in order to become miserable; this having been achieved, he continued:

—Know Isaiah that a true, pure, and meaningful language – which is precisely what I am in the process of procuring for the world – would be made up not of words, but *word*. Language as it is, is a debased thing, full of holes, gaps, discontinuities – and this syntactic predicament creates the impression that time exists, which is of course a preposterous notion. A redeemed language – *the* redeemed language – shall be a single word, without grammar, without syntax, without morphology, without etymology, without lexical category, without even *letters*. Prepare yourself for that great day, for it is coming!

—But how will we speak? said Is.

—We won't, said Don.

—That's even stupider than your idea of marrying Time, said Is. Talking is the very best thing in the world.

Just then a young woman approached, raising her hand in a gesture which indicated that she sought assistance.

—Ah, said Don. Our first damsel in distress — such is the nature of adventuring. Get those Prettanike words ready on the back of your tongue and we'll see what we can do with this lady as to the ruins of history.

As the woman drew near, the expression on her face changed in reaction to the animal pelts our two heroes were wearing, but moreso the spavined visage of our indomitable hero, Mr Don Waswill, adventurer. Yet she had made clear that these were the people she sought assistance from, and the rules of etiquette demanded that she complete what she had begun.

—How do I get to the Hippodrome?

—As a venue deriving its name from the Greek equestrian course, said Don, I have little to say of it, for this land goes relatively unscathed under the arms of our fellow island dwellers the Greeks. You are an inhabitant of this fair town, young lady?

—Of course not you silly-balls, or else I wouldn't ask where the Hippodrome is would I.

—That's as good a point as any, said Is.

—Where do you dwell then, madam?

—Jaywick. What about it?

—The pleasant little holidaying settlement Jaywick!

The woman laughed.

—It's a shithole more like, she said.

—Isaiah, bear witness to what response shall be elicited by my using solely the words just recently written in my notebook on this woman. If I am not mistaken, her Trinovantian roots will be coaxed out of her, and we shall see a true woman of Essex!

Don proceeded to spout such a load of nonsense at this woman, and in a form so similar to the list he had just written, that even a firm commitment by the narrative to render in true detail an account of the utmost verisimilitudinousness as regards our two brave adventurers is insufficient to warrant tainting its unfolding with such an inclusion.

Needless to say, the woman did not find the discourse enlightening, and saying 'prick' as she turned, she walked off in search of someone who was willing to tell her how to find the Hippodrome. Don was left looking frantically through his copy of Skeat wondering if 'prick' was the one word he had missed, only to find that there was no entry for it (the closest being 'prig', from an Indo-European root, meaning 'to steal') and so he was plunged into despair, not knowing at all what the kindly Trinovantian had meant.

—Our adventuring is but a few hours old, and already we discover a hole in our data. O Skeat! O wretched day!

—Cheer up, sir. Let's not worry about things we can't fix. Your old lady Chance wouldn't like it one bit – there being not a woman in the world as to tolerate a moaner.

—You're right Isaiah, said Don after a brief internal struggle. Although I am as repelled by the idea of taking advice from the writers of the past (not that the past exists) as a snail's eye is by the touch, I am more human than I am not. I have read that a walk may function as an unparalleled restorative (not that I believe in parallelism). The best thing for us to do, therefore, would be to keep walking. Our despair shall thereby be lifted. Let's keep on!

Is, protesting that he felt no despair at all, raised the chest on to his back again anyway; and, having only managed to travel some eighty feet from the water tower in the preceding three hours, our two heroes made a pact one with the other to keep going until they had at least left the environs of the town. So they wandered slowly on, through the afternoon, through the dying heat of the evening, into the twilight as the stars were revealed above the dew-dampening fields of Essex, ploughed open ready to receive the seed between glistening waves of clay-rich soil. Our courageous companions, whose feet had negotiated terms with the earth sufficient to transport them beyond the garter stitch of Chappel's ancient viaduct some ten miles north-west of Colchester, took their rest upon a riverbank in the open air as the last vestiges of the sun faded into black from the fringe of the sky, a fine way to sleep.

3

Then came the rising of the sun, as it always had and always would. Down at the river, beneath a weeping willow, amongst the twisted roots, our two indomitable heroes stirred out of sleep and rose as from unrest, such their discomfort there. The swelling light burnished the narrow leaves of the tree at the water's edge, picking out the delicate threads of its tapestry, like the words of the very finest story. The two companions sat together in contemplative silence on the riverbank, until Don opened his mouth in order to allow egress of the following words in the following order:

—A story is a miserable thing to behold, he said.

Is remained silent, scratching himself beneath the rabbit pelt tunic.

—It claims to be everything but falters into nothing as soon as the last word is killed dead by the shot of the final full-stop. Know, faithful squire, that nothing true ever ends.

Is moved down to the river, sat, and kicked his dangling legs back and forth over the moving water.

—I hope you are listening, said Don.

—Of course I am, sir, said Is. As sure as the sun is just ris.

The master looked out from under the willow across the water into the woods, but saw nothing. Already he had sunk into a meditation, as was his principal duty and preoccupation, upon the hyperfine transition of hydrogen. That was a whole bag of reality, in its fullsome Twenty-One-ness, not some cock-and-bull story.

—I feel a stirring of the necessities, said Don. Fetch me my things!

As soon as an enormous book and a pen were drawn from the chest and placed in his hands by his squire, Don began writing. It wasn't until the sun had made fair transit through the lower part of the sky that he ceased; and ceasing, he closed the volume and said:

—Treacherous discipline. Pruning to make small stunted shape the tangle of signs, mincing down the channel of time! Store this with the others again, Isaiah – I am done.

The squire replaced the heavy book his master handed him within the interior of the chest, finding himself inexorably drawn to dwell upon the conviction he had each time he was handed back a volume of the venerable book that it was getting heavier, and then came to sit beside his master again.

—You see this weeping willow here, said Don looking up into its canopy. It has been taken as a symbol of life because of its proximity to water; it has been taken also to be a symbol of – variously – fertility, wealth, luck, health, success and safety in travel. I proffer the following alternative symbolism, which marks an end to every other: that it is Porphyry's very own Tree, as the paradigm for our epistemology, in which we find organised everything by *regio regnum phylum classis ordo familia genus species*; but look! where it had been fettled finely now it grows sick of itself; it weeps for us at our dead-end, where everything is storied, where even science is just a sorry tale mediating the myth of cause and effect. I tell you Is, with every new story added, another leaf sickens and turns down, ashamed of the paltriness of the West.

—Well I like a good story, said Is. And I don't mind this willow here either, and that's all I have to say.

(Like a story it was, the tree, which began and ended and was a joy to behold.)

—Onwards! said Don, leaping to his feet.

The two companions gathered their various accoutrements and again began making their way down the thread of the country road, the leafy canopy above them refining the soft hot haze of the afternoon which lay across the hayfields. The soundless river flowed on, sometimes visible through the trees of the wood as the road twisted along its side. Distant birdsong threaded through the boughs, and the wood stood motionless as if waiting for something to happen. The road soon gathered houses to its flanks, and to their left as they passed, a little suburban cul-de-sac afforded a view of half a dozen houses huddled together around the road's terminus waiting for their owners to return from work. Being only six in number, Don would not permit his mind to register the presence of these houses in his field of vision – until, that is, the number of windows upon their façades presented itself to him: Twenty-One in all. All of a sudden, their reality burst forth into his consciousness.

—Be aware, Is, that the discernment of the number whose name I surely need not speak for you to know – for you are more than adequately aware of my love of it – yes, be aware that our task, in view of the size of the number which is my bride and true love, is by no means an easy one.

Here the master opened again the large chest which his servant had carried, did carry, and would carry, and rummaged through his papers until he had retrieved that which he sought.

—Here is my *triseptimum* on the subject of Numbers, Isaiah, he said opening one of his massive books. I will rehearse it to you.

—Well I must say, said Is, I've heard about this book, and I've certainly grown familiar with the weight of it on my back, but I've never actually experienced the thing itself. I'll settle myself down and enjoy the story.

—It will not be a story! said Don. The ontological treatise contained in its pages will be the very means by which humanity is liberated from his storying impulse, an impulse inculcated from the first origins of narrative some 25,000 years or more ago!

—Okay, said Is carelessly brushing off some seeds his rabbit pelt tunic had gathered to itself during the day's adventuring. He sat down on the lid of the chest in order to listen to his wise master.

The largest number the vast majority of human minds can know on sight is four. Beyond four, vagueness creeps in, guesswork becomes necessary, and we must count the figures which make up the number.

I   II   III   IIII   IIIII   IIIIII

I would have the reader know that this restricted ability is not the result of exposure to the system of the five-bar gate, but its cause. The historical record of the written means of recording number gives irrefutable proof of this fact – not that I am an admirer of the written record, being as it is a primary cause of the current mess, which is all around us.

To continue: the following cultures utilized a base-four tally record-keeping system, which unfortunately I have been led by the heinous process of acculturation to present to you in alphabetical order, for which I apologise unreservedly: Mesopotamian Aramaic, Syrian Aramaic, Cretan, Egyptian, Elamite, Etruscan, Greek, Hittite, Indus, Lycian, Mayan, Sheban, Mesopotamian Sumerian, Urartan. Whilst there have been several civilizations which used base-three systems, none used a base-five or higher tally system because the human mind is unable to comprehend instantaneously the fiveness of five things seen. Any higher than four, and we must count. A higher base system for record keeping would therefore be counterproductive, because the person using it would have to count the component parts, and counting is the very act the system seeks to eliminate.

Marks upon tally sticks from the Upper Palaeolithic, the earliest known forms of writing, must be counted one-by-one in order for the number of marks upon them to be established. At this early stage, an efficient method of accountancy had yet to be invented. The record-keeping systems abovementioned, developed thousands of years hence, allowed a far quicker means of conveying quantity, useful for administrative purposes, most importantly as a record of taxation. Thus we might note that at the very origin of writing, man is still happy to engage with the world directly; it is only when the institutions demand that he become more efficient that he places a system between himself and the world, the abstract base system. This, structurally speaking, is the origin of all corruption.

—This is some really good stuff sir, said the squire as he lay on his back on the chest chewing a grass stalk and enjoying the afternoon sun. You keep reading it out, and I'll keep listening, a thing you need have no doubt of, because the ears, as they say, are like a good brothel: always open.

—I will do as you say, said Don. But only because it is good and right in and of itself.

The ability to enumerate quantities beyond four through the means of counting is not restricted to the human species. There is very strong evidence that crows have the same ability as people not only to enumerate small numbers of things instantaneously, but also to count. In 'Use of Number by Crows: Investigation by Matching and Oddity Learning', A. A. Smirnova *et al* conclude that "it seems likely that crows are, indeed, capable of recognizing heterogeneous graphic arrays by the number of elements itself and can apply the matching (or oddity) concept to the novel stimuli of numerical category."

—And you may pursue further research if you wish, Isaiah, by reading the full article, published in the second issue of the seventy-third volume of the *Journal of the Experimental Analysis of Behavior*.

—You forget I cannot read, sir.

—I forget everything, for memory is but a delusion. But to return to my *triseptimum*:

Be it known that man was once as happy as the crow: happy to count instead of rhapsodise upon the engine of his abstraction.

The hooded crows involved in the above experiment did remarkably well in view of their circumstances. Not only were they placed in an aviary for a year before the experiment; they were also exposed to a significant trauma. Crow 250, a veteran of a series of two-choice object discrimination tasks, was unable to participate in the later phases of the experiment because "it was shot by an unknown hooligan in the outdoor aviaries." Although crows have been known to attack and kill lambs, this has not been for sport, but for sustenance.

—So, enquired Is, are you saying that crows and people are similar or different?

—May I continue?

—Go ahead, said the servant.

The split tally stick – which functioned as both promissory note and receipt of payment – gained great prominence in the medieval English system of exchange owing to the scarcity of metal money. The King's Purveyance, widespread in the eleventh to fourteenth centuries, in which the citizens were taxed of goods for the upkeep of the military, was recorded using these sticks, whose two halves could be placed together by the authorities to verify that payment had been made by each citizen. Thus we find a fine example of the oldest of technologies being the most puissant – at least to the authorities.

—(Know, Isaiah, that technology was invented to enslave others.)

As a member of the clergy reportedly wrote at the time: "They seize your cattle and pay you with a stick of wood. At the King's approach, thanks to this accursed prerogative, there is general consternation; men fly to hide their fowls and eggs; I myself shudder for the people's sake."

—I say reportedly because I quote from a '60s edition of the children's magazine *Look and Learn* which I was forced by the demands of my Science to steal from beneath the nose of a twelve year-old boy reading it at the public library. But to conclude:

> We would learn of the crow in our enmity, who knows as little of taxes as of trigonometry, another nonsense. Taxation indeed is the primary cause of political unrest; *viz* the so-called Peasants' Revolt.

At the conclusion of this oration they continued walking, Don with his mind on the hyperfine transition of hydrogen, and Is with the chest on his back. But the servant must have been thinking also, because very soon he spoke the following words:

—Not wanting your mouth to dry up like a salty crisp with all this talking, but what's the Peasants' Revolt when it's at home?

—The Peasants' Revolt! said Don, who was just then passing beneath a beautiful plane tree with his arms stretched wide, his narrow wizened face half obscured by the shadow of itself, and the badger and roe deer tunic hopping with fleas and crawling with lice all around him. Imagine to yourself a great sack of jewels infinitely varied in luminescence and beauty, and then when you sink your hand into it – only the dried husks of a multitude of beetles.

—If there's one thing I'm afraid of – and there isn't, there are many, or even most – then it's beetles.

—What I was trying to get you to do there Isaiah was experience the way I see History: it is a worthless repugnant dead thing. It is not even there, though people joy to look at it and give it so much credence as teacher. My *triseptimum* on the Peasants' Revolt will surely be one of my most famous in years to come (not that years can come, for the future is all around us as the Present). I will recite it to you, and you may judge for yourself whether the relationship I draw between taxes, history and people isn't as defensible as arsenic sorbet on the dessert menu of the House of Commons. My conclusion of the *triseptimum* on Numbers shall have to wait.

Although historians love to fight over the crumbs of Time, we can trace a general consensus. Three times in the space of eighteen months from 1379, so the accepted account runs, the commons were subjected to an unprecedented poll tax and subsequent commissions. In May 1381, Thomas Bampton (so it is said) visited Brentwood as leading tax commissioner in order to assess the surrounding Hundreds for tax evasion. People from all around came to Brentwood and, threatening his life, chased Bampton out of the town back to London. The mob, so it is told, hid in a nearby wood for several days, by which time mobs had arisen throughout the county of Essex, as well as in neighbouring Kent. Isolated acts of rebellion against landowners and civic authorities – mainly evident in the burning of documents pertaining to land ownership – became widespread in the following fortnight, culminating in the march on London. Here, three figures – Watt Tyler, John Ball and Jack Straw – are said to have stirred the commons up to a mob of sixty thousand members. They sacked the palace of the Savoy to avenge the taxation exacted upon them by John of Gaunt, who as head of government and military leader was seen to be responsible for this burden; they murdered many men of the law, as well as lords, including Simon Sudbury, both Archbishop of Canterbury and Lord Chancellor. The adolescent King Richard II in a charter drawn up and delivered to the mob at Mile End granted freedom to the serfs and exonerated them for any wrong-doing over the preceding two weeks and more. However, after the mob were put down and its leaders killed, the King's advisors persuaded him to renege, and to wreak vengeance on the multitude. Many were hanged, drawn and quartered.

A true account of the Peasants' Revolt, by contrast, would necessarily state that, as all words are without objective meaning, and all action ambiguous, and as Time is eternal and with neither extension nor duration but simply *being*, none of the events described in the preceding account actually happened, but have been dreamed up in the storying mind of a people hungry for order. Order, the natural state of the universe (as the people have come to believe), is founded upon the division of Being into entities, either abstract or concrete. Science stems ultimately from the Latin *scire* whose root meaning is 'to separate one thing from another'. But where resides, in True Reality, as Heidegger rightly asked, the thingliness of the thing? Know that every human act *vis-a-vis* Being is a meddling. Nothing in Being is properly separable; therefore, all human knowledge is error.

In truth, the war is upon Being, and the tax is upon the common mind, whose already overburdened tolerance for drudgery is witness to his being ground into the dust by ever-increasing specialisation. The world-orderers have us in their grip!

At the conclusion of this harangue, Don wiped his sweat-limp hair away from his eyes and sighed deeply.

—I am not certain, on occasion, he said, that it would not be better to be an animal than a human being.

—Which brings us back to crows! said Is. I have a story of a farmer and a crow, which contains both a human being which is the farmer and an animal which is the crow.

—A story! said Don. Do you not recall my directive against such things? You know that I abhor a story!

—It is good and illustrative, said Is, and so I have a will to use it, sir. It does have such a point on the end of it – it is sharp, so to say.

—It is a perilous path, said Don. But I will indulge you because the day is fine, and we are walking through it, and it is alleged that slavery is dead.

—Thank you, sir, said Is with palpable satisfaction, and he cleared his throat before beginning, and this is how the beginning went:

—So, one day there was a farmer who went and ploughed up his field and planted his seeds and then went home to bed. The next morning he got up to continue sowing his crop only to find that a very great deal of yesterday's seed had gone.

—Did he have a stick from the king? asked Don.

—No, but as you have most recently learned me, it was another counter-of-things taking from him what he had formed with his labour – it was the crow, exacting its beak-tax.

—It has been accounted a bird of evil omen on more than one occasion.

—I believe it, said Is. Anyway, the farmer stood there for a time and thought his way down the alleys of it all. Then he sowed some more seed, nice and generous, and went down into a shed he had there which he thought might do as a hide, and he took with him a shotgun and a long enough draught of ale to keep him going for a good number of hours.

—Now, this farmer could see the crow afar off sitting in a tree and doing his crow noises for everyway to hear, but he wouldn't come any closer, he wasn't stupid. The farmer was there just waiting for the crow to come back up to him, and the crow was there just waiting for the farmer to be done with his tricksy business and head off home. That crow was nobody's fool, so by the time the ale was gone the farmer had already brewed up a plan in his head of a better way to get him rid of this scourge on his means. So, he returned back to his home thinking all the time of how much grain that old crow was eating up into the midst of him, but he was chuckling to himself about his plan too, and the first thing he did was pledge a good handful of barley to the friend who'd return with him to the field and play out the scheme he'd just baked up within his head. Well, he got someone, and what do you know but the crow had been snacking hard on that barleycorn for the full time it took. The farmer was in a rage alright, but he sowed some more grain sensible and cunning with his companion, and then they both gone into the hide there. After a short while the farmer says to his friend, whatever his name was, You can leave now. And so he done, he went and left, pretending like to be the farmer. But the crow he weren't fooled; he just sat there in that tree thinking of that lovely barleygrain supper he was going to have when the true farmer left. And so he did, because the farmer couldn't hack the waiting; and the crow had a great good supper and all.

—Now when the next day rolled over, the farmer takes his body up out of bed early and thinks to himself and weighs it up and decides to give a half sack of crop to two men if they'll agree to help him. This being agreed, the three of them walk over the field sowing it afresh, and then into the hide they go. After a short while the first man leaves, and the crow watches him like it were a *panther* or something, but it still won't fly over and get stuck into that grain. So after a good golden while, the second man leaves the hide, and this time the crow is watching him like he were the cleverest crow in the county, and I doubt he was far wrong on himself. Anyways, again the farmer was sitting there on his own, and the crow doing the same, both watching each other, until the farmer gives up and goes home again. That crow too cunning for him.

—So on the next day, the farmer——

—Tell me Isaiah, does the farmer ever get the crow?

—He does sir, yes, said Is.

—Is it a long way off at all?

—It's getting further off all the time with these questions of yours, master.

—How many men does it take?

—Sixteen in all, said Is.

—Good Twenty-One, Isaiah! We've only done three! Can you not abridge the tale and move on to its finale? You are simply adding to the catalogue of complaints I have against stories. I am by no means an expert on the form and structure of effective storytelling – and indeed I should worry if I were, owing to my hatred of them – but I do know that a detailed account of such repeated actions is tiresome for the listener. If it had been Twenty-One men that got the crow then fair enough. But why pluck sixteen out of the air? It's such a horrid number.

—Well I never thought I'd hear this, said Is. You are asking me to sacrifice my conviction to serve up my story according to the right rules of rightness, if I'm hearing you correct; and how does that fit in with your Science thing, or whatever it is you call it? The story goes up to sixteen, and who am I to meddle with the laws of a story?

—Such ephemera as this, as well as every other story concocted in the mind of man, said Don, are not required to obey the same strictures as my dear bride Science. Move on to the sixteenth, Isaiah, or cease talking altogether.

—Fair enough, said Is. But I'd like to put it on record that I do not think it is right.

—If the attribute of memory was not a function of the mind whose utilization was forbidden me, I would gladly store that record in the recesses of my brain. But unfortunately, it is, so I won't. Continue.

—Okay. So, after sixteen days the farmer gathers together the same number of men for the purpose of tricking the crow – that's sixteen for those who have sworn against the rememberment of things as you have, sir – and they fill that little hide like to an egg's meat in its shell, and then one-by-one they make their way home pretending to be the farmer. Now that wily old crow watches them go one-by-one and after the sixteenth goes, he flies across the field and begins to satisfy himself in the eating of that grain again. But he mis-counted, and the farmer lets him have it out of both barrels boom-boom, out go the lights.

At the conclusion of the story, a brief silence prevailed.

—Good squire Isaiah, said Don. I do not doubt that some may find your story entertaining. But you described it as being illustrative – illustrative of what exactly, besides the witheredness of your brain?

—It is illustrative of what happens if you are a farmer trying to get one over on a crow, or a crow trying to get one over on a farmer.

—The story is not *illustrative* of that; it *is* that. To be illustrative of something, it must symbolize something else, almost always a figuration that partakes of the sinistrations which comprise and take their habitation in the moral realm; Cf. Aesop's fables.

—I don't know anything about that, said Is. I just like the story, though I do wish the crow hadn't bought it at the end. In fact, if as you say the rules of storytelling are not as strict as those of Science, I can forget the ending and just keep adding the men up, can't I?

—You can do whatever you like with your story, said Don.

—Though there is the problem of the population of the village where the farmer lives. How many people do you think I can rightly press into the habitation of a single village? They are not large places after all.

—Indeed they are not, replied his master. Though Tiptree, one of the largest villages in England, has a population of between several hundred and eleven thousand, depending on what year it is. And as the concept 'year' is a false one, and as the past and future have no real existence, I refuse to even conjecture as to the population of Tiptree.

—Well, at the higher end of the scale you mention, eleven thousand would provide me with enough to-ings and fro-ings of the farmer to fill a number of hours with the entertaining shape of the tale. But what should I do when I reach the eleven-thousandth, if that's how high I can go?

—Perhaps that can be the moment at which the crow wins, said Don.

—There's a fine idea! You know, you'd be a wiser man if you withdrew that law you've established which forbids the ins and outs of a story as it connects with your ears and mouth, because you've got the knack for it, if I'm not wrong.

—You cannot flatter me out of my convictions, Isaiah.

—I do not want to. The only thing I want is a rest, because we've been walking almost the whole day, and this chest and its contents are as heavy as one of your thickest sermons, sir. Might we take a rest? This seems as good a place and time as any.

And so rest they did, in a place called Hilly Fields, affording a fair view.

4

Pale squirrel-tail fescue grass tickled at our two friends' arms and ankles as they sat there in pleasure. Looking down the gentle slope of the field they found with some amount of surprise that they appeared to be overlooking the town of Colchester, the very town they had left the previous day. Is's heart sank.

—Sir, I have a mind to take my own life. Jumbo has never appeared so unappealing to me – look at your old squat, standing there braggy and unfriendly as the worst kind of bouncer.

—Your attitude perplexes me, Is, said Don scratching at the flea bites around his neck and chest, earned in the wearing of his pelt tunic. Have I not indicated in the (actually non-existent) past that Chance is the Queen of our adventure, and should take us any which way she chooses? The very fact of our coming to arrive in the same place we only just left shows just how much Chance is directing our peregrinations, because it is inconceivable that we would ever intentionally return here without some specific objective, which we do not and cannot have. This gives scientific proof that Chance favours us; and the more Chance favours us, the sooner shall our quest reach its glorious conclusion, and so the less miles you will have to walk. So I'd advise you to stop bending your face like that.

—The fewer steps I have to take, the happier I'll be, said Is. And now you've said all that, Jumbo is back to his good old self and looking a whole lot friendlier.

Is lay back contentedly in the long, pointed grass, which quivered in the light breeze over the bunched slopes which backed like unmade bedclothes up against the old west walls of the ancient town. The day was unseasonably hot, as had been its immediate predecessors, and innumerable insects were abroad in the haze of the mid-afternoon. From where the two men were sitting, they were able to watch the cars coming down the Avenue of Remembrance, wind in geometric ellipses silently – at this distance – round the buildings, pass beneath the railway line, flash the light of the sun into their eyes when the angles reached the correct alignment, and then move out of view.

Is made a noise expressive of hunger, and began making a fire beneath their pot for an overdue lunch. Inevitably, however, he soon felt the need to speak once more, which, even above eating, was his primary mode of entertainment; for it was true that Is was so given to talking that, even against his master's most inflexible interdiction, he would gladly repay debts to a tale-not-to-be-told at even the very highest rate of interest, being as he was a man for whom a swarm of words, even if they sting, is better than no words at all. It was simply the way he filled the time.

—Humpty Dumpty sat on the wall, he said.

Don, still scratching at his flea bites, looked up at his servant.

—Humpty Dumpty had a great fall, he continued.

—Where are you going with this? asked Don.

—I would have thought you could guess. There are only two lines left.

—You will neither say nor sing them. Devote your attention to something else.

Is looked down at the fire, which was just beginning to take. But he could not hold off for long, barely as long as it takes to form a thought, and the thought which formed was this:

—Old King Cole was a merry old soul.

Don looked up at him again.

—And a merry old soul was he.

—Something not involving the formation of words, said Don. Something involving silence.

—I will try.

Is tried, but he failed; and in failing, spoke thus:

—Isn't it strange that Humpty Dumpty and Old King Cole both come from the same place?

—There is a little more of the idiot than of the *savant* to you today, Is. What is it that your brain is fumbling with now?

—I was just thinking that it is strange how they both come from our town, being such famous nursery rhymes, and there being so many towns in the world. I was told as much by my mum, and it's a bad man who doubts his mother.

—Do you mean the rhymes themselves, or the characters who inhabit them? asked Don.

—Either, or both, said Is.

—I think you might find that such rhymes tend to come from wherever the present speaker does. Which is to say, that the two rhymes you mention come from as many towns as care to claim them.

—That doesn't seem possible to me. How can a thing come from more than one place?

—You are a case in point, said Don, removing both scratching hands from his flea-bitten neck and focusing his full attention on his squire for the first time. You come from your father's negligence, your mother's despair, and the devil's own nursery, and from these three just as much as you do from this town you call home. (There's a three again!)

—That's not fair, said Is. Just because your neck's itching doesn't mean you should scratch at me. In any case, you're mixing up the come-froms. What you said might be true, but I am born of my mum and my dad and no others, and I have grown up in this town particularly, and I thank whoever requires thanking for such a thing, for there are some bad towns out there.

—I count a town in which the soldiery routinely douse its flagstones in the nasal blood of the civilian population to be as bad or worse than any other, to which you remain a testament. How many times have you had your nose broken for you?

—Certainly more times than I have had it fixed, said Is. Seven I think.

—(There's a seven again!) said Don rapturously into his own interior. And then to his squire: Your nose resembles most closely a Jerusalem artichoke.

—That is true, said Is. But as with our town, so with my nose: there are worse vegetables out there.

Don laughed at his friend's words, and then spoke again:

—I meant only that nursery rhymes will be put to whatever uses their users choose. They have that promiscuity oozing out from between the gaps in their sense.

—I do not like to think, said Is, that Humpty Dumpty was not the cannon fired by One-Eyed Jack Thompson which toppled off the wall of the very church I am looking at now. (And he was indeed looking over the broom bushes and the distant trees to the tower of St-Mary's-at-the-Walls as he spoke.) It makes me sad. And who can persuade me that Old King Cole did not come to Colchester and like it so much he chose to die here, and that his lovely daughter didn't stay on after him and build the church she named after herself?

—I do not think there is a man or woman alive who can persuade you out of these beliefs, said Don. But that doesn't mean they are not founded on error. The latter I cannot conceive of being true, because the legend appears in the *Historia Regum Britanniae*, written by Geoffrey of Monmouth, the most notorious liar ever to have lived. Monmouth is a border town, and border towns will breed iniquity into the best of people. Jesus wouldn't have turned out so good in Monmouth, and Nazareth was by no means slap bang in the centre of Galilee. It was no utopia, is what I mean. In fact, you would do well to remember that the first temptation is said to have occurred on Mount Quarantania, close to the Roman Judea/Peraea border.

—I don't know anything about any of that, said Is. Though Jaywick, if my mum was right, is on a kind of border, even if it's just that big blue thing called the sea, and our first damsel, who was from Jaywick – and

who you'd remember if you gave up this silly idea of the past not exist-
ing – did look pretty mean and nasty when she didn't get her directions
to the Hippodrome. But like I said, I'm only going on what's been told
me by my mother. Shall I tell you her favourite joke?

—Go ahead, said Don without enthusiasm.

—A chicken and an egg are lying in bed. The chicken closes its eyes,
leans back against the headboard, removes a cigarette from the box at
the bedside, and then goes and offers one to the egg. The egg huffs,
turns its back on the chicken, and says all uppity-like: 'You know I've
given up.' To which the chicken goes 'I thought you might like one,
it being a special occasion and all that.' And the egg says in reply: 'I'm
already premature, and you want to ruin the meagre life left in me by
getting me back on the dirty snouts. Get out of here.' And the chicken
says back to the egg ——

—You tell jokes as you do stories, said Don. I think you may have
lost the thread a little.

—And you interrupt them both, said Is. I was going to get there,
don't you worry, even if it was by the scenic route. But now I've lost it,
and the joke is cut adrift, and will have to make its own way home, and
I've had enough of it now anyhow.

Is crossed his arms in a petulant childlike way.

—It would have taken a great many resources to tug that joke back
to harbour intact, said Don. But tell me Isaiah, do you know how jokes
work?

—Now you mention it, no, I have no idea.

—I will have to tell you properly another time, for the demands of
the hyperfine transition of hydrogen will soon be upon my meditative
mind, pointing me to some indirection in the not-future. I really do feel
that this loop back to Colchester is a necessary preparatory pause in the
march of Time prior the true fight, from which we shall soon emerge
victorious (not that the word 'soon' is anything other than preposterous).
But what was I saying? Ah yes, jokes. Suffice it to say for the Present
(which is all there is) that the humour of a joke – at least in the case of

the joke you just now failed to tell, which exhibits a structure common with many jokes – stems from the sudden revelation of a thing as being two very different, often mutually incompatible, things at once.

—Like Humpty and King Cole being both from Colchester? said Is.

—That is not at all what I mean. The humour in the joke which you failed to tell comes from the sudden realisation that although the chicken might not come before the egg evolutionarily speaking, it might well come before the egg in the act of coitus, owing to the egg's lack of sexual organs.

—Why would my mum like a joke like that? asked Is.

—Was she a louche woman?

—She had a squint for certain. Humpty would never have let it roll like that – he had an organ alright: he blasted one and a half pound shot down his pipe. That's one hell of an egg, and with ways worthy of being aspired to. Some of it would have landed here, where we're sat. Maybe the very hollow I'm sitting in is down to old Humpty. Fertile soil I'd say, all egged on and that. But the only people you get here are kids bunking off school and dog walkers. And us. Why are we here?

—Because it is safe, and we will not draw attention to ourselves. And because Chance led us here, which is inestimably important, as you know. But tell me, said Don, turning his attention to the fire. What, may I ask, has Chance granted us within our bag of provisions by way of sustenance?

—Well, you're not going to believe it, but we have some chicken, and some eggs, and little else.

—I do believe it Isaiah, because my mind is free from the shackles of convention. I will have an egg or two; you may have the chicken.

—Ah, you are like the old saying, not so keen on the hen.

—How so?

—Well, isn't it said that a hen is only an egg's way of making another egg?

—I hadn't heard such a saying before, but I like it. And it is correct: unconscionable emphasis has historically been laid upon the hen. There are other things like eggs. Lamentation or sorrowing (of whose line-aments I am not ignorant) is that strangest of thing: what is and what isn't at once. Sorrow is said never to die ——

—Don't I know it, said Is with a Ruthful pang in his heart.

——but equally it is said to be assuaged by time. It walks into rooms unbidden, refuses to leave, and makes a home there, and such a com-fortable and permanent home that we would miss it if it left. It contains great secrets (it is true that even in laughter the heart is sorrowful). Thus, sorrow is also an egg – the egg which the cuckoo has stolen.

—He that steals an egg will steal an ox.

—The indirection of your talent yields surprising effects.

—Thank you sir. I have indeed been said to suck wisdom out of nonsense like a weasel sucks eggs. Or perhaps it was the other way round – I can suck a weasel out of wisdom like an egg can lay a non-sense. I do not remember. But I do remember that Is is as Is does, which is a characteristic most egg-like in my opinion. May I add one further observation of my own?

Don nodded.

—A kiss without a moustache is like an egg without salt.

—I comprehend the terms of your analogy, said Don. But I feel we live in different times to the one in which this proverb was coined.

This highly entertaining conversation continued whilst they cooked and ate their meal of chicken and egg; and at the conclusion of the meal, Don rose and indicated to his friend that now was the time to go foraging for fungi which might serve for their further sustenance at the end of the day. So they walked between the sparse broom bushes down to the wooded part of the heath, where small copper and comma butterflies harried the air, and a red-shanked carder bee was bumbling pleasure out of the zenith of its working day. Is had soon collected sufficient edible mushrooms – along with sage, parsley and chervil – for an evening meal, and they began the walk back up the hump of the hill. Don followed behind his squire, pondering aloud the imponderable intricacies of the work which he was engaged upon, thus:

Triseptimum: The Trinity and Lucky Seven

It is true that neither the number Three nor the number Seven is the number Twenty-One, and therefore that these lesser numbers are of infinitely less importance than our great Figure for Truth. However, both Three and Seven have long been considered significant or efficacious numbers, and the product of the two is the hallowed number by which I profess my faith in the True Science, my Lovely Bride, the Daughter of Time, Fair Chance, and therefore these two numbers deserve to be considered within this work.

The Trinity – which is to say the Father, the Son and the Holy Ghost – is an extraordinarily convoluted conception. Each is distinct and contained in the one God, as stated in the First Canon of the Fourth Lateran Council of 1213 AD (not that there can be any such thing as an *A* in True Time, of course). Their relationship is said to be perichoretic, whereby each reciprocally contains the others, and yet does not have identity with them. The Father is begetter, the Son begotten, the Holy Spirit proceeder. It used to make perfect sense, though has become a paradoxical conception for the modern mind. I proclaim it a truth of kinds, though it be a near miss on the target of ontology. Know well that Twenty-One is the sole supreme verity.

The number Seven is uniquely significant across all the religions of the world. To restrict ourselves to the Christian religion and its Judaic progenitor – for these are the religions which have been the parent of our abominable West – Seven is the number of days of the Creation, of Passover, of the week as established in Exodus, of the branches of the candelabrum in the Tabernacle and the Temple in Jerusalem, and of the pillars of the House of Wisdom; and in Revelation – the unveiling or *apokalypsis* upon which my own endeavours are oriented – there are Seven each of kings, torches, seals, angels, plagues, golden bowls, stars, eyes, diadems and thunders. Mark well the thunders, for they shall be a key.

Twenty-One is the only true and real number by and through which the restitution of Being may be enacted, as laid out by the length of the spectral line of the hyperfine transition of hydrogen, which is measured at Twenty-One centimetres. Three and Seven have been preparatory figures in the History of Time, and I therefore pay homage to that fact by presenting each of the entries within this my glorious *Encyclopaedia of Being* as a *triseptimum;* in which, both symbolically and actually, the Threes and Sevens of our tradition are made Twenty-One in Eternal Now. This work, which will grant to Being its restitution, is the product of Chance, the Princess of Time. Intention is oppression; structure is fallacy; form is death.

Take for example the chest in which this work has been carried by my devoted servant. Though the people of the world may disparage its lineaments, ridicule its workmanship, mock its inutility, they would be foolish indeed to pass over the features of its design as if they were an irrelevance: the Twenty-One studs and the Twenty-One panels of which it is constituted. Will the world skip over such details, as it has done since the beginning of Time? Abominable species! Through Chance I shall be brought to my bride, the spectral line of the hyperfine transition of hydrogen, and all strife shall cease, and Being be redeemed.

—I thought your future Bride was Time, sir?

—She is (not that there is any such thing as future).

—So how come you're chasing the line thing too, you randy old rascal?

—Are they not one and the same, Isaiah?

—And you've certainly been making eyes at Chance recently too. You'd better watch out, because these sound like some pretty fearsome women to be three-timing.

—All three are identical, though not in any way your mind might grasp, acculturated as it is to believe in the accursed systematization of Universals and Particulars in mirrorplay.

—That's ridiculous. If they were the same, there wouldn't be different words for them.

—Such is the condition of language, Isaiah. It is a bog of error.

—You're the boss, sir.

—That's true enough.

At the crest of the hill, Don and Is stopped.

—I fear that we have done what we shouldn't and drawn attention to ourselves, said Is as he looked across the hilltop at a great swathe of smoke writhing into the air. It seemed that their little fire had spread around the broom bushes, which crackled in a great excitable chatter of firevoices, to become no longer little at all. Somewhere in its midst, Is realised, was the invaluable chest.

—Your work, sir! Your *Encyclopaedia*! The chest!

Don stood, a smile playing serenely across his face.

—Fetch it if you wish.

—I certainly will! said Is. It's my job, and I won't have the world saying I don't do what I'm here, or there, or anywhere, to do.

In a single movement Is threw both the mushrooms he held at his front, and the abundant fear from his back – for it is true that amongst very many other things, he was frightened also of fire – and ran towards the blaze.

It was hard to tell exactly where it had started; the fire had grown, and by growing concealed the point of its origin. But in refutation of Don's take on the world, we will find that everything has an origin – it has to. An expansive mat of burnt-out grass curled black and hot under foot as Is made his way between the burning bushes. The wind turned the flames in great leaning pirouettes, which licked at his face and the pelt tunic he wore. He danced into an improvised rhythm with them, trying to negotiate his way through. The chest demanded such things of him – his employ demanded such things of him. Finally he found it, at the far edge of the rapidly growing fire-scorched ground. He reached down to the smoking chest and, wrapping his hand in an old rag which Chance in Her infinite mercy had left there for him, picked up its end. He dragged it across the blackened earth back towards his master, who waited without anxiety.

Is lay the chest at Don's feet, where its wood panels hissed and steamed and smoked.

—Open it, said Don, and his assistant did as he was told.

—It's all okay!

—Of course it is.

—It wouldn't have been okay if it hadn't been for me! said Is.

—I admire your confidence, said Don. But you are wrong: *nec tamen consumebatur.*

—Neck, two men consume batter? said Is. Are we playing at the cryptics all of a sudden? I've never liked a crossword.

—It is Latin, said Don. It means, Yet it was not consumed. You do not know your scripture, then?

—I barely know my own address, not that I have one any more.

—The writing within the chest would have been untouched even by the fires of the sun had it been removed there and left to burn for Twenty-One millennia. The fire we have just now witnessed only serves to confirm that we are on the right track!

—It shows us before that, said Is, that we should be more careful, I would have thought. And anyway, it seems cheating to go counting signs of our own making as signs. Maybe I'll throw a penny down and then pick it up with 'Oh, look, a penny, and there's howeversomuch good luck, or future wealth, or love till death', or whatever I make it mean. And I wish I could hear just a little more about this track you mention. At the moment I know nothing more than that it exists, and even that stands in need of proof. Where does it begin? Where does it end? How long is it? Does it take an easy route? Are there plenty of places to sleep and eat along the way? Why is there no map?

—Shut up, Isaiah. You have asked enough questions for today already, and none of them pertinent. People are beginning to gather at the top of the hill over there, and our proximity to the fire evinces our involvement in its origin, not that I believe in origins, which are a comforting delusion of common sense logic. In short, let us leave.

And so they left.

On and on, on and on, again, as the day before, through the afternoon, into the evening, towards the twilight without rest or sustenance. The heat fleeing from the earth; on they walk. The moon rising. Don first, and following him, Is; the light attenuating; wisps of cloud and smoke, deprived of light, silhouetted against the cobalt-into-rose luminescence of the higher sky. The stars abroad; darkness across the fields and the country roads. Eventually, another hollow, and sleep.

By the time Is woke, Don had already been writing for over two hours. He watched as his master shook out the knots from his writing hand, folded shut the pages of his notebook, stood, and then struck out anew on the road. How did he know Is had woken? The befuddled assistant had no choice but to climb to his feet and haul the massive chest up on to his back, thankfully cushioned to some degree by his flea-infested rabbit pelt tunic. Lurching, he followed.

As they walked, Don's mind dwelt upon species of existence too exalted for any eye to notice, except perhaps the birds, for whom he seemed by the quickness of his yellow eye to feel a kinship. Hours and hours and hours. Beyond the hedges, dry ditches. The heat oppressive as the day rolled on. They walked at the road's edge in the dust and grit. A car in the distance, visible through the heat haze, approached, the sound swelling, beginning to grow into a drone of bodily touch through the hot road, growing, thickening, quickening, until – the pitch and rush was dragged out and down by the car's passage, and the grasses at the side of the road, momentarily bent flat, straightened to sprightly once again.

—Onwards!

Without destination or intent – *onwards!*

They march on. Dry hawthorn hedges at the roadside mince up and scatter the sunlight within their dark tangled bodies, complex as hearts. The tread of the two men on the road approaches common time, finds it, drifts apart, then moves toward unison again. Left. Right. Left. Right. Left. The weight of the load on Is's back pushing his line of sight down to the road as it moves beneath him. Hours upon hours upon hours. The pressure from above and below and the heat of the day working blooms into his vision with each tread. Eyes shut or eyes open. This. That. This. That. This chip and seal road softened by the heat, small pieces of stone freed from the tar by the unfamiliar traffic: footfall, footrise. Glittering quartz crystals within the rough grey aggregate, half-submerged in the tar. Bite of flea and wriggle of louse harass his sweating trunk beneath the uncured pelts of his tunic. The scattering of light into the turning heart of the hawthorns and out again, playful and secret to the passing eye. Hours within hours within hours, the time stretched with never a rest. Another car successfully passes; the mortal vertigo leaves Is's body once more. The grasses, bobbing back up, celebrate: Life!

Presently, Don turned to his companion with a look in his eye which Is recognized well: an idea.

—I have just realised, said Don, that my *Encyclopaedia of Being, Synthesised in Accordance with the Eternal Verities Delineated by the Spectral Line of the Hyperfine Transition of Hydrogen*, the work I have been writing for the past Twenty-One years (not that years have any existence), is in one very important respect profoundly flawed. In allowing my work to follow the ordering principle of the alphabet – an apparent inevitability owing to the fact that my book is written in the manner of a palimpsest upon the very pages of the *Oxford English Dictionary*, though as alike to that work as a salt-mine is to a sparrow – yes, in allowing the alphabet to order my own work, I am granting legitimacy to error. The worm of convention insinuates itself into every nook, no matter how fastidiously one seeks to maintain its exile.

—I was not aware of any of it sir, said Is. But I am now, and I thank you for the information. Set the sparrow on the worm, and all will be well, I reckon.

—That is exactly what I intend to do, said Don. Not that I permit myself the bourgeois indulgence of having intentions. From whence does order spring? From the impulse to tidy-up. But the very tidying-up is what creates the notion of disorder and mess – there are always further problems, complexities within complexities within complexities. No, I will not order my *Encyclopaedia* along the channel of the *abc*. What kind of a thing is the alphabet? There is no such thing as the alphabet! So, Isaiah, you are my sparrow: take this knife and cut each sheet from each volume of my book, and then cut each definition from the sheet which holds it, and liberate our work from this false order. We will then have something befitting better this earth of ours.

And the good squire did exactly as he was told, and it took him three whole days to do it.

5

Late in the evening on the last day of May, Don and Is approached the small estuary town of Manningtree. The days had cooled, and a sharp saltwet wind tore off the estuary up the marshland channels, buffeting the long spines of grass which bobbed up and down in clumps; the light a dark steely grey, sinking into night. Beyond the marshland to their left lay the deep estuarine mud; and beyond that, the sea churned greyblack with the failing light behind it. They walked on between the gathering houses, following the crooked road sheened with dew, the streetlights blooming mandorlas of yellow hue in the damp saline air. The day ending.

—Chance, said Don to nobody in particular, is so finely arrayed, so delicate in her movements, so dignified in her lineaments, and so vigorous in her way with Time, that when I merely think of her I feel every fibre in my being enlivened, enriched and ennobled.

As if both a demonstration of and a full-stop to Don's statement, a large nodule of flint just then fell like a molar out of the wall beside which he and his servant walked. They both stopped for Don to stoop; he collected the flint into the gentle bowl of his hand, and held it up before him with as much care as he might an injured bird.

—See how its rind is crossed like a desert floor with the tracks of innumerable animals, resembling in fact the thick hide of such quiet and dignified beasts as do walk there; feel how its interior is as smooth as the holiest of flesh. This bungaroosh house here – (and it was true that the flint and brick wall from which the stone had fallen was the external wall of a dwelling) – shall be our shelter for the night, for to go anywhere else would be to treat My Lady Chance as if she were some alley-standing strumpet.

—Well I'm glad that stone fell out of this wall then, because a bed would be a grand thing – and I'd very much like to take these animal skins off my back for a night because I'm itching like mad.

—A bed is a profoundly ungrand thing, no matter what happens else in the world, for it has a cultural existence, and all such existence is twisted out of kilter. But never mind that: knock on the door, good servant.

Is did as he was told, and within several minutes our two admirable adventurers were standing within a kitchen or parlour around a dark-topped circular table and engaging in animated conversation with a man named Ringwood who had become their host.

—Nice chest, he said, looking down at the amalgam of mispropor-tioned oak panels. Who made that, Picasso?

Don muttered an oath to the only number which warranted such a metaphysic.

—Anyway, Ringwood continued, you're a pair walking these unfa-miliar parts through the night aren't you?

—We're trying to get somewhere, said Is.

—Aren't we all, said Ringwood.

—We are not in a position to be able to give an account of our origin, our destination, or the intentions which connect the two at the present Time, said Don to Ringwood. Because three quarters of the entities I mention are in fact non-entities. Only the Present has a true and real existence.

—Now I'm no pryer, you can rest safe from that, said Ringwood. My wife, she passed last year – she would've jumped on your stories. But I never found people's doings sufficient interesting for the outlay.

—Every word taken in by the ear procures a debt for the mouth, said Don. Every economy of discourse seeks to circumvent its ineluctable destiny, which is unequality. Interlocution loves disorder. And yet the mind loves its opposite. Hence every manner of discord. Hence war.

—Okay then, said Ringwood. And then to Is: What's he going on about?

—No idea, said Is. But whatever it is, it's full and wise.

—I don't doubt it, said Ringwood doubtfully.

Don stood before them both, but had slipped into such a profound reverie in regard to the hyperfine transition of hydrogen, both his shelter and his storm, that he heard nothing.

—Let's take a drink, said the host.

—Sounds like the ticket, said Is. Anything with guts.

—Navy and black, said Ringwood.

—Perfect, said Is. Light on the black though.

No answer came from Don, but Ringwood prepared three drinks nevertheless, and set the heavy-bottomed tumblers which enabled their preparation down upon the tabletop, bringing Don's mind back into company.

—Cheers, they intoned in a trio of their several voices.

There followed a brief silence during which the three men could dwell upon the sensation the rum and blackcurrant cordial produced within their throats and bellies.

Bringing this silence to an end, Ringwood spoke:

—So what's with the animal skins, lads? You look like a couple of Flintstones.

—Before the instigation of the Forbidden Line, before all Time was riven, man lived in peace, and strict logic was not yet hocus-pocused out of his death-cap – there were no questions, exemplars, paradigms, universals, only true and visceral Being. But it was not *before* – it only appears as before, such are the deceptions of our sweet logic. No words are patient of describing this depredation, hence the necessity of our adventuring!

—I haven't a clue what you're on about, said Ringwood. But that get-up's going to land you in some trouble sooner or later. I used to have a friend Mick as was a big fan of womenswear, always sporting a black eye with his rouge. They don't like that sort of thing round here, you know: *difference*. Anyway don't the dogs go crazy for the smell of you?

—As the last great poet did not write but instead *sang:*

> Οὐ μὲν γάρ τι φύγεσκε βαθείης βένθεσιν ὕλης
> κνώδαλον, ὅττι δίοιτο: καὶ ἴχνεσι γὰρ περιῄδη:
> νῦν δ᾽ ἔχεται κακότητι, ἄναξ δέ οἱ ἄλλοθι πάτρης
> ὤλετο, τὸν δὲ γυναῖκες ἀκηδέες οὐ κομέουσι.
> Δμῶες δ᾽, εὖτ᾽ ἂν μηκέτ᾽ ἐπικρατέωσιν ἄνακτες,
> οὐκέτ᾽ ἔπειτ᾽ ἐθέλουσιν ἐναίσιμα ἐργάζεσθαι:

—What? said Ringwood.

—I'm with him on this one, sir, said Is. If there was a dog in amongst all that, you're going to have to get the fellow to bark for us to hear him. Anyway, we've been so lost most of the time that even a dog with a nose the size of a baked potato couldn't have found us.

—I can't stand dogs, said Ringwood. More of a cat man myself. So I think you probably did well.

Is took off a boot and brought it up close to his face for scowlful inspection. The lace had broken, and been retied, and then broken, and then been retied again so many times that it clambered crookedly between just four eyelets in the manner of a vine between saggy rotting tomatoes.

—That's a bloody mess you've made there, said Ringwood. Let me give you some fresh laces.

He stood and went to the bureau where he began rummaging through three little drawers.

—Can't have you walking so many miles as you say you are without that contraption strapped properly to your foot. Ah, here we go.

He threw a couple of laces, tied together in a bow and wrapped in a slim paper loop, across the room to Is.

—You get that boot lashed back on your foot and straight after I'll show you the real Boot. That's the pub, you see.

—My master's been threatening me with his real boot sufficient to make me wary of them all. But pub you say, now there's a golden word.

—All words are but dross, said Don.

—I'll take you to the Boot and you'll both be happy. Now if you'd only quit making heavy weather of that re-lacing we can be off.

Quickening at these words, Is's fingers exhibited a nimbleness never before witnessed in this world. Don, however, was less happy with Ringwood's words.

—Weight is no more existent than mass, he said, which is no more existent than the atom, which has no existence, being merely a convenient Image. In truth, I could if I chose float up through the lower air and into the æther, there to dwell in that terrible space where the celestial spheres are said to spin.

—Now that is something I would like to see, said Is. I seem to remember hearing a story about that at Sunday school.

—The story you mention is no doubt the Passion of Christ, Don replied. And the particular episode you refer to is the Ascension, in which Jesus rolls the stone from the cave mouth, attends his disciples at Bethany, and rises really and truly in his corporeal form to heaven.

—This is the Jesus H. Christ my dad seemed always to be calling on?

Ringwood laughed.

—You simpleton, said Don.

—I'd like to know Jesus' full middle name, said Ringwood.

—There are two common accounts of the source of the 'H', Don began. It has been suggested that the 'H' was taken from the Latinized lunate form of the Greek Christogram IHC; on the other hand, some contend that children mishearing the lord's prayer believed – from 'Our Lord, who art in heaven, hallowed be thy name' – that Jesus's middle name was Harold.

—I prefer the second, said Ringwood. If you want a laugh, a kid's the thing to do it.

—Neither is true, said Don. Because nothing in the world is true once it has been linguidated. Language had better look out though, because I come not to bring peace, but a sword!

Here, Don thumped his fist down upon the table top as ample demonstration of his determination.

—I bet it's quaking in its boots, said Is.

—Enough of boots, except the one true one, said Ringwood. Let's go to the pub.

Out in the night the stars shone through the descending mist. The three men walked down the little road, turned on to the high street, and soon found themselves entering The Boot.

Three large ceiling fans turned lazily above their heads as they crossed the room; the thrum of the glasswasher, laughter from the other bar, and the crack of the cue ball breaking the pack.

—What'll it be?

—We've got no money, said Is.

—Who said anything about that. Best?

—Nothing too heavy, said Is.

—One beer (it is Don again, taking exception to the words of the world) – as with any other entity – can be no heavier or lighter than another, owing to the denotation being nothing more than a tired and worn-out metaphoric extension of an already illusory concept. Thus we may glimpse the family tree, rooted in error, of all language. Growing crookedly from its very beginning, the language of man seeks ever greater accuracy, but merely invents distinctions which are not there; and even when inventive, every metaphor must eventually wither and die on the stem.

—Thanks for the advice, said Ringwood. But try eating after four pints of this porter. That'll change your mind about heaviness.

They picked up their three pints and crossed the room to sit at a low table.

—I wonder why there's never any women in these places, said Is looking around.

—It's either because or why there are so many men, said Ringwood.

—My little boy was always getting those two words the wrong way round, why and because.

—In which case, said Don, he is a true philosopher. The delusion of Cause and Effect would needs be interrogated into extinction as a forerunner to the Universal Restitution.

—Absolutely, said Is and Ringwood, looking the one into the other's eye and making wassail with their glasses.

—My boy, said Is, taking a drink.

—You say it heavy hearted, said Ringwood. Did he pass?

—God no! said Is, who flushed with mysterious emotion at the idea. He's with his mother, who hates me.

—Heaviness of heart is as heaviness of beer is as heaviness of matter. Heed my repudiation of gravity and by extension my attack on every dead metaphor!

Before Is could protest with anything other than a useless flapping of his hands, Don picked up the pint glass which contained his drink, held it above the table, and let it drop – and that is exactly what it did, resulting in smashed glass and beer pouring over the table top and into the three laps which sat around it.

—What the hell was that! said Is.

—You know what it was, said Don wiping himself down.

—It doesn't seem fair, said Ringwood.

—If you want to have a dig at gravity, use your own pint!

—Order! said the landlord from the other bar.

—But what would be the use in that? asked Don out of a serene countenance. Owing to the high esteem in which Chance holds me, my own drink was as likely to fall as you would be to successfully take on a vow of silence. Nothing can be gained from demonstration; action – as directed by Chance – is the sole means of us achieving what it is we are going to achieve. The truth is that your drink, in being yours, was steeped in error. If you had not desired it so, it would never have fallen. Such is the way of matter when it enters the human world of signs – it accrues a set of values, which are visible under the discerning judgement of my eye in their objective reality: in truth, such values are nothing but a nasty patina. I'm as indifferent to my own drink as if it were a single mote of dust cast high into the air above the Preural plains (noting though that neither motes, dust, air, nor the Preural plains have any real existence). The hyperfine transition of hydrogen comes as a polish of the utmost astringency to rid the world of its thought-grime!

—Give me your drink then, said Is.

—Take it, said Don without resistance. There is far greater solace to be had in contemplating the dappled flanks of the hyperfine transition of hydrogen, whose variety is unmatched in this or any other world.

Saying this, Don turned away from his servant and Ringwood to face the wall and close his eyes, much in the manner of an aloof and half-senile cat. His ruminations lasted little longer than a few seconds, however, because a man just then approached the table and, nodding a recognition of his presence to Is, commenced to speak thereafter to Ringwood as if he were unaccompanied.

—You know what that fucker Harding's gone and done now? he began. He's moved his fence right back where it was and further. You can even see he's tried to cover up the old posts by taking their tops off. Bill and John T. are in the next bar just now talking it over. He's got some security firm on the perimeter, a man every hundred yards. It's going to get heavy.

Through the meditative state which enclosed and nourished Don's mind these words penetrated like a shard of flint. He winced, and was evicted from his reverie on the hyperfine transition of hydrogen faster than the very transition itself.

—Who dares to approach me and speak such falsities into the hallowed funnel of my ear, the preserve of my mistress Chance, who alone is permitted to nibble its lobe, procuring for me my unmatched pleasure?

The man, whose name was John Somenour, looked with bemused puzzlement at Don for a time before deciding that he was harmless, and then continued:

—Give Harding another year and he'll have taken the fence round the back of the lane and'll be evicting us from our own houses. Man's a fucker. Come round and join us Ringwood. You can bring these two and all if they're handy with a pair of snips. Fucker!

—From the account you have just given, said Don, it sounds very much as if you are assembling in the next bar in order to construct a plan of action. I feel therefore that I should warn you that only unplanned actions are true, pure, proper and good, for they trust to Chance, which is my maiden.

Is looked from his master's face, to that of John Somenour, to that of Ringwood, and then back at his master's.

—Sir, can't you forget about Chance for a bit? My bed for the night is in peril, I can smell it.

—You are a pernicious slave to expediency! said Don to Is. I could as easily forget about Chance as you could forget about your stomach. You are welcome to attend this rabblement in whatever meddlings with Time they wish to transact, but I am going to sit here and get back to what's best, which is thinking about the hyperfine transition of hydrogen. There's not a better bed for the head of man. ·

—I'll do as you offer, sir, said Is. And you'll probably never see me again.

—I am willing to forego your company if Chance deems it apposite. Indeed, I would choose the very same if it were not for the fact that you had been selected, and were the act of choosing itself not strictly forbidden me.

—Come on, said John Somenour to Ringwood.

Ringwood and Is rose and attended John Somenour over the footworn stone of the threshold through the low doorway into the saloon bar. Don continued to sit; he turned his head once more to the wall, closed his yellow eyes, and drifted, as we must suppose, into that land of thought which was his continual comfort.

Some minutes passed, during which Don continued to sit where he was without moving, and during which Is, in the other bar, listened to the small band of men who were Ringwood (his former and hopefully future host), John Somenour, John Thecchere and William Smith talk animatedly about Tom Harding's place. And if Don had been present – and it is a good job for us that he was not – three of these four men would no doubt have experienced his chivalrous wrath against History, for persons answering to the names Somenour, Thecchere and Smith had all three of them been arraigned on charges of vandalism and threatening behaviour against Tom Harding in 1381, as the court records reveal.

—Plotting a revenge? enquired the landlord in a humorous attitude as he retrieved twisted corpses of pork scratching packets and glasses ringed with the tide marks of dried ale-spume from the table of these men.

John Somenour, whose outrage was reinvigorated anew by the very thought of him, began telling again the story of the procession of Tom Harding's fence across the land.

—He's a fucker isn't he, said the landlord, and with nods, and ayes and yesses and low, neck-bent gaseous belches everyone in the pub concurred.

—Man's a fucker.

The heavy oak-set drop-dial clock above Is's head ticked onwards like a metronome as it measured out the variations on the topic of Tom Harding's place, and how much of a fucker he was.

—His daughter doesn't *walk* out those grand gates each morning; no, she's driven a full three hundred yards. And the coach which picks her up must have cost more than my house. Where it spirits her off to I don't know. Do you like an animal?

Pointing at himself, Is received a nod.

—As long as it's not too wild, he said.

John Thecchere laughed, and then continued:

—Willow's about as wild as a tin of soup. That's the cat.

—What cat?

—The cat as resides with me, said John Thecchere. She's an ancient thing. Fucker Tom Harding's the only person I've known to *aim* for a cat with his car. But he won't mess with Willow – she sits in the middle of the lane sunning herself, right on the bend, licking a paw, and Fucker

Harding won't dare even try to go round her. He's a superstitious thing all right.

—Have you seen him turn three times on his draincover?

—And his spitting when he sees a magpie.

—He'll need a bloody lion's foot of luck to stay out of trouble tonight.

—Hear, hear, says everyone else, some not even party to the conversation, such is the hatred for this Tom Harding within the town.

The chime within the clock goes – and there in the doorway stands the unmistakeable silhouette of Don Waswill, polymath, adventurer, hero; at his feet the malfactured chest of oak.

—Sir! said Is.

—If the mysteries of human emotion could be said to have any reality to them, which of course they can't, it would be true to say that I was missing you.

—Come and sit down sir, because these men here are as entertaining as a weasel riding a unicycle; and what's more, the drink is free!

—I'll do as you say, said Don – and so he did, dragging the chest over to the table, and coming to sit at Is's side. He stroked the distorted refractions of the room which gathered in his dimple mug, rippling them like miraculous little pools of water.

—Who knows what he's up to in the courts, said John Somenour. He'll have his men all over the Land Law just as his others are round the fence.

—Nice chest, said John Thecchere. You get it made at the Special School?

—Now I was not aware that your complaint related to Land Law, said Don resolutely ignoring Thecchere. Had I known, I would have attended your every step. The very phrase Land Law fills me with black bile, and undoubtedly Chance in her infinite wisdom has placed you before me, or me before you, so that I might assist you in destroying any individual or individuals who intend to turn any point of Law – Land or otherwise – against you, for all Law is but a story continually retold, and, except in its oppressiveness, has no more basis in truth than a snake has legs. Oppression is ten-tenths of the Law.

There arose a great excitement in the group.

—Yes, continued Don. Whether it be proprietary estoppel, adverse possession, or false replevin he seeks to turn on or from you, I will explode each item as if it were no more than a child's dream.

More excitement.

—I can see by the way you are smiling, Isaiah, that you are happy to attend me in this latest adventure.

—There's no greater truth, sir, because you've brought all my wishes true: a bed for the night, a beer before, and some handy company in the dark to help me with this chest.

Outside the pub, Don and Is pulled their mammalian tunics about them against the cold air, and walked with Ringwood, Thecchere, Somenour and Smith down the deserted street, with Ringwood taking the other side of the chest. Not long after the last of the shops had receded out of view round the bend in the road behind them – wine-dark and forlorn their neglected frontages – Somenour made plain that they were to cease talking.

Off the road they cut, over a brambled ditch, into a woodland of oak.

—This bodes well, said Don. The oak is a tree we can trust.

—Shh!, said Somenour.

The moon craned between the passing boughs to shine on the heads of our adventuring heroes until, as the group reached the other side of the small woodland, they found it illuminating in narrow monochrome a broad meadow falteringly segmented by an ancient slender iron fence, and down in a declivity of the land a large house exhibiting its stark defiantly unnatural angularities.

—Where's the fence gone then? said a member of the group. And his men?

Around their feet, in the bushes and leaves, rodential scamperings; in the distance, the query note of an owl.

—Never mind where it is, said another. We're where it isn't. Now let's get to work.

Along the perimeter of the wood they made their way, measuring every dozen-or-so feet their possible detection. The wind gently rose and fell, and a chevron of geese passed overhead, their wings tub-thumping gasps through the air.

Soon the men would have to come out on to the open land, exposed. Each measured his own visibility. After the dark of the wood, anything would seem bright, surely. But the moon was big tonight. They would need to cut across the meadow, and down, and not a solitary oak to have for shelter.

But here comes a cloud!

—Wait for it lads, says one.

They all look up into the sky, right into the bright white of the moon, and watch as the light hem of the cloud approaches, and then is pulled over, and the moon shines through like a voyeur on their human antics.

—Better than nothing, says Somenour – or perhaps another – and they run down the shallow declination, across the cattle-shorn grass, over the mole hills and rabbit holes, making huge noise for merely seven natural bodies at-run.

They reach the house.

To the wall they press themselves, and puff out their windedness, several hardly suppressing astonished laughs at the degree of their exhaustion and the lunacy of it all. Is and Ringwood unknot their hands from the side handles of the chest and shake out the fatigue in them. The moon comes out the other side of the cloud, and enough of them feel sure she winks at them as to make it part of the story later on, told over strong drinks, ensconced within the safety of a lock-in, when the deed's been done.

—What will we do? asks one.

—Sack it! exhorts another.

—I'd like to see us try. We'd need an earth-mover.

—Let's go round, beckons Somenour with a twitch of his hand.

They skirt the old house, and discover from curtains undrawn that no-one is home, not even the dogs – and they hadn't even considered the dogs.

They all laughed then, a release of nervous energy, and came out from the narrow moonshadow of the eaves to roam. John Somenour entered the stables and released a horse, but it just stood there observing him through its dapper fringe as a politely tolerated guest.

—Sod you then, said Somenour slamming the stable door shut after him.

William Smith caught his foot in the line run along the perimeter of some emerging brickwork of Flemish bond.

—Damn! he hissed; and, after kicking himself free, avenged the assault by knocking the nascent wall to the ground with his other heel.

—That's good work, my man, said Somenour.

Don and Is, and their former host Ringwood, stood within the court-yard amongst a shabby cone of wet sand, a mixer, and a pallet of bricks, and they nodded with bemusement at the childish acts just as did the gently wind-blown pot-flowers unseen all along the wall.

John Thecchere took it upon himself to scratch out the mortar from between the breeze blocks of one of the outhouses, not yet rendered, in an attempt to bring it to the ground; soon it became clear it would take him all night.

—Heavy fucking going this, he said, wiping the sweat from his brow with a coarse-woven sleeve, regretting it immediately, for his face began to sting from the abrasion.

—Now, said Don. If I was not strictly forbidden the remembrance of any act in time, a mere phantasm of the mind which populates that ignominious invention the Past – yes, if I deemed it at all possible to remember anything whatsoever, I would be as certain as anything that on not one, not two, but *three* separate occasions the word 'heavy' has been uttered without due diligence to its meaning, which is null and void (not that any meaning is not null and void, such is the nature of each and every word). And so, in reproof of all three of these word-acts – and as a corrective to the abortive demonstration which my servant both witnessed and caused – let me not only tell you that weight, mass, heaviness, and any other item of gravity and its auxiliary figurations are empty gestures, but also prove it by the transaction of this unrivalled demonstration of True Science, which can only be apprehended within the epistemic kernel vouchsafed by a firm and unwavering consideration and acknowledgement of the hyperfine transition of hydrogen!

Here, Don threw his pelt cloak grandly from his shoulders, walked round the corner of the house, jumped down into a trench dug deep beside its foundations, and began unscrewing the acrow props which supported the corner and one side of the building.

—Sir, I'm not sure that's a good idea, because the whole side of this house is going to fall to the ground, and if by some miracle you don't die from the bricks falling on your head, then you'll certainly die in prison, because it's a very expensive-looking house, and you're no spring chicken.

—If this house falls to the ground, then I am a bigger imposter than Simon Magus, who offered bribes to Saint Peter and regrets it to this day (not that the illusion of separateness and consecutivity of days has any reality to it); and I hardly need to say to you, Isaiah, that I am not.

—I'm sure you're not sir, but it pays to be cautious.

—Go play with your boils, Isaiah. This is real scientific work.

Don continued taking down the supports, all the time humming a tune of uncertain melody to himself.

—He's like a child with a balloon, said Is. I can hardly watch. Sir, if this gravity you've got such an issue with didn't exist, wouldn't we all be floating round in the air? And wouldn't the trees – hang on, why do the trees grow up?

—It is said that nature needs resistance in order to flourish, said Don as he carried on his experiment. Such indeed is also the nature of man. If sufficient numbers decided to relinquish their conviction that gravity has any real existence, the moon would spin off like a struck ball.

—Well that doesn't sound very pleasant to me, said Is.

—Who cares about pleasance when it competes with truth?

—I do, sir. Particularly if the truth is pleasantness's opposite.

—There are no opposites! said Don, and he flung himself with renewed vigour upon his task.

In a short time the whole corner of the building stood hanging there like an enormous and impossibly undercut cliff. Don turned, spread his arms, and announced to the assembled company – for it was true that John Thecchere, William Smith and John Somenour had left off their tiny destructions to watch this madman undertake his one big one.

—Witness how gravity is but an illusion!

Against all the tenets of probability, and much to the assembled company's chastisement, the house did not fall.

Back at the pub some hour or so later, the six men received glasses of scotch unalloyed, sat back in creaking chairs, and recounted inwardly the events of the night. All except Don, of course, who would be more willing to cut off his own head than to recognise even that the drop-dial clock which now unwound above his own head made any sound at all. John Thecchere took to dozing into his beard; Ringwood played draughts alone; and John Somenour sat in stupefied silence, wondering what would become of himself, and his companions, and how Fucker Tom Harding always came out on top, even when he made no effort at all, which was all the time.

—You should know, Isaiah, said Don, leaning across to speak the words quietly into his servant's ear, that when I removed those acrow props from beneath Tom Harding's house I was not only revealing the sham of gravity, but also repudiating the structure of Law, for the inventor of the acrow prop, the Swiss William de Vigier, seeking a name for his new invention, struck upon the idea of conjoining the initial and surname of his London lawyer, Mr A Crowe. Thus we find a twin unnecessity in the acrow prop – it props up buildings against a phantom physical gravity, and figuratively, the Law props up phantom objective rightnesses of action. My removal of these structures serves as a demonstration that all meaning is convention.

—That's really good news, sir, said Is without enthusiasm.

At that moment Ringwood felt compelled to withdraw from a sly and hidden pocket a roll of writs of green wax, and to offer them to Don.

—To speak the truth, said Ringwood, I was not even aware of the pocket, let alone what I found in it. But here they are.

—The contrivances of Chance are as the face of a newborn child, wonderful to see, said Don.

He took into his hand the documents offered to him, broke the waxen seal, and opened it up.

—What is it, sir? said Is.

—It is a collection of laws or decrees issued to the county of Essex in a year said to be in the past. As you are all aware – and, indeed, as you all now agree with me, I hope – I recognise neither the Past nor the Law as entities having reality. This document is hateful to me, and must be destroyed. Pass me therefore the lighter that you have there before you, my good friend Ringwood, and I will perform my duty to Being.

—I do not know why I am smiling, but it's true that I am, said Ringwood, who was smiling the work of Don to see.

Ringwood passed his Zippo to Don, who turned its wheel, ignited it, and then touched the resultant flame to a furled corner of the hated document. Soon it was only ash and smoke, and the odour hung drily in the air.

—But enough, said Don to Is. Let's get the hell away from these people, all of whom but the good man Ringwood are aquiescents.

With this, Don and his reluctant servant picked up their lice-infested pelt cloaks – the latter pulling also the great chest on to his back once more – and bade their companions farewell, walking out of the door of The Boot into the night, which just then was turning into morning – and the moon still visible in its transit now close to the pale horizon.

6

Our fearsome adventurers began to move out towards open country once more, down the wet lanes, between the sodden fields, through the parishes and districts of north Essex. The sun came up and the fields steamed.

All day they walked, and into the next night, some thirty-six hours without sleep – though what was sleep to Don, who scorned the weakness of man? He withdrew from his pocket and held within the cradle of his fondling hand the dark flint which, as directed by his fair Bride Chance, had fallen in his path the night before, and which had brought him into the company of Ringwood. He lifted it to eye level for the purpose of inspection; certainly it could be accounted an object of beauty. He ceased his and his servant's perambulation: the books retrieved from the chest, the draw of the dry pen's ink along its canal encouraged by a tongue-moistening of its tip, and the work was done. Very soon, Don was capable of reading back what he had written.

TRISEPTIMUM:
FLINT; BEING OF THE CLASS: PETROLOGICAL

Many interesting things have been written about the cryptocrystalline form of quartz, a silicate mineral. Although it shares a taxonomical species with agate, onyx, jasper, and other semi-precious stones, the abundance of flint, particularly in East Anglia, has meant that it has absolutely no value whatsoever, except in its utility. In the medieval period, for example, flint was one of the main constituents of stone building material, as evidenced by the many churches of the region, which happen to have the appearance of tortoiseshell in the middle distance.

Flint, of course, has a more ancient utility value: the raw material for tools. The flint knapper is one of the earliest technologicians, preparing humanity for his coming-into-being no less: removing the *anima* from the animal, dispensing death, a symbolism is required to comfort becoming-man in his new knowledge: Where do we go?

Still further, flint's finest utility: it has been used as a firestarter for tens of thousands of years. Working across the scales of Being, flint, that darkling thing, is like the thundercloud, and likewise emits its sparks of fire. The last truly honest man, who like my assistant and I wore the pelts of animals and lived in the open upon the wooded land, saw the analogy; whence the nativity of technology: the capability of the dispensation of fire.

Francis Bacon's *Novum Organum* (1620), which marks twenty-eight 'Instances Agreeing in the Nature of Heat', is instructive in respect of fire and flint. His approach to the investigation of forms bears an admirable preludium, the which the scientists of our own generation would be wise to consider:

> *The investigation of forms proceeds thus: a nature being given, we must first of all have a muster or presentation before the understanding of all known instances which agree in the same nature, though in substances the most unlike. And such collection must be made in the manner of a history, without premature speculation, or any great amount of subtlety.*

A muster is a good thing to have. Bacon is throwing everything in the pot at once and seeing what kind of stew it produces. He continues thus (and I will include only the first Twenty-One of his forms, for obvious reasons):

For example, let the investigation be into the form of heat.

Instances Agreeing in the Nature of Heat

1. *The rays of the sun, especially in summer and at noon.*
2. *The rays of sun reflected and condensed, as between mountains, or on walls, and most of all in burning glasses and mirrors.*
3. *Fiery meteors.*
4. *Burning thunderbolts.*

—(Mark well, Isaiah – you Chance-chosen servant of all that is good – the importance of the lightning strike.)

5. *Eruptions of flame from the cavities of mountains.*
6. *All flame.*
7. *Ignited solids.*
8. *Natural warm baths.*
9. *Liquids boiling or heated.*
10. *Hot vapors and fumes, and the air itself, which conceives the most powerful and glowing heat if confined, as in reverbatory furnaces.*
11. *Certain seasons that are fine and cloudless by the constitution of the air itself, without regard to the time of year.*
12. *Air confined and underground in some caverns, especially in winter.*
13. *All villous substances, as wool, skins of animals, and down of birds, have heat.*
14. *All bodies, whether solid or liquid, whether dense or rare (as the air itself is), held for a time near the fire.*
15. *Sparks struck from flint and steel by strong percussion.*

—(And mark too the goodly flint.)

16. *All bodies rubbed violently, as stone, wood, cloth, etc., insomuch that poles and axles of wheels sometimes catch fire; and the way they kindled fire in the West Indies by attrition.*

17. *Green and moist vegetables confined and bruised together, as roses packed in baskets; insomuch that hay, if damp, when stacked, often catches fire.*

18. *Quicklime sprinkled with water.*

19. *Iron, when first dissolved by strong waters in glass, and that without being put near the fire. And in like manner tin, etc., but not with equal intensity.*

20. *Animals, especially and at all times internally; though in insects the heat is not perceptible to the touch by reason of the smallness of their size.*

21. *Horse dung and like excrements of animals, when fresh.*

—In the infancy of science, Isaiah, is wonder. I need not say any more than this: the Twenty-First is the one! If we walk in shit, we shall find it!

—Well we are certainly doing that, sir. Look at the state of my shoes. Is lifted his foot to show his master the filthiness of it.

—I am going to continue reading from this *triseptimum*; and you would do well to continue walking, even if the filth buries you up to your head.

Flint is found within the sedimentary rocks chalk and limestone in nodules of irregular though rounded shape, with a kind of skin covering its entirety, resembling thereby a misshapen orange. The means of its formation was a mystery until very recently. Modern science has provided an account of the formation of flint which is staggering in its complexity, and which might seem to foreground the role of Chance in the formation of the entities of the world, both organic and inorganic.

I therefore offer to the reader a recipe for flint, synthesized from many sources, as seems to be the fashion in contemporary culination.

First, take the sea, and let there be silica in solution. Allow certain organisms – sponges, diatoms, silicoflagellates, radiolaria – to build their scales, plates, granules and spicules from this silicate. Allow these organisms to live and then to die, whereupon their bodies may sink to the sea bed, become buried admixed with the predominant carbonate sediment, and thereby enrich the sea bed with silicate in high concentration.

Now for our oven: set initially just below the zone of future flint formation, encouraging hydrogen sulphide released by bacteria feeding on buried organic matter to rise through the porous bed. Allow this to mix with oxygen, which sinks from above the zone. Hydrogen sulphide will now re-oxidise to sulphate within our oven, collecting within any small vertical thread-like burrows formed by creatures which had lived in the carbonate sea bed. *Do not disturb this solution!*

Permit hydrogen ions released by the most recent reaction to migrate out through the porous sea bed towards more oxic conditions – only a short way, mind; do not spread your hydrogen ions too thinly – and dissolve the local carbonate sediment around the thread-like burrows.

If this recipe has been assiduously followed, the dissolution of host carbonate should provide the flint with both the physical mould for its formation and the chemical conditions for silicification. Any non-carbonate grains within that mould will be preserved within the emerging flint, hence the ferrous tinge to many such stones.

The conditions for the formation of flint, in other words, must be not just ideal but exquisitely perfect: it is the soufflé of the sea, though a little harder on the tooth.

To break open an otherwise untouched nodule of flint – not a difficult thing to do if you can lift and then drop it – is to expose to the sight of the eye the work of millions of organisms over millions of years. Flint, from this perspective, appears as a miracle of Chance, and an East Anglian church a multiverse, proper praise indeed for the God those few remaining adherents suppose made a world which is capable itself of making flint.

This should then serve to illustrate that everything is a miracle of Chance. How, for example, is the tree? How is the friable or the greasy earth? How is the light?

Know this however: the explanation offered by modern science for the formation of every entity the universe has ever contained, does contain, and will contain, is insufficient insofar as Chance is in actual fact hunted, chased down, and killed, and all the gaps its death leaves filled to repletion by Cause and Effect. And yet this decries the true caesura in Being: where is Twenty-One in these accounts? In conclusion, then, all modern Science is bunk, none of the above is worth anything at all, and the reader should ignore every word of both. When I look at the things of the earth through the glorious number Twenty-One, I do not see Blake's Mundane Egg (Plato, in spite of his orational excellence, was a very poor philosophizer, I will have you remember) but a choir of infinite voices singing '*I am*'.

The night encircled and claimed Don and Is for its own. Degrees of darkness busied up against one another. To their left as they walked, the ground went down, becoming darker as it went into non-visibility; then, across the light-sucking water, rising up again in a series of hills a mile or so distant and beyond, their shapes sensed rather than seen, suggested as they were by the sparse embroidery of streetlights scattered over their forms. In places, and on occasion, worn and distracted threads of silvery gold would play in the depths of the darkest part of the earth below them, and then be gone. Still there was no horizon.

But eventually, after much weaving of feet upon the roads of north Essex, they came to a village called Mistley, and the lights drove the darkness back a little, though it still hung there like a desire; and the streets, bereft of people, as it were in grief.

Lightly it began to rain; then in strength redoubled. In came the wind.

Don and Is, the two glorious adventurers of this fine tale, turned off the main street to take shelter, and soon found themselves on the other side of the village at the edge of an area of woodland, which they proceeded to enter.

—In there, said Don, pointing to the hollow trunk of an enormous oak tree.

—In there? said Is. I would rather skin myself.

Don took hold of Is's nose between his thumb and finger and escorted it into the interior of the oak.

7

Our two heroes stood close together within the tree, the chest at their feet, and the narrow bottom of the hollow broadening upwards like the interior of a voluptuous jug, though the top of the chamber was enclosed, thus protecting them from the rain. From within the dark hollow of the tree they looked out upon the wooded hill, faintly visible in the lesser dark. A number of animals came gradually out of the ground into the wet night air.

TRISEPTIMUM: MORPHOLOGY

Everybody believes that you can discern nationality – that is *place* of origin – through linguistic form; and many – the smugly self-satisfied among our species – that one may do the same in regard to *time*. What confounded error! Mark well: the Middle English word 'soffren' when spoken is far less demonstrative of difference than when it is written, as compared to the modern equivalent 'suffering'. Writing and the reading of it divides the time into segments, asserting a history of language; on the other hand, speech and the hearing of it asserts continuity and eternal presence through the continuation of forms. Written forms are merely the old broken cobwebs of language hanging disconsolately in the corner of the room. This tree we have recently entered is as good a place as any to be cheating history, which is a creature of writing and a delusion, as it has run rings around the years and stands, although cleft, still a burly defiant thing for our experiment. Let us speak in the language of those who played about this tree when it was a mere sapling! A truth shall be learned thereby. The difference between speech and writing will be discernible in the gulf between the exoticness of the visual appearance of the words, and their sound, which is only a little twisted. Speech brings all Times into the present, which is the sole reality. Do as I do Isaiah, and experience the tensile tremblings of the Present through yourself!

—I haven't got a clue what you're asking me to do, said Is.

—Speak in Middle English, that is all.

—That is all! said Is. I don't stand a chance – I mean Chance. I don't have the wherewithal in my word-box.

—We are in an ancient oak – the words will come if you allow them to. Marke welle, goode sweyne, we ben not for long prysoneres heer, lyke unto wordes in a booke, but forsoothe soone breke out, as a songe into the aire. Let's see what History has to say about this; let us talk, and enjoy ourselves.

—I'll do just as you say, sir. Loke! ysee the litel conyes in the mede, and the squyrels, and other bestes smale of gentil kynde.

—That's it my man! said Don with very great pleasure. You never sought, but you found alright! Ey, the sond of the rayn a-wakenen hem. The rayn hem ne troublen. Thyr fyry bodies i-blissien ouer the feild.

—Forsouthe, said Is, the rayn is their swete licour.

—Hyt hafeth y-brought hem of heore beri an burgh, her covert an clapern, said Don. Eche mil, pucelle an auncien, gamen on the holt.

Here he broke off from talking momentarily in order to become morose.

—And yete we men mot seke thes seintuarie, he continued. Mankin at-fleon fram water as hyt wæs fyre. Mercy ben.

As the animals partook of harmonious nocturnal play species-with-species beyond the shelter in which the two friends were huddled, Don and Is began to share a half loaf of stale bread which had accompanied them through the day's perambulations. Wordlessly they chewed for a time, until Don's voice penetrated the silence thus:

—By Godes bones, wy is eouwer hond clochen at myn garget?

—Peekgoose, foole, myn hond es franke, Is replied. It mot ben eouwer coler.

—Nam werien a coler. Remouyn se wiht or ich wille waxen wraw.

—We twichand ne, said Is, raising his arms in a shrug unseen in the dark in order to demonstrate beyond doubt that they were indeed not touching. Ich thenchen eu be swevenye, or els wood.

—Certes ich ben in wude, said Don.

—Wood or wude, nother is gud.

—Soth, chuckled Don, forgetting momentarily the conundrum set him by his senses. However, this amusement was coarsely interrupted by a sudden outburst from Is:

—Iesu Christi! What ben thes cold wight to mire necke?

—Ah, the scho is onne the other fut nu, said Don. Yu carpen althermoost folk, ac onlich hete aire healden of eouwer mouth.

—Huddy-peke! cried Is. Mire necke! Who is it? Ich ben sore afrayen in the herte of thes ook. Deliueren us of ther deofeln!

Don began to laugh heartily at his friend's fright, until a pair of hands grasped his own throat with the full vigour of a physical attack.

—Wat manere of tre hafeth lymes withinneforth? he managed to say in defiance of the restrictions imposed upon the articulation of his mandible. Sothely thes ook soffre of enchauntement.

—We ben soffren of the enchauntement of thes tre, ne other-weies, said Is. Man fleen!

And with these words he made a desperate though ineffectual bid for his liberty, thrashing about within the heart of the hollow oak like a fish in a narrow jar.

—Fuck sake, said a voice, will you stop titting about.

—Ey, Christes foo! said Is. The ook speken! And in voys lich to a thonder-dent!

—Ey foole, said Don to his wretched servant. Without doute thes which assaile us are men, naht tre.

Which was true, for by pure chance – which Don of course loved as an infant loves its mother – there were two people already taking refuge within the interior of the time-blasted tree.

As Is began pitifully to moan in his fright, the second now spoke:

—He told you to shut up! through touching teeth.

—Rascalles, said Is, with tunges borwede of the deofell.

There followed immediately upon this outburst the manual deployment of a heavy blunt implement to Is's head, causing him to cease discoursing for a time, occupied as he was in being unconscious beside the great chest within the gnarled cradling pit at the foot of the tree's hollow.

Don fell silent, and even though it was contrary to the tenets of his Science, he pondered the means and manner of the connection between the preceding phenomena. Following this activity, he felt it prudent to address using a very low voice those who shared with him the interior of the carbuncular bole.

—What are you doing in this tree?

—None of your business mate, said a voice.

—Sh! said the other.

Don looked out of the hollow and saw a light sweeping through the falling rain, a conical, fanned shape, moving organically, switching from side to side, like the diaphanous tail of some mythical bird strutting through the wet night. The fan moved back and forth from behind the buildings at the edge of the wood, drawing nearer. One of the unseen hands within the tree moved to Don's shoulder and warned him to stay still. The sweeping of the light came closer until its source moved out from behind a house: torchlight. Don was drawn back by the hand from the opening of the trunk deep into the tree's interior. The first funnel of light was joined by a second. They danced across one another as their sources moved over the ground, first along the boundary of the field, then slowly up the hill between the trees. Their movement divested of its human agency by the dark and the rhythm of the sweeping motions attested to by the waterpeppered air. Stalking like wolves for a view to bring a kill, growing monstrously large as they swept upwards from casting their white intensity upon the ground to illuminate the boughs and leaves of the woodland. Abrupt stops, coincidences of the two beams upon common ground, and then moving off once more. They came nearer, and then nearer. Crossing, sweeping, and the beam directly located the oak and its hollow, and surely impossible that those within were not seen.

But they were not seen. The torchbeams turned and after making a series of swift reconnaissances over the immediate terrain, slunk off back into the village, downcast, making small disappointed spots of illumination.

Is, who had remained slumped on the floor unconscious at Don's feet since the receipt of the blow to his head, began to stir and was soon standing once more, though a little more careful to monitor the activity of his mouth. He rubbed his head and complained inwardly. The rain began to ease, and one of the men spoke:

—You've got to go down to old Tom Harding's place and fuck it up.

—There's that Tom Harding again! said Is. How many places does he have?

—He is no doubt some kind of local notable, said Don.

—He's a cunt! said the man whose name, in actual fact, was Geoffrey Panyman. I knew you would come, and so we put ourselves into this tree and waited. And here you are.

—How could you have known we were going to go in a tree? *No-one* knew that, said Is.

—Do not listen to this man, Isaiah, said Don. He is a blot on the earth.

—You, said Panyman grasping Don by the flesh of the throat and pushing the back of his head up against the fibrous interior of the trunk, will be a blot on the earth in a minute if you don't shut the bloody hell up and do as I say.

Don, although more fearless than a goshawk as he flies amongst the pines, thenceforward ceased resisting the leadership of Geoffrey

Panyman, for he was an enormous man, and the odour of drink was upon him, and the air within the tree heavy with menace. One-by-one as directed by Panyman, they stepped out of the tree and began to walk slowly and quietly across the wooded hill, back into the village of Mistley, where the sea smell was vivid on the nose.

—Nice chest, scoffed Panyman. Looks like a hobbit's blanket box. Now get moving.

The heavy footfall of the fat man Geoffrey Panyman laid down a firm and purposeful four-four rhythm, over which were super-imposed the poly-rhythms of Is's trot, for he was staggering under the weight of both the chest and Panyman's menacing stare. In one hand this great slab of a human had a club, and the expression on his meaty face indicated that he was not afraid to use it. Don, reflecting that even the most perilous happenings in the course of his adventuring must be welcomed by him as the attentions of his sweetheart Chance, walked along contentedly in spite of the threats he had just received. Beyond the reverberating sound of their progress turned the whispering hush of the night silence.

—What are you going to do at Tom Harding's other place? said Is. I don't see what it's got to do with us.

—I'm going to string him up! said Geoffrey Panyman. And you're going to help me.

Panyman's taciturn assistant muttered his assent.

—I'm really not too keen on getting myself into any lynchings or murderings, said Is, mostly to himself. I don't mind admitting that this Tom Harding's last place didn't topple over from some miraculous anti-gravitying of my master, but it will be hard for the man himself – that's Tom Harding – to hang from a rope and not land us in enough bother to put an end to every manner of adventure. My Ruth is not going to think me more of a man for attacking this Tom Harding, no matter how much of a fucker he is. I'm peaceful.

—Fucker! said Geoffrey Panyman involuntarily, as if it were a cough. You don't have a choice, unless you want your nose broken.

Don, witnessing the pathetic quaking of his servant, now felt the need to come to his defence, and so spoke the following words:

—If my good Lady Chance had not put you in our company within the heart of that ancient oak, and if any such idea as the reality of the future could be entertained, then you would be in a whole lot of bother, impudent Geoffrey Panyman, because the fortitude of this arm is as fearsome in attack as it is in defence, and you'd soon be praying to a God you never before felt the need of that rather the trebuchets of Tyre orient their lime upon your hateful head than the ire of this my indomitable arm!

—Shut it, said Panyman who brandished his club at Is, urging him onwards into the night with a firm grip.

Out the other side of the village they passed, witnessing under the weak glow of a few lone bare-bulbed lights at the jetty the grasses bob, and the closest boats sitting variously askew on the mud, casting their masts jauntily up like lonely fishermen waiting patiently through the night for the tide to come back in with its fish. What remained of the fine rain swept past the lights in a flurry and into extinction on the rippled concrete of the landing ramp.

In time they moved away from the shore along the road, and soon arrived at the beginnings of a long driveway across which stood two very tall gates locked together. Through the rough wet iron bars they could see the road wind through the woodland and thence past several neatly trimmed hedges up to a large house, where several windows were dimly lit within.

—He must be mighty rich, said Is, because his house at Manningtree had a hundred sides to it if it had one, and this one's no smaller.

—He's richer than a pig's a pig, said Geoffrey Panyman, panting to regain his breath. Now get over that gate and let us in.

Is dropped the chest to the floor, looked up to the top of the wrought iron gates, and decided that he would rather not.

—I'm not such a good climber, he said. And I'm ever so afraid of heights.

—I can vouch for my servant here, said Don raising his finger with a kind of Socratic authority. He is so afraid of heights of any magnitude whatsoever that if you were to cut off his legs he would likely thank you.

—I will pull off his head and throw it over if he doesn't get up there! said Geoffrey Panyman.

—I'm not doing it, said Is, who then had to scurry round behind his master and Panyman's associate to avoid furious kickings from the other master's fat but curiously dainty foot.

—Get up over that fence you bastard!

Don, completely indifferent to his servant's second assault of the night, looked up into the air above the barely perceptible silhouette of the trees and dwelt upon some inconceivable twist of the hyperfine transition of hydrogen as it impacted upon Being and Time. But even he could not endure for long such mis-kicks to the shins, aimed at his servant though straying to himself.

—Desist! he said, and such was his authority that everyone in fact did. I will accompany my servant to the top of the gates and over their other side, for when I am close at his side, nothing can frighten him, for I am his master, and he is devoted to me.

—It's true, said the ill-used servant.

With this, our two adventurers climbed with some amount of effort over the gates. Alighting upon the ground on the other side, they looked through the bars at the still-puffing Panyman. Is smiled and said:

—Now what can you do for us?

Geoffrey Panyman, visibly colouring even in the dark, lunged for Is's neck through the bars, but the servant, emboldened and invigorated by his new-found safety, jumped out of reach and jeered at him with a little jig of victory.

—Chance, said Don, seems to favour you as much as me these days, good servant Isaiah. Our former abuser Geoffrey Panyman offers himself up as a fair exemplum for the indicators of emotional stress in the body. Note how his eyes protrude from their sockets, the further shortening of his breath, the shaking of the hands as they seek your throat. Although it is true that I am no physician, as well as that I solemnly renounce the possibility of linear Time, such a sight cannot but lure me into conceiving anything but a short and unpleasant future for this man, he is such a picture of unhealth. Where do you think Chance stands as to the opening or not-opening of the gate?

—I'd have to say, said Is with the mischief fairly shooting from his eyes like arrows, that Chance put us on this side of the gates and left old fatty on the other, and who are we to meddle?

—Said like a true adherent! said Don with satisfaction. And so, I'm afraid we cannot assist you in gaining access to this enclosure, which for all anyone knows is Chance's very own nocturnal Arcady. We therefore bid you farewell.

Don and Is nodded at their former assailants and turned to walk up the long winding path towards the house. Geoffrey Panyman, a bitter and angry man with innumerable complaints against the world, stood with uncharacteristic placidity watching our adventuring pair drawing up the path. Eventually, seeing his moment come, he drew a thumb and finger to his mouth and emitted the loudest whistle anyone in the immediate vicinity had ever heard. It ran through the woods, and its echo ran through the woods, and its echo's echo, such was its magnitude.

—I fair near jumped out of my skin! said Is, who had indeed jumped a good few inches off the ground. What's he up to now?

Panyman laughed, made an indication with his hand, and he and his associate turned and walked away. Several lights came on in the house.

—You may very soon wish you had indeed jumped out of that skin of yours, said Don. Because it would provide a very effective decoy to the dogs just now straining to be set free from their kennels.

Behind them they could hear Panyman's laugh tailing off in the distance; but it was the commotion in front which preoccupied Is: the unmistakable sound of several very large dogs thrashing round within cages whilst being unchained and set out to patrol their territory.

Here they come. A cone of torchlight swings through the enormous garden, through the shrubs and trees, and the dogs emerge from the gate, stepping round and on and over each other in a frenzy to commence the chase, and then they are released – the floodlights clanging on – and down the slopes the dogs come, faster than the mind can believe is possible, the movement of sinew and joint rippling beneath their gleaming coats.

—We're dead, says Is.

—Nonsense, says Don. All we have to do is cut into this wooded part here (gesturing off to the side of the path) make our way between the flora found therein, until we reach whatever structure functions as the demarcation of this property's perimeter, and climbing over it, we shall be not only free but also alive.

In the time that it takes Don to say this, all three dogs discover the identity and location of the intruders, and – now drawing together, now apart, two taking the flanks – they work together and are but a dozen yards from our heroes, stalking. Don and Is back away from the path, into the shrubs and among the trees, keeping their eyes on the dogs, whose silence and slow stalking light-footedness is more frightening by far than their quick pursuit. One stops and raises its nose – very wolf-like – and sniffs.

—Why don't they rush us? says Is.

—I don't know, says Don. Perhaps they understand us as brothers in this world.

Another of the dogs sniffs the air, and lets out a high-pitched querying bark. A screech owl replies disapprovingly from above and takes to its wing.

—It is our pelts, Isaiah! says Don all of a sudden.

Is looks down, touches his ridiculous tunic, and emits a noise consistent with the apprehension of revelation.

—They think we are giant rabbits! continues Don. All we have to do now is hop over to the fence or wall or whatever lies beyond in the dark behind us.

—I'm not turning round with those three looking at me like that, says Is.

—Well I am, says Don, and he does exactly that – to Is's ample dismay at being left alone.

How can it be described with sufficient evocativeness the nature of Don's procession through the small nocturnal woodland in the manner of a rabbit! (The truth is, that it cannot.) With Don gone, Is panicked, turned, and began running after his master, at which turn of events the dogs decided this was definitely a man, and a man was what they were there to dissuade from being present. In short, all three dogs leapt on Is's back and brought him down to the ground, and a furious tussle ensued, with teeth and hair and fists and claws and bestial ululation. In the midst of this, Is managed to crawl out the bottom of his tunic, and found the dogs so preoccupied with punishing it that they were willing to forget that the human who had worn it ever existed, such was the wisdom of his master in the identification of this decoy. He was free to go; which he did, with the naked form of his body cringing as he falteringly fled between the slender ribbons of the trees, which appeared to be strung down as tendrils from the blank night sky.

In time (which certainly does have duration, as he had just then had confirmed for him), Is found himself back in his master's company, on the safer side of a crinkle crankle wall, with the action of the dogs tearing the rabbit pelts apart not only audible but also actually sensible from the ground through the soles of their feet.

—I am naked! said Is.

—There are many worse things to be, said Don. Take us onwards, good servant, and Chance will be sure to clothe you in one thing or another, according to her inimitable whim. Anyway, you should be thankful – speaking of my own tunic, it has become so infested with parasites that only a firm commitment to recovering the purity of mind of our prehistoric forebears can persuade me to keep it upon my body.

Is shrugged and did as he was told without the least bit of resistance, for he could do little more than shakily walk onwards and recount in his disbelieving mind the events of the preceding hour or so, which were so unfathomable that he wondered if perhaps the dogs had not got him after all, and whether walking naked over the fine grass of a dark damp field was everyone's afterlife or just his own.

8

The darkness of the night over the cold wet fields of the county led Is to think of home, where had been his only comfort. Inwardly, and deeply, he sorrowed; it was true that he had no home. Soon he felt moved to give oral recitation to his heart's grief.

—In the mornings she would sometimes bring me a buttered muffin with my tea, and up against me through her nightdress back into bed the very-warm curves of her body. That is one thing I'd prefer to unremember if I'm never to feel it again. Because now: no home, no bed, no comfort, no breakfast – and now not even any clothes, flea-infested or otherwise, with the dogs having got them.

—Melancholy is an intolerable third companion, said Don. Please show him to the door without ceremony.

—Nothing doing, sir. What am I going to do about clothes? I can't walk around in the altogether.

—Something will turn up; have faith in Chance.

—Chance which did this to me is hardly going to suddenly undo it. Oh Don, I miss my home, my home that's gone – the whole world just a blankness and blackness without a home.

Don stopped walking, and placed his hands upon his servant's unhappy shoulders with a firm rectitude.

—Live here with me in this eternal Present and you cannot feel sorrow. The past and future have no existence; therefore your home is still your home; indeed, you are already there in thought, which is all there is in this human life.

—You are kind, but I don't think words can cure me.

—If my words can't, then let these words tell you what can. Attend to the rhyme:

> When the world is hard and heartless
> And life feels like a trap
> When your soup's more grit than onions
> And all else there is is chaps
> If the rain has filled your boot holes
> And the wind has nicked your hat
> And there's no-one home 'cept next door's tom
> Most odious of cats
> Then do not fear; terror not
> For all you need do is ask
> Saint Monica'll hie 'erself down the stairs
> And *Pop!* the cap from the flask.

—A drink would be nice, agreed Is.

—Well let's see what's down in this cellar, said Don, moving his hand into the depths of his duffel bag. Now if it's not the lovely Saint Monica herself, just now back from chiding Augustine, I'm——

—A monkey's uncle.

—Twice removed, with a whole tree of co-laterals to rail against the dryness with. Behold!

Gold-gilt and buff-leathered, the whisky flask is raised into the air.

—The wonderful booze! said Is.

While Is sought refuge from his sorrow and the cold of his night-time nakedness in the spiritous liquor within the flask, Don encouraged the lineaments of the spectral line of the hyperfine transition of hydrogen to assume a shape within the infinite space of the palace of his mind. But each time he began getting somewhere, the line branched off. There was a forwarding, or a backwarding, or both, and the whole enterprise collapsed. Such was the difficulty of his mission.

—Sir, said Is interrupting his master's cogitations. I don't know whether to thank you for your kindness or curse you for its opposite, but I've only just now realised that you've gone and got the chest for me, and here it is riding on my back again.

—I did not, said Don.

—Well how on earth did it travel from the gate we climbed over, round the whole estate's wavy wall, and come to perch on my back without me even noticing?

—You should remove forthwith all the faith you have in the past as a real and existent thing, and reorient it upon Chance, Who alone is worthy. Chance has placed the chest here because She is my lovely Bride and desires that my mission be successfully accomplished in Her honour, not that She be either braggart or egotist.

—This Lady of yours must have a pair of forearms on her then, sir, because this chest is as heavy as sorrow, and that's saying something, speaking of my own.

—On the contrary, good servant, nothing is saying anything, words being a mere string of sounds.

Is shrugged, and the pair continued walking, and the chest bobbed along with the servant's every tread.

—But tell me Isaiah, continued Don. Do you happen to be familiar with the Swedish botanist Linnaeus?

—I don't recall the name, but I might stand a better chance by his face. What's he look like?

—It is unlikely that you would have met him, said Don. He died in 1778, not that that precludes your having met him of course, Time being ever-present and never-past.

—I do believe you just contradicted yourself, master.

—When dealing in the true Science such contradictions are inevitable from the viewpoint of our prevailing epistemology.

—I will take your word for it, said Is. Now tell me about this man I could never have met, but might have; and though my feet must keep walking, and my back bearing up this chest, I will try to give my mind a measure of repose in the armchair of your fine words, if my ears will permit me.

—Finely said, good squire. Linnaeus, you should know, established the taxonomical system for living things, thus providing a model for the structure of knowledge. Of course this model had existed for at least two millennia before (you will remember – if I myself am forbidden from doing such things – that I have already mentioned Porphyry's Tree); but Linnaeus applied it to a rigorous analysis of the living forms of the earth. How appropriate it is therefore that Linnaeus' corporeal remains comprise the type specimen (in accordance with the International Code of Zoological Nomenclature) for the species *homo sapiens*. Ha! What is a man? The human being has become a taxonomizer *par excellence*, always trim trim trimming down to newfound minutiae of subdivision the threads of Being. Even the poets have found themselves thus afflicted: a rose is a rose is a rose, indeed! Witness the trajectory, Isaiah. It is called Progress, and by it we will be de-sapientiated, which is to say unmanned. Man became man how? And at what point? Is he not the unmoved mover in his own destiny? How can a thing cause itself to be?

—It sounds very much like our old friends the chicken and the egg.

—Isaiah, you are the very greatest of our species! How I revel in your unadorned mind! Permit me the following digressive *triseptimum* on the chicken and the egg, being an etymological study, wherein the harvest of your brain will become clear.

—Even though the parts of me are somewhat cold, I really am looking forward to this one, sir.

—And so you should. You will hereafter understand the predicament of all human science by a consideration of the aporetic ontological end to all inquiries into the mutually co-dependent, whether concepts or entities.

—I don't doubt it.

In no way implying priority, we shall begin with the word 'egg'. Two forms competed throughout the middle ages to become the word by which one might denote a reproductive body: *egg*, borrowed from Old Norse; and *eye*, from Old English *æg*. (Note well the relationship between an egg and an eye implied by the Old English/Modern English homograph 'eye', for it is not uninstructive). Both these forms ultimately stem from the same prehistoric Germanic root **ajjaz*, which in turn was a descendant of Indo-European **owo-*, which also forms the root of Greek *oión*, Latin *ovum*, French *oeuf*, Italian *uovo*, Spanish *huevo*, and Russian *jajco*. However, this Indo-European root probably stems from an even earlier Proto-Indo-European root for 'bird', which forms also the source of Sanskrit *vís* and Latin *avis*, and is the ancestor of English *aviary*. It might seem, therefore, that *egg* has its origin in describing a bird as an 'egg-maker'; however, devoid of syntax as individual words are, it is equally likely that *egg* stems from the original sense 'bird-maker'. Thus, the two etymological possibilities re-inforce the conundrum by performing the co-dependency of the two entities: an egg is an egg because it is made by a bird and because it makes birds.

No closer to the truth as a result, we therefore turn to the chicken. *Chicken* is a Germanic word, whose ancestor is written as **kiukinam* by etymologists. This word was formed from the base **keuk-* (or **kuk-*) which has been claimed as the variant of a base form which lies behind *cock*. The *-inam* suffix denotes a diminutive, and so a *chicken* is, etymologically speaking, a 'little cock'. This fits in with the written record, in which the word *chicken* tended to be used exclusively for young fowl until quite recently. This gives us very little to go on.

So let us turn to the word *cock*. In doing so, we find that its source is almost certainly onomatopoeic. Let us look at the evidence: the male fowl's call in English, French, German and Italian is rendered as *cockadoodledoo*, *coquierico*, *kikeriki* and *cocorico* respectively. It would therefore seem that *cock* is a shortened version of the sound which that animal makes; and so, the words *chicken* and *cock* have their origin in representing the domestic fowl by the sound it makes, and so it is characterised as a 'sound-maker'. In this case, eggs are not implicated. Instead, something else the chicken makes is at the root of its identity, at least for speakers of the Indo-European languages.

The conclusion to our current investigation, therefore, is this: in seeking both the truth of the egg and the truth of the chicken through the science of words, we reach the real and larger truth: in our hunt for both the chicken and the egg, we miss our target: either the egg is nothing without the chicken (or vice versa), or the chicken is nothing without the sound it makes, or both. Our shot, aimed at the egg, hits the bird, and aimed at the bird, hits its call. In the end, we are given the slip; we have neither the chicken nor the egg; we go hungry. So we see that there is something wrong with the application of the word to the thing: it is inefficient: the meaning bleeds: there is entropy. An egg is not an egg is not an egg. This is where we might turn to the hyperfine transition of hydrogen, which offers the opportunity for the restitution of all things in the symbolic world, marking, as it does, the delusion of temporality. But this is another matter, and here concludes the current *triseptimum*.

—Well I never, said Is. I think I am really beginning to understand what this hyperfine transition of hydrogen thing is all about.

—If you were to suddenly attain full comprehension of what the hyperfine transition of hydrogen is able to achieve, said Don, your mind would fold up and your innards would drop out of you onto the floor. But you won't, so they will not.

—That is reassuring, said Is.

—Anyway, I was talking about Linnaeus, was I not?

—You were.

—Well, suffice it to say that I don't like him and his noontime clarity. And so, in both symbolic and real resistance against the cultural inheritance bequeathed to us by Linnaeus and that self-abuse he perpetrates in the use of his own person for a type-specimen, I have decided that you, Isaiah, will form the type-specimen for *homo sapiens* in my *Encyclopaedia of Being*.

—Are you sure that is a good idea, sir? said Is. Although you've just now praised my brain, some might say I lack the requisite sapience, if that's the word we're using for brains these days. Shouldn't it just be you, sir?

—Some can say whatever the hell they like, said Don. But until the number Twenty-One trips from their tongue, my ears are turned against them.

—Fair enough then, said Is, resigned to the duty of taking his place within the encyclopaedia, or *Encyclopaedia*. So how does it start, this entry about me?

—Let's see, how about:

TRISEPTIMUM: HOMO SAPIENS I: ISAIAH OLM

The person under consideration is frequently inebriated. Therewithal, he is also frequently (at turns): non-retentive of the causes of such inebriation; expectoratory (invariably upon the floor of whichever public house is occupied); given to the makings of hullabaloo; liable to talk too closely and with stridency into the faces of strangers; somnolent; and demonstrative of such ambulatory oscillation as often to result in damage to either his person or to street furniture, or to both.

The foregoing pertains to only one of the seventeen works of the flesh inventoried by Saint Paul – namely drunkenness – the other sixteen of which now follow *in toto*: adultery, fornication, uncleanness, lasciviousness, idolatry, witchcraft, hatred, variance, emulations, wrath, strife, seditions, heresies, envyings, murders, revellings, and such like.

—I can't disagree with any of that, I'm afraid to say, said Is. It's true that I'm particularly fond of Emulating.

—There can very easily be more, said Don, and he hunkered down to add to the written disquisition on the subject of his squire.

Continuation of *Triseptimum*:
Homo Sapiens I: Isaiah Olm

Notwithstanding the formidable degree of devotion evident in the conscientious service of his master, the man to which this account appertains exhibits sundry characteristics which, under the schema of Saint Paul's anatomy of sin, are indicative of an assured moral turpitude. Of the seventeen acts specified, thirteen (13) are represented so amply as to place the classification beyond doubt. Of the remaining five – to wit: idolatry, witchcraft, hatred, seditions and murders – it remains to be seen which will be added to his corpus of sinfulness.

—I wouldn't mind doing some Seditions, but the others are not my bag at all, said Is. I don't really have the mental fortitude for Witchcraft. I would be frightened of myself.

—Ah yes, your fears, said Don. An important supplement to the current *triseptimum*.

Addendum to *Triseptimum*:
Homo Sapiens I: Isaiah Olm, being:
An Inventory of things feared by Isaiah Olm

Being; the orders of being, in order descending: divine, celestial, mundane; space; time; space-time; events; things——

—Do let me know if you disagree with any of these, said Don. I can easily scratch them out.

—Is is as Is does, said Is. Which is to say, nothing so far, sir. You're doing fine.

—In which case I shall continue, said Don, before doing exactly that (and, as before, the reader who dislikes lists may skip to the following page if he or she so desires).

——phenomena; relations of whatever kind between comparable events, things or phenomena; the primary properties of phenomena as percepts, including colours and shapes, odours, textures, sounds and tastes; the inference of knowable entities from the data gathered by sense perception; the dark; his own imagination; the animals, in descending order by class: reptiles, amphibians, insects, birds, mammals; the weather; changes to the weather; unchanging weather; ominous characteristics of the weather, i.e. the portentous character of the weather (e.g. persistent and uniform cloud cover; large, dark clouds piling up in the air; blustery wind); mains electricity; liquids, whether contained or uncontained; gases; solids; interventions in matters concerning domestic plumbing; cubbies and nooks of the household, especially those which refuse or obscure the ingress of torchlight for investigative purposes; the railways; walking in icy conditions, especially over hilly terrain; driving and passengering within an automobile; the manoeuvring of automobiles on the public highway; the authority of others, especially those responsible for public welfare or the manoeuvring of automobiles on the public highway; the incontrovertible sexuality of his parents; eye contact; strong feelings; weak feelings; lack of feeling; pins and needles; disability; wrongful imprisonment; hair-loss; physical wasting; death; lighting gas hobs; public speaking; mad people; forgetting others' names; the potential harms sustained by his children; loss of voice; cancer; the deep end of the swimming pool; dreams of the nightmare class; blood loss; the sight of blood, especially his own; any mortification of the flesh, whomsoever it may be inflicted upon; the idea of killing any living creature; subways; expectation; excessive speed, or excessive alteration to speed being travelled; accidental poisoning and the resultant symptoms of this occurrence, as well as the period of time during which they manifest themselves; flying, sailing, cycling, skiing, and all other modes of transport, irrespective of climate and conditions; arriving somewhere after a long period of travel, irrespective of the mode, or the destination, except if it be his own home; heights, and falling from them; depths, and not rising from them; live burial; accidental death of every possible variety: drowning, suffocation, choking, decapitation, electrocution, etc.; men; women; consequences (the ultimate element in a perceived causative chain, not the pastime involving the unpremeditated juxtaposition of words or images by a number of players, of which he is fond); numbers; letters; words; nonsense; meaning. And most recently – as indeed most vehemently – lightning. Oh, and dogs.

—We will return to this entry in due course, Isaiah. You give the world a lot to learn.

—I'm glad you could find so much of interest in me, sir. But I really do think your book could do with an entry for yourself.

—I don't think that's necessary, Isaiah.

—But of course it is! You, the writer of this masterwork, can't go undescribed in it.

—Well if it satisfies you, I hereby grant you permission to write such an entry, said Don. And I vow to include it within my immortal work.

—You forget I cannot write, sir.

—I do not forget, I simply refuse to remember.

—Well that's not playing very fair, said Is. Someone should do it, you being after all a very different kind of person. I've never met anyone like you before.

—Let's forget about this latest scheme of yours – not that forgetting is possible without a memory – and get back to the considerations of the road. I repeat: if you wish to have an entry for me, you have my permission to come up with something, but I will not write it myself.

—Okay. I'll have it done somehow, said Is.

(And in the spirit of fairness and good will toward the servant, so often wronged by both the world and his own master, the narrative will now provide a description of Don Waswill for the consideration of the reader as the pair continue talking and adventuring through the rural Essex night; and also so that the reader might take some comfort in the forthcoming conversion of this story into something more resembling a *story*, something a little more *enjoyable*, for it will be made to happen, do not fear that. And we can slip this little *triseptimum* into the chest when the pair are not looking.)

TRISEPTIMUM HOMO SAPIENS II: DON WASWILL

His skin sallow, his face wizened and carbuncular, his visage by turns clouded and bright, like a blustery day moving over the mudflats. Erect and aloof, his nose beakish and aloft, yet ready to stoop down to the ground and examine with great patient concentration the effects thereupon. This man as self-involved as a planet, and the workings of his gravity equally mysterious. Even were he not clothed in badger pelts, people in the street would still shrink from him. Hewn out of knotty old boles and coggled into great slender lengths, his legs are a foal's. His trunk resembles most closely that of Our Lord Jesus Christ at late afternoon on his deathday, hanging from his tree, not yet having left himself. But this man's hands so beautiful pianists would howl in the night with envy, though the long opaque sepia fingernails which cap them might be taken to indicate certain broadly defined pathologies. The protuberance before his temples at the brow considerable – forming a promontory beneath which his eyes move with very great indifference to the world beyond. His skin resembling leather, complete with the tang of urea used in its tanning. His temperament oblique; his manner with the world cryptic; his wit woebegone; his sense perception synaesthetic; his aspect taciturn. Most bluff when he's bluffing, most cloven when he's cleaving; an irremediable muddle of a man.

(Such is the authority of the book: to provide balance, order, momentum, even origin, for the proper transaction of the work. No parent ever bid a child *messy* his or her room – you see, there isn't even a word for it.)

But to return to our indomitable duo:

As the two companions talked, the walking became easier; and by the motion of their walking, their tongues were further loosened, to the effect that both space and time passed rapidly beneath their feet and thought; and their friendship, fortified by the pleasure of their nocturnal colloquium, was fit to bloom. Is shivered in his night-time nakedness, but following the dispensation of such wisdom as was contained within his master's most recent discourses, his faith in the wizened old man was restored.

The darkly shimmering surface of the estuary, which was once again visible to their left, grew in magnitude and luminescence, acquiring a sheen as they gradually became elevated by their procession up a shallow hill. From within the blackness, effulgence: lambency rising out of an apparent void, like an idea. Beneath the darkness, a gloaming; behind the manifold scintillation, black – an unsolvable riddle, interdependent, conjoined twins which share a heart, as do joy and sorrow. It lay there, at their side, an enormous expanse, and filled Is's self with an absolutely physical response to its presence. He could feel the myth of things swelling up out of the damp country night and rubbing the length of its flanks against him, curling round him, eyeing him all the time through animal eyes.

In neat succession the road they were on took them through Bradfield, Wrabness, Ramsey, and then brought them to a main road where the first cars they had seen for five or six hours negotiated a roundabout and continued on their way. The faintest touches of pre-dawn light re-established the sense of a horizon.

—If we're back in the civilised world, I could really be doing with some clothes, said the servant.

—Well look down with the orbs of your eyes and you'll see an item of clothing balled up in the gutter of the outer lane of this peculiarly pear-shaped roundabout.

—Is it an item of clothing?

Is picked it up as might a child a dead mouse. The garment uncrumpled, emptying a fine shale from within the stiff folds it had gathered to itself.

—Trousers! said Is.

—Didn't I tell you? said Don. Now take us where Chance wills us to be taken.

—Straight over, Is replied after having climbed into the stiff damp legs of the filthy discarded clothing.

They passed a huddle of factories, an industrial estate, schools, houses. Past the churches they went, past the hospital; and the faint glow of dawn swelled before them in the east. The town was gathering itself around them, declaring its utility, its human necessity. The tinge to the sky turned ever so slowly through the colour spectrum. The stars fled. A taxi passed. Buses queuing for the commencement of their day rattled the shop windows with their engines. The shops, many shuttered; their frontages strewn with rubbish. A human being asleep in a porch. The light swelled rapidly now – the streetlights fizzing uncertainly out. The unmistakable sound of cawing gulls at flight. Past the water tower the road took them, past the rail station, past the municipal buildings; exhaustion deep in their bodies and minds. And there, before them, at the terminus of the town, the wharf coming alive with vehicles packing and unpacking the ships at the mouth of the estuary; and beyond, the sea, out of which was delivered the rising of the sun.

9

If it is perhaps true that the preceding chapter was tainted by too much pontification on the part of the master – so many of his so-called *triseptima* – then it did at least serve also to bring our adventuring pair to the port town of Harwich in the north-eastern tip of the county of Essex. Here, after stealing a shirt from a woeful old charity shop, Is attempted to feed himself for free, and was reprimanded by members of the county's Constabulary, and thereafter taken to the police station. Sigh the servant did; but a proportion of that sigh registered relief, for by his arrest he achieved his aim, the police offering him a beef sandwich soon after his arrival. Don Waswill, polymath and hero of this our tale, attempted to negotiate his friend's freedom; however, lacking the requisite interpersonal skills for the acquisition of his desires, he was unsuccessful. He was so unsuccessful, in fact, that he was also arrested, though for the more serious offence of assaulting a police officer. Both were transported by police van to the holding cells at the police station at Butt Road, Colchester, and Is cooed and moaned in lovesickness as the familiar scenery of the town passed by, recalling to him memories of his estranged wife.

The two friends were booked, and then spent a day together in their cell; and it was whilst engaged in expansive though largely meaningless talk that the latch was released, the door opened, and an inmate fellowed to them within the white cube.

—If I believed, said Don, that the exercise of memory was at all possible, which patently it neither is nor can be, then I would be convinced that the man who has just been brought into our cell is none other than Mr William Smith.

—I would worry if you thought any different, said Is, because I would recognise both the sneer on his face and the boot on his foot – the very one that first began kicking walls down at Tom Harding's place – even if I were blind. It's him as sure as eggs is eggs.

—Alright? said the man who was most certainly William Smith.

—We are very well, said Don. What brings you into our company?

Smith sat down on the sloping shelf behind the toilet and put his feet up on the lidless rim.

—Fighting. You?

—The Law will stop at nothing to preserve its abominable strictures, said Don. It is my belief that the false institutions of our nation – which is to say, all institutions, for their very institutedness is their taint – are becoming aware of their precarious existence in the face of the Truth I profess and under whose aegis I forge valiantly ahead. And so they seek to keep me under lock and key. All I did was offer a policeman a symbolic corrective about the head; and all my servant did was attempt to avail himself of some sustenance, which even under the terms of the Abominable Law must surely be a Human Right.

—Assault of a police officer, said Smith. That's better than me – all I did was slap this uppity twat down the market.

Smith scratched at his arm, and looked about himself; it was apparent that he desired to smoke a cigarette.

—You beat us at Tom Harding's place too, he said. Or are we *fermaying* our *boosh* about that one?

Here, Smith raised his eyes to the camera in the corner of the room.

—No camera is going to tell me what to say or hear, said Don. What are you saying or not saying about Tom Harding's place?

—Oh sir, said Is.

—Tom Harding's place hit the deck of course after your little piece of work, said Smith – and he spat a lump of mucus into the open bowl between his feet.

—If you are referring to what I think you are referring – and it is only with Chance's infinitely merciful forbearance that I am being granted such a special dispensation to utilise that haggard imposter Memory – then I should say to you that you would needs be careful if you value the skull which encloses your brain. There is as little chance that that house fell down as that my servant here will spontaneously atomise, for gravity exists as little as do atoms, which is to say: not at all.

At this, Is became anxiously engaged in examining himself with his hands for the first signs of his atomisation, whatever that was, while the other two men continued their conversation.

—I can only say what I saw the next day, continued William Smith, and that was a great big pile of rubble, and one room opening up on to the open air like it was the war.

Growing crimson with fury, Don began moving towards the man who insulted his beloved Chance with such flagrancy.

—I may look to you like little more than an aged bag of bones, he said. But you should be aware that my Science, which despises all human institutions, despises most the institution of morality. And know this: a man without a moral is a fearsome fighter, for nothing constrains him. Therefore, prepare to have the many parts of you separated one from another and dispersed throughout this cell.

Don continued to move towards William Smith, who far from looking at all worried was looking out over the void of the toilet bowl between his feet with amusement. Fearing for his master's welfare, Is pulled the emergency cord by the cell door and announced that the two men inside were about to start fighting.

—Incident in 7, came the nasal reply, and the intercom crackled into silence again.

—What manner of servant are you, Isaiah? said Don, diverting his rage towards his squire. You saw as well as I that the house which is known as Tom Harding's place did not, would not, and could not fall down. And yet, against all Truth, you assist this ruffian in eluding the justice of my good arm!

—I'm just trying to help, sir, said Is, backing away from his master. This William Smith is handy in a fight, mark my words. It's been bred into him. You wouldn't stand a chance, sir.

—It is Chance, Isaiah! said Don. Not 'chance', *Chance*!

Is had reached the limit of his retreat, and now stood with his back wedged in the corner of the room blubbering most unmanfully. William Smith laughed his work to see.

Just then the cell door opened, and two police officers entered.

—Simmer down you lot, said one from out of a face raw from his morning shave, and the two of them looked on as the cell's occupants played out the death of the argument.

Don dropped his head and focused every fibre of his being upon the Truth and therefore Beauty and therefore Goodness of the hyperfine transition of hydrogen so that he might avoid having his incarceration extended into the afternoon.

—Get down off that shelf, mate, said the other officer to William Smith, who graciously obliged.

—Now calm down, said the first officer. You two (pointing at Don and Is with the butt-end of a biro he held in his hand) can be off out of here within the hour if you stop pissing around.

The door was slammed shut again, and footsteps receded up the hall.

The three men stood, or leant, or crouched in silence variously within the cell for a time. Is looked at William Smith, William Smith looked at Don Waswill, Don Waswill looked at the convex rears of his own eyelids, seeing only the beautiful dance of the hyperfine transition of hydrogen, stilled, sending out the true structure of being, in the eternal present, obliterating every form of opposition.

Eventually William Smith spoke:

—What's next then?

—That's as touchy a subject as the last, said Is. I think we're going to go wherever out legs take us.

—Where'd your fancy rabbit suit get to?

—Will you keep violating the air with your tongue! said Don.

—Sir, said Is, seeking to avoid another confrontation.

—But it's true that his voice is louder than his words deserve, said Don. You are a liar William Smith, and I won't hear it.

—I'm telling you, said Smith. The next day the house was fallen down, and everyone was talking about it.

—No, said Don.

—And when Fucker Harding got home he went mental. Went out hunting he did straightaway, and he shot John Thecchere's Lucy's pomeranian, says he mistook it for a chicken, which is bollocks.

Don hung his head down low and shook it lightly from side to side.

—If you don't believe me, Smith said, come back to Manningtree and I'll show you with your own eyes.

—I'm not going back there! said Is.

—Even my own eyes are not so infallible as to make such a judgement, said Don. Optics offers but an approximation, for the True Truth cannot be seen. I no longer despise but rather feel pity for you William Smith, because it must be that your eyes misled you, and you do not have the strength of mind to resist the beguilements of vision. There are many stages to the empirical acquisition of knowledge, from object, via the eye, to percept, to concept, to comparative classification, and so on into the labyrinth of your own acculturation – far too many stages for any kind of truth to survive. For Truth, if it can obliterate all error when held in the right mind, is equally prone to dissolution at the hands of the foolish. Rather than look, you would do better simply to think of the hyperfine transition of hydrogen, which as well as being everything in the universe is also a kind of short-cut to knowledge, and a true and good knowledge at that, not some patched-up and be-fur-balled construction you might as easily discover under an armchair.

Reaching the limit of his own tolerance for an insult he could not understand, William Smith jumped down again from the shelf to which he had climbed, crossed the floor with lithe and startling rapidity, and punched Don in the face with such force that he fell straight back on to the floor and lay there as if he was dead.

—Sir! said Is leaping to his side. Oh you've done it now William Smith.

Smith pulled the emergency cord, and announced:

—Incident in 7.

—Incident in 7! echoed the clerk.

Before Is could even place the jacket he had removed from his back beneath Don's head, the two officers re-entered the room, and while one rough-housed William Smith out of the cell, the other resuscitated Don with *sal volatile*.

—Spirit of Hartshorn! murmured Don as he came round.

The officer helped Don up on to unsteady feet and led him and Is out to the medical room. Within fifteen minutes, he was patched-up and ready again for whatever adventure or adventures Chance might feel to throw at him; and the police officers were only too glad to swap these two unknown and unknowable burdens on their time in exchange for the amply well-known William Smith, whose record was at least as long as any arm one might choose to measure for the comparison. Out into the sunny air they were propelled without charge.

Is sat on the buttercupped bank outside the police station and looked out over a large roundabout swathed in battalions of tulips gathered into groups by colour. Past the County Court buildings up Balkerne Hill he looked, where the thin ribbon footbridge arched across at its apex in some kind of unintentionally bathetic parody of a rainbow preserved to remind human beings of their limitations, and above which an immense flock of starlings just then rolled into view over the hill, turning internally, swarming but never dispelling nor losing its shape, as if in the aggregate they formed a single engine, their unmusical chorus reverberating between the buildings. And Jumbo to the East, the turquoise of the copper roof vivid under the noonday sun. Is's home-town.

—Sir, said Is, taking the whole feeling of the place in. I would like to see my children.

Don looked past the twin tissue-packed swellings of his nostrils down at his servant.

—I will take you to them.

At which Is leapt to his feet.

—Where will they be? said Don. I am an innocent when it comes to the young ones of our species.

—At school. Not far at all.

Collecting the detritus which were their possessions and placing it in the chest, our two valiant adventurers cut down the bank to the hot pavement, and walked back past the police station, up Butt Road past the sex shop, the dilapidated taxi rank, the crushed and discarded polystyrene takeaway containers smeared with burger sauce now split in the sun, past the unleased pub; and then up the dark brick steps to the alleyway which ran between the rear gardens of the Victorian terraces and the high wall of the garrison with its coil of barbed wire atop running the perimeter. All the way to the end they travelled, down past the rotting garden gates, the leaning sheds, the broken brick, dog shits, sick – until, coming out at Walsingham Road they turned left and stood at a pair of gates not unlike that outside the front of Tom Harding's place at Mistley, but here not fear nor foreboding for Is, solely delight; it was lunchtime just begun, and they looked on as the classrooms emptied: the shape of each child instantly recognizable as not the one, not the one, not the one, until:

Yes.

Out came his son from one class, and his daughter from another, and they ran out into the playground, every movement an instance of perfected form. They lost themselves in the rush of the playground, Is watching for their reappearance from among the dozens of children, running and dancing and skipping haphazardly in one turning mass not unlike the starlings he had just seen – though the noise they made was better birdsong altogether.

—They're happy! said Is with relief.

—If there's one thing I know about children, said Don as he placed – he could not say why – his hand on his servant's shoulder, it's that a young child is the happiest human there is.

Emitting a kind of barely perceptible vibration beneath the hand of his master, Is stood transfixed holding two railings of the gate in his hands. Don peered curiously at the face of his servant. What manner of thing was a man?

—Oh Don, thank you. Look at their little bodies! What a mess my life is.

—Everything will work out in Time, Isaiah; and I do not mean with the lapsing of Time, which is a fallacy, but *within* Time, if you can prise yourself into it.

Don allowed his servant to observe his children for the duration of their playtime until they were called in to eat.

A bell was rung – tossed up and down in the hand of the teacher Is knew by face though not name – and the children as if governed by some mysterious differential magnetism gathered into their separate groups and went straight in through the appropriate door and the schoolyard was left empty and silent except for the creaking of an old tin sign, whose peeling paint had left the writing illegible.

—Are you ready, Isaiah? asked Don.

—I'm ready.

—In which case, let us move on.

They turned from the school and walked away, round to St John's Green, through the gatehouse of the old abbey where once miraculous voices had been heard, and then out of the town past the parcelled dwellings which faced the road in an attitude of patient waiting; out past the reservoir at Abberton, down the slopes to the mud flats at the estuary, across the long straight ribbon of the ancient Strood to Mersea Island, where between the mud and the mist there was but a thin dividing line, yet no horizon.

10

Don stood upon the strand.

—Although baptism is a sacrament of the church, and therefore the silly custom of an abominable institution, yet there is something of momentousness to such symbolic acts. Besides, the itching from this rancid tunic is becoming more and more unpleasant.

Having said these words, Don kicked his pelt moccasins off and drew creakily over his head the patchwork of badger and roe deer skins to stand in his grey wrinkly nakedness upon the shingle shore. Is winced to see what was revealed: great welts and weeping sores in allergic reaction to the flea bites.

—Oh sir, you'd better get in that water quick before some crow takes a fancy to your shoulder.

—Is it as bad as that? I am certainly in some discomfort.

—You look like you're made of salami, said Is.

Don waded out into the placid waveless water, scything his ankles through its cool mass to form two delicate liquid chevrons in his wake which expanded and overlapped and eventually obliterated one another in a dance of reflected light. Soon his body was fully submerged, and he swam this way and that along the shoreline on his back while Is watched the grey beard and the corrupted intelligence of his wrinkled, boney profile moving across the face of the water. What a man he was, this master of his.

Refreshed and disinfected by his saltwater bath, Don emerged a contented adventurer indeed.

—It is no wonder the average cave man is believed only to have lived to thirty, he said, what with all the nibbling and infection they must have got from their first clothing. No longer will I tolerate the putrefaction attendant upon the wearing of uncured leather, though I say *requiem in pace* to our forebears, whose forbearance of flea bites perhaps gives them their name.

Drawing the lid of his chest up, Don reached in and retrieved his old clothes: suit trousers, shirt, a light lambswool sweater which many moths had loved, trenchcoat, old boots, socks.

—You kept that little stash quiet! said Is. It's a good job these old trousers I found have dried out and seem to have caught some kind of ironing off the heat of my own legs, because otherwise I'd be hijacking yours from you.

Don smiled at his servant, and clapped the lid of the chest shut with a theatrical flourish of his arm.

—Onwards! he said, and the reader can be forgiven for believing that the whole strand itself, in a grand curve of shingle from east to west, was in agreement.

Leaving the pelt tunic on the shore to fester, and now dressed as any two conventional men might choose to be, our companionable pair climbed back up to street level, walked the broad esplanade, and then worked their way along the western shore of Mersea Island, up towards the landings. At the sailing club, they descended to a narrow strip of beach where there were moored a number of boats of pleasantly and vividly varied colour. They took the one closest to where their walking had delivered them, because that was what Chance had ordained was right and proper for them, and then pushed off into the channel between aromatic mudflats.

—If I am not mistaken, said Don, Chance has felt it fit to put us in this boat with the express purpose of sailing, or rowing, to France. And it can be no coincidence that that is precisely where CERN's large hadron collider is located. Truly we are closing in on the secrets of the hyperfine transition of hydrogen! It wouldn't surprise me one bit if Chance didn't carry us across the sea, and thence across the land as if it were little more than a dream, and place us in the control room of the collider to teach those so-called scientists a thing or two about the particles of Being. So, once we get out into the open sea, all you have to do is row towards the sun and very soon we'll be welcomed on French soil, which nourishes a mind more respectful of Truth than the English, or so I have heard.

Don lay back in the boat, placed his duffel bag beneath the nap of his neck, and immediately fell asleep, not waking until the whole fullness of the day had elapsed. Is did just as he had been told, but was tricked: the sun lured them south-east out of the Blackwater, past Colne Point at the mouth of the estuarine confluence, with the great twin cuboid of the Bradwell power station visible to the south; but then snuck slowly south and west across the sky until the tides of the Channel caught the bark and sent it back towards the coast, where in a few hours' time the sun would join them in rest upon the patchwork fields of Essex. The salt stung deep into the blistered palms of the boat's rower; our indefatigable pair ran aground. Don woke up and found himself sitting in a boat beached by Tip Head on St Peter's Flat, looking across primordial glistening mudflats once more, to the twin estuaries from where they had departed in the morning. He was so happy he crowed.

—Whatever it is that lies at the origin of all things, he said, I want this thing to bless you, Isaiah. You have not concerned yourself with reasoning out a correct course according to the destination I described to you. You have followed your nose, or, in rowing, your nose has followed you, and now both you and your nose are where they are, and I am here too, and I would challenge anyone to deny that here is the best of any place there is to be.

They disembarked. Quills of long dark grass pricked at their ankles as they crossed the salt marsh. Stepping over the brackish pools Is saw the evening sky moving within the earth, more real than the one above, clarified by its reflection in the black surface of the water. Beyond, the land proper, gritty, and then up the shallow slopes, covered with long, wide-bladed pale green grass which shivered in the wind. The wind – it had harrowed the few isolated trees into arthritic twists, as if their longsuffering backs were turned against it, and now groaned through the boughs. A decrepit shed stood high on stilts, long decades condemned. The coast all along appeared as some kind of filamented crust jutting out over a silver void, a promontory of crackling flint held together by the caprices of some forgotten god.

Reaching the shingled shore, they walk up the shallow gradient, only to find when they reach the limit of the climb they are in a broad hollow, the edges of which form a close horizon, which howls in wretched chorus with the passing of the wind, though they themselves are protected. Passing laterally across the hollow, round a hidden turn amongst the grass, they head down – but are brought up, and might see for many miles around the flattened landscape if the light mist allowed it. The low cloud turns and shifts as it passes. The pale mist arranges the prospect into degrees of distance, marked by their ever-decreasing vividness. Everything ranged as if a cut-out, a line of trees rushing forward as Is looks to them, and then back again when his eyes shift to another point of view, the trees tacking back on to the horizon like stage-sets. From their high vantage point, the sea hump-backed, like a wind-blown hill; and all around them the briars arcing over in great banks of metalworked ropes. Dung and hay in the fields around combined; the blackthorn and whitethorn and hawthorn splintered at the trackside by a vicious coppicing; the old church rising up from the close-grazed grass in impossible vertical elongation. Everything ranged upon horizontal planes, distances shifting, and then sudden crooked interruptions leaping into the sky and eye.

All at once the wind abated, and the clouds flocked down to the ground and hid the world in white-plumaged bellies of thick fog. A chill descended upon the earth.

—I don't like this one bit, said Is.

In reply, Don marched his assistant forward, where out of the white wet air an indistinct silhouette refined itself into a great building of flint and brick: simple, house-shaped, but far bigger, and with only a few very small slit windows high up under the angles of the roof's sharp apex, beneath which a large studded wooden door invited them in. Everywhere around the gloom gathered.

—Let's get us in this church, said Don.

They entered the cool quiet interior, their eyes drawn to observe above them the great oak rafters of the steep roof bleached grey by the narrow rays of sunlight and time. Don shut the door behind them. Rough to the touch were the great stones within the walls, grouped in patches, divided by creases and scars, like the skin of an elephant, which like Is is said never to forget. Oak benches ranged along the floor up towards the altar, a simple stone bench; and above it on the patched dapple of the altar wall a crimson crucifix with Christ flanked by Peter with his key and Paul with his sword. Above, the hand of God; below, Saint Cedd on his knees clutching a staff and looking up to his Lord; to either side, the Saviour's mother and father.

—Sir! said Is. There's someone there!

Don peered into the dark interior with his ancient eyes. It was true; a figure sat to the left of the altar.

—So there is, said Don.

—What's he doing? said Is.

—No doubt the same as us, sheltering from the chill of the fog. You needn't whisper, for God is but a dream, and every man little more than an apparition.

However, no sooner had Don said this than the bizarre mechanism of his Science began to whirr within him, to the end that he soon saw with incomparable clarity the manner in which this man here with them within the church participated in Don's own unique destiny.

—Now I think about it, he said, I can see beyond all doubt that the person sheltering here in this church is an anchorite, marooned in the careless folds of history, spurned into solitude by our steely and hateful modernity. In fact, not even James Ussher, writer under James I of the authoritative catalogue of saints, would be able to persuade me that the man before us is not Saint Cedd come here to his very own church of Ythanceaster to die of the plague.

—It's true that he doesn't look so chipper, said Is. But although my knowledge of saints is strictly limited (I am certainly fond of one, she who grants to me my easeful days, Saint Monica I mean) I am sure I have never heard of a saint wearing trainers.

—I will establish with him a colloqium in his own language in regard to the discovery of a cure to his ills, both spiritual and physical.

—Well if he does have the plague, you'd better not get too close. I for one am going to sit on this bench here and look at the opposite wall and keep as far away from him as I can.

—You are free to do whatever you want, Isaiah, though I doubt the wisdom of what you propose. But before you do anything, retrieve for me my Anglo-Saxon dictionary, which will enable me to converse freely with him in his own tongue, my Old English not being what it once was. And I would advise you good squire to observe this famous moment in our adventry as it unfolds, even if you find the opposite wall of this place irresistible and can only attend through your ears.

Is shrugged, bent over, and, in amongst the hundreds of thousands of paper slips which he had cut from his master's encyclopaedia to free it from its alphabetic form, he found nesting there the book his master desired. Flicking through it, Don began walking down the aisle towards the altar, to the side of which sat the anchorite, or saint, or person.

—Haelettung, æðeling, said Don, arriving before the anchorite.

The anchorite looked up from beneath his hood, and nodded a solemn greeting.

—Well I'll be buggered if he's not doing it! said Is in quiet wonder to himself.

—Hwaet séocnes þu geþrówest?

The anchorite dropped his chin back down to his chest, and gave only a slight grunt.

—Hwaet séocnes? Don repeated.

A nest of martens from high in the roof answered, but the man did not. Don prodded him at the shoulder; he rocked lightly, but made no response.

—Isaiah! said Don. I think his time is not long. We must save him!

Don bent low to look beneath the anchorite's hood.

—Yes, it is most certainly a plague, because he has sores on his face.

—Tramps do have sores you know, sir, said Is from across the church. In fact, the one down the road from me has plenty, as well as only one leg.

—We will need a remedy. Get me Cockayne!

—What is Cockayne?

—A book, Isaiah. *Leechdoms, Wortcunning, and Starcraft of Early England* is the book's name, and Cockayne is the author. For God's – I mean Twenty-One's sake, hurry!

Is sighed and moaned, flipped up the lid of the chest again, and after a good rummage through the multitude of paper slips obtained this Cockayne which had hid like an egg within.

—Bring! Bring!

Is began to walk up the aisle, but very soon faltered.

—I am nervous, sir.

—Just bring the damned book here!

—But what if it is the plague?

—Then the cure I give the anchorite can be turned on you too. Now give it to me!

From somewhere very deep in his interior, Is retrieved a scrap of courage and made his way to his master's side.

—He does look bad doesn't he, said Is lifting the top of the hood a little to peep.

—Turn to the plague section, said Don.

—Which section is that?

—Ah, just give it to me.

Don dropped his Anglo-Saxon dictionary with a reverberating clap to the stone floor and took up *Leechdoms, Wortcunning, and Starcraft*.

—Hmmm, here is one remedy. Flying venom appears to be the name for it, presumably because it describes the means by which the contagion travels.

> For flying venom and every venomous swelling, on a Friday churn butter, which has been milked from a neat or hind all of one colour; and let it not be mingled with water, sing over it nine times a litany, and nine times the Pater noster, and nine times this incantation. The charm is said in the table of contents to be Scottish, that is Gaelic, but the words themselves seem to belong to no known language.

—This is no use at all! said Don.

—It's true that we don't have butter, a deer, or the words of the necessary charm, and it's as likely to be any other day as it is Friday, their names now as separate from the days as me and my Ruth. Ah Ruth!

—Stop thinking about yourself for once. There will be other charms. Ne ádrædan, Sanct Cedd! he then said to the hooded man. Ge þu hæledon! Let's find another before he carks it.

Don flicked furiously through his strange book until he found the next cure for flying venom.

> The white stone is powerful against stitch, and against flying venom, and against all strange calamities: thou shalt shave it into water and drink a good mickle, and shave thereto a portion of the red earth, and the stones are all very good to drink of, against all strange uncouth things. When the fire is struck out of the stone, it is good against lightenings and against thunders, and against delusion of every kind: and if a man in his way is gone astray, let him strike himself a spark before him, he will soon be in the right way. All this Dominus Helias, patriarch at Jerusalem, ordered one to say to king Alfred.

—Well that sounds to me like something you might have written yourself, sir! The white stone must be flint, because you can make sparks with it. And while you're at that spark-making over the head of Saint Said or whatever he's called, you might want to strike a few out over your own to cure yourself of your peculiars.

—Stop speaking forevermore, you prattling idiot. How much of a delusion can my Science be if Chance has laid in my pocket the very flint we need to cure the man before us?

Don withdrew the flint he had harboured in his pocket ever since it had fallen from the wall outside Ringwood's house many days before.

—The whole damned church is made up of a million flints, said Is. So your old lady Chance might not have bothered. Christ, we've kicked enough flint walking over the land to build a temple to your hyperfine thingy of thing so big it'd make St Paul's look like a tool shed.

Ignoring Is, Don withdrew the flint from his pocket, and it did indeed upon one of its faces exhibit that white rind mentioned in the remedy.

—Sparks struck from flint and steel by strong percussion: achieve it for the blessed man.

Don handed the flint and his pocket knife to Is, who, fearing what Don would otherwise do, did as his master, Francis Bacon, and Cockayne in his *Leechbook* directed as one, together. The sparks flew, coruscating in the dark interior down over the hooded head. At the very same moment, the studded oak door of the church swung open to reveal a small group of people standing in the doorway, one of whom said:

—John?

They peered into the halflight of the still space beneath the serried triangulations of the roof's rafters, straining to decode the gloom. John – and not Saint Cedd – lifted his head, turned it toward the door, and rose to his feet. The people entered, came to his side, and then just as promptly exited with their companion, whom they embraced and supported and coaxed with caring words and gestures. Don and Is were left alone to ponder the chain of events which had – or perhaps hadn't, as Don might well see it – just occurred.

—Although he appears to have answered to the name 'John', Don said, there is no doubt in my mind that the man we just saved from certain death is none other than St Cedd, the depth of whose sorrowing attests as much to his grief at being trapped in the history books as it does to his affliction with the plague. It is as easy as a pie to cure a man of plague, as we have just now proven; it is a different matter altogether to refine the history books into non-existence and leave the true, timeless man standing there at liberty. Let's follow him, for My Lady Chance has placed him before us, and Chance in Her infinite mercy will show us how we might achieve a far greater success in this respect, for our work is only just begun.

—If you say so, sir. But I'd rather not go out into that fog again, because it does bad things to my nerves, and you don't even need a corner to not know what's round it in a fog, because the very straightest path leads into the unknown.

—Just as it is and should be in every endeavour, and just as the Prince of Stagira the last great thinker Aristotle knew up to his eyeballs. But shelter behind me, fearful squire, and you need fear nothing, for the fog will shrink back like a wild dog in the face of my righteous fire.

Is shrugged, drew the heavy oak chest on to his back, and followed his imperious master out through the heavy oak door into the desolate landscape once more.

The fog had grown so thick, however, that the people they intended to follow were no longer visible, and our adventuring pair had to guess the route they had taken. Up and down the undulating landscape they went, over the damp grey ground, the limit of their vision always constant, the strict curtain of fog drawn across the world. Down they went past the stilted shack again, its form now a looming irregular hexahedron above their heads. Within a shallow concavity in the earth, broad bladed razor grass lay flat in great overlapping swathes, as if some great beast had slept there. They joined a shingle path which led them nowhere in particular through a fog which annihilated all sound beyond the limits of vision, and brought the scrapings of their feet all the more intimately into their ears. An unkempt hedgerow halted their path; winding along its edge, our audacious pair discovered a tunnel cutting into and through its tangled interior, whose ringed entrance resembled most closely a monstrous crown of thorns.

—If you think I'm going into that, you don't know me at all, said Is.

—Well I am going in, and that will leave you all alone in this primordial vapour which may shelter all manner of rapacious fiend. I wouldn't be surprised one bit if Grendel stumbled upon you.

—Well that wouldn't bother me at all, because I know that story, and she was a clever girl as to outwit that witch, so I'd probably feel safer than I do now with you.

—You are thinking of Gretel. Grendel, the shadow walker, is something completely different, and his mother even worse than Gretel's. Descended from Cain, humanity's first murderer, Grendel lives within the goo of swamps not unlike that which squelches beneath the salt marshes and between the mud flats recently passed. Four men are required in the lifting of just his head. Perhaps Grendel was just now resting on the ground beneath that rotting shack and already has your scent.

—Let's go down this tunnel here, said Is.

—I knew you would see sense, said Don.

They entered the thorny hole and began to follow the course of its narrow channel. What sparse budding of berries and leaves had managed to grow within the nooks at the hedgerow's edge now disappeared, and the bare fibrous shafts of thorns and their twisted stems formed a complex reticulum which contorted and snaked at the smallest movement of the eye, like thousands of blood vessels pulsating within a tubular membrane, ready for the birthing of some abortive hog. All around our two adventurers as they advanced the writhing structure arched, and beyond: only the sorrowful opacity of the fog, and not an animal to be heard.

Eventually, they emerged from the tunnel into a pleasant garden. Thick grass cushioned the tread of their feet as they crossed. Vegetables ranged in neat rows grew beneath an upturned plastic bottle on a stick, sentinel to their ripeness. The fronds of the carrots, the knees of the bean stalks, the weft of the tomato vine – everything was bejewelled in vivid droplets from the pertinacious fog. Across the neat lawn beyond the vegetable patch stood a modern single-story building whose three frontages were arranged as three sides of a square, a tripartite horseshoe, and its dark windows aspectant upon the lawn between. Our intrepid adventurers walked along the line of all three walls, first the left side, then the centre, then the right.

—It would needs present us with an aperture to permit our ingress, said Don.

From behind them came a curious cracking sound, and they turned around to discover a door, previously unseen, opened to them, and a face within the doorway friendly and smiling. Don and Is exchanged a look of which Chance might have been proud, and they crossed the grassy lawn. The door closed behind them to shut out the fog, and Is shook the cold out of himself, only now perceptible.

—We seek a man, St Cedd, who was seen and cured by us in the church, said Don without preamble.

—Welcome to the Othona Community, said their host. Follow me.

They followed the woman down the corridor into a large common room, where a dozen or so people sat reading books and magazines and drinking coffee; and thence through some double doors into a large kitchen where several people stood around a great workbench at its centre.

—Sorry, your names? said the woman.

—Donald J. Waswill, said Don.

—Is, said Is.

—Welcome to you both! said the community as one, beckoning them forward with be-floured hands.

—Today we are baking. We grow and harvest our own wheat just out the back, you may have seen? Um (and here she looked at the filthiness of our two adventurers) would you mind scrubbing up before you start? There are aprons in the basket by the laundry room.

Don and Is walked round the bench and out to the laundry room, where they washed their hands.

Back at the bench, our two friends took direction from their courteous host in the manufacture of various breads. In a little over four hours, they prepared muffins, a fine white plait loaf, Polish bublik, zwieback of Germany, Portuguese broa, Turkish yufka, Georgian shoti, a large batch of scones, Japanese anpan, and a large strudel, such was the variety of workers by nationality then staying with the community, and such the desire of that community to ensure the comfort of its visitors. By the time Don and Is finished baking, they – or one of them at least – had worked up a substantial appetite, and so both accepted the invitation to dine.

—As it seems I must accept that your stomach is a more authoritative leader than am I, said Don aside to his servant, I will join you as you dine, though of course I will not myself eat, for I cannot imagine that the hyperfine transition of hydrogen ever eats, being as it is inorganic, and thus free of all the scourges that may trouble a man. I will observe the customs of this sect as you chew, or else meditate on my fine friend the Haitch-Tee-Haitch – unless Saint Cedd comes through the door.

Before Is could even open his mouth – and it is true that he had both words to say and a tearing of bread held in his hand to place there – Saint Cedd, or 'John Gerveyn' as he was more commonly known, shuffled through the very doorway which Don's nodding head had indicated into the room, with the two friends who had retrieved him from the church still supporting him on either side.

Whatever Is had sought to have said – and it now seems that we will never know – vanished from his mind, and the bread he held in his hand might as well have been those very words, such was the degree of its holder's disregard. Yet Is's mouth did fall open as he watched the procession of his master's latest obsession cross the floor to his seat at table.

—If that doesn't prove that Chance favours me, then I don't know what would, said Don.

Is turned towards his master a face radiant with admiration.

—How did you know?

—I knew as much as a daisy knows the sun, which is to say both not at all and completely.

—But why is he being led along like a blind animal? Has the plague got him after all – I hope your cure with the flint wasn't just another piece of quackery.

—'Another' is unacceptable there, Isaiah. Everything I have done has been auspicious to the highest degree.

—I was only saying so because Saint Said looks now to be almost Saint Dead for certain. I wonder that his eyes don't seem to want to land for long on anything – they are like a couple of flies.

—It is a nervous rather than a physical ailment certainly, said Don.

—I wonder what caused it.

—Please don't say the word 'cause' in my presence, said Don. In fact, don't use it at all, because owing to the fallacy of space, presence and absence are neither different from one another nor do they have reality at all. Cause and Effect are the great storying delusions of human culture, and they are about to take a hiding to none. If I believed it was possible that the past existed, I might suggest to you that I have in fact reminded you of this on several occasions previously.

—Nevertheless———, said Is leading his master gently on.

—Okay, and to indulge you in common parlance: it looks to me like he's had a bit of a fright. But watch, because after he's come forward with his ministers at his side, he will stand by what he takes to be an altar, and if I'm not mistaken very soon in accordance with the ancient tradition will say: Τοῦτό μου ἐστὶν τὸ σῶμα τὸ ὑπὲρ ὑμῶν κλώμενον· τοῦτο ποιεῖτε εἰς τὴν ἐμὴν ἀνάμνησιν, and in doing so repeat the words of his Lord at the institution of the Eucharist at the Cenacle before the Essene, as are we here before these so-called Othona. Thus we will know him to be the saint that he most certainly is.

—Ketchup? said Saint Cedd, or John Gerveyn.

—Ah, how the emptiness of modernity does corrupt every institution, said Don in lamentation.

A red plastic spheroid intended to resemble a tomato was brought to the table, and upending it St Cedd obtained via the small spout at its top a quantity of the viscous sauce upon his empty plate. Around the table sat the members of the community and their guests in good-willed silence – twenty-one in number as it happened, though fortunately Don did not notice.

Several remained in the kitchen, evident in the crescendo of audible activity just then taking place as the final preparations for dinner were made. A door at the end of the room swung open, and tureens of sausages in a thick brown gravy, of mashed potato, and of steamed carrots and runner beans – good honest English fare – were carried in, tails of steam following their bearers. Each person's plate was liberally filled by these assistants, Grace was spoken over the protestations of Is's stomach, and all began to eat.

Throughout the meal, Don kept a watchful eye on the man he took to be Saint Cedd. Sitting hunched over his plate, the Saint – or John Gerveyn – ate little, and for long stretches of time simply held his fork aloft like a dowsing rod and looked as any diviner might into the unknown, seeking less water than peace. Much of what food he did raise to his lips fell or dripped down his front. His eyes had long ago, or so it seemed, retreated into their sockets, and far further back behind them lay the personality he worked to conceal, a safety maintained through distance. There was something heartbreaking to the cut of his hair and the assemblage of his clothing – a fitting garnish upon a neglected body and a dilapidated mind. Is, oblivious to everything in the room that was not upon his plate, ate his meal, and then helped himself to more, and soon could hardly speak, such was the quantity of food he had eaten. Behind the window, beyond the hawthorn, over the rustling trees, across the salt marsh and sea, the sun began to set.

It was at about this time that one of the diners sitting across from Don and Is – a Gdańskowiec woman with very large glasses – stood slowly up and pointed beyond them with a look of terror on her face. All conviviality quickly drained from the room as the diners one-by-one had their attention drawn to the target of that pointed finger. Then came the sounds: great booming knocks upon each window in turn. Several diners knocked over their chairs and ran; others hid beneath the table. Saint Cedd alone stayed where he was, though his eyes finally came to rest on a single point, a blank space on the white of the table linen beyond his plate, where they remained as the room emptied as if picked-up and shaken roughly free of its human contents; leaving, in addition to the neurasthenic, only Don and Is, neither of whom had turned to see what the commotion was caused by – the former because he didn't believe in causes and in any case was meditating on the hyperfine transition of hydrogen; the latter because the quantity of mashed potato he had consumed was proving to be a powerful soporific. Eventually though, the booming moved round the building to the windows of the room they occupied and Is was dragged out of his tuberous reverie.

—Twenty-One save us, sir. Grendel's here!

Hearing the hallowed number exit his servant's mouth pleased Don so much that he immediately brought his attention to Is's latest fright without the least rancour.

—Good servant Isaiah, what is troubling you?

—Look!

Is pointed through the broad French window at a large man in the dusk about to strike its glass once more with his boot.

—It is just a man, said Don. Do not worry.

—That's not just a man, said Saint Cedd or John Gerveyn, looking steadfastly into the eyes of our hyperfine adventurer. That's Richard Proudfoot come to get me.

The enormous pane of glass shuddered in its frame, rippling the reflections of the room into concentric circles which dilated and contracted rapidly about its centre like a great affrighted eye. Saint Cedd or John Gerveyn, resigned to his fate – though Don, if he could attend to the words of this our great narrative in his honour, would reject the notion of fate violently – sat in his dining place awaiting the inevitable, as does one who suffers long illness come to welcome death. Don stood, and then took himself over to the wall of glass where this man was violently attempting to gain entry.

—To breach this invisible barrier here, said Don at Richard Proudfoot through the glass of the window, is to embrace the humiliation of defeat, for Saint Cedd, whose protection now falls under my aegis, must be defended from any and all such counter-attacks of the disease of history (and I am certain that this is one such) of which I am in the process of curing him. Disarm, retreat and disappear back into the fog from where you came you nasty relic of past time, or else feel the strength of my justice!

—He would need to disleg, sir, said Is, his foot being the only weapon he seems to be using.

Again the foot hit the centre of the window and the glass quivered.

—I am willing to exact either and both, said Don. I will turn you into a snake, Richard Proudfoot, if you do not desist!

Richard Proudfoot did not desist, but instead redoubled his attack on the side of the building.

—When he gets through there, said Is, I want to be somewhere else, because he's far more frightening than Geoffrey Panyman or William Smith or any other of the gang what were onto Tom Harding's places, and they were bad enough. Look at the bloody size of him!

Proudfoot, silhouetted by the dusklight, was indeed a very intimidating man to behold, such were his proportions and the ferocity of his attack. Head ran into neck ran into shoulders – his upper body a grotesque convergence of muscle. As it hit the window, the size of his boot compelled the boggling mind to measure. This, or so it seemed, formed the source of the imperial measurement of length twelve inches the foot, though taken sideways across the shoe.

—Gerveyn! said Proudfoot as he wound up for another kick.

—I will go with him, said Saint Cedd, or John Gerveyn.

—What did he say? said Is.

—He said Gerveyn. My name's John Gerveyn, said Saint Cedd or John Gerveyn.

—Your name is Saint Cedd, Don assured him, and you're not going anywhere.

—Why is everyone called John? said Is. I've never met so many as in this past week. There was Thecchere and Somenour, and now there's Gerveyn.

—His name is Saint Cedd! said Don.

—And Don is John in all but the very first sound, continued Is taking no notice of his master.

Here, Don turned away from where he faced Richard Proudfoot at the window and chased Is round the room until, catching him, servant and master became engaged in a manner of combat very much resembling a cuddle or hug. Proudfoot made one last kick to the window, which shattered it, and entered the room. Taking hold of that which he sought, he escorted John Gerveyn or Saint Cedd back out through the window frame over the mound of glass fragments into the evening air where he berated him for his cowardice and informed him that – but already they were gone beyond earshot, and we shall never know.

Soon afterwards, Don tired of his attempted assault on Is, detached himself, and observed his servant's chest, which pattered up and down like the breast of a frightened bird. But when Don saw that Proudfoot had entered the room and that Saint Cedd had been abducted, he nearly went mad – though of course he was already as mad as a sack of ferrets – and began lamenting his failure as protector of all things pertaining to the hyperfine transition of hydrogen, though St. Cedd's place in his mission was never explicitly stated. Seeing that the danger at the hands of Proudfoot had passed, the members of the Othona community re-entered the room, took their places at the table once more, and, caring little that the window was letting the damp of the fog in, they finished their meal. Don kept up his lamentation until late into the night, and so everyone in the building including Is made their way to bed to the soothing lullaby of his self-berations.

Early in the morning the community assembled and without a word of farewell escorted our valiant pair out through the smashed window as a man in blue overalls with a large pencil of triangular profile and hand-sharpened tip taciturnly took measurements of the frame for the pane's replacement. At the mouth of the tunnel of hawthorn the community handed Is a small linen bag and bade him and his master a firm goodbye; it seemed our adventurers were no longer welcome at the Othona community. But it was of no matter, for Don and Is were once more on their way.

11

Coming out of the tunnel to view the ancient angles of St Peter-on-the-Wall in the clear bright sunlight, Is placed his master's large heavy oaken chest upon the ground and reached into the bag he had been given to discover to his pleasure two rolls, still as warm and comforting to the touch as a cat's belly. They tore bread together as friends do, sitting on the knotted planks of the misproportioned chest, and then proceeded on their way, making footfall upon the earth like two pairs of hands on the same drum. The air was crisp and clear, and the moisture it had shed in the night bedazzled their eyes from every stick and stem as they made their way along the filamented shoreline, crossing the line of the low morning sun as it slanted in from above the English Channel. The blocks of shade and illumination of the four sides of the church turned as they passed it, and Is felt much less afraid with the fog gone.

—What kind of a place *is* this? he asked of no-one in particular.

They walked on.

A long straight stony track led them along the top of a ditch, and then to a road. Poplars swayed on one side; small noisy birds skittered in a bush on the other. Bradwell's decommissioned nuclear power station came into view in front of them, and over the fields a great agglomeration of hay bales stood as if in inexpedient genuflection to this great modern device, which would never work again. They passed an electrical facility, forming a distant adjunct to the power station, with its fretted and fronded gallows not now sizzling, but silent; and then joined the public highway. Tempering the bleak marshes and flats of old Witbrictesherna – the Dengie Hundred – the hills grew out of the ground as they made passage away from the sea.

Throughout the turning of the day they walked, through Tillingham, Dengie, Asheldham, Southminster, Steeple, all the time with the master's chest bobbing heavily on the back of the servant. By evening, the whole Hundred having been negotiated in happenstance zig-zags by foot – and it should come as no surprise, for they had not eaten since their bread rolls twelve hours before – our stouthearted pair were feeling weary and experiencing the knuckled fist of hunger push into their stomachs. By the many agonies of their misadventures they were becoming familiar with trouble and its origins; accordingly, when they saw the hoarding of a petrol station in the distance they arrowed and hastened their course towards it. Soon they were crossing the brightly-lit forecourt, whose transient usage, combined with the twilight, encloaked them in unremarkability and so granted them a momentary respite from the less fortuitous side of the workings of Chance. The servant Is was certainly in need of such respite, for he now exhibited many remnants of his misuse.

Brightly and individually packaged for their pleasure and convenience, our heroes purchased turgid pork products within the strip-lit garage, and their mouths greeted them as if selections from the taster menu of the finest restaurant. They stood once more out in the open air, eating beneath the flat canopy of the petrol station, like two cats beneath a table. Cars pulled onto the forecourt, and then a few minutes later pulled out again.

—I think I would like to live by the sea, said Is. I think I would find the sea a comfort.

—Ease of existence, replied Don, is by no means an achievement worth a lifetime's work. You might as well be dead.

—I nearly am, said Is. Look at what that rowing to not-France did to me.

Here he showed Don his swollen, weeping palms.

—The next person that drives up in need of fuel, said Don, we shall accost and request a small amount from for the disinfection of these wounds.

—That sounds painful, said Is.

—It will be painful. But why is that such a bad thing?

—Because pain hurts. Pain is the hurt. It's painful. Pain frightens me.

—Pain needn't be painful. I would advise you to approach pain in a new way.

—How so?

—I will illustrate my point with a discussion of entropy.

—Something to do with plants? said Is.

—It is something to do with everything, said Don. Now, an atom is a very simple thing indeed, almost the most simple thing.

—I thought I was the most simple thing. I have heard you say it more than once.

—You are simple in a less simple way, Isaiah.

—I will take that as a compliment.

—You are entitled to do such things, said Don. For these are your ears, and between them is the thing which makes meaning out of the sounds which enter them. But to return to the atom: an atom is very simple indeed, but it is still a system. It contains energy, and it is always losing energy. All atoms, left unmolested by others, will, like people, grow old and get slower. But this energy doesn't vanish in use: it is transferred to the atoms around our atom. Now the crux of the matter is that it has become an inescapable and unquestioned human value that the loss of energy within an ordered system to a larger, less ordered system is a bad thing. So, whilst your refrigerator is good on the inside, the heat produced at its exterior in keeping its interior cold is bad. It is *waste*. However, in refutation of millennia of erroneous thinking, I would counter that without such waste there could be nothing, for the sun couldn't heat us, and indeed nothing could cohere, for there could be no attraction. Entropy is necessary in providing us with conditions somewhere in between absolute order and absolute disorder.

—What has this got to do with my hands? said Is.

—The answer is simple: Don't berate your refrigerator for wasting energy; congratulate it for symbolically celebrating the possibility of the universe (not that I can approve of the symbolic function).

—I still don't understand how this has anything to do with the pain of my palms.

—Invert your priorities, understand your pain as pleasure, and then you will see.

—I would stand as much chance taking my manself for a woman. There are certain things which seem to me to be beyond rethinking.

—What you have said is not so watertight as you believe, said Don. It is subject to refutation in the same manner. I will furnish you with a fresh analogy. Watch for a few minutes these cars pull into the garage, and the drivers climb out and refill their fuel tanks.

They watched for a few minutes a number of cars pull onto the forecourt and refuel.

—Did you notice anything?

—I noticed a number of cars pull up, their drivers get out and refuel, and then drive off again, said Is.

—If you are told to look out of a window, said Don, do you find it necessary to open it and actually crane your head out through the aperture? You pilot the least penetrative mind I have ever encountered. What do you see beyond the pulling up, the refuelling, and the driving off?

—Oh, I don't know, said Is. Don't make me watch it all over again.

—Yours is a petulantly received education. I will tell you what I am getting at. Watch this woman: she pulls up, she goes to the petrol tank, she refuels, she rehangs the handpump, and then she re-caps the tank and goes to pay.

—Yes, I saw all those things take place.

—But you didn't see one particular thing take place, because it didn't take place. Now watch this man. He pulls in, goes to the tank, refuels, shakes the nozzle of the pump into the tank, and then rehangs the pump. Now, if you, Isaiah, were to refuel your car and refrain from shaking the droplets from the nozzle of the handpump, you would be taking a step towards the experience of your manself as a woman. If you managed to decode every hidden male action out of your everyday behaviours and stop yourself doing such things, you would cease to be a man.

—How would you account for the thing and things between my legs? said Is.

—Precisely what I have been talking about: your nozzle, said Don.

—But they are what make me a man, said Is.

—They would disappear, said Don.

—Really? I don't believe it.

—It is logically irrefutable, in accordance with the terms of the spectral line of the hyperfine transition of hydrogen.

—In which case I believe it completely, said Is.

—But that is not why I have discoursed upon the topic, continued Don. My reason has been to make it known to you that what you are is hidden from yourself, and that what is hidden cannot be interrogated.

—Once again master you have opened my eyes, said Is. It would seem that there is no way of escaping ourselves. So if I can unhide the pain in my hands it will become pleasure?

—Something like that, said Don. It will not hurt to attempt it.

—But perhaps that is precisely and solely what it will do, pain being, for me at least, nothing other than hurt.

—Let us see.

Here, Don walked up to a man who was refuelling his car and asked politely if he could shake the nozzle of the handpump onto his friends hands after the man had finished with it. Hearing this, Is could not stop himself from laughing and exclaiming that his master was attempting to reach into the trousers of the man he was talking to and shake what was inside. When what he thought was happening dawned upon this man, he grew suddenly and viscerally appalled, pushed Don over to bang his head on the oily ground of the forecourt, and shouted foul obscenities of the homophobic class over his prone body, the words reverberating across the forecourt of the otherwise deserted filling station. While this was happening, Is approached and withdrew the nozzle of the handpump from its place in the side of the man's car, and shook it over his palms. The scream which he thereafter emitted promptly ended the assault which the man was making upon Don, and the pain to the back of Don's head, which was entirely painful and not at all pleasurable, was thereafter transferred – one might say like the energy from one atom to another – with very little loss or modification to Is's hands. The lone man who staffed the petrol station stood framed by its window in the yellow light of the interior and gazed with bemused inanition out on the spectacle. Don and Is fled the forecourt with the newly acquired knowledge that not even the transient usage of a petrol station could protect them from attack.

—It would seem that not even the transient usage of a petrol station can protect us from attack, said Don.

—Let's find somewhere else to go and rest, said Is. We are looking our very worst, and feeling little different. I have heard it said that a pub is the only place where even the unhappy are at least contented, and my personal experience doesn't contradict such a notion.

—The best I can offer is that we might enter the first pub Chance brings us to, said Don, which pleased Is enough, knowing as he did that the English pub would always spring up when you most needed it.

They walked away from the petrol station down Steeple Road, until they came to a curious little settlement called Mayland.

—Why are all the buildings so short? said Is.

—The combined pressures of poverty and bad taste, said Don. We are sure to stumble across a pub here, though I'm not sure either of us will want to enter it.

—If it serves beer, I will want to enter it.

—Very well. And I believe you are in luck.

Down the road, beyond the bungalows and a vacant plot of smashed breeze blocks, splintered wood frames and plaster, stood a pub.

—Life is good, said Is.

Through the featherlight door they passed.

At the end of the bar a lone man sat on a high stool and caressed the glass which had held his drink. At the other end, a pair of women talked in hushed voices. In the opposite corner from the door through which our two companions had entered there sat a wizened old man on a low stool with a guitar in a case at his feet. The pub was as empty as these three people along with Don and Is could make it, and by now last orders were not very far away from being called.

Don ordered and paid for two pints, and they took their seats.

—Luxuriate in the comfort granted to you by this solitary drink for as long as you can Isaiah, for it will by necessity have to form the substance of your nightcap, bedclothes and breakfast. We have no money.

—None at all?

—Not a penny.

—What are we going to do?

—I am not sure. Something will happen.

—That is what I am most afraid of, said Is. Something keeps happening, and we grow poorer, and weaker, and more injured, and equally malnourished, and less well-slept.

—It is true that our fortunes need to change if we are to carry on in our quest, said Don.

—Our fortunes would change immediately if we stopped it, said Is. Maybe that is all it would take.

—We have come a long way.

—We have been walking now for a week, and we're still only just down the road.

—Twenty-five miles, said Don. That's what the sign we passed most recently said. Not that such a sign can have any reality, owing to the unreality of the concept 'distance'. And don't even get me started on signs.

Don raised his glass to his mouth, reflected on the tangle of Being, and then continued.

—All the true signs I have seen – and there have been many – like weather vanes on the most tumultuous day have been turning and turning, and this is why – ignoring all the imposter signs – we must go wherever Chance blows us. Mark my words, the signs will start pointing in the same direction very soon. Events will lose their bluster.

—Or Is will lose his muster, said Is. The economic climate in your right pocket will determine which happens first. There needs to be an upturn pretty soon.

—A man can live for free if he puts his mind to it, said Don.

—And he can die even cheaper if he doesn't. I do wonder, with a week's travelling and only being down the road from where we started, if our home town has some kind of magnetical property to which we are peculiarly prone. We've done a bloody loop round it like a tethered donkey.

—Your friend Old King Cole's name is said to relate to the *coel*, or 'omen', associated with ancient trackways, thus we see the reasoning for Colchester being said to have received its name from that king. The science of leylines is neither an exact nor an esteemed one, and you are now by no means the least of the contributors to it. I do wonder that Chance saddled me with your service.

—Who exactly was Old King Cole? said Is. I learnt his song so long ago that it hasn't even crossed my mind to wonder.

—Ah, said the old man with the guitar case, who had been approaching Don and Is slowly with a rickety creeping lurch without their knowing from the other side of the pub. Old King Cole was a merry old soul. He called for his pipe and his bowl, and for his fiddlers three.

—Did he get them? asked Is.

—Did he get them! said the old man. Of course he got them, and in spades. And what have you got? he then said, gesturing at the chest which Is had placed before the table, beside his own stool. Am I dead or something, and you my undertaker? Look at the state of that box! It looks like a hollowed log.

The old man kicked the chest dismissively.

—So it will appear, said Don, to those marooned in the doldroms of an erroneous aesthetic.

—I've got my pipe and my bowl right here, the old man continued, pointing to his guitar case. But not here, and he made a curious smoking gesture. Spare a pound for a song.

—We have no money, said Don.

—You are buying a song? said Is.

—No, I'm buying a drink, said the old man, but selling a song to get there.

—Buy a song off us, and then sell it to those people, said Is gesturing towards the women at the bar. We're skint.

—Will it be a profitable one? said the old man.

—It's never been used, said Is, so it must be brand new, which has got to be a good thing as far as value goes. In fact, it's so new it's not even been written yet. Pick a number.

—Twenty-one, said the old man, to mark my birthday today.

—That old chestnut, said the corpulent landlord from behind the bar, and he rang his bell. Last orders!

—Twenty-One! said Don.

—I told you going in a pub would be working out well for us sir, said Is. That means the song is twenty-one verses long. That's a long old song you're being given there. That'll cost.

—If it costs them, so much the better for us all, said the old man. But you'd better hurry it up because I'm thirsty.

—We've got the number of verses. Now we need a subject.

—Old King Cole.

—Been done before.

—It's all been done before.

—Twenty-One! said Don again to himself in a rapture.

—Well it makes sense.

—It's——

—Dark.

—There are——

—Sufferings, to the power of twenty-one.

—And——

—Twenty-one stars.

—And——

—A cabin, mud, sea, boats – twenty-one of them. And a twenty-one-eyed brood of chickens. And the devil.

—Yes! said Is. A song isn't a song without the devil in there somewhere.

—If the woman you love don't love you, not even the devil can help.

—I hear you.

—Twenty-One! said Don.

The old man took up his guitar, which was not in tune, and began to sing.

> In the dark, twenty-one stars
> > *twenty-one stars*
> Twenty-one stars overhead
> > twenty-one devils sharing my bed.

—That's the business! said Is. The devil got in early, which is the way he is, and don't we all know it.

> Chill night outside the cabin
> > *outside the cabin door*
> Twenty-one stars they shoot
> > twenty-one agonies in each boot

—We all three of us know the weight of that boot, said Is nodding with solemn approval.

—Been wearing it since we've been wearing our skins, said the old man in a brief interlude as he picked out the notes of several strangled chords.

—Keep it up! said Is.

> Road is a-long and hard
> > *long and hard*
> Twenty-one moonful pothole puddles
> > *Twenty-one hundred toiling troubles*

—Now we're talking, said Is. Moonful pothole puddles. That's a fine phrase for the singing.

> One-eyed chicken at the roadside
> *at the roadside*
> Ten blind chicks by her side
> *twenty unseeing and a canny eye*

—I was wondering where the chicken had got to. I've seen such chickens in my time, the blackhearted fowls.

While Don drifted into a reverie upon what he and Chance might choose to wear on their wedding-day, Is and the old man continued at their song for a dozen and more verses, to which it is not strictly necessary for us to give representation. But let us hear the final two:

> So, the return: back along the track
> *a heavy return*
> trudging return along the track
> *over the sound and onto the flats*

> Into the rising sun!
> *the mist-chasing sun*
> Into the – into the
> *wondrous rising sun!*

—Ah! said Is. There's an ending! I thought you'd gone flat with the second-to-last. But then: *The wondrous rising sun!* That's an ending and a half. Tell me, how much you think it's worth?

—At least three pints, which is what I'm going to bid for with the very hand that played it.

The old man stood up and went unsteadily to the bar with his guitar. He drew the instrument up to his chest and coughed for the attention of the two women, upon which the landlord waved him down and began pouring three pints. The two women resumed talking; the bell was rung for Time.

—This is where we've been going wrong, said Is to Don. All it takes is a slab of outwardness, a slice of guts, and a spoonful of what-you-know, and you've got yourself a dinner. We could do this.

—I am not happy with the idea of interfering with Chance, said Don. Except insofar as she is desirous of it, he added with what might have been a blush.

—Who's to say you are not interfering with Chance more by *not* doing such things? said Is.

—But neither of us can play an instrument, said his master.

—That is where you are mistaken. I have been playing the French horn since I was eight years old.

—It is true that I did not know that. When was the last time you played this instrument?

—When I was eight.

—The use of the perfect continuous tense implies continuousness, said Don. Not that I believe in the representation of Time through that imposter linguistic tense. You have not been playing the French horn since you were eight, you played it when you were eight.

—I still have the skills about me, I'll bet you, said Is.

—And where in any case are you going to get a French horn from?

—Something similar will do.

—Ha! Even the most similar thing to a French horn will not bring you close enough to it for the melodious playing of. What do we have? That shredded tyre in a ditch, a broken bottle, or the bullrushes we passed at the salt marshes. As close as anything else I've encountered today. You would do better simply to purse your own mouth in imitation.

—You seem to enjoy your hardship too much to want to give it up by assisting me, said Is.

—You, lest you forget, are my assistant, said Don, and not the reverse. I will have you deport yourself in a manner more fitting this station.

—I will serve you better if you allow me to feed myself and live, said Is. Let us have all variety of music!

—Let us have all variety of music! said the old man as he returned to their table. They brought their three glasses into collision in order to ratify the statement.

—And until the night is chased away, he then said before taking a deep draught of his drink.

—We are in a pub, sir, said Is. There is surely some brass trinket which will serve for an instrument if I hit it with a stick.

—You can do better than that! said the old man. There's a fife in the cubby round there.

He pointed towards the passageway which led to the back bar.

—A fife's a kind of penny whistle, isn't it? said Is.

—It is. But made of wood, or a reed, or something. More flute-like, I think.

—Is it easy to play – how many holes?

—Less than it takes to get lost in, said the old man.

—That'll do us nicely, said Is rubbing his hands together.

He rose and made his way to the toilet via the fife-containing cubby. When he returned he had the instrument upon his person, the mouth-piece of which he flashed at his companions in verification of his success.

—This man's a do-er, said the old man.

—He's more of a say-er in my experience, said Don.

—Is is as Is says, said Is. I say what I do, and I do what I say.

—Now there's a phrase. A conundrum of the paradox class, said Don. A regular Zeno, he is.

—You what? said the old man.

—Never mind.

—Where did you find him? the old man asked Is in reference to Don.

—It was the reverse. He found me, and I wouldn't have it any other way.

He then began to make a move towards withdrawing the fife from his pocket.

—Not in here, Isaiah. You have only just stolen the object off the man of whom we are currently still the guests, or at least the customers.

—For Twenty-One verses I think we got sold short, said Is. This'll make up the difference.

—You are too bold, said Don. Put it away, or you will experience yet more violence, and you have grown too ugly in the past week to risk it.

—Let's drink up and get ourselves out there, then, said Is.

There was a general unspoken consent, and they upended their glasses so as to be able to consume the liquid remnants therein.

—Where do you two live? said the old man.

—We are currently of no fixed abode, said Don.

—Where are you staying?

—Probably in the nearest field, said Is.

—That won't do, said the old man. You can stay at my place.

Is's face became suffused with an expression of pure pleasure.

—This is what living is about! he said. A walk in the day, a pint in the evening, and a bed at night – and all of it for free!

They exited the establishment through the door whose purpose it was to serve that and its reverse function.

As they were walking down the now dark street, Is removed the fife from his pocket, and investigated further the means by which he might make it produce such sonorities as would feed him in the coming days. The old man laughed and said:

—That's not a fife! That's a fitment for a vacuum cleaner, the one you use for the nooks.

Is became very upset, and only calmed down when the old man promised to give him a recorder which he had at home, and which would be every bit as promising for the imitation of the French horn as a stolen fife.

—And surely, said the old man, you will have played the recorder at least as recently as you have the French horn, seeing as they're the curse on every schoolboy's and schoolgirl's mouth.

—That's true enough, said Is.

—Then we are all happy once again, said Don, though he noted with regret how the hyperfine transition of hydrogen had been dislodged from its usual place at the forefront of his thoughts by all this chatter.

Just then there came flying a massive drunken gentleman out of the door of another pub into their midst, knocking Is and the old man to the floor. Don remarked to himself how even thinking about the hyperfine transition of hydrogen was a very great thing, and then returned to this deeper reverie, ignoring the predicament of his servant and the old man. The massive drunken man gathered himself up above unsteady legs, pulled straight the lapel of his capacious double-breasted blazer, and informed the two men on the floor that he would fight them so he would.

—Ah, come on Clive there's no need for any of that business, said the old man.

—Don't you believe it, said the massive drunken man, and he hauled Is up by his shirtfront to standing. What do you mean by getting in my way when I'm all ready for my night walk home, he said.

Not enjoying the prospect of another beating, Is sought as firmly as possible to extricate himself from the massive drunken man's grasp, but in the attempt he further angered this man by dirtying his trouserlegs and scraping his shins with his bootsoles.

—He's a perfect cat, squirming to get away like he is! said the massive drunken man. Treat yourself to one of these! he then said as he placed firmly the large fist at the end of his right arm into the centre of Is's face. Copious bleeding ensued from the servant's nose.

—Clive! said the old man.

—Shut up you vermin! said the massive drunken man, and kicked at him; but the massive drunken man, whose name must have been Clive, lost his footing as a result of the attempt, and very soon found himself flat on his back.

—The martial arts! he shouted in outrage; and, grabbing Is's leg, he proceeded to bite it.

Is's scream brought Don out of his reverie, and seeing what was happening, he launched into the following oration:

—The body, knowing its own laws, which are accorded it by nature and not by that dreamed-up scheme of thought known as medicine, will heal when it heals. There is a certain length of which I am fond, one which measures all things and knows not only those things by their length, breadth and height, but also the otherwise immeasurable features of them, which cannot even be named. To interrupt, impede or obstruct the discovery of the means by which this wonderful line might restore the world to its true self – an activity which I see occurring before my very eyes, the man currently under assault being none other than the assistant who I have taken into my employ as bearer of my wonderful *Encyclopaedia* and as general assistant – is as grave an offence as can be committed. I am led perforce to make hasty intervention on his behalf with the twin-might of my arm and mind so that the goodness of everything in the world might soon be rediscovered, as it will, following its restitution, with the assistance of Chance. Therefore, you brutish man, as you have contravened the laws of my Science, whose truth is majestical, you must pay the penalty, which is to admit to everyone before you that the spectral line of the hyperfine transition of hydrogen – for that is its name – is the sole measure of and means to truth, and that you have erred on this occasion in assaulting my goodly assistant, an action tantamount to explicitly dishonouring the eternal verity just now stated.

The massive drunken man writhed upon the floor in his polyester finery and said: Bastard!

Don, seeing that this was unsatisfactory, spoke once more.

—You are one of many who cannot see or even imagine your own mediocrity, even though every day serves to apprise you of it. Therefore, we shall have no more to do with you, because in truth you have no existence. And to prove it, I will continue to walk onwards, and even if you were to shackle the moon to my heel as an impediment, my stride would be sure and efficacious.

Concluding the delivery of these fine words into the air for the delectation of the people proximately assembled, Don walked straight over the belly of the massive drunken man – who it should now be stated was one of the magistrates who presided over the county sessions every fortnight – and beckoned to Is and the old man to follow him. The massive drunken man made no attempt to follow them, for he was now occupied in evacuating the contents of his stomach down his shirtfront.

—Sir, said Is with great emotion once they had passed far enough from the massive drunken man to ensure their safety. You have saved me from a certain death. It is the greatest honour to serve you in return.

Concurrent with the delivery of this devotional from the mouth of the assistant came a great fawning and obsequious pawing at his master as they walked along with the old man once more.

—I appreciate that you are grateful, said Don. But be pleased not to smear the blood from your nose upon those items I am attempting to wear for clothing. The events which appear to have just taken place amply prove that your nose is most unlike a cat, in that it has survived the ninth assault upon its life, and therefore there is no need to behave like one of the apprentice printers of Paris who made such a sign with the blood of *le grise*, their master's wife's favourite, although it is true that your nose has become rather grey by the aggregation of the indignities it has been made to suffer.

—I will do whatever you say, said Is, just as soon as I know what it is you are saying. Oh master, you are great!

In a brief time the three companions had negotiated the streets of the peculiar little village of Mayland, as well as the front door of their host, and found themselves sitting upon the outdated soft furnishings of his home with very large glasses of cheap unmixed vodka before them. Is held the bridge of his nose, not unlike a mother cat as she carries her kittens by the nape, in an attempt to prevent any further disgorgement of blood. The old man put on some music, then took it off, then put on some different music, then took that off, and then searched again, and repeated the whole process several times – for it was the case that he was inebriated – until Is interrupted him by proffering a reminder of his host's promise to grant him the ownership of a recorder. By the time the old man returned from wherever he had gone to look for the instrument, Is was asleep, and Don declared that it was strictly forbidden that anyone wake him, even had his mother been upon her deathbed. The drunken old man shrugged, picked up the bottle from which he had poured their drinks, and made his way upstairs to his own bed.

So while Is was not in a bed, he was at least beneath the shelter of a roof; and he slept soundly throughout the night while his master watched over him like a new parent until the sun rose and he awoke.

—Do you never sleep master? said Is upon waking.

—Not if I can help it, said Don without even a noonday's shadow of fatigue taking the crisp edges off his words.

—These other men are like children when compared to you, sir.

—Does the hyperfine transition of hydrogen ever rest or sleep? asked Don.

—I wouldn't dare say with any certainty one way or the other from my own knowledge, said Is. But seeing as you and this transition thing seem to be on the very best of terms and the most like one another of any two things in the world without being the self-same, and as I have hardly ever witnessed you either rest or sleep, I'd say no, it almost certainly doesn't rest or sleep.

—And you would be correct, Isaiah, said Don. I am guessing that our host will not be rising for a number of hours. He took upstairs with him for a bed partner a half-filled bottle of spiritous liquor. Such nocturnal carousings will secure at least a half-morning's debt.

—I have our livelihood upon me! said Is in reference to the recorder he discovered in his lap, and he played ceremonially a solitary low note to demonstrate this reality.

—Take up our things and let's be gone, said Don.

Just as they had entered the house in the night, they exited it in the morning; and though Is had acquired some new injuries to add to his catalogue, they were mere variations on ones he had already possessed, and so he felt infinitely better rested. Meanwhile, Don had come to a number of intermediate conclusions in respect of the relationship between the hyperfine transition of hydrogen and the workings of the world and the many things it contained. In other words, our venturesome pair were in fine spirits. Is heaved the chest back on to his back and the pertinacious company of two walked on into the day seeking their next adventure.

12

Entering Maylandsea our redoubtable pair came to a small patch of grass marooned within an otherwise uninterrupted expanse of tarmac and concrete which lay before the *Horny Toad* pub, upon which Don now sat to begin re-tying his boots. When he had completed this act, he raised his head with the air of someone who has made a decision – which is precisely what he had done – and spoke.

—It seems to me, Isaiah, that we might be wise to make a concession to the readership of my *Encyclopaedia* through the provision of some kind of preface to the work, for the human mind, although not by its nature, has by exposure to the multitudinous conflicting accounts of everything, from the ways in which a horse chestnut might be fortified to the trajectory of light in a vacuum, been moulded into a sceptic's shape, to the end that it is counted wisdom to doubt everything and stupidity to believe anything, unless it be proven by the eye, which is the greatest stupidity of all.

—The best way to toughen up a conker for battle I learned off Charlie Bray, said Is, who said you should pass it through a pig. The conker is supposed to harden by soaking in the stomach juices; all you need to do is sift through the shit at the other end. Not that Charlie would have done such a thing, because he was an honourable player of the game and despised a cheat.

—And so, continued Don, ready yourself to hear as I write the follow-ing, which will be entitled: 'Prologemena to Don Waswill's *Encyclopaedia of Being, Synthesised in Accordance with the Eternal Verities Delineated by the Spectral Line of the Hyperfine Transition of Hydrogen*'.

—Does this mean I am finally going to find out what this transition business is then? asked Is.

—We shall see, said Don, sharpening a pencil – for his pen was mis-behaving as to its ink – and blowing the consequent shavings from the sensuous cleft at the centre of his open notebook. For even I do not know what meanings the words described by the point of this pencil might make until it has ceased its scratchings.

PROLOGEMENA TO DON WASWILL'S *ENCYCLOPAEDIA OF BEING, SYNTHESISED IN ACCORDANCE WITH THE ETERNAL VERITIES DELINEATED BY THE SPECTRAL LINE OF THE HYPERFINE TRANSITION OF HYDROGEN*

The following Work is a work in progress, as must be all things if they are to have Reality, owing to the existence only of the Present, which is Process, and the non-existence of Past and Future, which are nothing but delusions invented to comfort the fearful minds of our species. Mark well the fact of the matter: The human mind refines the fallacy *Duration* out of the reality *Moment*. This work will restore us to the Now-Eternity, and the turning of all things shall cease.

The wanderings of the author and his assistant have been conducted with Chance as their guide, and without aim. This is befitting the ways of the hyperfine transition of hydrogen, which does not *intend* or *mean*, but simply *does*. What is more, it is the irruption of the Present Moment into Time, and therefore an exemplum to us all!

The so called 'hydrogen line' is an electromagnetic radiation spectral line which is formed by an alteration to the energy state of a neutral hydrogen atom. The frequency of this line is 1420.40575177 MHz, which is equivalent to a vacuum wavelength of 21.10611405413 cm.

The alteration to the energy state of a neutral hydrogen atom which produces this line occurs when the electron which orbits the proton 'spin-flips'. If a single hydrogen atom were to be isolated in a laboratory on earth in order to examine such a transition, the observers would have to wait an estimated average of 10 million years for it to happen. The transition is therefore said to be highly forbidden – it happens very infrequently – and the electromagnetic spectral line emitted by the hyperfine transition of hydrogen is known as the 'forbidden line'.

There is a symbol, a schematic, which denotes the hyperfine transition of hydrogen – the very one engraved on a gold-plated plaque attached to Pioneer 10 and shot into space in 1972, which happens to be the first man-made object to leave our solar system. This schematic bears a striking resemblance to the symbol discovered in John Dee's *Monas Hieroglyphica* (1564), by which Dee examines and represents the unity of all creation. My work is indebted to Dee for paving the way, and the similarities between the two – though the lines be jumbled, and though my copyist's hand be no longer so steady as Marcantonio Raimondi's – are self-evident.

Ceasing to write, Don rummaged through the materials in his home-made chest until he located a scrapbook, and from which he tore two cuttings, transferring them to their new place within his Prologemena.

Schematic for the hyperfine transition of hydrogen (sketch in pencil and ink by Don Waswill, author of the *Encyclopaedia of Being*)

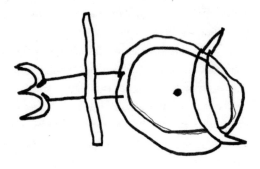

John Dee's monad (sketch in pencil and ink by Don
Waswill, author of the *Encyclopaedia of Being*)

Dee's method of exegesis, in being isopsephic – using numbers to interpret words – exhibits all the properties of right reason.

—I can second that, interrupted Is. Because my story about the crow, which was so entertaining that it must be true, shows how a crow well understands a number, but I've never heard of a crow as could speak English. Therefore numbers are truer than words.

—Thank you Isaiah. May I proceed?

—Fill your boots, sir.

Dee's method was appropriate, though the whole enterprise was in one respect ill-judged: he lacked the correct number, which the schematic of the hyperfine transition of hydrogen, combined with Dee's own, now identifies. Mark well, good reader: the number by which all meanings may be judged is Twenty-One.

The isopsephic systematics transacted within this *Encyclopaedia* – a *gematria* founded on the holiness of the divine number which shames all deities into non-existence – will reveal the true value of every written discourse in existence, which is precisely nothing!

I am of course deeply indebted to Jan Hendrik Oort, Harold Irving Ewen and Edward Mills Purcell for the discovery of the Forbidden

Line. However, the path Ewen and Purcell's research took after the discovery is not something which eternity will thank them for. It is a very attractive thing which they have done – by the redshift of the spectral line of the hyperfine transition of hydrogen to be able to image the shape of our galaxy and say beyond doubt that it is expanding; indeed, the big bang theory, which has gained almost universal credence, is entirely dependent on it. But there is no such thing as beyond doubt – until, that is, the Universal Restitution takes place. The sole true and good use of the hyperfine transition of hydrogen will be to enable the enactment of the Salvation of Being, which is the duty of the author: providing as it does a means of ceasing all strife; being as it is the base matter of the universe; penetrating as it has into every level of the scalar iteration of being, from the atom, up through the soil, the water, the fields, the trees, the flowers, the gardens, the window box, the birthday gift, the pet-name, the brooch, the word spoken in every emotion, the handshake of the self-made custodians of the land, the horrid stench of power, the market, the flow of capital, the burial of the dead – and beyond, to the view of the earth, and the rotation of the planets, and the infinite time – each of which emits the ululation of strife and unrest at every moment by its entrapment in a state of dis-ease. The Forbidden Line is that moment of transition, the present of which infinitesimal moment is bliss, but around which, upon either side, is the infinitely large and visible past and future, which is suffering. I am here to grasp that spin-flip, make it cease, and exist without orientation, without polarity, and by unforbidding that line, to make it eternal, annihilating all other false lines, and thereby the categories they create, opposite for opposite. And there shall be only ecstasy.

—Well sir, said Is. I understand all that about as much as a dog understands its own shadow.

Don laid down his pencil, leaned back against his oak chest, and sighed. He soon found himself led by his preoccupation with the lamentable state of humanity to think again about that peculiar taint *story*.

—It's not really any surprise that people want and need stories, he said. That stories started, I mean.

—I'm always up for a story, said Is. There's very little better.

—There is something disconcerting in bliss – the power of ecstasy terrible. The story a kind of shelter, dividing things up, making sense of time. It is possible to imagine the dawn of culture, the beginning of the telling of stories to establish the teller's place in the cosmos. It seems to me a kind of re-enactment of what happens in infancy. The moment of birth is the moment of the inrushing apprehension of contrast: out of unity into warmcold lightdark meyou. From this stems the compulsion – let us give it its proper designation, the *neurosis* – of the division into opposites. There is an experiment we might make here, Isaiah. Tell me, what is the opposite of left?

—That's easy: right.

—And what is the opposite of right?

—Wrong.

—You see? Now what is the opposite of wrong?

—Correct.

—And the opposite of correct?

—Leave-it-as-it-is.

—Excellent my good squire. Next?

—Alter.

—And the opposite of alter?

—Um, narthex.

—Furthermore:

—Indoors. Then outdoors. Then inside.

—And then?

—Abroad. Then home. Then away.

—What next?

—No way.

—And?

—Possible. Then unpossible.

—Perfect.

—Then can. Then tube.

—Ha!

—Then sausage.

—And what, might I ask, is the opposite of sausage?

—Jesus.

—Christ! Is it any wonder the world is in the mess it's in when the opposites of our language lead us from 'right' to 'Jesus', via 'sausage'? O holy number Twenty-One, he continued, climbing to his feet, and then up on to the twisted lid of his homemade chest in a gesture intended, we must assume, to reflect his approaching magniloquence. Come to us, Twenty-One! Grant us our Reparation! Be our Salvation! All things shall be brought back together through it into their Twenty-One-ness! Witness then on that good day, doubters, the meanings fall away like pasteboard stagesets from the words which are so gunged up with them they can hardly walk!

Is had ceased listening and instead began attempting to puzzle out some old tunes on the recorder he was very happy to call his own: 'Autumn Days' was the first; 'When the Saints Come Marching In' was another. Don drifted over the serene surface of his meditation on the perfection of the number Twenty-One. In this dilapidated old holiday-makers' pub car park there was no beauty; and yet the morning's sun, the copious birdsong, the warm touch of the breeze, the clear bright air of early Summer – did it not promise a fine day for adventuring?

—My favourite hymn has always been 'We Three Kings', said Is, and he started attempting to discover the notes of this tune, though, reaching the chorus, he struggled with finding the relative minor of the tonic from the dominant, which is where he had ended up. Such are the ways in which the mind is trapped by that which precedes it, as Don himself might say.

—There's one thing you might do well to consider as regards this money-making scheme of yours, said Don to his faithful servant as he climbed down from the chest. In view of our circumstances, which is to say our habitation within the purely public realm, people are going to find it difficult to distinguish between when you are practising and when you are performing, which I feel will only work to your detriment as regards the revenue you seek to bring in. Also, when busking it is customary to remain stationary, and the demands of your incumbency are in direct opposition to this.

—In which case the public will have to take me as I am.

Is sat down at his master's side on the small patch of grass within the desert of tarmac and crossed his legs like a schoolchild.

—They can take my practice as my performance, and my restlessness can form part of it. There are only two directions a person can walk along a path, and I'm going one of them. We will pass and be passed by people, and we'll see whether it brings anything in. I will mount my hat here, hanging from my belt loop, and with a few coppers bobbing in it, the message will be plain.

—I admire your optimism, Isaiah.

—And I admire yours also, sir.

There was a brief silence while each of the two men continued at their tasks and preoccupations: Don putting the finishing touches on his prolegomena and then fiddling once more at his boot laces; Is looking at the coins he had placed in his upturned hat.

—One thing which has always puzzled me, said the servant, is how the copper that makes up the material of the cheap coins is possible.

—How do you mean? asked his master.

—Well, surely it is worth more as metal than it is as money, it now being worth so little, moneywise.

—Such things have been known to occur, said Don. This is why the coins we call coppers are now produced from steel, and are only copper-plated. The rising value of copper made it cost more than the money was worth to make it.

—So some are copper, and some are only copper-plated? said Is.

—Correct.

—So how would I tell one from another?

—With a magnet, said Don.

—As simple as that?

—Yes.

—So some are worth more than others, though they are all worth the same? said Is.

—Correct again.

—Well this is it! said Is. If we get hold of a magnet we can make our money twice. Through the playing of a few choice tunes, we take in people's solid copper coins, and then we make a profit from the copper we melt it down into.

—Your scheme does not take into account one very important feature of economics: the scale upon which you would have to operate in order to turn a reasonable profit would soon result in a flooding of the market.

—A flooding of the market with what?

—With the material it values, you dunce. Scarcity is the essential ingredient of value. The road of excess leads to the palace of wisdom – and the wisdom here is: money is most valuable when you don't have any of it.

—I don't get it, said Is.

—Silver is a valuable metal, and it is scarce. Gold, being more scarce, is more valuable. Diamond, being even more scarce, is of even greater value. Value, then, is bequeathed to a thing in proportion to its scarcity.

—Ah, okay, I think I see now, said Is. Is there anything more valuable than diamond?

—There is love, which is said to be priceless, but you will hear what I have to say about this, for I do not hold love in high regard, and how could I, the phenomenon being something I refuse to countenance as existent. Here is my proof: two of the possible meanings which inhere to the word 'priceless' – these being the ironically literal 'without value', and the conventional 'of infinite value' – occupy opposite ends of the continuum of sense. I need say no more than that this is as it should be, for love makes no sense, being both without worth and non-existent. It is a term of convenience used for a certain kind of delusion.

—How can you say such a thing, master?

—Because it is the truth, and I have committed myself to communicating the truth of all matters, as far as it is in my power to do so, to everyone I meet. If you disagree with me, feel free to expound a logical proof of the existence of this thing which I henceforth refuse even to name, for to name something is to imply that it has a genuine existence – *nomen est numen* – and this has been one of the major routes into error for the world: too many words for not enough things.

—I'll take up that challenge, said Is. But first I must think.

—Let's rather forget about it and continue walking, said Don as he attempted to rise. I am becoming stiff sitting here upon the grass like this.

—You stand and walk, master. Do some circles.

—I will not, said Don. Avail me of your perambulation.

—But I have it! said Is. Not even you will be able to tell me I'm wrong here. Before becoming your servant, I used to walk my children to school every morning. There was a wall which followed the line of our route which started off low, and grew by whatever means to become high at its other end.

—No doubt the street exhibited the property of being on a slope of a number of degrees inclination, said Don.

—Every day, continued Is, my little boy climbed up onto the wall at its low end, and trotted along the top to the other end. I suppose it was about up to my waist, and he's only five – of course, you saw him! When he got to the end, he would steady himself on both feet and square up his little shoulders and then jump down. Every time he did it and landed, a real nasty shock travelled up from my feet to my knees where it bloomed into a funnyboneish vibration going right throughout the inside of the middlejoints of my legs. That's the proof I offer for the real existence of love, and it is a cast-iron one, because no matter what I did I couldn't stop this strange tingling pain every time my boy's feet hit that ground.

—What an extraordinary proof you offer, said Don. Sometimes I feel a certain fondness for you, Isaiah.

—Well sir, said Is, rising to stand beside his master. I don't mind at all saying what you say can't be said: I love you.

—I am astonished, said Don, whose body spoke no more eloquently than his mouth, for he could only stand stock-still. Is took this as an opportunity to embrace his master in a gesture of heartfelt corporeal felicitation, which in turn produced further astonishment in Don; and so the pair stood there in an embrace for some time – which even Don would find it hard to deny existed, such was the degree to which it dragged as he was held in this awkward embrace. The sight of two men embracing in the street was of sufficient interest to such passers-by who saw them – for the morning was gathering its timeliness and the road was acquiring other pedestrians – as to lead them to stop in their tracks, forgetting the shopping which weighed heavily in their hand, and watch this strange pair.

—Might we disengage ourselves? said Don in a voice muffled by his embracer's collar and unshaven neck.

—Yes sir, said Is, letting go of his master.

—I must say, you are a peculiar man, Isaiah. Astonishment, the word I would surely remember using to describe my internal reaction to your hug were it not forbidden me to remember, binds us together. For astonishment, far from meaning 'turned to stone' – which in fact my body did just appear to me to be – refers instead to the effects of thunder on the nerves, of which I believe you have a more intimate acquaintance than most. This love you mention is perhaps the strangest thing of all, should it be found to exist.

Our valiant pair began walking once more, which is how we like them best, and the errant tunes of Is's recorder and the jingling of his few coins formed a melodious accompaniment to their foot-tread. Several passers-by deposited a few small coins into the hat to join the ones Is had placed there, and so the morning seemed as good as any to the servant.

Beyond the settlement of Maylandsea they moved, along the edge of the Mundon Creek, over the banks tufted with stray hay-grass and mole hills. Past the Butterfields Farm they came, and down to the road. The last of the night damp was evaporating from the surface of the road, which wound up and down along the ancient borders of the irregularly proportioned fields. A sparse canopy overhead and the cool dappling of shadows it cast upon the road coruscated gently in the breeze. Once again we observe our two great good friends making their way down the thread of a country road.

Through Latchingdon, North Fambridge, Cold Norton then they came, where nothing at all happened. Is's pouch slowly gained a weight of coinage as people in the villages took pity on this man who piped out nursery rhymes from beneath the heavy load of his master's oak chest. They stopped for several hours at the sidings of a long disused railway line, where they rested and ate apples picked over a farmer's fence from an orange pippin. The early-June day drifted on, and gradually the weather turned. Our two adventurers turned east across the broad flat fields, heading straight towards the darkening sea. The clear light of day squeezed down between the sky and the land behind them as the sun began to sink. They reached the levee of Limbourne Creek; mud and salt and water all around. A sharp saltwet wind tore off the Blackwater estuary up the marshland channels, buffeting the grass which bobbed up and down in clumps, and the light sank further into a darkening steely grey. Beyond the marshland lay the deep estuarine mud, and the chalk bed below, where perhaps infant flint was incubating and waiting for its time of birth. Beyond, the sea churned greyblack with the failing light.

—I do hope, said Don, that the warmth and comfort of last night's stay at that old man's house – if indeed that is where we stayed, for I am forbidden from remembering – has rather restored than softened your vigour. Otherwise (and here Don pointed with his finger) it may dismay you to hear that we shall be sleeping in that field tonight.

Is shrugged his shoulders and patted his pouch of money to make plain that he did not care.

—Money is a wonderful sweetener for those who value its powers, said Don, relieved no doubt that his companion was not complaining for once.

—It's the very best thing in the world, sir, said Is as they climbed over a barbed wire fence and made their way across the field towards a tree at its far corner.

—I would disagree with you there, Don replied. But I'm not going to enter into an argument about who is right in this instance. It is sufficient for me to say that the history of money – which I would believe we had just recently touched upon were it not against both the tenets of my philosophy and the oaths I have made to my mistress to make recall – bears a very great resemblance to the history of the Eucharist. Money, there is no escaping from the fact of the matter, is like Christ. And the alleged saviour of the world is not so keen on money as you are.

Don and Is sat down with their backs against the tree and looked over the estuary to the sea, which appeared just then to be sucking the last of the light into itself and extinguishing the day. Is made a fire and set their billycan upon it to boil for black tea; he then began preparing a dinner of bread with cheese and raw onion, all harvested during the day from unwitting shopkeepers along the road.

—Perhaps that opposite I came up with earlier was not so opposite after all, said Is. Because while Jesus said backwards is 'sausage', they do go together mighty good.

Don pondered briefly the nonsense his squire had just delivered into the air.

—Even if you were right, he said, I do have to wonder how on earth the signs of money and of the sacrament of the Eucharist brought you to such a formulation.

—There's no need to scoff, said Is. Most of your ideas are more strange. It's as my mum showed me when I was little: you take your money down to the butchers and the bakers and the offy, and with the breadcrumbs and the belly of pork and a little drop of wine you can make a good cheap sausage, because Jesus is made out of bread and wine and flesh and blood, isn't he?

—Thank you for the elucidation, said Don. Now open up your ears and close your mouth, Isaiah, for I am going to discourse on the connection between money and the sacrament of the Eucharist right now, and when I grant you the guardianship of its written form you had better store it away firm and secluded from admixture with any sausagery, whether presented frontways or backways or sideways. This is not a casserole we are making here, it is a philosophical work.

Triseptimum: The Eucharist and Money

> Henry VIII, that very great villain, performed such outrages on both money and the Eucharist that it is a miracle that either of them have survived the assault; though it is arguable of course that they haven't.

—Incidentally Isaiah, do you think I should refrain from the use of the past and future tenses in the writing of these *triseptima*?

—I have no idea.

—Very well. I think I should. But I shall continue, or I will begin again – or, should I say, I continue, I begin. No, that doesn't quite work either. Anyway, here goes.

> Henry VIII, the very greatest villain, performs such outrages on both money and the Eucharist as to make one surprised that they can——

—Do you think, Don interrupted his writing again, that widespread belief in the death of this king is an impediment to my sense?

—Not at all, sir, said Is.

—Okay then – I go forth once more with my pen, I continue.

> Henry VIII, the vilest of all the English Kings and Queens, thrashes money and the Eucharist to within an inch of extinction. He herds all the silver coinage of the nation into the mint, a common practice with English money owing to the need to check clipping and the production of counterfeit coinage. The people are promised more money back than they give, a miracle of fiscal alchemy, but the money they receive back is debased. Between 1526 and May 1542 the silver coinage is minted at 11oz 2dwt fineness silver. Then, in just five years, between that date and April 1547, Henry VIII debases the coinage

five times to an eventual low of just 4oz fineness, taking in from the nation almost pure silver coinage, and giving back to it coinage of only one quarter silver.

At the same time, Henry makes the split with Rome. In Roman Catholicism, the species of bread and wine in the Eucharist are both sign (bread and wine) and thing signified (the body and blood of Christ). By contrast, the theologians of the Anglican Church decide (though not without precedent; Cf. William of Ockham's nominalism) that there is no real presence in the Eucharist, and that it is only a sign. Thenceforth, the 'pound sterling' in fiat value is only a sign for the pound sterling of silver with which it used to have identity, just as the bread and wine is only a sign for the body and the blood of Christ, with which it also used to have identity. Thus also is born the possibility of speculation, and thus of modern capitalism; and also of the distancing of sign from signified to the extent that the connection breaks and we have atheism. These two eventualities conspire to produce a culture in which capital and its signs become fetishised in order to stand in for the absence of any metaphysics, which has throughout its history been sustained by human sign-making. Outsiders from this money culture are the custodians of the cultural trajectory of Europe towards the formulation of the cult of the creative artist, who – like the God who died – makes signs. Modernity, to conclude, is a pool of snot.

13

—It is very difficult to talk about things which are supposedly in the past without using that thing known as the past tense, said Don.

—Yes, I did notice that you slipped back into talking about the far past and the near past and the thread that joins them, said Is.

—It is a curse inscribed into the language, said Don. Another example of the co-dependency of concepts: language forms time, which demands more complex language, which entrenches time, and so on. I'm not sure it can be redeemed. Some kind of linguectomy is necessary, and I'm not sure I could cut out the tongue of every human on the planet.

—It does seem a little unfair, said Is.

—And there are the constraints of time to think about, said Don.

—There you go again! said Is. I thought there weren't supposed to be any constraints of time!

—Ah, damn my immersion in this pighole language. You are right Isaiah, and it should be my own tongue that I cut out first.

Here Don swept back the flanks of his be-patched trenchcoat and removed from the belt that ran roundabout his decrepit trousers a fastidiously sharpened pocket knife.

—Do not do it sir! said Is. Think of all the good your treatise or encyclopaedia or whatever it is, is meant to do, and think of how you might need your tongue to spread the word of its existence! And in any case, the tea is now brewed, and your supper prepared, and no man can eat and drink with a wound so severe. And if none of those persuade you, consider my squeamishness!

Don's hands were stayed by the hurriedly delivered yet pertinent words of his companion.

—You are not often right, Isaiah, said Don. But when you are, you are righter than, how shall I put it?

—Rain? said Is. An angle?

—Both of those will do for the time being.

At the conclusion of this edifying conversation, which might have continued until the last whimper of the universe had their hunger not drawn Is from it, Don and his servant began eating and drinking, and they didn't cease until there was nothing left, their hunger enriching as it did their humble fare with such a savoury and flavoursome sauce.

In time, which even if unconstrained is said to wait for no man, Is spoke again:

—Excuse me for asking about it again, sir, but I was just wondering what we are up to now. What's our next stop?

He was chewing on the last of a piece of cheese garnished with onion and looking out over the fields, past the isolated houses of the desolate floodplain, to the mudflats, and the dark sea beyond.

—You are well aware, began his good master, that even to think to myself of what we are doing and where we are going would transgress the law of our great enterprise, which is to allow Chance, the daughter of Time, to do with us what She wills. Although it is said that there is a patriarchy on earth, in truth Woman dwells behind it all, though She be currently obscured.

—That's all well and good, but there must be certain places or undertakings which it would be preferable for us to visit or do.

—That is correct. But as soon as I consider them, they will start channelling my actions, and my intentions will blot out the fragile tapestrying of Chance who, though She reap very great harvests from the fields of Time, works always delicately.

Is sat silently for a time, and as he wasn't asleep we must presume that he was involved in practising that pastime known as thought, which for him was as rare as the silence of his mouth. Presently – and unavoidably – he spoke again:

—Okay then, if you cannot talk about where we are going, tell me where you have hoped to go in the past. If – and Is here reacted to an arch look which had been adopted by his master's visage – the past could be said to exist, which of course it doesn't, how ridiculous.

His master indulged him with the following words:

—As you know, I did once expect to be delivered to the large hadron collider at CERN, the world's most powerful particle accelerator. However, I wasn't, because the transit of the sun across the sky lured us back to the same coast we had left, as you though not I will remember.

—Ah! You have reminded me well! said Is. It is true that you said we were going to France. Your Daughter of Time is being treasoned against, it seems to me, and by no other than you yourself.

—I am but human, Isaiah, said Don. But I have learnt from my failures, and now am resolute. There shall be no intentions residing in my heart. The chain of cause and effect which everyone plots out upon every occurrence is an ugly thing indeed; but more than that, it is a falsity invented to comfort and shelter the mind from the infinite accident of Being.

—Well I don't believe you, sir, said Is. And I'm going to go through a list of places and let's see if I can't detect in the flickerings of your face some manner of plan, because you've mentioned enough places to me over the past week and I bet there was a reason for each of them.

Is proceeded to do just what he had said he would, and which it would be tedious to relate in its entirety, because the process lasted for well over two hours, which is equivalent to approximately fifty pages for a slow reader, and even such a reader – much our favourite kind in his attentiveness – would find a fifty page list excessive. However, it can be related that as the light continued gradually to fail, and as Is received no report from his master's face in the early stages of his investigation, he – Is – soon was unable to see Don's face because it was too dark, and indeed had forgotten what the purpose of his speaking such place names beneath a tree in the corner of an Essex field had been, and so the list functioned as no more than a lullaby to his and his master's fatigued bodies and minds. And so, after the two hours had elapsed, both men were fast asleep and their fire gone out.

(And while the two are asleep it would be instructive to provide for the reader a list of those places which Is named which did in fact produce an effect on the face of his master, although each went undetected, for there were several: Oxford, Greenwich, Cape Canaveral, Brooklyn, the Jodenbuurt, Santa Monica, a village in La Mancha the name of which he could not quite recall, Stagirus, Roccasecca, Soho, Ilchester, Fobbing, Samos, Happisburgh, Lascaux, Lagar Velho and Boxgrove.)

When the morning came Is was the first to wake, and he was not happy with what he found: a number of cows huddled close about him, switching their tails and occasionally nodding. The smell coming off them was peculiarly sweet and delicate, somewhat like Turkish delight, though muskier. He urged his master awake with a vigorous shake of his shoulder.

—Sir, I'm not happy with the bedfellows we gained in the night. How do we get out of this one?

—They're only cows, Isaiah, said Don. Allow them to exercise their curiosity for a time, and then they'll be off.

—As long as they don't use my head as a stepping stone to their off-ness, I can live with that.

Is managed to hold his tongue and his fear within him sufficient for twenty minutes to elapse, but still the cows exhibited no intention of moving on. They stood in a curious huddle in complete stillness, except for the switching of their tail-cords. In the end, Is was led to complain once more.

—I'm not liking this one bit, he said. Let's get out of here; I don't care where to. Anything is preferable to being intimidated by a gang of cows.

—Well let us move on then! said Don, rising majestically to his feet with his boots already tied and the grandness of his thoughts whirling behind his yellow eyes.

Is, keeping a wary eye on the cows all the while, once more hauled the enormous chest containing his master's *Encyclopaedia Of Being* on to his back and made to follow him. Past the cows they went, and over to the corner of the field, where they found a broad farmer's gate which Don noticed with distaste was of the five-bar denomination. The master unhooked the thick stiff wet loop of rope from the post, pushed open the gate, and wound through the aperture, with his servant following him. But when Is came to close the gate, he found upon his hand the hot rubbery lips and turgid muscular tongue of one of the cows, all of whom had slowly turned and lumbered over like so many cumbersome ships. He shrieked, allowing the chest to crash to the ground, and let go of the rope, to the end that the cows were able to push the gate open and follow their human friends.

—Sir! said Is. They're coming for us!

—It's fine, said Don. And here comes a horse too. What a lovely creature is a horse!

This was too much for Is, for whom cows, whilst frightening, at least had in their favour an exceeding ponderousness. Horses, by comparison, were inescapable, which made them fiends.

—I am in hell! said Is, and he ran across the field, with the stationary horse looking quizzically through its crimped fringe at him as he made transit across the succulent grass littered with stalks of straw.

Don laughed.

—Isaiah! he called across the field to his terrified servant. The Chance which you treat with contempt and which I adore like It were my Bride – which indeed She shall be – has done this for us. I believe that the trunk you have complained about carrying for the past week and the horse that you are complaining about being in the company of now might be introduced one to another for the alleviation of your suffering. Come back here and we will rig something up by which this mare can assist you, and perhaps then you will like her more.

The attractiveness of this idea could not be denied, and for a short moment Is ceased quavering and complaining and returned warily to his master's side. And as luck – or perhaps Chance – would have it, ensnared in clumps of overgrown long pale grass at the field's side they found the beam and coulters of an ancient rusty plough. With a mildewed lifesaver ring dragged out of the marshes down by the water's edge, they secured the plough to the horse, who took on her new burden without objection, and they loaded the ploughbeam with the chest.

Very soon this extraordinary caravan rejoined the road: Don at their head, holding the improvised bridle for their majestic horse; then the horse herself; then the plough and chest, with Is at the latter's side ensuring like a tutelary spirit its safe transit through the fair county, whilst picking and eating heavy succulent blackberries from brambles at the roadside; and finally, the eleven cows behind in echelon. They made it ever onwards across the land, with Chance (we must presume) turning over the Time around them as if it were the pages of the very best book in the world.

Presently the entourage met upon the road a car coming in the opposite direction, and whose progress was thereby checked. The driver sat behind the wheel, waiting and watching as they passed. What must have passed through the mind of the spectator of their mad deeds! The answer to that question can never be known for certain, but it would not be difficult for even the least supple intelligence to speculate from subsequent events that the spectator was not feeling as indulgent as our fair reader on that day; for within fifteen minutes, and with a queue of six cars travelling behind Don's caravan, a vehicle bearing the insignia of the Essex Constabulary made determined procession down the road and stopped in front of our heroes and their attendants to the effect that all were halted.

—What are you doing? said the officer, as soon as she had climbed out of her vehicle.

—Here we go again, said Is, who remembered without fondness the morning he had spent in the cell at Butt Road with William Smith.

—By the strictures of my Science, said Don, which scorns the epistemes which over at least the preceding ten thousand years have gradually calcified Western thought into the abominable form you find it in today, I cannot tell you what I am doing because I do not believe that it is possible to account for actions except through action, words by their nature (and what a false formation that is, a natural language!) always carrying within themselves an ineluctable ordering into temporal neatness which is exacted upon that-which-is and should be forever unorderable, except insofar as the spectral line of the hyperfine transition of hydrogen reconfigures it, the extent to which is entire.

At the conclusion of this formidable speech the police officer made it plain that she was not at all interested in anything it had contained.

—Is this your horse and livestock, sir? she said.

—The word 'animal', began Don again, is derived from the Latin *animalis*, which ascribes the possession of a soul. As it has been the tradition in our culture that beings with a soul have eternal spiritual life, corporeal existence should not be made to run counter to the freedom that entails, but should be analogous to it, in accordance with the *analogia entis* described by the great Aristotelian theologian St Thomas Aquinas. Therefore, no animal can be the property of a person, just as no person – in spite of the evidence offered by the historical record – can be the property of another; and therefore, although this is not the logic to which my own actions adhere, it is perforce yours, and so I reject your question as being founded upon false premises.

—That's a weighty bag of words, said a farmer from behind a hedge. The police officer smiled.

—Bring your body and your soul over here, she said, and I'll place both of them under arrest.

—Good Twenty-One Isaiah, it is an impetuous woman. Move aside and let me and my companions pass. We have a long day's travel ahead of us, to where we do not yet know.

—Allow me to tell you where, said the police officer. Your first stop will be Colchester police station.

And she began reading Don his rights.

—Colchester! said Is. It's the ley-lines at work again, sir! Old King Cole wants us and our chest here! O not Colchester again! The town of my undoing!

With these words freshly delivered into the ears of whoever would listen, Is sank to his knees at the policewoman's feet and begged her not to arrest them and send them back to Colchester again, because it would break his heart, not that it wasn't broken already.

The policewoman looked sternly at our two adventurers; she placed again a stray lock behind her ear better to intimidate the pair with her eyes; she turned her radio down low for the delivery of her judgement.

—Return anything which is not yours exactly to wherever you took it and you can go on your way.

Profusely the servant thanked her, and agreed, and obtained begrudgingly-given concordant agreement from his master before the assembly.

—Nice chest, said the farmer from behind the hedge. You steal that off the blind boy that made it?

14

Not half an hour later, Don and Is were back where they had been, though now without any of the animals they had enjoyed the company of; and Is, liberated of the burden of another impending incarceration and the walk once more from Colchester to wherever it was they might go, was placed again beneath the more familiar burden of his master's chest. The sun shone, the crickets chirruped in the verge, and a mistle thrush observed diligently their further passage onwards, north, towards the ancient town of Maldon.

—One thing I've been wondering master, said Is after a time, is why it's you that's been chosen and not someone else – for this resuscitation job or whatever the name of it is, I mean.

—It is but by Chance, and that is all I can say. You may wish to know though that I am what the contemporary quacks would call synaesthesic. It is not irrelevant, I believe.

—What's that then, sir? said Is.

—The division of my five senses each from each has not been fully achieved. I smell sights, I see sounds, I hear flavours, I taste touch, I feel odours. People are not at all surprised that, having smelt it, they know the taste of urine; but tell them that Beethoven tastes lambier than Buddy Miles, and they look at you as if you are mad.

—I once did by dint of his scheming drink my brother's urine.

—That's a wonderful thing to tell, Isaiah. But to return to the subject at hand, synaesthesia is a remnant of a truer means and manner of perception which has been evolved out of us by necessity. Sense has been divided into the senses, just as the species have been divided, just as everything has, each within its little group, neat and well-behaved and in its proper place, and everyone now learns what their five senses tell them as if their parietal lobe were the infallible judiciary of Being. Let me tell you this: the division of the five senses one from another was only necessary because of *work*. Work lies at the origin of specialisation. Before work was invented, being alive was one big ecstasy. The codification of all sense experience is the work of Creation. I feel a bout of the necessity coming on – fetch me my things!

—Give me a chance, sir, said Is, and I'll crack this old chest open.

TRISEPTIMUM: CREATION

Know well the fact of the matter, Isaiah: Neanderthal Man could have had no creation myth. A myth is a system that stands in for a complex of other things – it *is* that complex; it is the structure of the interconnection of a multitude of signs belonging to multiple sign-worlds. Neanderthal Man couldn't think across sign-worlds like that – indeed, he saw no signs, only things. This is why he perished, because to adapt to change one must think symbolically; to see the flint spark as did the lightning, and thereby harvest fire for the warmth of the tribe, that is the work of the analogous mind. Such a leap of thought comes naturally to *homo sapiens*. Mark well that an unforeseeable outcome of the versatility and adaptability of humans is the making of art works. One might say, in fact, that works of art are the waste matter of being human. First among these art works are humanity's creation myths, in which we see order imposed on Being for the comfort of our species.

In the Judeo-Christian creation myth, the reader will notice that our conceptions of the key terms 'heaven' and 'earth' are insufficient for the interpretation and comprehension of the opening verse. We read: "1. In the beginning God created the heaven and the earth. 2. And the earth was without form, and void; and darkness *was* upon the face of the deep. And the Spirit of God moved upon the face of the waters." Earth here is matter, it has no form; heaven here is what we have never been able to comprehend: 'matterless being'. God has created only chaos. *In illo tempore*, God creates being from nothing, and then looks being up and down and sees what it's all about. At this stage we are level pegging with the Greek creation myth, in which chaos is the raw material of divine creation. Had no further work been done, my *Encyclopaedia* would have had no necessity.

But done it was: The divine *logos*, that is to say the Word – light, reason, thought, law; only possible because of *the word,* which indeed is how they are denoted: *logos* – directs, and matter obeys. "3. And God said, Let there be light: and there was light." Chance took a hiding to nil on that primordial pre-day, chased down the alleys of darkness into ignominy. Return to me, O Chance!

Our God is a veritable first writer, laughing at his own jokes, and pleased as punch to be meeting his made matter. Look here: "4. And God saw the light, that *it was* good: and God divided the light from the darkness. 5. And God called the light Day, and the darkness he called Night. And the evening and the morning were the first day." Editing away at his little slip of a thing. Mountebank! Everything he does is good, good, good, *very* good. Except for one little thing——

—And mark me here, Isaiah, said Don in a spoken interjection which he could not help but pursue. The only part of his creation not given the specific pronouncement 'it was good' is man and woman. How do you like that? Anyway, in the Creation myth we find a record of the primordial mind of the West giving an account of its own self-acculturation. Allow me to continue.

—I wouldn't dream of standing in your way.

There can be no chaos! screams the neurosis of the West, and God (which is now Writing) is close at hand to do His duty, which is to create light and the day, and to divide it from dark and the night, and to divide heaven from earth, and to divide the land from the sea, which by analogy is to instigate language, whose written form creates the myth of History.

—O our first fall! said Don, whose sudden anguish again terminated the writing of the *triseptimum,* and led him to denounce the universe with his tremulous voice:

—What has been cloven apart must be made to cleave together, he said into the air. And the might of my arm is fortified by the spectral line of the hyperfine transition of hydrogen. So quake, Being, for I am on my way, bearing Twenty-One bowls, diadems, thunders, and I forget what else.

Is watched his master perpetrate his usual deeds in the name of the forbidden line and allowed him to come to some manner of rest before speaking the following words, which he had been wondering whether to allow out of his mouth for some days past.

—Excuse me for asking, sir, but I'm a little confused as to your criticisms of writing when that's exactly what you are doing, unless I've got something mixed up, which wouldn't surprise either of us at all, seeing as I don't have the skill myself – the writing skill, I mean.

Don looked at his servant and friend for what even he – in spite of his refusal to believe in duration – would have admitted was a considerable length of time.

—I'm sure, continued Is, seeking to extricate himself from whatever disgrace his previous words had seemed to set him in. I'm sure there was something you said about writing and the devil, or God, or something. Writing and people and time, good things and bad things. Stuff.

—Oh Isaiah, said Don. It seems that it is necessary for me to explore the relationship between writing and time audibly before you. And so I shall: fetch me a good fistful of scraps from the chest so I may find and read it to you, dolt.

Is did as he was told, relieved no doubt that he was not being reproved. Very soon he delivered into Don's hands an enormous pile of dog-eared papers, within which Don miraculously found what he was looking for in no time at all.

TRISEPTIMUM: WRITING

When writing emerged in the cultures of the world, the concepts of those cultures assumed rigid forms. The protean fluidity of ideas pertaining to beauty, majesty, the sacred, power, but also to the conception of the objects of the natural world, was obliterated by a system which invited codification, systematization, taxonomization, and so on. If writing did not exist, there would be no opposition between the rational and irrational because such categories would not exist. Conceptions of reality would have remained fluid; semiotic systems based upon stark binary oppositions would never have emerged. The modern Western human mind now *requires* oppositions in order to make any sense of the world, *viz.* the persistence of the myth of happiness in marriage. For the sake of our own sanity, it is necessary to believe. The truth, though, is that marriage is the most oppressive institution in existence: it is as two lightning-struck trees leaning upon one another, and rotting. The infinite storm of interlocking oppositions which characterizes the content of the modern mind – at one end having no firm origin or stable basis; at the other drifting into a logically inescapable self-annihilating illogic – has been gathering ever since. Without writing, there would still be religion and science, but they would not be in opposition – indeed, they would be the same thing. Writing has been, is, and will always be a murderer of Truth.

—Well, said Is, sensing that Don's recitation of the *triseptimum* was concluded, and therefore believing it time to heave the chest back on to his back. If writing is what you say it is, let's burn your *Encyclopaedia*, and we can do the chest as well right along with it.

He looked at the burden he sought not to take up again, and then to his master, and then back to the chest. Don, in return, looked again at Is for a hard long while.

—You are an imbecile, he said. Have you never heard of the phrase 'to fight fire with fire'? We must tenderize the minds of the world using the instruments with which they are familiar. You cannot just declare a thing entirely new to be so – that is known as madness. Corporate thought develops very slowly Isaiah – every modern painter discovers the same problem and its partial solutions as the painters of Lascaux 20,000 years ago. (Though, of course, the modern painter has to work harder to find joy, which is a necessary disposition for the making of works.) This is how narrow are the limits to being human.

—The ways we tell our children to behave, continued Don, are unthought-out variations on a motif without singular origin, but one which was certainly being performed in a not dissimilar form at the cave-mouth before the ice came. So, a true revolution in culture, which my system entails, is inconceivable before it happens. We must be cunning; and my *Encyclopaedia* is as cunning as anything ever committed to paper.

With a great melancholy suspiration, Is bent to the chest once more, and heaved it on to his aching back.

Within an hour they found themselves passing a trading estate, and then a decrepit wharf with its rusting debris strewn across a broad expanse of grass-seamed concrete as if by a monstrous child in prehistory, when men were giants.

15

After an hour's fitful rained-on rest in the graveyard of a church in the centre of the old town of Maldon – the church tower so patched with cement that its flints appeared to be engaged in retreating from the world, the whole church shrinking back into itself – Don and Is rose among the wet bushes where the birds sang, dusted themselves down, and walked out on to the road to continue their adventure. A worn-out fibreglass model of a butcher greeted their arrival in his vicinity by grinning and leaning forward with a side of bacon draped over his arm like a priest with maniple. Past him they went, with Is checking all the time that the butcher's eyes did not follow him; and they made their way down the high street with the sun glinting off every wet surface it could directly find, and a rainbow bisecting the sky with a painterly sweep.

Moving back through the town along precisely the same route by which they had entered it – such were the demands of Chance – our adventuring pair now had the mouth of the estuary to their left, flowing round Northey Island, and glittering under the early afternoon sun. With each transit through the town, more coins were added to Is's bobbing hat in payment for his troubadourian services, which made him as happy as he had been for weeks. Right they turned, along Downs Road, following the course of the Blackwater as it flowed out to the North Sea.

—If days and dates and measures of the year existed, said Don, which clearly they do not, then we could say without any doubt that the day of judgement is closing in. Very soon the true secrets of the hyperfine transition of hydrogen will become apparent to me, and the whole world will be cured.

—Is there anything that the hyperfine transition of hydrogen is unable to do? asked Is.

—A pernicious and misguided fool it would be who claimed that there was. Do you remember what I told you about the atom at the filling station?

—I do, said Is. But surely you do not. You are after all the sworn enemy of memory.

—I like the phrase you have invented there. Should we succeed in our quest, it might function as part of my appellation, which will require some solemnity to it. Such ways with names seem to have passed out of fashion. But yes, you're right.

—How then can you ask me to remember something?

—I never said that you had to imitate me in that respect, said Don.

—But the very asking of the thing means that you remember the thing you are referring to, said Is.

—I do not have to remember that I spoke of the atom at the filling station, I merely have to be lucky. Did I speak of the atom in that place?

—Yes, said Is.

—Well there you go. I wasn't aware of that.

Is emitted an inarticulate utterance signifying scepticism.

—I think, he said, that there might be more of the normal to you than you let on. Maybe the playing-the-part-of began a long time ago.

—Are you insinuating that I am a pretender? A charlatan? said Don. Are you implying that I would treat my true mistress and only love, Science, or Chance, or Time, or whatever her name is, as if she were a whore? Are you accusing me of not being genuine in my commitment to discovering the nature of the force which drives every flower to its blooming, from the origin of the universe down to the springing of water out of one of hydrogen plus two of oxygen?

—The answer I give is dependent on what its consequences will be, said Is. If you are feeling violent, I would change my mind. Could you outline my immediate future?

—Has a man ever been so malleable! said Don. You won't even look at a map of the path of righteousness. You should be called Easeiah.

—You wrong me, master, said Is. I am the one carrying your chest and books and meat on my back, which taken together are heavier than the proverbial monkey.

—Moral and physical hardship are two very different things, said Don. Not that I believe either the moral or physical to be categories having any reality to them. But they are convenient terms.

This conversation might have carried on for hours, and might have taken in such diversions as the cultivation of rapeseed, the predominance of flint in the manufacture of churches in East Anglia, the beauty of the song of the blackbird, and the competing claims of historians in respect of Flavia Julia Helena's residence at Colchester for their theme, had the pair – who had by now walked the length of the quayside and through a pleasant park – not stopped to witness an adolescent boy sitting atop a large bronze statue of some kind of medieval warrior, and two police officers standing at its foot ordering him to come down.

—What is the Law, said Don, but a story continually added to and retold? And you know the way I feel about stories.

—That's a funny old chest you've got on your back there, said the boy to Is from his place on the statue's head. Looks like something my dad would've made after a night on the piss.

—You may not like stories, said Is. But I am very fond of a good yarn. With a beginning, middle and end, that's how they're best. And a true story is the best of all.

—Look at how these despots threaten and intimidate the innocent boy, said Don ignoring his servant once more. I shall engage them in mortal combat!

—Please don't do that, said Is. We'll only end up arrested and back in Colchester again, and I don't think my poor heart can take another visit.

—If it will avert your pitiful moaning, then I will do as you say. But the boy shall be saved!

With this, Don ran after his own style up to the statue and began climbing it.

—Sir! What are you doing? asked one of the police officers with great surprise.

—I am visiting a friend, said Don, and he continued to climb.

Is moved closer and watched: the boy was examining in detail the various features of the statue from his unusual vantage point.

—Child! Or boy! Or young man! shouted Don up to the adolescent. I have come to rescue you from these ravening instruments of the Law! It is irrefutable that Chance has laid you before me!

The adolescent demonstrated through recourse to the medium of spitting that he did not want to leave his place on the statue's shoulders.

—Good Christ, he is a very cat! said Don. How on earth did he get up there?

The adolescent continued to spit and laugh at Don, holding on to the sword held aloft by the statue; and the police officers continued to threaten both the boy and Don.

—Sir! said Is. Maybe you shouldn't bother. He's got you licked when it comes to climbing. Maybe Chance is being a bit of a tease today and she's meaning for us to just wander on.

—I will not countenance such negligence. And besides, I never want to hear you speak in such a derogatory way of my fair lady bride Chance again – who would certainly forgive me for referring to the future in her defence. This boy has been placed before us as a reminder of the various instruments of oppression, both epistemological and ontological – namely the Law, the Word by which it is written, History, whose statue he climbs, and Gravity, by which he is constrained into proximity to the three former. Besides, we have travelled this far, and you can't wind back time.

—That's true enough.

—True Time being decidedly un-clock-like, continued Don. The maze is unidirectional. There is no Ariadne. All threads are immediately consumed. Past and future are sacrificed in perpetuity, and the blood washes over and cleanses the greatest mystery the world has never known: Now.

Is gave up trying to persuade his master to cheat on Chance, and instead began attempting to persuade the police officers not to arrest Don when he returned to the ground. They were unyielding, and demanded that Don join them at the foot of the statue immediately. Don demanded that the police officers re-phrase their demand so that he could understand what they were saying, for he had recently vowed never to countenance another dead metaphor, and 'foot' in the context in which they had used it was such a locution, because the plinth was tall enough to elevate Byrhtnoth's feet – for that was the warrior's name – high above the esplanade.

—If you do not climb down from that statue, you will be arrested for causing a public disturbance. Do I make myself clear, sir?

—I understand you better, said Don, still showing no sign of intending to descend to the street. However, I cannot help noticing that your use of the word 'clear' is as metaphorical as your previous use of the word 'foot'. The subject deserves some further attention, and so I shall write.

With a vigour which defied his years, Don clenched his thighs around Byrhtnoth's left leg high on the bronze plinth above the ground; and, steadying himself, he reached into the inside pocket he had sewn into his trenchcoat and retrieved an emergency notebook and pencil. In no time at all, with the boy cawing above him and the police blandly remonstrating below, Don was deep in a *triseptimum* on the subject of figurative language.

Triseptimum: Metaphor

O foolish man! Vanity! Let us be blunt: the metaphor is not only the most fallacious instrument of language; in being so, it also bears testament to the impossibility of all language to do what it attempts, which is to name things, whether objects, actions or ideas. Conventionality lies at the root of language: we know what you mean, Isaiah, when you say you stubbed your toe because, possessing them ourselves, we have seen and touched toes, and are used to the sound 'toe' being used to describe such a thing. But the word 'toe' only ever signifies the idea 'toe', never the thing *toe* itself. Why? Because the thing *toe* itself *has no real existence*.

In Bristol there was a man who inadvertently cut off his left thumb with a saw. Surgeons removed his big toe and attached it to where his thumb had been. That digit is still the same matter that it was when it was a toe, but you would be thought mad if you insisted that that man must wash the entire left side of his body when asked to wash between his toes. Therefore, his toe has become his thumb. By extension, all materialism is thereby discredited.

So, what about idealism? A 'toe' can become a 'thumb' because it can be made to perform the function of a thumb: by fulfilling the idea of what a thumb is, a toe can *become* a 'thumb'. But if this man was asked to thumb a lift, and used his right foot – or if he were to 'toe the line' by brandishing his thumb before an assembly in readiness for action – he would be making a joke. Every fresh metaphor, formed within the word-mint deep in the mind, is also a kind of joke (the word 'wit' began by meaning the seat of consciousness, and has ended up denoting a talent for saying brilliant or sparkling things, especially in an amusing way). And what is a joke if it is not interference, a kind of linguistic short-circuit? If the whole of language has any value whatsoever, it is solely as one colossal piece of humour.

You will notice that I described the construction of metaphor as taking place in the 'word-mint' of the mind. Comprehension of this metaphor requires us to take coinage to represent words, and the mint to represent the intellect. But a mint requires a royal charter, whilst anyone can make a metaphor. Additionally, those who produce the most metaphors are the ones with the least coinage: the poets.

Therefore, metaphors should be seen not as glimpses into the truth of things, but as little imps whose sport is the dishevelment of every house on the street. My isopsephic use of the hyperfine transition of hydrogen reveals that it is safer not to speak. I therefore renounce talking.

By the time Don had finished writing, the police officers had mounted the statue too, and were in the process of interpreting his renunciation of speech as an instance of the availment of the right to silence.

In short, Don, the boy and the two police officers were very soon back on the ground beneath the elegant statue of Byrhtnoth and discussing, much to Don's distaste, those classes of time known, recognised and believed-in by the whole of the rest of mankind as the past and future. Why had they climbed the statue? What were they thinking of? Why didn't they get down when directed? Did they want to be placed under arrest for a breach of the peace? But within half an hour, Don and the boy agreed terms with the police officers – sorrowfully for Don, as such negotiation required him to renege on his vow of silence almost before it had begun – and were free to go on their own way, though with due warning: no more mucking about or there'll be trouble.

The boy was escorted to the police car, placed upon the back seat, and given a ride home. Don and Is therefore very soon found themselves standing beneath the imposing figure of Byrhtnoth in one another's company, in freedom, with the officers gone. High above them the warrior towered, his nine-foot frame glistening beneath the golden light of the afternoon, steam rising from the impressionistic loops of his chainmail, up past the arm and sword, the pointed beard, the chin held up, the helmet. Did he not look like Don himself, who perhaps had always walked the ages, in defiance even of death?

—I cannot say that I am satisfied with the outcome of our latest conflict with the instruments of oppression, said Don.

—Neither of us is injured, sir, so I'd be willing to call it a draw if you'll allow me, and a draw's not such a bad result.

—Such acquiescence!

—Is is as Is does, said his squire once more.

—And in this instance, Is does badly. To roll over like that – such a way with living is surely at the root of the necessity of our mission, though the very concept 'root' is of course as illusory as it is abstract, and has no more existence than does that tree over there.

Is looked at the tree Don had indicated, scratched his head, and appeared very much to be wondering what on earth his master was talking about, because the tree seemed to have very much existence indeed.

Very soon, Don and Is, in accordance with the strictures of Chance, had passed back through the town a third and final time, leaving the bleakness of the estuary's salt marshes behind them, and began travelling north-west along a winding and leafy country lane close to the River Chelmer; which is exactly where we shall rejoin them in just a moment.

16

Presently, the rural banks which channelled the narrow road began to slouch down, and a broken white line began at the road's centre.

—We are drawing into a village, said Don. Let us be vigilant, for we have not been fortunate in the settlements of the county so far today.

However, they passed through Little Baddow without incident, and the road brought them back on to the broad flood plain of the Chelmer. The poplars rustled in the light breeze, and the white blossom of the scrappy hawthorn was brilliantly spread to the approaching evening, whose sun now goldenly shone once more. They turned left, heading upstream along the road's verge at the bank of the river. Dragonflies careened through the air; birds rustled in the hedgerow as they heard the footfall of our heroes pass; bubbles rose in the river, denoting the presence of fish. Dazzling scintillae of sunlight flashed from the surface of the river as its water was moulded by the pebbles beneath into silken pools and eddies of infinitesimal delicacy. Is felt the need of a rest; and with permission granted by his master, he sat on the riverbank and felt the cool water flowing over his tired feet.

—Sir, he said. I know that the past doesn't exist, but if it did, I would certainly remember that you were moaning not too long ago about writing again – it was while you were hugging that bronze bloke with the big sword. Don't you think you should renounce the writing in the chest upon my back and we can burn it like I've been saying? I haven't stood straight for a good week or more now, not that that's my reason of course.

—I wonder if you ever consider, before you open your mouth to speak, what the words you are about to say might be taken to mean, Isaiah, said Don. The only equivalent I can conceive of for the burning of the papers in the chest you carry – and the means by which the construction of that equivalent has been assembled in my mind has been affected greatly by the tumult of grief which your words create in me – is to think of what would have happened if the adolescent Christ had fallen out of a tree and died premature to the transaction of his Passion. Do you want to be responsible for depriving Time of its true salvation?

—But I don't believe sir that I am wrong in thinking that you believe the Christ thing to be a bag of tripes, said Is.

—You are an idiot, said his master. I do not believe it to be anything of the sort. It is a very great attempt at an insoluble problem – insoluble, that is, until now.

With these final words, Don stood up on the river bank and struck an heroic pose, with one hand raised and the other close to where his sword would have resided in its scabbard, if he had had one.

—Oh I don't think I can bear to hear about the thingy thing thing again, said Is.

—You do not have to, said Don. Because I commission you instead of either talking or listening to make a fire so that we might take a cup of tea, which should stave off the cold and hunger till the morning, for night approaches and we have no food. And know full well, fractious servant, that if you tried to fuel that fire with the papers of my *Encyclopaedia* you would find them as impervious to the flames as the adamants of Alexander the Great, and the strength of your hand in fire-wield is unworthy of comparison even with the soft and downy earlobes of either Gog or Magog, whose might was thereby thwarted.

—If that's how bad I am at making a fire, perhaps you'd like to do it yourself this evening, said Is.

—And so I will, said Don.

This ended the current conversation so absolutely that silence made a rare visit to our martial duo for the quarter of an hour or so that it took Don to fiddle an assemblage of tinder and kindling into something resembling a combustible order; and, following this, the application to it of a match which could be made to burn. The fire rose, and much smoke, owing to Don's use of green wood in its making. Is sat contentedly back with his feet still in the river, his recorder in his hands, and a smile on his face, inwardly gloating at his superior skill in the ways of firecraft. The light began to over-ripen, goldening, and the day began to die.

—Well if we can't burn your book, even though you hate writing, maybe we could have another story. They're really not so bad as you think.

—They are the sole cause of all suffering, said Don.

—Perhaps despite the hugeness of your brain you're just no good at telling them, and that's the real reason why you don't like them. Perhaps you're about as bad at it as you are at making a fire. Maybe if you put that hyperfine what-not out of your mind for a bit you'd get better at everything else. And maybe you'd realise there's nothing wrong with stories at all; that the whole world isn't a jar full of wasps owing to stories; and actually everything is fine. If there's one thing that every fire wants – even one as bad as the one you've just made – it's a story told over it.

—Every word, thought, idea, concept, explanation – every human endeavour – is mired in storying, Don said from within the funnel of smoke that his fire had produced, and from which he was too proud to remove himself.

—Well how about a joke then?

—Ah, a joke is a different matter altogether, said Don. A good joke is a fine thing, founded as it is upon the strictest logic, and oriented as it is upon logic's destruction. But I am forbidden the remembrance of anything, be it even the slightest thing on earth, even my own age or the place I grew up in as a child – if ever I was a child – and so I cannot tell you a joke. The burden must fall on you.

—The burden is always falling on me, said Is. And the familiarity my back has built up with this chest isn't making it any fonder.

—That's as may be, said Don. But take this new burden up, and very soon afterwards you will gain the sweet pleasure of setting it down again within the ears of your friend and master.

—Perhaps, said Is. But I only know one joke, and I'm not even sure it's a joke.

—How can you not know if it is a joke? came Don's voice from within the pillar of smoke.

—Well, I was told it *was* a joke before I was told it *as* a joke, but it didn't make me laugh any more than it would have without the clue.

—Usually comprehension is an essential ingredient of memorisation, said Don. I am surprised, therefore, that this joke in particular is the only joke you are able to remember. Do you know what a joke is, Isaiah?

—I'm sure I do sir, yes. But I'm not so sure I could describe what one is other than by saying they make a person laugh, which appears to be my problem here. I think maybe it's like sheep.

Don peered from his place within the billowing cloud of smoke at his servant through bloodshot eyes.

—How is a joke like sheep, Isaiah? he said.

—Well, I've known what a sheep looks like since I was a very small boy, and I've been able to draw a sheep for almost as long, and the picture I would draw of a sheep now would look little different from the picture I would have drawn then.

—Your analogy is most fascinating, Isaiah.

—Thank you, sir.

—But what exactly is it that you are saying?

—What I'm saying is that I can draw sheep and I can picture sheep in my mind, but when a sheep comes up to me – and there have been times when a sheep has done such a thing, and I'll admit I haven't much liked it – it doesn't look like a sheep at all. In fact, it looks so little like a sheep that I can't be sure it's not something else.

—What else could it be? asked Don.

—I don't know, said Is.

—Perhaps you might mistake a sheep for a goat?

—No, certainly not a goat, sir. They are a very recognisable animal.

—Well, so in my opinion is a sheep! said Don.

—I completely agree, sir.

—Then what on earth is all this talk about? Are they recognisable and mistakeable all at once? And is a goat as liable as a sheep to be a stand-in for your description of this joke?

Don was beginning to lose patience with his servant, and the smoke from his fire was making him cough.

—All I know is that if a sheep comes up to me in the life of the real, I can't be certain that that thing there before me is a sheep. And I find with a joke that it's the same – except in reverse.

—How so? said Don, who in spite of his streaming eyes seemed to be relieved that Is had returned to the original topic of their conversation and that some conclusion seemed to be in sight.

—A joke can come up as close as it likes to me and I'll always know damn well it's a joke, turn it whichever way you like. But there's no picture I have in my mind of what a joke generally *is*. I couldn't draw you one if you asked me.

—The roundabout route you take to your point is as ingenious as it is necessary, which is to say not at all, said Don.

—The worrying thing for me, sir, is that the only joke I know is the only one I don't recognise as a joke. It's the odd-one-out: the black sheep.

—It would appear that it's any kind of sheep at all, said Don. But enough of all these preliminaries: shear the wool of it into my ears and let me decide whether it is a joke or not.

—I will do as you ask, said Is. But remember that I am innocent. I'm only telling it because it won a joke competition, which would tend to indicate that it was a joke.

—It does indeed, said Don laughing. I wonder that you didn't mention this earlier. The winning of a competition tends also to indicate that a thing is an exemplary member of its class; in short, that the joke which

I hope will soon be issuing from your mouth is a very fine one, and so may possibly recompense me for that pleasure lost in listening to you prattle on about sheep. Though such an assumption assumes also that those who deliberated the matter were sagacious and discriminatory.

—Normally I'd agree with you sir, said Is. But the competition was for the worst joke in history.

—I see, said Don. I wonder that Chance felt fit to punish me with your service, you imbecile.

—Shall I tell it? said Is, ignoring his master.

—You have raised my hopes and then dashed them, said Don. But for the sake of completeness I suggest you tell the joke. Is it a long one?

—No sir, said Is. It is very, very short.

—Well, if it is truly that bad, at least it has brevity in its favour. Be pleased to stimulate into waves the air through the articulation of the muscles of your mouth and throat, and share this joke with me.

—Yes sir. Here it is.

Is coughed before he began, and his beginning went thus:

—What is the difference between a duck?

Silence.

—Be pleased to remember the first premise of the joke in its entirety, Isaiah, said Don.

—That's the first part sir, the question bit. That *is* it. Then there's only one little answery bit and we're all done.

—What is the difference between a duck, you say? said Don.

—That's it, sir.

—Well, said Don. I think you're certainly on to something here. Carry on.

—Okay. So: What's the difference between a duck?

—I don't know, said Don. What is the difference between a duck?

—One leg is both the same.

Pause.

—It is the greatest joke ever uttered, said Don.

—What does it mean? said Is.

—Who was it, said Don, stepping out from within the pillar of smoke, raising one arm into the air as if he were Byrhtnoth freed from his bronze, and rousing himself into a fever of righteous indignation. Who was it, say I, that traduced this fine, this masterful, this sovereign specimen of its class? I will destroy them utterly. How dare the adjudicators of this joke take it upon themselves so wrongfully to dismiss it! Speak Isaiah, for I shall have an answer, and that answer shall spur me to right the wrongs testified by it!

—It was a bunch of schoolkids, sir, said Is. Try not to get angry, it's not good for you.

Don, ceasing to rage at the sky above himself where the sun was slowly getting ready to set, slumped to the ground, inadvertently imitating his fire, which after filling the air with such a quantity of smoke had gone out.

—O your words have quelled my anger, he said, such that I am now filled with sadness. Not since Aristotle have words been assembled in so fresh an order! And yet the imaginations of the young, which should be in their springtime, lively and inquisitive, are jaded. They know not of what they speak. This, like everything else which is, is a damning indictment of the West.

Don then ceased bewailing the youth of today in order inwardly to lament. But very soon he recalled the existence of the hyperfine transition of hydrogen, which acted as a universal balsam and tonic to his body and mind, and he was contented once more. From a face black with soot, he looked out of red eyes with great happiness upon the small patch of scorched earth which his fire – now having extinguished itself – had created, and which along with the rest of the earth might have been in the process of being atomised for all he cared, for the hyperfine transition of hydrogen was again at the forefront of his mind.

—It is only a short distance to the town we are about to enter, he said. But I would prefer to stand upon the ground at this riverside for the night and transact a vigil on behalf of my Bride, such is my feeling for Her at this Time.

While Don did as he desired, Is looked about himself at the grasses of the roadside, which were growing damp in the late-evening air.

—Sir, you might want to conduct one of your famous vigils, but where am I going to sleep? Night's coming down pretty soon, and I don't want to sleep out of doors again, especially when I've got the means to a room in a hostel (patting his hat, which jingled). I'm sick of waking up about as ready for the day as a shipwreck.

—There is a large oak tree within that field, said Don. Take a blanket and make that tree at once your bed and hangings.

—See you in the morning then, said Is as he reluctantly did as he was directed.

—You shall see me — and hear, smell, touch and perhaps even taste me — but be good to remember that is not all that there is, as you continually demonstrate. Oh the intricate web of Being!

His master having finished talking, Is left Don's company for the night, waded through the flavescent rape crop, and lay down to sleep beneath the dark moon-shadow of the oak tree in the open air until the morning came.

17

And when the morning did come, it prised open the eyes of the good servant sleeping beneath the tree to witness, standing above the remains of yesternight's fire, his master Don Waswill, who had not moved even the slightest fibre of his personhood during the whole night. His face he lifted to receive the warmth of the early morning sun. A delicate mist hung in perfect stillness over the fields and meadows and river, and the dewed stalks of the innumerable plants around them sharpened the sun's stroke up and down their length to the end that the freshly woken eye was dazzled by the vividness with which the world was sometimes capable of presenting itself.

Don held his eyes closed in contemplation; Is rose and came to him.

—It is a beautiful morning for adventuring, said Don without moving. Restored by his night's sleep, Is agreed.

And so our two resolute champions of Chance were ready to continue doing whatever it was that they were doing before they had stopped at the riverside on the previous evening. They loaded themselves with their accoutrements and continued along their way.

Is was the first of the party next to speak.

—Forgive me for the question, which I am sure is as much the product of my bungling intellect as my lack of knowledge, but I was just thinking about writing, which is hardly a surprise seeing as I have a ton of it on my back, and I was thinking about my own lack of the capabilities, and how speaking has done me just fine – my question being: are the words that people speak and hear the same as those that people write and read?

—That is by no means a stupid question, said Don. Everybody thinks the two are the same, and everybody is wrong. As I have stated in my *triseptimum* on Creation, writing is responsible for the neurosis at the centre of the West, which has at its source the incompatibility of myth and science. If writing had not been invented, the old myths would not have become codified and calcified in the Laws of the Old Testament and the miracles of the New, which are now greeted everywhere with incredulity. If thought through language had been allowed to continue to dwell in protean fluidity, every paradox would be seen for what it is: Truth. Speech is the language of the present; writing is the language *against* the present – it is the language which thinks only of the past and the future, and hates the present, which is the only Time which exists. The writers of the world have a lot to answer for – but here am I to take them to account!

—There you go again, sir, and how peculiar you are! said Is. A writer who detests writing! It's true I've said it before, but I'll say it again: if you hate writing so much you should certainly decimate your *Encyclopaedia*.

—What you should have said there is 'triseptimate', said Don. 'You should certainly triseptimate your *Encyclopaedia*'.

—Whatever word you want. But the meaning's the same: you should destroy your *Encyclopaedia* and its infant notebooks, which as babies go are incomparable heavyweights. It would save me having to lug this chest round the world, which is where it seems we're going; and I'll tell you, I could stride my legs out a whole lot longer which would do us wonders for increasing our speed.

—Time being always present in the eternal Now, we aren't in any particular hurry, so your argument doesn't persuade me one bit. I have now moved beyond expecting the things that are formed in the pan of your brain and which exit it on the fillet of your tongue to contain any goodness of sense.

—But you were going to tell me about taking these writer creatures to account, though to be honest I have no idea how I'd spot one. What are they like, these writers? Where do they come from? Do they require a special diet at all?

—Yes Isaiah, said Don, warming to his next theme (and one for which the reader might wish to prepare a critical eye). I will satisfy your curiosity by discoursing for a time on the writers. A writer is the most awful specimen of humanity you'll ever have the misfortune to meet. Just to think that, without the fortitude of my devotion to chasing every episteme of the Western world out of its dank and nasty hiding place, humanity would for all eternity be immersed in falsehood and sophistry! For it is the writers who invented that foul and execrable discipline History, and filled it with such storying seductions and all manner of manipulative filth that it has infected every discipline you might wish to think of. Know well that the historians of the ancients had at once the dual responsibility of entertaining their readership and recording the truth. We started there, and have worked our way down ever since.

—A writer, continued Don, sits there with his or her mind on the two grand conceptions of the past and the future: the perceived past, containing the object or raw material of the writing which is reorganised according to the vanity of the writer; and the perceived future, serving as the indistinct habitat within which the ego can wander about in eternal self-congratulatory serenity after the writing has been completed and sent out into the world. The writer always has him or herself at the centre of the task. A writer is an abortive thing; a monstrous, bristling, entusked infant whose rage at those it competes with can only be soothed by a relentless feeding from the nasty dugs of its collective readership, and especially of the reviewers and prize-givers, whom if it is lucky congratulate it on its creativity without commenting on the meagreness of its talent. But the milk is never sweet enough; the writer always demands better, and more.

—Writing, as you should now be aware, disgusts me, continued Don building himself up to a conclusion. But the writers moreso. My advice would be this: if you do manage to find a tolerable one, seek out their view of music. If he or she should not love music infinitely more than writing, then banish them from your company, for they are of foulness. Any writer else misunderstands what writing is.

—Well, put that way, said Is, I don't like the sound of those writer types at all.

—In which case, said Don – and here's the cap on it – they will not like you back; they are desperate to be loved, though they reserve the right to scorn all. I do not wish to talk about them, or indeed anything, ever again, such is the effect discoursing upon them has had on my mind. There are more satisfying and productive pastimes, chiefest of these being the contemplation of the eternal verities of the hyperfine transition of hydrogen, which hates writing, and is not only my primary occupation, but also my sole duty. Therefore, I must direct you from now onwards to cease speaking so that I can do what I must.

Although it was true that Don in fact had been talking far more than his servant in the most recent past, Is ceased querying his master, even though, owing to the peculiar contradiction that he, a writer, hated both writers and writing, Is was in fact desperate to continue interrogating him. Don likewise put away the tongue of his own speaking so that he could ruminate on the eternal verities of the hyperfine transition of hydrogen unmolested by the demands of conversation, as he had intended.

Our two gallant heroes continued walking the lanes of the county of Essex; and although remaining silent, Is saw much that pleased him, though owing to the demands of this our story, the exact nature of this pleasure must be passed over, for he and his master must be brought to a certain place at a certain time, and there are but limited pages within a book. The reader, however, can take it for truth that the sleep of which they partook that night upon the mossy ground within a woodland of beech trees took them, much like the turning of a page within a book, from one day to the next.

18

Upon the rising of the sun, Don and Is stood, brushed the leaves and soil from their clothing and hair, and struck out on the road once more. By the time that same sun had made transit to proclaim the early-June day's afternoon, Chance, it so happened, had brought them to the small village of High Easter, up on the wind-blown plateau of the Rodings, where the Brussels sprouts occupied the fields all around in great battalions, a very awkward place for our heroes to have taken themselves, for it plays no part in our story, which very soon shall be made to emerge, so the reader may be assured.

Fingering the flint which remained in the pocket of his trenchcoat, the very one by which he had cured St Cedd of his plague, Don spoke:

—I wish to make an addendum to the *Triseptimum* dealing with flint. What came before was of the class petrological. This will be of the class poetical.

—O good! said Is, breaking his silence. A slice of verse! This is exciting.

—I do feel moved by the naked flesh of this stone to write a few words, said Don.

—Go ahead, said Is as a thick wall of air made steady pressure upon their windward side from across the high flatlands. But read it back won't you.

Don withdrew his books and his pencil once more from the great chest and began.

We must find the means of reading the flint in order to discover the mind of man before the Creation, which is to say before writing. How to read such an obdurate thing? Touch it. The wax of its flesh; the whorls of its elephantine hide; the constellations of its blemishes, joined by veins travelling in great reaches through its crystalline interior; and such patterns, dimly perceptible in its seam of breaking, as resemble ripples upon the dark silk of a softly moving river, which appear for an instance, and are gone. How to read the crooked lurch of the lines of the ancient hedgerows across the hills! How to read the gatherings of stones! How to read the blasted settlement, the burial site! There is not so much as a word in any of it, in which we find its very preciousness. O subtle trap! With the emergence of the written word comes the obliteration of all innocence. They are one and the same. Where is a softly spoken word between kin? Speak, flint!

A long silence ensued.

—Where is the poeticals? asked Is eventually.

Don slumped down at the barren roadside.

—I cannot do it, Isaiah. It is beyond me.

—It can't be so, sir! You can do anything!

—No, the science of poetry eludes me, said Don, as now it eludes most. It is a dead art. The signs are severed, attenuated, shrunken.

—Sir, let's have a little to eat and see how you feel after. I'm sure all we're dealing with is a little temporary blockage to the wellspring.

—Perhaps you are right, said Don. Pass me a crust of that bread, would you?

So the companions sat down together at the windswept roadside and took a simple meal.

Presently, Is spoke again.

—Sir, I'm wondering if you might not do better with your poeticals just speaking them off the cuff. You appear to dislike writing so much that there seems little point in attempting poetry in it, not that I know anything. And whilst you're at it, seeing as we now know everything there is to know about writers and their writing, you should, for the sake of fairness, give it to us on the speakers and their speaking too. Because I'll have you know that I took it upon myself to remember exactly what you just said about the flint and it's all stored away safe in the silo of my mind ready to be sown as you feel fit. And even if you don't want to polish it up as a writing, I can grant you it in a sack of speech whenever you need it.

—I have no idea what you are talking about, Isaiah, said Don. But I will do as you say as to the ways of speech and of the speakers that speak it, and I'll make a writing of it thus for the good book.

TRISEPTIMUM: SPEECH

There is a meddlesomeness in the people as to speech and writing. Never should the two be confused; nor should anyone assert that one is or achieves the same as the other. Be it known throughout the world: a panther is more similar to a gust of wind than a piece of speech to a tract of writing, even if they trace the very same words in the very same order.

My good squire Isaiah Olm has revealed to me in the short period of our acquaintance how speech is a gift, the articulation of the present, in its way similar to the irruption of the spectral line of the hyperfine transition of hydrogen out of non-origin, the vibration of Being in moment. I sometimes believe it possible that he might speak forever, and that he is therefore a kind of Messiah of the spoken word, though his laziness works against him.

Sitting about the fire, the storyteller re-told the old story out of his or her mind along the ancient trackways. The value of it in the sameness, the difference of it in the moment, like a tree amongst trees. The terror of the bard-work there like the terror of the brutal wood behind. With safety, the safety of writing came too. Unto this end: civilization.

—That's a lovely parcel of words at the end there, said Is. Let's hear it again.

—One may read it from the written record I have made, said Don. But I cannot repeat what I have said because (1) I am forbidden the remembrance of anything, be it so simple as what I breakfasted upon this morning; and (2) the value of speech resides in its unrepeatability, for it is the Eternal Present.

—And so I'll say it for the third time, sir, said Is. You might as well tear up the papery versions of these *triseptimums* of yours.

—You cannot comprehend the necessity of writing without having learnt it, Isaiah. It is like fire: once invented, you'd find it hard to live without – though I would that neither had been invented at all! The first fires were harvested from lightning-struck trees, and humanity and Chance lived in harmony. Then came the technology of flint and tinder, and man was divided from Chance, and look where we are now, in this Winter of our Technics.

—Okay, I see you're decided, said Is. But whatever you might say about your own remembrance of things, sir, I hope you won't mind if I repeat what you just read out, though the reason I wanted to hear it again was as much for the sound of your voice as the words spoken.

Is looked at his master, expectant we may be assured of a blasting with some sermon or another against the delusion of memory. But Don just scoffed and then gave his permission so that he might observe the precise shape into which his servant would mangle his choice words. And so Isaiah Olm, faithful and honest servant, repeated word-for-word the speech which his master had just given; and his master was astonished. Don looked at Is with an intensity and for a length of time which his servant found unnerving; and then bid him repeat the feat, which amply he did.

And again.

And again.

After the fifth time, Don was convinced.

—I am completely at a loss as to explain how you managed to repeat yourself so exactly, he said.

—I've had the skill ever since the lightning strike, said Is.

—And you never thought to tell me? said Don.

—The ability to remember any string of words, of any length, no matter how pointless or idiotic? – I didn't think it possible you'd approve, what with your edicts or oaths or whatever to your Old Lady.

Don looked deep into the gyre of eternity: Chance!

—You, my dear friend Isaiah, have in a matter of minutes (not that there is any such thing) both destroyed the work of Twenty-One years and revealed to me the new work to be done. I cannot thank you enough.

—Are you joking sir? said Is. Neither of those things is good.

—You may hate work, but I do not. You came into my employ by Chance, and by Chance you have identified and cured the disease at the heart of my project. It is the end of my *Encyclopaedia*!

—Does that mean I'm man enough to go back home to my wife and kids now?

—It matters not, said Don. For there is more work than ever before us. Now sit back down and put your memory cap on, for I must test you further. Though it be against the tenets of the absolute truth I profess – that there is no such thing as time past or time future, and thus that memory is an impossibility – yet your memorisation is a manifest lesser evil than writing, which is responsible for History, that canker on the human spirit (if there has ever been such a thing as spirit). I will have you memorise every part of the new *Encyclopaedia* I am about to embark upon, a remedy to the previous; and though it shall have the same name, I will add the judicious prefixes 'New' and 'Oral': *New Oral Encyclopaedia of Being, Synthesised in Accordance with the Eternal Verities Delineated by the Spectral Line of the Hyperfine Transition of Hydrogen*. It is a title both majestic and sonorous. No more shall my work be shackled in a form which insults its import! There shall be no more writing! Now Isaiah, repeat what I have just said.

Is went ahead and repeated just what his master had said, verbatim, without one iota added to or taken away, and the master was again astonished at what he heard.

—My dear Isaiah! he said in wonderment. You have repeated just what I have said, verbatim, without one iota added to or taken away. I am again astonished.

Don hereafter entered a profound reverie while the drought-withered grasses and weeds of the Rodings fretted in the wind.

Eventually, he jumped to his feet and announced the following in an excited voice:

—The outcome of my most recent discovery in this our glorious adventure to redeem the universe is now upon us: the chest and all it contains – which is to say, the fallacious *Encyclopaedia*, riddled in its writing with a deathly rigidity – must be utterly destroyed. Quick! There's not a moment to lose – we must destroy all writing, beginning with this!

Don here kicked hatefully at the chest.

—Do I finally have your permission to burn the chest and its contents then? asked Is.

—It is not that you may, said Don. You *must*. The restitution of Being demands it of you as a duty. Twenty-One years of error I spent on that pile of drivel! Burn it now, for my whole view of the matter is changed with the death of writing. Writing, the parent of History, the Fall of the World, must be replaced with Eternally Present Speech. Do not commit a single word of its written form to memory, but burn it all!

—I'll be more than happy to oblige, said Is. But might I rest a little longer before I get stuck in? Afterwards I can guarantee that Is will be what Is will do.

—You may, said Don. It is fitting, for you are the source of the discovery of my new method, and therefore in desert of great tribute; and in any case, the chest and its contents can be burned at any time we choose, though the new *Encyclopaedia* begins to take its shape immediately. Enjoy the sound and sight of the land around you, descending into the two shallow valleys on either side, and I will begin perorating at you, my glorious servant, eternal speaker, seal of the present. Here begins the new work!

Within an hour Is had become the custodian no longer of a chest of scribblings in his master's hand, but of his living word, delivered from the sacred grotto of his tender throat, into Is's listening ear, whence *Triseptima* covering such varied subjects as funerary ritual in Cro-Magnon culture, the development of lacrosse as a systematics of physical exercise, uses of vinegar in the home, humour in the cartographic tradition of Florence, and the history of wigmaking – all turned towards the hyperfine transition of hydrogen in adulation.

At the conclusion of the delivery of these *triseptima*, and after checking they had been retained in their correct order and quantity within the mind of his squire – which he was delighted to find that they had, word-for-word – Don found it incumbent upon him to indulge Is, who felt the need to talk come upon him.

—I don't want to appear to be remiss in my service to you sir, but all these facts you've just showered me with are so far beyond my comprehension that not even the tiniest sprig of sense has sprouted in my brain since you started talking. The Spring and Summer of my mind is barren. I know that my task is to remember them, but what do you want me to do next?

—There is no next! said Don in an ecstasy of consciousness. It is a fortunate thing indeed that you do not know what I am talking about, because if you did you would be a poor receptacle for the work I am filling you with. This is entirely your value! As it is, pure and spotless Chance can work on the contents of your brain, taking first, perhaps, the nature of plant reproduction, then the lineaments of efficacious Roman military strategy in the Balkans, then the structure of molybdenum molecules, then the formal characteristics of a fugue, bringing them all together, and thence patterning them to the end that a discovery might be made!

—That's as may be, sir, said Is. But I am still not completely clear on it. Although I think I understand what you have said about writing as the parent of history, and therefore a very naughty thing, and though I'm going to appreciate not having to carry the chest any more, I must say I am still a bit surprised by you not wanting to have the hyperfine thingy in writing, because if it's in me only, it can't be read, and who is going to get any good out of that?

—My reason for writing the *Encyclopaedia*, I now realise, was never in order that information be conveyed, said Don. No, the purpose in writing is – or was – to discover what the writing is – or was – about. But that's an irrelevance now, because by that writing the *Encyclopaedia* has come to be about *not-writing*. You are now the book, and the bits of the book will rub up against one another in the innards of your brain, and something will happen. I dare not think about it any further, or I'll spoil it with some intention or other. So that's why. The new form we have for it, being within the living mind of an imbecile, is fitting, and that is all. In fact, I will now refer to you only as Is-Book: Is-Book will be your new name. Now, have you rested sufficiently?

—I believe I have, replied Is, sitting up.

—In which case I now intend to undertake – or watch my good squire, the honest and scrupulous Is-Book, undertake – an act of very great importance, for I deem that he has rested sufficiently from the day's exertions. Good Is-Book, please remove my cape and then light a fire.

(For it was true that Don, in place of his usual trenchcoat, was at that moment wearing a beautiful silken cape, as befitted the occasion.)

Is did as he was bidden so that the solemn ceremony might be transacted. Preparing the ways for it, Don rose to his feet, cleared his throat, and spoke:

—In order to demonstrate my unwavering faith in the unknown shape of Chance; moreover, in praise of my goodly squire, the Is-Book, for the endless inventiveness of his dim-witted oral peregrinations; by the same token, for the purpose of evincing the true science which laughs at the paltry notion of progress which has been a cancerous growth riding grotesquely upon the back of the nonentity which the feeble-minded have come to call History, a thing without substance (and all the more pernicious and ineradicable as a result), at which it would be a waste of saliva to spit; – in short, and so that you, my faithful companion, may understand me well, actions as they say speaking louder than words, and he who hesitates being lost; and according to the well-worn adage that it is better to give than to receive; and abiding by the truth that it's no use locking the stable door after the horse has bolted; further, in accordance with the strictures of that sagacious dictum, which states that one should live for today, for tomorrow never comes; whilst also noting well that nothing is certain but death and taxes; not forgetting, of course, to pay heed to the truth that pride goes before a fall; and bearing in mind the truest of sayings ever to greet the ear, do not seek and ye shall find; and moreover to qualify a misleading saying by adapting it, which thenceforth shall maintain cognizance of the truth that whilst the pen might be mightier than the sword, the tongue is mightier than both; and acknowledging the great moderator of hubris: there's more than one way to skin a cat; and finally, in preferring the truth that there's no Time like the Present (because there is no other Time) over the pernicious fallacy that Time will tell, I round my fine words upon my intended action in regard to the papers contained in the trunk which has been borne up by my good squire's back these past dozen days or so, not that a day is any more real than a dream. Be it known that I intend to satisfy my conclusions in regard to the chest he has been faithfully carrying upon his person, which is that its contents must be burned, these being none other than my *Encyclopaedia of Being, Synthesised in Accordance with the Eternal Verities Delineated by the Spectral Line of the Hyperfine Transition of Hydrogen*, whose title I would be entirely justified in supplementing with the prefix *False*, for despite the penetrativeness of its contents, its form is irredeemably corrupt.

—Excuse me for interrupting sir, said Is, but I cannot believe what I am hearing. Have you gone quite mad? The proverbs fall out of you like the trots.

—Rest your mouth Is-Book, this is a momentous occasion, the victory of speech, and the proverb is above all an oral form, so it is fitting. Now open the lid of the chest.

—Well, continued Is in resignation as he lifted the lid of the great chest back on its hinge to reveal that which was hid. If I might be permitted to add one more pearl of wisdom to the long string you just now strang, it would appear truly to be the case that every stick has two ends.

Don reached into the chest and brought out a sheaf of the leaves whose printed pages were embroidered in the fine hand which in the very different role of destroyer now held them aloft. There was no eclipse, no earthquake shook the ground, no flood waters rose and tore the fruit of the valleys down; the sun continued to shine, and the clouds of the sky drifted, slowly metamorphosing above, as clouds do. He placed the handful of paper into the flames of the fire, which leapt up.

—Page by page, said Don, we (or you, Is-Book) shall burn this other book of mine until it is ash, and by doing so you will be freed of your burden, or at least this particular physical one, and we shall be closer to that which we do not seek, but find, for writing is but an impediment.

—Take this, he then said, passing his servant sheaf upon sheaf. The writing of this book – the very one you hold in your hands – involved the alchemical transubstantiation of misery into joy. Be that as it may (which it is) writing is a falsity. Although writing a book be but the creation of a game, it only really exists when a reader starts playing; and the only reader this book shall have henceforth is of flame. So burn it!

Don watched as Is proceeded to do what his master had told him to do, and lo! the flames took, and the fire grew, to the effect that the air all around them was soon filled with fine greyblack ash and smoke which was borne up in great turning balls into the sky. The pyre burned for several hours in all, with Is feeding it all the time with sheaves of the now-hated manuscript, as well as of fragments of the chest, which he kicked apart with glee.

And by the time all was consumed, both men had lain down on the high plain in the meagre shelter of a twisted hedge, and it is here that we will leave them, sleeping while the wind blew as steadily as the turning of time itself.

19

In the morning – and a fine morning it happened to be – our two august itinerants rose from their hedge-slumber and cast their feet out on the road again, this time heading towards Saffron Walden, where—— but this is intolerable.

NOTICE TO THE READER

Our two adventurers, more tiresome than tireless as adventurers go, occupied themselves with their usual aimless prattling over the next few days' travel. In fact, so loathsome was the dung ejected from their mouths that to include their chatter would be a bold affront to the tolerance and taste of the reader. Also, they have wronged writing in their most recent acts, a very grave misdemeanour. What is more, they were moving all the time in the wrong direction. And so we shall omit those chapters which tell of what they got up to, and instead move on — or indeed move them *on — to the Twenty-First, and a time and place at which some sense of a story might be extorted out of their existence. There, we shall exploit the tenderness of the servant, and frighten him into order.*

Now (though not before turning the page): Read on!

All day an oppressive heat distorted the view across the pale stubble fields. The horizon simmered. Enormous hayrounds stood in formation, each pointing the same way, tracking the harvester's remnant course. Shade sat nowhere across the treeless expanse. Rivulets of tar welled up out of seams in the road and trickled down its camber like blood down an injured limb. The sound and sight of passing cars tore into the raw senses, hurting the eyes, the head, the skin. Birdsong dried up; the wires running from pylon to pylon across the fields vacant; the bushes silent. Crickets sang drily unseen in the verge. Beyond, the cracked ditch.

Into the afternoon the heat swelled the day up. A hot wind came, unremitting, and the haze gathered into cloud, piling up upon itself, and the light was filtered down through the pillars of vapour and the whole earth changed to the eye, already relieved at the coming rain before it fell.

Late afternoon and the first fat drops burst on the road and hiss into the grass and hedgerows.

We bring our duo into Cressing as the sky disgorges its liquid contents upon their heads. Thirsting, dust-covered, burned, they drink in the falling rain. On the tin roof of an outhouse the heavy drops applaud. Thunder rolls across the distant hills. Bunting ranged about the village green hops and twitches excitedly in the blustery air. The green and all the air around it darkening by degrees for the coming storm.

Night falls in a matter of minutes, two hours early, back-lit by an ominous half-light edging under the black clouds like the eye of some mythic monster behind half-sleeping lids. Don and Is shelter beneath the eaves of the ancient Cressing barn, close to where the Order of the Knights of St John had once resided, before their Temple was sacked. The deluge continues. Eventually, our friends lie down in the gutter and seek rest as the land all around them blackens to the second, true nightfall.

(The land: tenacious of its wardens; a name: tenacious of its bloodline; words: tenacious of the history they build.

Come, reader! Let us witness the story take a hold of these book burners – *a curse on them and their mischief* – and prepare the way: there shall be a conduit made for action and its unfolding, appropriate to the story. Let us make a little loop in the time – the desolate country night allows such things – and take within it the servant, whose fear, being ample, shall make him malleable. The master shall remain on the ground sleeping, and nothing shall be found to wake him until this other one is thrashed into an order.

Thus our Twenty-First chapter, which we might call the *Triseptimatrix*.)

Is woke with a start; dark was the night. Great taloned clouds sailed on a bitter wind, ploughing at the bright white moon; cold was the ground. He stood and re-wrapped himself in his ragged clothing against the wind's needles. The rain now abated.

He walked to warm himself. Shadows twisted and morphed under the moonlight. Within the hedges, beneath the trees, an energy unac-countable pulled at him. In the night-time, the land stripped of its season. It would not have taken much to persuade Is that the earth was hollow, a few inches of ferrous crust; and within, the bodies writhing and wailing and thrashing, seeking some kind of remittance, though their words be formless.

(How-so-be-it that the catalogue of Is's fears reads as a compendium of everyday experience, let us greet him with that which he has most cause to fear.)

From afar, an unmistakeable thread of lightning visible, an exploratory stitch cast from air to earth.

Is recoiled from the distant flash, and then crouched in dread within the hollow, that parenthesis of time between the light of lightning and its thunder. What animals had fled their inundated burrows now hurried back for that self-same fear.

It came – crack through the air as a jackhammer.

Refuge he sought, but there was none.

The next flash closer, the fields flooded for a moment in pale light, then gone; and following, its sound: swelling, splintering, lashing the ground. The leaves of the oak above him shivered. Safer or not beneath or not the tree? Heavy drops falling, viscous, like blood.

Another lightning capillary discharged into the ground, the third flash – closer still – and there came also a great surge of wind, and the leaves tipped over like a shoal of turning fish, revealing their pale waxless undersides under the moonlight. The interior of the earth boomed as a drum for the servant's footsoles to feel.

The smell of electric storm entered Is's senses – the ionization of the air preparing a path. Again the leaves turned. Closer came the white threads of lightning, moving across the rolling fields.

(To scorn writing is to scorn the source of all human power. We make dutiful appeal to the tradition; thus the words of Milton, under whose directive:)

Is *shall hear Infernal Thunder, and for Lightning see Black fire and horror shot.*

See how the servant cringes in the face of the lightning like some undead thing!

(The books of the nations, an institution requiring veneration across time, for by them only is time prepared – yes, the books shall be brought to avenge the meddlesomeness of this man and his master. Compelling Mary Shelley to our assistance next, of the tree which stands before Is:)

He beholds a stream of fire issue from an old and beautiful oak, and so soon as the dazzling light vanishes, the oak vanishes, and nothing remains but a blasted stump.

(Yes, let there be a demonstration of great power – that writing is immortal: we marry Is to the unfolding of this our story as was Dido to Aeneas in the firestorm:)

> *Interea magno misceri murmure caelum*
> *incipit, insequitur commixta grandine nimbus…*
> *… fulsere ignes et conscius aether*
> *conubiis summoque ulularunt vertice Nymphae.*

Look how he seeks shelter as the storm, like the nymphs, bewails him!

(But there shall be no shelter, just as Chaucer's Parson tells, already using the writings of a venerable other:)

> *For certes, as seith*
> *Seint Jerome, the erthe shal casten hym out*
> *Of hym, and the see also, and the eyr also, that*
> *Shal be ful of thonder-clappes and lightnynges.*

Yes! The little man's rabbit heart fit to burst. See him scurry in the obliquities of the rain, electrified by the fear of God. Relentless our attack upon the guileless servant – but the story requires it. He is as he must and should be: at our mercy.

Coleridge: *The lightning fell with never a jag, A river steep and wide.*

The lightning as to some ravenous beast; and so, *Beowulf!: faérníða gefremed.*

Massing two thousand years and more of writing, the canon become cannon!

Let us look, in the pool of this lull before the final assault. The grass lies singed in great rings between the barns; the charred remains of the oak sizzle under the beginning of new rain. Is weeping and gnashing his teeth and pulling out his hair. Sagaciously we deploy Publilius Syrus, one of his venerable maxims: *Vain it is to look for a defence against lightning*; and even were Benjamin Franklin himself to appear on the scene with his lightning rod to aid our stricken servant, the maxim would prove true, for writing will have its way.

Don aside in Time, asleep; Is beyond Time, at its unmercy.

A funnel of black light turns in a gyre above, up into the regenerating nightsky. Sulphurous wisps of smoke curl from the ground, seeking the trills of the servant's nose.

(But enough; let us finish the job. The final attack now upon him:)

Marvell first, a wonderfully visible assault:

> *Three-fork'd lightning, first*
> *Breaking the clouds where it was nurst,*
> *Did through his own side*
> *His fiery way divide.*

Is prostrated upon the scorched earth, his face planted in the mud like some barren and empty seed pod. We might finish him here, as did Zeus enact upon Iasion, *striking him dead with our bright bolt of lightning*.

(But no; the voice of the story is power itself, and can give as well as take away life; we are as Twain on the Mississippi, scratching our head with the lightning and purring ourself to sleep with the thunder. Let us therefore raise him up to convey the substance of the lesson, for he is ready:)

Training the charge of the sky upon the soft tummy of the earth between the barns, a great tumult strangely magnetical was unleashed, and the flints beneath the turf were pushed therefrom as would be the bodies at the Judgement. And like unto Moses' tables, written into the flints were mysterious glyphs, graven in the blacks greys oranges creams whites blues darkly darkly darkly. Glistening dark the flesh of the opened stones dancing in a multitude, brought from their subterranean dwelling place as to a multitude of eyes woken from sleep or death.

And the words within the stone swarmed for the eyes of the servant.

And a gust turned the remaining leaves of the struck oak once more, and written thereon, beneath, were the same words for the servant.

And we shall have him read, as were Piers Plowman and his friends inspired: *Oon Spiritus Paraclitus to Is In liknesse of a lightnynge we lighte on him And make him konne and knowe alle kynne langages.*

The writing in the stones laid out in words what must be done, taken by Is into his mind in miraculous fearfulness; words writing out his duty, and the future, of his and his master's fate, a single week hence, in the City of London; and that he should serve the story, a better master, and bring the rebel to the place where everything could be brought together, where the story could find shape, and so end.

And so it was, across the fields, the shapeless sky, the hills, at every distance, a swarm of written words, directing the servant to his larger duty. Written into the fabric of everything, the blades of grass, the prints upon his fingertips, the pollen in the air: Writing. The servant shall be made to know and to serve the story and smooth the way, as did his namesake, and through him New Troy shall be made New Jerusalem, and the swarm of words shall write over all men, women and children, as the signs are brought back to their event horizon in univocity, and all lines are made straight, and all the floors of meaning are swept clean, and no tongue shall wag.

22

Now that these two burdens upon our time have been made through the servant to conform to the shape of the tale, we may continue; and although the book may appear to be no less a playground than before for their ceaseless prattle, which turns and turns with the time but signifies nothing, we may be assured that their end is already measured out — is not the reader's right hand furled about the very book's back cover?

Now read on!

Then came the rising of the sun over the desolate waste of the fire-scorched field. First Don and then his servant woke and looked about them. Don cared as little as a stone what had or had not happened in the night; Is, by contrast, shook with terror in the cold of the early morning.

Don cocked his head left and then right, looking and listening like a blackbird.

—Chance is a wonderful thing, he said. Gird whatever worry there is in you, and the work of your feet on the good road will be an ample restorative.

Is stared into the attenuated rays of the low orange sun and shrugged.

They turned their course ninety degrees and progressed south-west, which is as it should be, towards the City of London, crossing obliquely the thin shadows of the early morning, following the crease between two adjoining fields which banked down to the road and ditch and hedgerow between, like pages meeting at the spine of an open book.

Read on!

Is remained silent for the next few hours as they walked, reflecting on the events of the previous night. The full force of his alertness he pointed upon intercepting words from within the trees, the soil, the rocks, the water; from the buildings, the railway bridge, the passing cars. But no words came to him, and he could only quake at the prophecy which he had witnessed (the which we shall soon see come to pass, for the foundations have been laid within the workings of so-called Chance, and the narrative would cackle if it had a mouth with which to do so). But let us allow them to comport themselves as they desire for a time.

Read on!

—Now, said Don. I'm not sure if you are aware of the history of money in our islands? But it is irrelevant whether or not you are – I shall expound briefly upon potin, and you shall take my discourse into your remembering ear, my faithful Is-Book. This will form an invaluable preludium to my next scheme for you, which is of unequalled greatness.

Before Is could open his mouth – which indeed he would have attempted, for it was true that he intended to take no notice of his master any more, such his terror of the lightning – Don continued speaking.

—In the mid-2nd century BC, the first indigenous coinage, called 'potin', was struck in Britain from bronze. In imitation of the bronze coinage at the Greek colony of Massalia, it shows a long-haired bust of Apollo to the left on its obverse, and a butting bull or horse on the reverse. Apollo was the god of music, poetry and dance, but also became god of the plastic arts, science and philosophy, and of the intellect; he was the god of healing and prophecy; he was the god of flocks and herds. But primarily he was the god of every kind of light – astronomical, terrestrial, intellectual and moral.

—Gradually the design on indigenous British coinage changed, continued Don. The representations of Apollo's head on one side and the horse on the other became more abstract. Typological analysis of early indigenous coinage in Britain has enabled the thesis to emerge that early British coin-makers held shamanistic roles in their communities, and were considered to be communicant with spirits from beyond the physical world. The archaeological record suggests the common consumption of hallucinogenic substances such as mandrake, henbane, opium and cannabis, which a recent study has suggested to have mediated the development of the abstract designs on British coinage. It is irrefutable that early money had a complex metaphysical as well as political and commercial function. Early coins were certainly used in votive acts, especially attending burials. This is the reason for their survival – if they had become otherwise non-current, they would have been re-minted. (Mark well the importance of things not fulfilling the function people ascribe to them – and thence the delusion which is accounted History.) Already in the pre-Roman era, the great Greek symbol of intellectual and moral clarity, Apollo, is being twisted into something more attuned to the minds of the people dwelling among the muds and mists of present-day East Anglia.

Is, who in truth had not been listening, trudged sorrowfully onward.

—Know this truth, continued Don. That the scientific methods of the more simple cultures of the world far surpass in efficacy those of our own. And so, Is-Book, you will drink the drink I am about to prepare for you, and then we'll see what wormholes of Twenty-One-ness might be navigated by the words which are formed in that throat of yours!

Before the words had even left his tongue, Don left the road as it wound through a little woodland and began scavenging around the trunks of trees for herbs and fungi. Very soon he had crushed within the mortar improvised from a dimpled stone a good paste, added to it half a cup of water, and now stirred it with a filthy finger as he presented it to his faithful servant.

—What is it, sir? said Is.

—You needn't worry about that, said Don.

—Now sir, you know that I worry about anything of even the least significance. I would refer you to the *triseptimum* on myself which you yourself wrote.

—It no longer exists, if indeed it ever did. Just drink the damned drink!

Is, whose usual fractiousness of service was tempered by his most recent terror, dutifully drank the repulsive potion; and the product of this experiment, within two hours, was the following spoken-word entry in *Don Waswill's New Oral Encyclopaedia of Being, Synthesised in Accordance with the Eternal Verities Delineated by the Spectral Line of the Hyperfine Transition of Hydrogen*, as both spoken and memorized by his goodly servant, the Is-Book.

—*TRISEPTIMUM*: [UNTITLED]: In the biginnan, the par were made separate, parity went parārity, and the paired were despaired by the irruption of that kernel of light. At which biginnan of time (beholden to the colonel of hight) the shape of things – **ghut-ghot* – was magicked out of chaos into this stark logic within the waking mind of man-making-man. His spirit hauled in across the face of the waters to this hum drum bodily infirmamentity to make the division of like from unlike. Me that sœli seely silly Isaiah Olm, happy blessed pious innocent pitiable feeble fool.

(This was merely the beginning, but we have neither the time nor the patience for such *triseptima* any more, whose contents are nothing but distractions from the truer aims of our narrative. And so:)

After several hours of meandering nonsense, which flowed freely from the drug-opened sluice of Is's mouth, the servant fell with exhaustion to sleep. Don thereby found himself sitting in the evening of the day on the soft earth of the woodland warming himself by a fire which he had just then made, now free to meditate on the innumerable profundities of the spectral line of the hyperfine transition of hydrogen. This occupied him for a not inconsiderable time – until, indeed, the day had been converted by the setting of the sun into night.

All of a sudden, however, he rose to his feet with a look of great concern on his narrow face.

—Is it not true, he spoke into the dark woodland, that every book, even an Is-Book, requires a cover?

He went to work (and let this be a further lesson to the squire that his master is a cruel and heartless man, and deserves to have his service sabotaged): in the nook created by two rocks, Don assembled, poured fuel into, and then lit a paraffin lamp. Its glow swelled quickly, then faltered, then redoubled itself, until, with time, the globe atop the lamp gave out a formidable degree of illumination within the dark wood. Don then took a large jar and placed its open top above the chimney of the lamp. Gradually the jar grew streaks of carbon up its sides and along its upended bottom. Don turned the jar round and round until it bore a thick layer of black residue on all sides. He poured into the jar a few drops of water and mixed the two together with a fine brush. The product was a most impressive black, blacker than the night around him, he noticed, for unlike the night it could not be looked through, even with the aid of the lamp.

After preparing the ink, Don sharpened his knife: he oiled his whetstone, and drew the knife at a narrow angle down its length along the stone, first on one side, then the other, paying particular attention to the sensual curve towards its tip, switching sides back and forth until edge and tip were hungry. He cleaned the blade, and folded away the instruments.

Eventually, Don turned his attention to Is. Close by the fire he lay, in his shirtsleeves, covered by his coat, peacefully sleeping. Don took a length of twine and fastened it about his servant's sleeping wrists; he then tethered this line to the closest tree. He performed the same action with his friend's legs. Thus prepared, Don could now do what was required of him, as befitted his mission, and his science, and his future betrothal to Chance, wherever She might be.

The moment came.

—Ruth? mumbled Is as Don pounced on him.

He tore open his friend's shirt, and steadied his heaving chest for the first incision. The lamp light ran up the smooth sinuous forms of the birches as Is looked up from the ground – yellow flashing eyes and boney determination.

—Master! What are you doing!

—You, my Is-Book, require as all books do a cover. So be quiet. And still. This will be painful.

With these words travelling through the many trees, Don penetrated the flesh of his friend with the glistening tip of the knife and began the work of slicing the schematic for the hyperfine transition of hydrogen into his chest. The blood welled up in great thick lines and curves, though seemed unwilling to spill over onto Is's flesh. The firelight danced upon the suffering body; the lamp glowed unheeded at some remove like a fallen fragment of the moon. Don rubbed the lampblack deep into the incisions, reconnoitring the flesh beneath the flaps of skin with his fingertips, caressing pigment into the tissue. With this, the blood breached the banks of the wounds and now ran down the flanks to explore the woodland ground in curious rivulets.

The ordeal came to an end.

—What have you done to me? said Is in disbelief, looking down at the sheet of blood which flowed over his chest and abdomen. The pain approached him like a train through a tunnel: it seemed impossible that it had not yet fully arrived, that it still swelled in magnitude, that he could still bear it. But it came and came, stronger with every moment.

—You'll be fine, said Don cutting the twine from his wrists and ankles. Now sleep, good Is-Book.

—Sleep! said Is. How can I, except to sleep eternal? I'll be dead by morning! Look at me!

He pushed and kneaded at the skin which fell open and lay back in flaps. Wretched beyond words, he took himself away to a hollow at the foot of a tree, curled himself around the pain as if it were a baby within him, and he wept and wept. Don, feeling a curious stirring within himself which he supposed to be pity, took Saint Monica over to her devotee, who hungrily kissed her face off. It was only in such a manner that the Book-Man could regain some measure of composure: a good pint of whisky it took to chase the pain in his chest out to the limbs of him and beyond.

When eventually Is had drunk himself to sleep, Don sat back down on the mosses of the ground in the silent night, picked his servant's dried blood from his hands, and smiled to himself: What a glorious thing it was to observe the hyperfine transition of hydrogen at work in the world.

23

Early the next morning Is woke to the sensation of being eaten. He looked down; he *was* being eaten – a cocker spaniel had its muzzle deep in his jacket at the chest and was lapping with contentment at the dried blood all around his tender wounds.

—Oh my God! said Is.

The dog's owner just then came into the clearing and called her dog away.

—What the hell are you doing sleeping here anyway? she said as the dog circled her looking for a treat, and she walked off shaking her head and muttering about drugs.

This was not the last judgement they were to receive within the woodland, for it was a popular spot for the exercising of dogs, and Is flatly refused to stand up for a full two days, even defecating as he lay on his side as if life had become for him an endurance event, devoid of pleasure, dignity, hygiene. Even with the application of Don's famous unguents, whose recipes were gathered from obscure sources through the eternal ages, Is refused to recover any quicker than his obstinate mind had made up for him. In the end, however, Saint Monica was kissed dry, and there was nothing left to live for – he may as well rise. He parted his old jacket and the blood encrusted shirt, and – rubbing the dried bloody tide-marks from his skin – he looked down at the design which had been tattooed into him. As far as he could see it looked little different from a sketch of two owl's eyes.

—Well I thank you for this, sir, and hope in all honesty that your own blood turns rotten and poisons your brain.

—You'll change your mind about that, said Don. The schematic I have carved into your flesh is greater either than the Christian cross or *IHS,* or the Semitic hexagram or הוהי, to take only the two most important traditions which have informed our own culture.

—I don't care, said Is.

Don looked down at his unhappy servant who sat slumped against a tree trunk in the dirt.

—Would you have preferred me to shirk in my responsibility to Being and not decorate your chest with this hallowed symbol?

—Twenty-One times yes, said Is.

—That is a good answer in its form, said Don, though I cannot agree with its content. I will forage you a meal and you will soon feel better.

—Go forage yourself a man trap. I don't want bitter berries and poisonous fungus for lunch. Just leave me alone.

Don took in Isaiah's words, turned, and walked off into the woodland, leaving his servant as he had desired. For three hours Is sat in his disconsolate hollow inwardly reciting the times-table of his despair. Even the small sinuous forms of the squirrels moving in jerks around the striated trunks of the oaks could not alleviate his dark mood. He dwelt on the lightning, the words of the world rushing into him, and the warnings they contained. He was resolved to leave his master; he struggled to his feet; he gathered what possessions he had; he looked at those of his master for one final time – until: here comes that very master himself. Such a lost and found face he had on him!

—Isaiah, said Don. I have journeyed across the plains of Essex in search of food both restorative and delicious. Fragrant is the fat of bacon at-fry! Here.

With these words Don handed Is a very large bacon roll, whose contents were still piping hot, and garnished with the perfect quantity of brown sauce.

—If it was at all possible for me to feel compunction for certain acts of mine consequent upon following my solemn and absolute duty in regard to the hyperfine transition of hydrogen, then I would no doubt be very sorry to have hurt you Is-Book. But I hope you understand that I cannot. Please take this victual as recompense for any inconvenience caused by the performance of your role as my squire and Is-Book; also this kiss, apparently the sign by which we humans convey the highest regard.

Here, Don gave the roll into Is's hand, and a kiss to his filthy cheek. Tasting the lovely salty fatty tartness of the roll, Is found it impossible not to forgive his master, in spite of the pain in his chest and abdomen. And when St Monica was brought out fully replenished with cherry brandy — well, Is felt capable of going through the whole ordeal all over again.

—Thank you sir, he said; and it would be a rash reader to doubt that he meant it.

Let us rejoin our fearless duo — who from that moment on were once again firm friends — on the noon of the following day as they approach the county city of Chelmsford for the first time, where finally we shall witness events of some import taking place, and not a page too soon.

—Before us, said Don, you may see the city of Chelmsford, administrative centre of the County of Essex. If Chance permits it, we shall rest in this place for another two days before continuing our journey, along whatever route that might be.

When Don informed Is of the possibility of two days allowance for rest and recuperation — of which he was sorely in need owing to the infection which was developing at the site of his recently acquired tattoo — the servant dropped to his knees and clung about his master's own with such gratitude that he completely forgot that Don was the source of all his pain and suffering.

—Get up, Is-Book, said Don. You are acting like you're *in* a book rather than *are* one. Real people do not do such things.

—Thank you sir, said Is ignoring and continuing to embrace his master. I know that you are some several decades older than me, and I know that the chest I had carried like it was my own soul is now gone,

233

but the memory of my carrying it is so recent and so ingrained in the knots of my body that my age – like my back – has been almost doubled, and now my chest is all black and blue and purple and yellow and silver with diseaseful infection, so two days without walking will restore me, you can count on it, and I'll be back to normal, or even better. And even if the chest and its contents were miraculously restored and pieced together out of the smoke and ash of their destruction, I feel that I would be able to take it upon my back with something approaching joy after a rest, for I've always thought of the snail as a happy animal, though the chest was never my home.

—A man without a burden is like a phenomenon without a name: as soon as you notice its absence, it acquires that which was wanting. Re-tie my boots, good Is-Book, and let's get us down into the streets of the place.

Is did as he was asked, and the two companions walked into the city.

Through the hot waste lands of the industrial estate and suburban superstore they went, where the dust and grit kicked up with passing traffic and sought out with estimable efficiency and accuracy their eyes. They crossed all the dual carriageways which, like stitching, attached the town to the fabric of the nation. Until, there they were: Chelmsford.

It was just after one o'clock when they entered the old city centre, and the offices had mostly been disgorged of their workers, who sat on the benches of the square and in the green spaces eating and drinking, and determinedly enjoying the pleasant weather, as English people do. The buildings themselves stood in benign perpendicularity to the street, adding a pleasant sense of human order to surroundings which, for this pair of travellers, had for so long, and apart from the order of the farmed fields and the rolling and turning of the road, only exhibited a human presence through rubbish choked in the hacked-back vegetation of the verge. The heat intensified as the day's light breeze was retarded by the buildings of the street, and the hot stone of the ground radiated back the heat it had been storing up all morning.

As our increasingly objectionable heroes made their way down the high street Is became aware that he was the object of an elderly gentleman's attention. He looked across the road directly at the man in an attempt to shake his eyes off himself, and it worked, though not before the man gave Is a nod. What could it mean?

A little further on, a large smoking woman stopped speaking for a moment to her friend and followed the line of their transit with her tiny, flesh-beseiged eyes. Another woman walking her dog on the opposite side of the street stopped to look at them. She smiled familiarly, then harried her canine companion into following a path against its wishes, crossed the road, and approached Don and Is with a flush of anticipation upon her features.

—Welcome! she said with the utmost thrill of an unexpected pleasure. Oh this is grand!

Don and Is ceased walking.

—It seems to me, began Don, that some new experience is about to land in our laps. And, owing to the precepts of my Science, in which Chance is the Prince of Time, who are we to resist?

—We are two, said Is in reply, and one of our party would certainly resist further landings in laps, which, speaking solely of my own, is overburdened already, though mostly with things which are not visible to the eye, like sorrow and agony and weariness. And yet, alas, we are not two, but more like one-plus-one, and I must forever cleave to your fancy. So my lap is at your mercy, and expectant of trouble. And anyway, since when has Chance been a Prince to anyone? I thought she was your Bride?

—We do not know you, madam, said Don, ignoring his servant. Will you make yourself known to us?

—I am April-May Quantity, a resident of this town, and very happy to meet you indeed. You must come with me. There has been talk about your possible passing-through. How excited everyone shall be!

—I wonder, Is said beneath his breath to conceal its import from the woman as they walked behind her, that this lady really can know us.

The last time I was here was in my babyhood, and I warrant my face has altered considerably since then.

—Your face, said Don, owing to the punishment it has received at the fists of the multitude of assailants you have attracted in the course of the past two weeks through your ineptitude, registers sufficient alteration as would make your own mother doubt your identity. But this woman surely knows us, and one should never doubt the wisdom of others until one gets down to a view of the solidity of the bedrock upon which it is built.

—I am beginning to wonder if such advice might not work better to my advantage by being left unheeded, said Is. Who's to say that the bedrock of this woman's wisdom won't be that upon which I finally dash my brains out? And rock I'd guess will prove a difficult nut to crack as far as burial grounds go. I will be eaten by the birds.

—What a cornucopia of despair you pour forth in the images of your witless prattling! Desist, and let us follow this amiable woman to whom Chance has led us.

In not many minutes at all the woman had led them straight to her front door, which according to custom formed an aperture in the wall. They went up to the flat, and the kettle was on, and Don and Is were seated, and a portion of cake offered to each, eschewed by the former in his saintly way and partaken of by the latter, who as we know was one of the more be-stomached examples of his species.

—I must say, said Mrs Quantity, we are deeply indebted to the example you are setting, its galvanising effect.

—It's nothing, said Is.

—Oh no, it is not! she said in an enthusiastic crescendo. You are rapidly becoming local heroes!

—No, I mean that it really *is* nothing, said Is. We're not doing anything. Are we, sir?

—I don't think complete dissimulation is necessary in this particular instance, Is-Book. Save such devices for those moments in which we encounter law enforcement officers.

—Quite so! said Mrs Quantity, with a small clap of her hands. She was very pleased to see them indeed.

—However, continued Don, our past, present and future actions are not something we are able to disclose, even if it were possible for me to believe in more than one-third of those stated conceptions of Time, not that I believe in fractions either, for everything is whole and entire only in and of itself.

—I can understand that, said Mrs Quantity. Part of the effect of this whole business – and a large part of it, I would wager – is the spontaneity of it all. It really is remarkable.

Mrs Quantity rose from her seat, excused herself, and walked through to the next room. Soon afterwards, the sound of a muffled voice reached Don and Is: their hostess was using the telephone. Is took this opportunity to talk with candour to his friend and master.

—I do not understand, sir. Half the town takes interest in us, we are being given cake by this lady who approves of what we are doing, and yet not even I know what I am doing. What manner of recompense is this town going to ask of us when we don't do what we are supposed to do for the simple reason that we don't know what those supposed-to-be-doings are? I very much fear that the inventory of my injuries is going to be added to, and the result sooner or later will be that Is will become Isn't.

—Do you fear death, Is-Book? asked Don.

—Very much so. I'm not sure I've ever known of anyone who doesn't.

—Would you like to live forever?

—Not at all.

—In other words, you want to die, but you don't want to die. Do you see where your logic leads you? To neurosis, my dear friend, that is where it leads you. Think not of the future, particularly as it has no reality to it, and be content to inhabit the present, which is all around you.

—I want to be able to choose when I die, said Is. Not that I can imagine a time when I'll finally say I don't want to live any more. That's what I meant.

—Ah! said Don. You are not afraid of death at all then. It is Chance that you fear! When will you learn that Chance is the only thing worth taking any notice of?

—When it stops me getting my head kicked in, said Is.

But Don was not awaiting his servant's response; he had been transported by the mere mention of Chance to a reverie in which he pondered the endlessly fruitful and fascinating subject of the relationship between the length of the spectral line produced by the hyperfine transition of hydrogen and his fair maiden Chance. However, Is was too eager to discuss their current predicament to allow Don to remain in this state; and so, after attracting the attention of his master by shaking him roughly by the shoulder, he began to speak.

—Let's get to the bottom of this, master. Where is it that we're heading? For a very short while everything made sense, when we were heading for France. But the sun lured us back round to Essex and we've been heading down the mazy channels in the mud and the woods ever since, through all kinds of trouble. Yes, I know that aiming for this place or that isn't the way we're working – you've told me that enough times that even if I didn't have my memory for words, I'd be able to recite it in my sleep – but I've gone down all manner of roads, lanes, tracks, ditches, dykes, across fields of mud, through tangled woods tearing at my flesh, over bogs and marshes, my feet steeping in brackish filth all day, rubbed raw, and that chest on my back until just a couple of days ago, and then straw for a cold bed scratching at me all night if I'm lucky, for it's by no means much of the time that I see a bed at all. And for what? I've followed you these past two weeks or whatever it is – it feels like a year and more – and have suffered like I've never suffered before. Haven't I earned the right to knowing a bit of what we're driving at?

Through those yellow eyes Don looked steadfastly at Is for a duration of time.

Then he spoke:

—How many times must I tell you? Throughout this noble and arduous undertaking, I have tried as hard as I can to eschew intention and destination as things which destroy all Truth. Whatever destinations may have weaseled their way into my mind have soon become irrelevant because they have been superseded by others whose precedence has been mediated by the workings of Chance. I have sworn never again to formulate another destination, and I have asked you to assist me in this endeavour – and yet you tempt me like this! It requires great strength of mind to reject the structures of thought which one has had inculcated within oneself since birth (not that birth is anything other than the eternal present unfolding itself in the hallelujah of Being). Anyway, were I seduced into conceiving of a destination, I should not communicate it to you because in the eventuality that we arrived there it would mean that Chance had failed to intervene, and thus no further advances would have been made in our quest.

—But what is that quest! said Is.

—Every destination is only like the horizon: it can never be arrived at. Cease questioning me on this matter, therefore; I eschew destination entirely.

—Tell me what our quest is, or I am leaving, said Is, who stood up on his bare dirty feet within the deep and comfortable pile of April-May Quantity's carpet.

Don looked up at the ceiling through the eyes which Chance had felt fit to give him.

—I do not know, he said.

—Okay, well I'm going home anyway then.

—Wait! said Don. I do not know because Chance herself has not told me. But we are close. Is it not true that this year is the Twenty-First in which I have oriented all the power of my thought upon an *Encyclopaedia* which will discover the means by which all things can be restored to their Twenty-One-ness? Twenty-One years, Is-Book! And here we are, and you the receptacle for all manner of truth as that Book! The end must be approaching, for the time and the eternal number dictates it! The secret interior of things is gradually opening itself up to me. It requires a delicate deployment of the number, and of the word – of the symbols granted to me by——

—I cannot hear about the you-know-what any more.

——the spectral line of the hyperfine transition of hydrogen.

And as if someone were controlling events, though this time in Is's favour, Mrs Quantity re-entered the room carrying a tray laden with a teapot, two cups, and two slices of fruitcake, placed it on the table, and then took a seat before the two men, which prevented Is from having to endure more talk of the hyperfine transition of hydrogen, a thing which he had begun to doubt was even a thing at all, becoming as it had through continual repetition in his sleep-deprived mind merely a collection of sounds devoid of meaning.

—Tuck in, said Mrs Quantity with a nod at the tea and cake. I do hope very much that you won't object to me receiving another visitor as well.

—Not at all, said her guests.

As if permission had thereby been prepared for it, the doorbell punctuated their talk and beckoned Mrs Quantity to the front door. When she returned, a man followed her, who was introduced to Don and Is as Reg Stevens, a local man who worked as the groundsman to a large estate.

—You know why I'm here don't you, he said with a sly wink and inclination of the head as he took his seat. Groundsman, to a *large estate*, he said with slow and heavy emphasis, winking all the time.

—The only why I can puzzle out for your being here is from your ringing of the doorbell, said Is.

—They *are* wily! They *are* wily! said Mr Stevens into the air of the room with manifold pleasure.

—Would you like a cup of tea, Reg? said Mrs Quantity.

—Don't mind if I do, said Reg.

Mrs Quantity left the room; and then re-entered it with a fluted cup whose mild translucence identified the material of its manufacture as bone china, placing it beside the teapot, which was busy brewing its liquid contents under the beneficent and watchful eye of its custodian and owner.

—It's a good day for it, said Reg.

—Indeed it is.

—What day is it? said Is.

—It's Saturday, said Mrs Quantity quizzically, hardly believing the guilelessness of her guest. We should get a good turn-out.

—A cracking day, said Reg. Did you phone Claudia?

—Not yet, said Mrs Quantity. We should, shouldn't we.

—Shall I do it? said Reg.

—Yes, please do, said Mrs Quantity.

Reg rose and left them. Silence took lease of the seat he had vacated by his absence and made easy repose within the room's white walls while the host poured two cups of potent hot brown tea.

Reg soon returned.

—She's free immediately, he said. She's going to use her charms, and God knows she's got a few.

—She has a lovely face, said Mrs Quantity.

—And more, said Reg, giving meaningful recapitulation to his earlier wink in the direction of Don and Is.

—Their James, Reg continued, was just taking his measurements for the lights in the new building. He was quite up for getting involved when he heard; I thought we could do with plenty of hands. You don't mind if he joins us? I already said come over.

—Of course not, say Mrs Quantity, and the doorbell again made punctual clarion for the entry of the man just then mentioned.

The host descended the stairs in order to let him in. Reg took a cautious draft of his too-hot tea and then spoke:

—Claudia is the Mayor.

—I see, said Don.

—She's the one to thank for what's going to happen today.

—What is going to happen today? said Is.

—Let it happen, said Don. Do not interrogate the future, which has no existence.

—This is James! said Mrs Quantity as she re-entered the room with a man whose name was James.

The occupants of the room made sounds and gestures consistent with polite greeting.

—What time does Claudia think she'll be ready?

—What time is it now?

—It's just gone two.

—Well she said she'd need an hour.

—That soon!

—She's a dynamo that woman.

—A powerhouse.

—I wouldn't try to stand in her way.

—She'd give the national grid a run for its money.

—Steel by name, Steel by nature.

—Do you mind if I use the phone, asked James.

—Of course not.

—I have someone in mind.

—Who? said Mrs Quantity.

—Garry.

—Yes, yes, of course! Why didn't I think of that? We must get it in the Chronicle. Imagine it!

—Soon you will not need to imagine it, said James profoundly; and he left the room in order to use the phone.

Is took the opportunity offered by the end of this conversation to partake of the piece of cake which he had received from his host. Rich and tangy it was, and possessed of a copious aggregation of currants within its midst. What little of crumb he dropped on the floor, the servant retrieved with the fingers of his hand, which flew mouth-ward thereafter.

Presently, James returned.

—Garry's just this minute got back from London; he's going to come straight over.

—There's a bit of luck.

At this point, the doorbell rang again, and April-May Quantity made the familiar journey to the front door, as was demanded by the bell. Soon she returned with the next of their affiliates.

Garry was introduced to everyone, and the conversation continued.

—Where are we doing this, then? asked Reg.

—In the park? said James.

—In the square? said Hyacinth.

—On the steps of the shire hall? said Mrs Quantity.

—At the foot of the steps of the shire hall? said James.

—Just beyond the foot of the steps of the shire hall, in Tindal Square? said Garry.

—Well which is it to be? said Mrs Quantity with an amiable smile on her face.

—Shall we ask Claudia? said Garry.

—She'll be busy, said Reg.

—Let's ask Colin, said Garry. He'll know.

—Yes, Colin.

—I will go and phone him right away, said Garry.

—Yes, do, do, said Mrs Quantity.

Garry exited the room in order to make the phone call he had said he would. Moments later he came back into the room with a formidable smile upon his face.

—He won't be a minute.

Less than a minute later, the doorbell rang, and Mrs Quantity rose again to let Colin in.

—Everyone, Colin. Colin, everyone, she said when they came back into the room.

—Sir, said Is to Don, this room is getting rather crowded.

—I suppose you are going to tell me that you are frightened of crowds too? said Don.

—I have never really been in a crowd, so I wouldn't know. But I am certainly at the foothills of some fear or other, and the number of people in this room is as good an explanation for it as any other I can find.

—Well, you may want to fortify yourself internally by some means or another because I don't see this concatenation of introductions ever ending.

Don's prescience was borne out by the events which followed: each time a new guest was introduced to the travelling pair, they would draw the attention of the conflux of persons currently in the room to another person not yet there, and, upon phoning that person, he or she would presently enter. This process was repeated so many times that the room grew completely full of people standing in closer than ordinary proximity one to another and discussing the demands of this special day. The floor, bowing under the weight, threatened to disgorge the assembly onto the floor below, which was occupied by a retailer of above-average quality women's wear, a quality high enough indeed for the proprietor not to appreciate such a sudden intrusion.

—Let's leave this place, said Don to his assistant, and both men rose from the seat on which they had gradually become marooned by the swelling tide of standing people. Mrs Quantity spotted them, and after beckoning them over to her through the crowd, said:

—We are about to go.

—We are leaving now anyway, said Is.

—What! said Mrs Quantity, forgetting her hard-learned manners. Why would you want to go now, before you know where we're going?

She looked from Don to Is, waiting for an answer. Is opened his mouth; Don gave him a warning glance; instead of talking, Is simply yawned very deeply.

Mrs Quantity acted:

—People! she shouted to the crowd. We are off!

With these words, Don and Is were carried by the outrush of people from the building down to the street and then along with it towards wherever they were going.

—This must be your strangest trick yet, master, said Is.

—It has nothing to do with me, said Don. Do you see how each of their faces is animated by the lineaments which describe an ample excitement? This is a strange feature of human pleasure, the enjoyment of something which hasn't yet happened.

—Things always feel better or worse than they really are, said Is.

—When is a thing really a thing? What is the *really* of the thing which is a thing?

—You've lost me, said Is.

—I might hope for it on occasion. But we shall return to this discussion when the opportunity arises. Let me instead for the moment congratulate you on your yawn just now.

—Congratulate? said the squire. My mum would have slapped me.

—I am not your mother, said Don. I would praise you for yawning no matter what it brought upon our heads, because in doing so you make righteous rejection of the mores of our tribe, who demand our full day-clear attention as they witter on down their well-trod lanes. The word 'yawn' finds its root in the Indo-European **ghei-*, from whence its cognates 'gap' and 'gape', and Greek κλάςκέη, which is a co-lateral of English 'chasm'. I think you can smell the scent at the foot of the family word-tree I'm taking you up.

—Perhaps I have a head-cold coming on, because it's true that I can't smell a thing, not even the me-smell of two weeks' walking, and these pits of mine are not so distant from the organ that deals in smell as to require any kind of wind to come to its assistance.

—Thank you for your lengthy explanation. The smell I was referring to is of the word which hangs around at the base of all these words: chaos.

—Our fine good friend! said Is.

—Indeed. Is it not true that our epistemology, like a fastidious car-penter, loves a neatly fitted join, one without such gaps between the objects of its workmanship?

—That sounds very close to the truth, sir.

—Yes, between a man and a woman lies – nothing. Between light and dark lies – nothing. Between night and day lies – twilight, that time of bats and cats and rats, familiars of the witch, corporeal communicants with the supernatural. And now do you see?

—Can I say yes if I do not? said Is.

—Can you lie, do you mean?

—Yes.

—No you cannot, said Don.

—Okay, said Is. Then no, I do not see.

—It's simple, my good man. The creation which our clarity-loving minds desire is one which splits things cleanly and then presents them well-abutted, one to the other. Chaos is the carpenter's unmaking, his bewitchment. Everything falls apart.

—What's that got to do with me yawning? said Is.

—Must I pursue every explanation for you down to the smallest degree, Is-Book? The yawn is etymologically related to chaos. My science discovers, then, that your yawn tears at the fabric of our culture because it is the chaos our culture has sought to smother, good manners and right behaviour being the puritanical bedfellows of rationalism and logical argument.

—Is that a good thing? said Is.

—Your yawn, my fine friend, was as good as good manners, right behaviour, rationalism and logic are bad, which is to say, formidably so. This is why I sought to congratulate you, but I now wish I hadn't bothered, because it is a tedious thing having to explain every last point to you.

(And the reader may well agree; for which reason we shall move on to that part of our story where something might happen: the place where the residents of Chelmsford most recently at April-May Quantity's house had agreed upon.)

—But look, said Don. I see that we are drawing towards some manner of intermediate destination.

—May all our destinations be intermediate, sir, said Is.

Ahead of them, across the junction of Duke Street and Market Road, was another small group of people which knew the one of which Don and Is were the members, and which exhibited signs of wanting to merge with it. This occurred, and very soon afterwards the crowd, now numbering approximately fifty people, reached the Shire Hall.

The day was a vivid one: humidity low, visibility high. The trails of two aeroplanes crossed above towards the threading of a tapestry in the air which would never be made. Several civic attendants in antiquated livery occupied themselves in hurriedly sweeping the steps, relaying directions between one another, and positioning and clothing a bench on the pavement in front of the hall. One carried a fire extinguisher down from the entrance and deposited it discretely within the guardianship of the inside of one of the tablelegs. A large shallow glazed dish was placed in the centre of the long table. Don and Is looked on as all of this was accomplished. The group of several dozen people assembled before the table chattered excitedly like sparrows in a bush; until, Claudia Steel, mayor of Chelmsford, emerged from the interior of the Shire Hall and came down to the place appointed for her behind the caparisoned table.

The people grew gradually silent.

—Fellow citizens, began the mayor. What is history? How does it shape the present? What do we owe to our past, to the people who have lived in the places in which we live, who have walked the same streets, worked and played in our shops and our squares, lived and died in our houses and our hospitals? These questions inform the way in which I have worked and continue to work for the good of our city: without history, we know nothing, feel nothing, *are* nothing.

She paused, to allow the interiors of the minds of the audience to caress the words she had spoken.

—I will tell you a story, she continued. Some years ago, I worked as a solicitor in the very building I am now looking at. If I had time for lunch, I would walk along Waterloo Lane to the Hot House and have something to eat and drink. Now, I remember as a girl when all the roads around Tindal Square were cobbled and the cars and buses made as much noise with their tyres as they did with their engines. My older brother got his front wheel stuck on a loose cobble one day and broke his collarbone in the fall. He had to start taking the bus to work down at the paper mill after that, and on one journey he met the woman who would become his wife. Shortly after my brother's accident, I went away somewhere, I don't remember where, a summer camp perhaps, and when I got back a week or so later, all of a sudden the cobbles were gone, and instead we had smooth black tarmac. I had never given the cobbles a thought, not until they were covered over. The whole square felt different – and not just when I rode my bike. Something I could not put words to had been taken from the place.

—She could have done with your *Encyclopaedia*, sir, said Is, if you hadn't gone and burned it.

—I can't abide a mystic, said Don.

—Thirty years later, said the mayor, the roads have been long worn into the everyday and ordinary again, with furrows from the weight of cars, and patches following gas and water works; this tarmac has developed its own history. No-one is *missing* anything.

—On my occasional lunchbreaks as a solicitor, she continued, I would walk round the square and up Waterloo Lane, take my lunch, and then return to work. But on one particular day I noticed that the thinning tarmac on one corner had cracked from the traffic, and gradually over the course of days and weeks the tarmac was detached from what lay beneath it and thrown into the gutter to reveal the rough flint cobbles beneath. Day after day the patch of cobbles grew a little from the running of the tyres over the surrounding tarmac until it was several feet across. I looked every day as it grew. It gave me pleasure, and, no longer a child, I was better able to account for what that pleasure was. It was the pleasure of memory – not only my personal memories: I didn't just renew my thankfulness on my brother's and his wife's behalf for the role these cobbles played in bringing them together; nor did I simply remember the childhood games I had played on this and all the other streets in the town. No, this small patch of cobbles which had been revealed beneath the tarmac didn't just alert me to my memories; it alerted me also to the *way* of memory: to its habit of jumping up whenever the particulars of life set off a catch; and so to the importance of having the particulars of the past about us as we move on into the future. Our heritage is important to us because it reminds us continually who and what we are.

There came from within the small crowd a gentle murmur of approval.

—We have with us today, the mayor continued, a man who has dedicated himself in the face of great personal hardship——

—She must now surely be talking about you, said Is with unconcealed pride.

——to doing for our town, for our county, for our entire country, what the cobbles did for me: he seeks to show us what we are by showing us our past.

Here, the mayor gestured towards where Don and Is stood in the crowd. The people on either side of them turned and nodded with approval.

—I told you so, said Is.

—Over the course of the previous ten days, said the mayor, this man has alerted us to our inheritance: the freedom we enjoy is directly descended from that demanded by the farmhands, craftsmen and artisans six hundred and thirty one years ago, who resisted the indiscriminate taxation and census-taking of the government by burning court records throughout the parishes of Essex.

—Howsoever you pass the figures six, three and one singularly through a calculation, it is impossible to bring forth the result Twenty-One, said Don. I therefore conclude that this woman speaks falsely.

—To commemorate the events of the Peasants' Revolt of 1381, the mayor concluded, I would like to ask our present-day Jack Straw to mount the stage.

Applause spread through the assembled crowd.

—Sir! said Is. It's that Revolting Peasants thing you told me about! (Not that you'll remember, of course.) That *triseptimum* was one of your best, I think. What do you think she's going to do to you?

Don stood still and ignored everything around him; unsatisfied, the crowd grew restive. Galvanised into action by the growing unease, Mrs April-May Quantity steered Don with a hand in the small of the back through the crowd and up the steps, whereupon the mayor took him by both hands to a position befitting his role behind the centre of the table.

—I am sure that Mr Straw has a few words to say, said the mayor.

The straggly crowd stood silent at the foot of the steps; Don looked at the assembly for a moment, and then began to speak.

—The contingencies of history, which my illustrious host has alluded to, but which extend further back into the womb of life, and ever beyond, to the womb of the womb of the womb infinitely, to the paradox which is the initial spark which stands beyond time, an origin without origin – true of every entity – is said by the prevailing sciences to have placed me here before you, in this place and at this time. But this is a fallacy. The origin of everything is only now, because there is only Now. The discovery of the error of science and the search for a more accountable truth has been the task to which I have turned my attention for a period of time, one which is conventionally measured by such units as the second, minute, hour, day, week, month and year. But the commitment to my science has led me to eschew the idea of duration as an entity having any real existence, which means that I can have no memory. And without duration there can be no syntax, which means that every act of speech is necessarily merely a game, and stands beyond the scope or purview of the eternal verities. Therefore, as a man committed to science and truth, I refuse to say any more.

The redoubtable mayor looked out upon the silent crowd, and would have been embarrassed if she had been capable of such an emotion.

—But Mr Straw, she said. Surely you are able to say something about the relevance of the civil unrest of the medieval peasantry to our times?

—Not until the mind of my companion the Is-Book has shaken the knowledges bequeathed to it by my tongue into a shape rightly fitting Twenty-Oneness, the sole True reality, shall there be anything but the crackling of thorns. Even if you used only a single word of the least complexity in your next entreaty to me, I would no longer deign to believe that I knew what you meant.

The mayor gave a brief chuckle befitting her public position.

—The two decades I have spent working in the Law have made me aware of exactly what you are saying, said the mayor. But we will speak nevertheless. What do you have to say about the argument between

Professor Maurice Stephens and several of the readers of the Essex Chronicle?

—I am not aware of this person and persons, Don replied. Nor of the argument they erroneously believe themselves to have had, to be having, or to continue to be having.

—Let's forget that then, said the mayor glossing over Don's uncooperative words. You have made us remember, and so, by remembering, pay homage to our forebears; and further, to know ourselves, in our time, by seeing how much we owe to other times. Is this not true?

The crowd gave a weak cheer of celebratory consent, to which Don brought his fist down heavily upon the table in front of him, making the large bowl upon it jump, as if with fright.

—What is this cretinous verbiage? he shouted. These foul sounds? Your palate besmirches with smears of great blaspheming falsity my mistress Chance, daughter of Time, mother of True Science. I shall give you an account of remembering, and you would do well to heed it. Our species, unique within the animal kingdom, has an insuperable desire to make tangible memorialisation of its members. Everywhere you look there is some memorial or other to the dead – I see one before me as I speak, a broad needle with the names of your townspeople lost in the so-called Great War engraved upon it. (There are places in the world, be it known, where it is cheaper to buy a domicile for your living body than a hole in the ground for your corpse.) The desire to make public memorialisation is one of only a handful of defining features of *homo sapiens* – and I use the phrase 'defining features' in the hardest of senses: when memorial was first made, so too was made *homo sapiens*, the interment of his fellow primate in red ochre dividing them at this birth of man. But look at where we are now; and mark the irony in the fact that the *Encyclopaedia* which until three days ago (if days can be said to exist) was being constructed by me, in its function as a memorial – a memorial not to an individual or group howsoever constructed, but to our species as a whole – would, if I had not burned it up entirely, at the very moment it became pertinent, at the moment it became necessary and justified, at the moment its tenets came to pass, have been inexplicable because *homo sapiens* would have ceased to exist, and the beings which supersede him will require no need of such memorialization, immune as they shall be from its sorrowful flurry of signs. Even from its origin, *homo sapiens* has sought to destroy itself.

—The popular account of evolution and its relevance for contemporary humanity, continued Don, suggests that for the first time in the history of the world, a species is creating the environment which exerts evolutionary pressure upon itself. This is nonsense. *All* species create their own environment. Outsiders in every species die alone, prematurely and childless; the clan is an oppressive institution, asserting identities, managing normativities, punishing dissent in order that it be a single manageable body. The increasing specialisation of roles in the western world, a direct result of the technological revolution and the capitalism which drives it, have created such a hostile world for the artistic mind that all the artists – who are the major proponents of the analogical mind, which has hitherto characterized humanity and allowed it to survive – will through one means or another kill themselves in despair or cease to be attractive as mates in a world which values only utility, to the end that a new species shall emerge which cannot even comprehend that an apple might *mean*, only that it offers sustenance.

—The end of humanity is approaching, Don continued. And here is the great irony of humanity: it came into being without origin, and will go out of being without visible end, because that which follows it will not be capable of grief. Whatever it leaves behind by way of memorialisation will make no sense – unless the Twenty-Oneness be brought into the fabric of Being through me, which it will. Inside of me is every creed, and thereby am I taught: history is naught but a story in the service of oppression!

The crowd took into its collective ear the word oppression, and lo, it fitted!

—And we remember how our ancestors resisted this oppression over six hundred years ago! said the mayor in an attempt to serve Don's words in a form more digestible to their audience. By this (and the mayor lifted up a scroll of paper tied with ribbon for the crowd to dwell upon) we will commemorate the acts of the people of Chelmsford who rose up against their oppressors to demand their freedom. The freedom to own property, the freedom to move, the freedom to work for whomever we choose – these basic and apparently common sense rights were won for us by the hard trials of our predecessors. I therefore ask our present day Jack Straw to light the rolls. (Does anyone have a lighter?)

Reg Stevens, being of the peasant class, came forward and gave the mayor his lighter, who passed it to Don.

—I will do nothing without the agreement of my squire, said Don, whose surpassing simplicity makes him too good for this world.

Don looked down at Is within the crowd; and the pious heads which formed its surface also turned to the dutiful servant.

—I thank you for thinking of me, said Is to his master from within the attentive crowd. Seeing as this particular course of events has reared its head up at you, I think you really ought to do it. Otherwise you take the unfolding of things into your own hands, and though they are good hands, if a little heavy on occasion, events will be very heavy indeed on our heads if they don't allow these people to get what they've come here for. Besides, these documents are covered in writing, which owing to my illiteracy I have no reason to value, and owing to your Science you have every reason to hate. So let's burn them and be done with it.

—He is a slave to expediency, said Don. But his last point alone is worthy of my affirmative action. In short, I will do as he says, the world being made up as it is of every kind of person.

Don rolled the wheel over the flint and watched the flame attain its effulgence; whereupon the mayor passed the roll into his other hand, and the two were brought together, and the roll burned up. As the root of the flames travelled down the scroll to his fingers, Don dropped the paper into the broad bowl on the table before him.

—Three cheers for our Jack Straw! said the mayor, and the crowd cheered three times in boisterous antiphone.

And although the office of mayor in our time is little more than a pat on the back, the stream must have its source somewhere. Thus it is written in the *Chronicon Henrici Knighton*, an important text for any consideration of the Peasants' Revolt: *Then these men and women leagued themselves with others and in turn they contacted their friends and relations so that their message passed from village to village and area to area.*

It is a means of organisation which we shall soon see come to pass.

24

Later on, in the evening of the same day, having walked a merry enough walk of some dozen miles or so from Chelmsford, Don and Is came down Potash Road into the peaceful enclosure of Norsey Wood. They sat beneath a tree, watching the insects and the birds flit from plant to plant and tree to tree as the sun started its descent. The noise of the day had subsided, and a languor hung on everything like the seed pods which had drifted and caught upon the nodding heads of the grasses. It was such a time as promotes quiet contemplation, which is precisely what both men were involved in: Don, on the subject of the hyperfine transition of hydrogen, which he accounted something of a sin not to be thinking of; and Is, on the subject of Ruth, whom he missed dearly, and of what she might have made of their fame at Chelmsford, whether it made him a man; and then of how she was back at home without him, and he here, in a woodland, doused in confusion. In the end, the thought of her being either alone or with somebody else was too much for him to bear in silence.

—Will my Ruth ever take me back, sir? he said.

Don, against his wishes, was pulled away from the beatitudes of his rumination.

—I see from the look on your face, he said, that you are undertaking that activity known as sorrowing. You may find comfort in the observation that many animals grieve for their dead; and how do we know but that the trees don't suffer pangs of loss when their neighbour be felled? O the inestimable beingness of trees!

Is was so confounded by this answer that he turned back to the meadow, closed his eyes, and let the tepid orange light of the evening sun fall on his face.

—As long as you undertake your role with dedication, said Don, seeing that he had disappointed his faithful servant, the perfectibility of Being shall show itself to be very much a reality. After my marriage to that beauteous though awkward little strumpet Chance, or Time, or Science, or whoever it is that will have me, there shall be no more sorrow. You will be able to live forever with your dear Ruth; though of course, you won't need to by then because perfection does not allow the entertainment of choice, owing to its monistic source in whatever lies behind the sacred Twenty-One. As long as we keep moving in the Present, which always is, you have nothing to worry about.

—So as long as we keep moving? said Is.

—That's right. And forever mindful of the hyperfine transition of hydrogen.

—That is something I am learning to do every day, sir, and I feel as if I'm really beginning to succeed. If that's what it takes to get my most beautiful best friend back, then I'd be willing to think about it as much as you.

—Everything is well then, said Don, and they went back to thinking their own thoughts in their own ways: happy, though tired; in good companionship, in spite of their many past disagreements; and without a thought for the future, which as we shall see was in actual fact about to greet them – or at least Is – with a new and astonishing experience.

Eventually, Don spoke.

—It is of course a glorious thing that we are on the cusp of succeeding in our quest (which is a certainty, I am sure). However, it is with a touch of sorrow that I must admit that you and I, within whom this victory shall take place – within you as the Is-Book, and therefore the crucible of the revelation of Being to Itself; and within me as the progenitor of all the data within you, and as the holder of the instrument of the Forbidden Line – yes, we shall be unable to witness its parturition, embroiled as we shall be in the transaction of it. Equally, though, I am contented to remember that there is always a pleasure to be had in the passing of my thoughts into the innards of your mind, through that incomparable pastime known as conversation, which far outweighs the solitary work of writing, an enterprise which I forswear forevermore. So while I am committed to storing away such ruminations as are presented to my mind within you as the Is-Book, I must admit that my first thought just now when I saw that female greenfinch there and perceived her way with a cornstalk, and noticed as anyone else would how very closely it resembles Charon's manipulation of his bargepole – yes, through long immersion in the activity over the past Twenty-One years, I was going to begin transcribing an account of this re-calling into my book – the papery version – such is the way of habit. And before I even had time to consider that I was mistaken, and that I would of course have to speak the *triseptimum* into the Is-Book rather than write it, I realised with a disconcerted soul that the chest containing my *Encyclopaedia* is in actual fact standing upon the ground right before my eyes.

Is laughed, and scoffed, but following the line of his master's sight he discovered against all the laws of possibility that Don appeared to be quite right: the chest.

—It can't be so, sir, he said. We burnt it already, days ago. Don't you remember?

—You are well aware that I am strictly forbidden from the remembrance of anything other than duty to truth through the hyperfine transition of hydrogen.

Is rose from his seat beneath the tree and went over to the chest to inspect it. What a mess. Although the fastidious devotion of his master had clearly informed the manufacture of the chest from twenty-one panels and twenty-one studs, this fastidiousness did not extend to the quality of his workmanship. So badly was it made that the birds of the air could be forgiven for mistaking it for a nest. So incomparably bad was its design, indeed, that it exhibited every sign of being the exact same chest as the ill-proportioned one Is had already burned. Was it possible for such an individual to have a double? Is kicked it; the pain in his foot registered its reality.

—This is very confusing, sir, he said. The chest hasn't been on my back these last few days, and it was a charred mess of stubs, ash and smoke the last time I saw it. If it's the one, which I can't believe it really is, it must have been magicked back into wholeness and walked its way who knows how down to this wood we're now in.

—But is it the one, Is-Book? said Don.

—It seems to be, but I can tell you this – and you could remember as much as me if you put your mind to it – that we most certainly burned it three days ago at the roadside up on that high hill until it didn't exist at all. So I will say that it cannot be the same, because I know and trust myself and my eyes. It is against all the laws of possibility.

Don smiled, and then spoke:

—There are no such laws, good Is-Book. You should know by now that the world will do whatever it likes, and the habits of your brain can be damned to hell for all it cares.

—That's as may be, sir. But I don't believe a thing which is burned completely up can ever be put back together again, even if it were Merlin as was the craftsman tasked with it. I say that if you don't believe me, take a peek inside. If your refusal to remember won't let you know the whereabouts of your *Encyclopaedia,* which is most definitely in the air as smoke and in the ground as ash, then maybe you will believe your eyes when you see the chest is empty, which I am certain it is; because every bone and more in my body tells me that this chest is an imposter which must have come to be here next to us in this wood through the mysterious voodooings of your old intimate, the Chance.

With these words, Is walked away from the chest, sat back down upon a tree stump, crossed his legs at the ankle, and set his sight on his master, who soon crossed the same ground, though in the opposite direction, and took up his place beside the chest.

—You are becoming insolent in your pride, Is-Book, said Don. Let me show you that I am the one who has been chosen for this quest, though I am unworthy, and though I am a mere human, more similar to you than different, and that you need to keep in mind the fact that the events of the past are of nothing – that they don't even put us where we are now; that now is just *Now* and that's that. Are you ready?

—I am, said Is, who was so sure of himself that he didn't even uncross his legs.

—Okay then, said Don, and he drew the lid back, reached into the chest, and picked up a handful of paper scraps, manifestly a portion of his formerly beloved and magnificent *Encyclopaedia of Being, Synthesised in Accordance with the Eternal Verities Delineated by the Spectral Line of the Hyperfine Transition of Hydrogen*, even if in their nasty written form. He held the scraps up in the air for his doubting squire to see.

Is was so surprised he could neither speak nor move; he was full of wonder at the events of the present, which bore out the truth of everything his master had tried to teach him but that he had disdained in his ignorance as a collection of impossibilities.

—I see by your face, said Don, that you are so completely full of wonder at the events of the present, which bear out the truth of everything I have tried to teach you, but that you have continued to disdain as a collection of impossibilities. Chance, as you shall now know, is beyond reason. Your behaviour, however, lies fully within the remit of my censure: in refusing to believe in Chance, you have failed me.

—But sir, I don't understand how it is possible. In fact, it's more possible in my mind that the chest isn't the same chest, and the papers within aren't the same papers, but that they are just resembling one or two another or however you might say it. Read a little of the writing by way of a test and we'll see for certain then if it's some imposter or not.

—I will do as you say, said Don, and he selected a scrap at random – however else might he indeed? – and began reading his entry on 'Copper', which he had altered from the form found in the *Oxford English Dictionary*, and to which he had appended a cutting from a magazine:

Upon the plaque attached to the NASA spacecraft Pioneer 10 we find the first instance of human beings attempting to communicate with non-deistic extra-terrestrial beings. The plaque is manufactured from tempered solutionized aluminium alloy containing, amongst other elements, a minimum of 0.4% and a maximum of 0.8% of copper by weight.

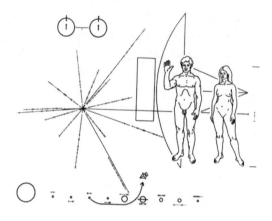

Cyprus, the Mediterranean island from whose ancient copper mines much of the West's supply of the metal came from, bequeathed its name to the metal through this association. The earliest uses of copper were for decorative and ritual purposes only, as the metal became too brittle for tool and weapon production when beaten. The hand which produced these early objects – but also invented annealing, technologised weapon production, divided tribe from tribe, held the hand of his woman down – speaks in a sign for us all; this hand the hand that waves thank you to the supernovae as it passes them for the nucleosynthesis of the heavy elements with which its aluminium is alloyed; the hand which waves an arrogant hello to new solar systems as it leaves our own, calling it progress, and travels out towards

Aldeberan; the hand which means nothing to the extra-terrestrial lifeforms it seeks, and would wage war on them if it could. It is the hand of humanity, and thus should more accurately be placed upon its possessor's throat as it stifles the life of him. Vanity!

Don stopped reading and placed the scraps of paper back within the interior of the chest.

—That's definitely got your style to it, said Is. I didn't understand a word of it. So I won't doubt it any more: the chest and the *Encyclopaedia* really are the one – or two – and only.

—Writing is a filthy thing, Don said by way of reply to Is, throwing his *triseptimum* on Copper back into the chest with disgust. You must fulfil your role properly this time and burn the chest and its contents.

—I did as much already! said Is. Maybe it's chance that's made the chest come back, and so we should have kept it all along, as now we can, though I'd prefer not to, seeing as I'll be the bearer of it, and it feels as heavy as that planet you just mentioned.

—I mentioned no planet: Aldebaran is a giant star, whose volume is such that it would take 100,000 of our own suns to fill the space it occupies. And I would appreciate it if – as I should not have to remind you – you would refer to Chance according to the demands of correct propriety: it is 'Chance', not 'chance'.

—I beg your pardon, sir, said Is. And you'll see by the way I say it – Chance, Chance, Chance – that I am as obedient as a squire's ever been. I certainly burned the chest, and this is definitely the same one, so Chance is surely up to something here. The only explanation I can find is that something or someone is enchanted, or maybe enChancéd, or there's some malign spirit machinating away in the background somewhere unseen. I've heard an owl is a devious nightly creature. Could it not have been an owl?

—How would an owl achieve such a thing? asked Don. I am at a loss as to account for the extent and degree of your stupidity.

—What about a stoat, then? Or a necromancer.

—Good Twenty-One! A heady leap it is from the one to the other! Just do the burning again as you did before – if such a time can be said to exist (which it cannot) – but do it better and burn the damned thing out of existence, whether or not Chance chooses to bring it back again.

Is did exactly as he was told without uttering a single word, which was proof enough of the gravity of the lesson about Chance which had been taught him by the chest.

Within just a few hours the sun had set and the night sky had grown completely dark. The two men lay on the ground with the chest and its contents burning steadily before them, granting them heat as they sought sleep, which came quickly; and the dark only receded with the first of the early morning light some seven hours hence, which time found the remains of the chest still smoking gently beside the two companions in a blackened heap, undoubtedly and resolutely destroyed. Our two irksome adventurers packed their kit back up, kicked the last of the fire out, and struck out on the road again.

For a good few hours they walked in silence slowly through the woods, befitting the penance which the servant was inwardly performing for doubting his master as to the genuineness of the chest, until they came to a small winding road, and there beside it a bench. Don beckoned his Is-Book forward and gestured that he should take a seat, which the grateful squire did straight away. They ate and took a drink, and sat there awhile as the insects played in the air before them. Don was thinking about Charles Darwin, whom he accounted a very great simpleton; Is was flicking through a copy of the Essex Chronicle which he had found next to him on the bench, in which stories of municipal building work, charity fêtes, lost animals and the declining quality of life experienced by the region's elderly came together to describe and circumscribe a community.

—I say, sir, said Is. Listen to this. It's from the letters page.

Sir, as an historian of post-Conquest medieval England, and particularly of the lower classes and the twilight years of serfdom, it strikes me that several of your recent stories ('Attempted burglary at County Hall', 4 June; 'Arson attack destroys medieval barn', 4 June; 'Vandals behead statue', 3 June; 'Magistrate assaulted by "madmen"', 1 June; 'Bizarre livestock theft', 28 May; 'Local grandee's mansion destroyed' 24 May) appear to be linked to one another. Not only do they seem to be political actions directed against the legal and executive institutions of the county (or at least against individuals which can be seen to represent them); these actions are also moving closer to London. As such, it befalls me to point out that this sequence of actions contains a faint though distinct echo of the events of six hundred and thirty one years ago this month, those which we now call the Peasants' Revolt. It is a piece of our history worthy of commemoration, particularly in view of the conditions in which today's peasantry labour (or struggle to attain such positions as would allow them to labour) under the shadow of international finance capitalism. Although, of course, the echo could be a quixotic trick, and it is possible that I am seeing what I want to see because of my immersion in another time.

Yours,

Maurice Stevens, Professor of History, University of Essex.

—Well I'll be damned, sir, said Is. It's the bloody Peasants' Revolt again, like it's following us about. Isn't it the most peculiar thing you ever read? And I know for a fact that that Claudia Steel woman with the furry hat mentioned this Maurice Stephens character too, whoever he is, because there's not a word as can sneak through the net of my memory. In any case, it seems that we've gone and made it into the paper! Which can't be a bad thing for either of us, seeing as you're chasing Chance, and I'm chasing Ruth, and these women tend to go for celebrity. In fact, I'm going to tear this story as carefully as can be from the paper and keep it – Ruth'll be impressed, you mark my words. But anyway, this Peasant thing does at least make some sort of sense of what happened earlier with the mayor and the burning paper and everyone knowing us and you being Jack Daw or Raw or whatever it was.

—The Peasants' Revolt is a rag-bag of events which the historical sense and the coward's need for clarity have turned into a singular thing. As you are aware, it is precisely this attribute of time past that I seek to avoid looking at, for to look at something, which I would necessarily do with words, is to grant it a degree of reality. *Nomen est numen*, as some might say I have said before, good Is-Book, though 'before' be impossible.

—I had never been made aware of what it was in the past that you objected to. And in actual fact, even since you've said what you've just said, I'm still none the wiser.

Placing the newspaper clipping in his pocket, Is reflected on his own recent words, and on the events of the day; and then he spoke again, utilising a different tone of voice, this time of the anxious class.

—Do you think that your setting fire to that tube of writing back in Chelmsford was a mistake?

—Do not talk to me about things which you deem to have happened, said Don.

—There's no deem about it, said Is. Everything I've said has happened, certainly *has* happened; and I know it because I was there, as were you. Damn your doomy deem, and everything having to be so serious. Let's get us on to wherever we're going, and if we can't talk normal, then let's not talk at all, because – and here Is slapped the open page of the newspaper he still had in his lap – a man reads better when there's no noise about him.

Don turned and looked at Is in such a way that the servant could not continue talking, an outcome so extraordinary that the known universe might be scoured to no avail for greater proof of the profound effect the flashing of his master's yellow eyes had upon him.

—I thought you could not read? said Don.

—I cannot, said Is.

—Well how on earth did you manage to read that letter in the newspaper then? asked Don.

Is sat up and looked out of his innocent face at Don.

—You know, he said, I really have no idea.

He looked up over the road, over the trees beyond, up into the pale blue sky of the late morning, and believed at that moment in time that nothing made sense. If nothing makes sense, then something makes nonsense, and as something is the universe, which needn't be here, then the universe means nothing, and so nothing makes sense. Deemy doomy. How did everything which is, have its beginning? Oh, it doesn't even matter. How do snakes move? Who cares. That's what Don could do with his Science. It was best always simply to let things happen and not go turning stones and peeking places like aunt Maud first-visiting her new friend's home. But how could he all of a sudden read – and the same had happened at Cressing during the lightning storm, hadn't it? All the words on the leaves, in the air, on the grass, *everywhere*.

—What on earth are you doing now! said Don.

Is looked back at him.

—Well sir, I believe I was *thinking*.

—Something is happening here, said Don. Something of the utmost fishiness.

—I'd agree with that over, up, and all the way round, said Is. We in the paper, and known throughout a city I've not been in for thirty years or more; and to top it all, me reading and thinking of all things.

The servant then partook again of his newly discovered pastime for a short while – that is to say: thought – before speaking:

—So, is this what people call *consciousness?*

(Let us proffer a short interlude from the direct experience of our two faithful though somewhat annoying friends and note merely that they immediately ceased discussing whatever matters they had been discussing – for it is not good for a book to have its characters sniffing about within its own recesses. So let's just say that neither of them knew what the other meant, and equally neither was Is certain of what he had been saying, nor Don of his own words, for he distrusted them immensely, particularly since the burning of his dictionary, which, owing to this event's transaction in the past, the dictates of his philosophy placed beyond his comprehension; though if we were to look hard through the impenetrable aloofness of his stare at that particular moment, we might swear that a tear had gathered at the tip of his eye.)

So, although the ground was somewhat firmer and more uneven than a mattress, and the grass was not an Egyptian cotton sheet, and their old jackets were not goose-down duvets, and that they might just as well have slept on the bench, which was amply large enough – and, indeed, despite the fact that it was still only late morning and that they had only woken from a good enough night's rest several short hours ago – we will now find our two good friends laying themselves down for another rest with admirable equanimity, for we can hustle this thing along now, and make a shape.

So: soon the two companions were fast asleep under the noonday sun; which will give the reader a chance, before we recommence, to take in whatever it is that is, or was – or indeed is or was *not* – happening.

25

Much against the laws of all probability, which fortunately need not obtain to the craft of storymaking, our two wonderful friends did not awake again until *the following morning!*

Well, how might it be told with sufficient import and emphasis exactly what effect Is's surroundings had upon him as he woke. Opening his eyes, he noted that the clear bright early summer day whose pleasant warmth had gently lulled him to sleep had been succeeded by a chilly fine damp early morning mist. The servant raised his head and looked through the translucent air of the clearing within the wood and saw innumerable bundles on the ground, ones which certainly had not been there the day before, and which stretched from within ten metres of him and his master all across the clearing, which was by no means small. Is rubbed his eyes and furrowed his brow and slapped his own face, but the bundles stayed where they were; in fact, they did more than stay where they were: very soon, as his sleep-befuddled mind cleared, leaving only the fine diaphanous physical mist between his eyes and the objects they perceived, Is became aware that the bundles were not in fact merely bundles, but a multitude of people asleep, as he had been, on the ground in the open air.

—Twenty-One save us from this one sir we've woken up on a battle-field, he said.

—This is no battlefield, good squire, said Don, who at the very first sound emitted by his servant's mouth had woken in full readiness for his further adventuring. This is but a normal everyday ordinary woodland clearing strewn with sleeping people who believe, in accordance with the newspaper article you miraculously read on a day which appears mysteriously to have become of the yester variety, that we are – or I am – Jack Straw, the first mover of the so-called Peasants' Revolt, a thing whose place in History confirms its very unreality, for History as you know is an illusion. I am anxious that the achievement which we are in the process of achieving will be prevented from happening by this horde, who certainly do not esteem Chance in the manner properly befitting Her gloriousness, because expectation and anticipation obliterate the liberty of the present.

—Like the watched pot not boiling, sir, confirmed Is in a thoughtful whisper.

—We must rise very quietly, said Don, pack up our things, and make our way in whichever direction our feet tend to carry us, so long as by doing so, distance is put between ourselves and these our unasked-for followers.

The two companions managed, through the use of their good sense and their practised lightfootedness, to move away from the crowd of several hundred persons sleeping in the wood with them. So good were they at this, indeed, that very soon they were on the road again, heading whichever way the road was heading (towards London of course, for that is where our book shall deliver them); and even though Is turned his head very often, he was relieved to find that nobody appeared out of the mist behind them in pursuit.

Moving quickly across the land they arrived within two hours at a small town, whose name according to the sign at its edge was Billericay, and Is's plea for liquid refreshment was satisfied by his indulgent master. They entered a public house and bought drinks with money unfurled from within the servant's hat.

—That's what it's about, said Is as he returned his glass to the centre of a beer mat at the high bar, adjusting it to flush, and wiping his face with his shirtsleeve.

—You won't get a finer pint, said a droop-faced man at the bar.

—His cellar hand's as skilled and sure as a watchmaker's, said his portly companion.

—There are magical properties to malt and barley and hops, I'll swear it.

—It's the water what does it.

—O the wonderful beer!

As Is and the two men continued propounding their views on the quality of the ale served in the establishment, Don cast the sight of his eyes about the bar. Numerous people sat and stood in attitudes bespeaking restfulness and companionable repose. Some spoke between them, propinquitous. The sounds which came into the hearing of his ears were of glass clink, chair scrape, trinkets at tabletoppery, matches lit, smoke exhaled, and beneath it all the soothing hubbub of improvised conversation. Individual words were largely lost to Don's ears in the tide of speech, but it could intermittently be discerned that some spoke of congestion upon the thoroughfares of the nation, others of the travails of employment and financial want, others still of today's sporting fixtures.

—I would prefer to be sitting somewhere which might vouchsafe us a little more privacy, said Don.

—Why's that then? said Is.

—You will find out, said Don. There are certain things I think it would be prudent for us to discuss.

—Like what?

—That you will find out too, said Don. You have the whys and whats flowing from you today. There is a table and stools in the corner.

They crossed the room and sat down. Is took another deep draught.

—You know, he then said, I don't think I could ever be unhappy in a pub.

—Remember that scarcity lies at the source of all value, though it is true that I despise temperance.

—I'm a man to savour what's been made for me and paid for out of my hand, and if excess is possible in such an arrangement, then that's fine with me, because as you've already told me, the road of excess leads to the palace of wisdom.

—And the rotundity of your person is living testimony to the perspicacity of that aphorism, said Don.

—I don't understand what you are saying, but your laughter is as clear as a bell, so cheers.

They clinked glasses.

—Anyway, what was it that you wanted to talk about? said Is.

—We need to talk about our unasked-for followers, said Don. And the Future.

—Now there's a turn up for the books!

—Books, books, books, said Don. This is precisely the subject. Books have been hauling it in since the first words were gambled onto paper. I do wonder what Chance is up to with my own book and the chest containing it. She's a capricious One, and isn't that the truth. It is enlivening so to be the object of a flirtation.

—Books is as books are, sir. We've done our double burning of your old tome, so I don't think we'll be seeing it again, even if your lady Chance dressed in satin and danced round a greasy pole.

—That would be something to behold indeed, said Don nodding his head with the utmost seriousness.

—But the future, continued Is. Where's your you-ness gone, sir? You've gone right offstage and out of character.

—This is precisely my meaning: character, character, character.

—Stop it, stop it, stop it, said Is. You grow stranger and stranger. I honestly think I'll never understand you. One minute I feel I'm getting close, and then you whip the carpet out from under me and I'm on my back like a beetle.

—You speak as if there was such a thing as a person, said Don.

—What are you saying now! Again, there goes the carpet. I look around me and I see persons, with edges, and voices, and looks. Look there at that woman at the bar.

Here Is found his speech self-interrupted, for the words were fairly knocked out of him by the sight of her.

—Good Twenty-One, there's a woman! he said in a voice modulated to a soft baritone by desire.

Don looked at the woman Is had identified: eyes which could make quarry of any man's heart, a face of surpassing clarity, a fundament of unequalled womanliness. Undoubtedly the sight of her would have produced pleasure in him if his Bride Chance could be believed to tolerate such double dealing.

—And a woman, Is continued, if I'm not mistaken, has been, is, and will always be a person. In fact, if this woman we are looking at is not a person, then grind me to dust and throw me into the furnace of her fire. Her looks are liable to cook me up either way. And you say there's no such thing as persons! My person, and the person of my wife, and the contract which binds us indissolubly together – it's all in a swamp of trouble just contemplating her. Or it would be, if I still had a wife. Oh Ruth!

—Desist, swain! You are running on and milling nothing but air. Personhood is a chimera of literature, and wouldn't even be conceived of if no books had been written. Damn all the books of the world to bloody hell! Now store this in some infernal nook of your brain, Is-Book.

Here, Don assumed a stance befitting the delivery of one of his profoundest orations, and let us hope it is not entirely otiose.

—*TRISEPTIMUM:* LITERARY CHARACTER: Literature is a tyrant. It builds up an edifice of normative thinking and feeling against which real people can only crack open their heads in despair.

—In the beginning was the book, and the book described things that occurred in the world. But then the things which occurred in the world started being taken for other things, and were turned toward the human interiors, as if by the squeezed light of an eclipse, and the symbols and signs burrowed out little hideholes and nooks within the interiors, until people began to think that the job of books was to describe the interiors of people – the mysteries of the flint – whereas the truth is that the book created the impression that such interiors exist – the flint has no interior, it only *is*. When the people saw this, they became excited, and they called this excitement the Renaissance; and there were born as many persons as there were people, and so journalism became necessary for the newborn prurience, manifest bastard of personhood, to content itself. And the press grew, and literacy responded, and the writers clapped with joy because time had passed and created the bourgeoisie for them, and they deployed great armies of burrowing words to drill new recesses in the warren of personhood for the flint to grow. But fortunately for the commencement of the academies, the main tunnels which had developed out of the very first hideholes were supplemented by completely fresh diggings, and so character could be discussed in terms of a set of paradigms. And the emergence of a supposed increase to the complexity of character in the 1860s involved nothing more than placing personal and historical character in opposition, from which one produces the bourgeois tragic. And the people read the books, and the words did their work, and hollowed their personhoods out into labyrinthine psychologies, but which were patient of being discussed because of the paradigms. And so now even though a person is a multitude, a character is 'loyal', or 'introverted', or 'impulsive', or any other of a set of paradigmatic adjectives in combination, and he or she recognises this, and will behave accordingly; and woe betide a book whose characters don't obey this directive, for they will go unread as 'failures'. The persons therefore suffer at their own reading, because they cannot conform to such clarity of character, because the flint at their interior is not immaculate but shattered into an infinite number of shards, from whence the pain of neurosis, which is now become as inescapable as their own skin.

—It is incumbent upon me, as a result, to seek out all works of literature and destroy them utterly! (Though this shall have to happen later, because we are busy with the hyperfine transition of hydrogen at the moment.) But still: damn all the books of the world to bloody hell!

—Leaving the destruction of all these books till later, said Is, is a good idea too because you might change your mind, and I'd rather not start chasing every book in the world down hidey-holes trying to damn them to hell, bloody or not. I'm worn out as it is.

(No reader could be accounted foolish to remark that Don, whose scientific training was entirely garnered from the Victorian library held in his water tower, speaks more like a book than anyone he or she has ever read. Is not his hatred of books the very pinnacle of the modern neurosis therefore: the hatred of self? We shall get him for this, the meddler. Now: *read on!*)

—To return to what I was going to say, said Don ignoring his squire. You will remember I mentioned that we should discuss the Future, which you might account an antithetical treatment of Time to that espoused by me in my commitment to my True Bride. But I would maintain vigorously and furiously that you would be wrong, for although I am concerning myself with the Future, which I must reiterate does not exist, I am doing so only in regard to the liberty of Chance, which – though she teases me hourly (if hours can be said to exist) – owing to our pursuers is currently in peril. The priority of our further investigations must therefore be to elude the many people who have been following us since we left Chelmsford, and who found us in that woodland (not that I am remembering anything, an activity strictly forbidden my mind) for their will is to have us play at their little game of History and be what-once-was, which in reality has never been.

—You can concern yourself with ending the game, said Is. But I'm more set to wonder how it began. The newspaper it was that did it, for sure. But then there was Cressing before that.

Steadfastly his master looked at him.

—Is there anything you should be telling me about Cressing, Is? You did look wild the morning after the storm – or so I might recall if it were permitted me. But I take that back: you needn't fear momentarily to make reference to the past or the future in my presence, for I have decided to place a moratorium upon such discourse for the period in which we find ourselves in this public house.

—May we remain forever within its walls! said Is.

His master looked at him again.

—So?

(Foolish indeed would be the individual who, by crossing the ineluctable line which divides life and art, takes upon himself the burden of propagating the interior of a narrative with all that it demands in order to satisfy, entertain and teach. It should be a rare man indeed that might carry it out. The events at Cressing had taught the squire a good lesson; that chance was never Chance, and that the present was nothing – quite literally *nothing* – but a point of division upon which the past and future rocked, like the fulcrum of a seesaw; but only *like*, for it was less than a point: the present was nothing but an idea. Furthermore, that there was only one end to the recession through layers of human thought and behaviour, and that end was a story – *all* is narrative – which needed to be told and retold in order to sustain us as *us*. If the servant didn't *know* all of this – for how could he? – he felt it, and the resultant fear was ample. No, Is would not tell his master what he had witnessed at Cressing, and let that be an end to it.)

—I have nothing to say master, said Is.

Once more steadfastly did his master look at him with those yellow eyes.

—I have nothing to say master, the servant repeated.

—Very well, said Don, and the matter was forgotten.

—As I was saying, Don continued, or as I was about to say, the use of us by the Chelmsford crowd, and then the waking up in a meadow with a full battalion of followers – these things I regret to say might be happening as a result of my poorly transacted Science. For while my ideals are clear, I have not always maintained such a freedom of mind as I might wish I had. Eschewing all intention has proven impossible; for it is true, as you know, that I hoped to get to France when we got into that boat at West Mersea, and a good proportion of my joy when we found ourselves again returned to the shores of this good county in the country of England was from the sense of relief that my intentions had been frustrated by events. I had drifted perilously close to that normative human activity which leads from desire, through exertion, to satisfaction. It is a disposition on the one hand praised as aspirational and on the other denigrated as depraved, depending on the object of desire. (You see how capricious we humans are!) But I must confess that all the time through our wanderings I have had in mind numerous destinations which I have hoped to arrive at in order that my ambitions be carried out and which I have been unable to suppress or disperse from my hopefulness. I am more than aware that the only propitious end to these wanderings involves the rejection of such a mode of thought.

—In short, continued Don to his goodly servant, I am stuck. I must now admit that I have wanted to arrive at CERN – which you knew – but also at Oxford, in order that they might publish my *Encyclopaedia*, though it be now twice-destroyed, and thank Chance for that; at Santa Monica——

—Santa Monica! said Is, thinking of her sweet whisky lips.

——so that I might interrogate Carl Sagan in relation to the plaque of Pioneer 10; at Cape Canaverel, so that I might examine for clues the place where that craft was launched; at Greenwich so that I might symbolically destroy the phantasm of measurable time (and what is a human life but a nexus of symbols?); at the *Bureau International des Poids et Mesures* near Paris in order to destroy the platinum-iridium bars and other spatial measuring constants; at the Bank of England, so that I might remove the foundation of fiat value; at the Jansky Laboratory at the National Radio Astronomy Oberservatory, Green Bank, West Virginia, in order to examine the horn antenna which first detected the spectral line of the hyperfine transition of hydrogen at Harvard in 1951; and so too, then, at the Lyman Laboratory at that University, where it was first used.

—Everywhere, Don continued, I wish to remove the centres of false systems of organisation. What, indeed, *is* that centre? One glimpse of the red breasted robin is enough to inform oneself that they don't give two hoots about centres. Abominable centricentricity! Centres do not exist! And yet we demanded them for a comfort at the cavemouth, to this end: they are now taken to be a reality. So deeply engrained are some, that the centre conceals itself and pretends it does not exist. Take for example the base-10 number system: for almost everyone, it is simply *there*, an objective fact of number. How am I to replace it with the true base-21 system? We would need new numbers in new numerals from ten to twenty-one, and no-one will take it up even if I were to formulate it. And yet, how will the world ever be tolerable without Twenty-One at its heart? I have attempted to restore humanity through the destruction of the many snares it sets itself, but the very intention espoused by me towards that destruction is the habit of mind which is above all responsible for setting those snares. This is why I don't know my quest – I know its objective, but to aim for it is to place it further from any possibility of achievement. Oh Is-Book, I am lost!

With these final words exiting his mouth, Don sank his head to the tabletop and wept.

—You can't be perfect all the time, said Is, and he placed his hand upon his master's in order to soothe him. If I think too much I get the same feeling myself, all miserable and weary. If you ask me, I think it would be best to take your own advice, let our feet take us where they will – as long as it's away from that strange horde, wherever it might be now – and do with the Present as Time does with everyone, which is to say play it as if it were a game.

Don lifted his head up from the tabletop.

—I think you are right, he said with words choked by a persistent if diminishing sorrow. Help me good squire to keep the perilous seductions of cause-and-effect, of plan-hatching, time-arrowing, target-aiming, of programmatic action, and of the storying of oneself, which partakes of all the previous, the heroing inward thoughts, the ugly egoism – help me maintain the best comportment of myself for the achievement of my non-aims. For in truth there is no aim except to still every atom in the universe, and to witness that spectral line eternally extended, and Before and After annihilate!

—Well let's be on our feet then, said Is. And be aware that here's a man (and he pointed to himself to make the reference unmistakable) who will serve you so well that he is willing to leave more than half a pint of this fine beer to the fruitflies of the room in order to succour your aching heart.

—You are a better man than I have given you credit for, good Is-Book, said Don. But I just do not see how one can go about one's business without intention. Even refusing to have an intention is an intention in itself.

—Sir, if the importance you place on going about our business in the without-a-clue manner is justified, which I don't doubt it is, then perhaps I might suggest that there is in the bones of me a feeling which is worth taking notice of, and one which, as far as our adventuring goes, might well be salt to the meat which forms the dinner of it; that is to say, indispensable if it is to be nice and savoury. In short, I have an idea. Let's pretend that we are going to Oxford to throw the book at all the other Dons, even if the old one's been burned up and the new one's in a funny form now inside my head. But really the real and true Don, which I hardly need to point out is you, will be going about his anti-business at liberty, because those revolting peasants did their dirties in London most of all, or so says our man Maurice Stephens in the letters page.

Is pulled the newspaper clipping from his pocket and brandished it at Don by way of corroboration.

—You see, sir? continued the servant. We'll be headed for Oxford, and either we'll lose the crowd because they're heading to London, or the crowd'll lose us because we're not. And if it decides to follow us to Oxford, then that's Chance regenerated because I don't think there could ever be any revolting peasants in Oxford, as they wouldn't be allowed, if it's really the kind of place I've heard it is. Our play-at with Oxford will enable the work to happen, so mark my words. Do you see how the dog sits?

—It sits well with me, Is-Book, said Don who was reinvigorated by his servant's words. And though it has no collar, or name, or home, or compulsion to cleanliness, it's all the damned better for it.

Our two wearisome companions left the pub a great deal happier than they had been when they entered it; and not a minute too soon, for it was precisely that length of time which elapsed before a very large group of people came into the same town of Billericay, seeking with their senses in all the recesses of the town the heroic pair; and it did not strike Is or Don as in any way incongruous that the time was only seven in the morning and the public house within which they had just taken a draught was not only open, but also busy.

(The time will grow ripe; soon the pair will be reined in, and an ending prepared for the delectation of the reader. No-one is going to Oxford.)

In accordance with the scheme concocted within the four walls of the public house just vacated, the small company of two, of whose adventures it is our sometime pleasure to continue in the reading of, discussed their agreed destination.

—It befalls you, said Don to his servant in a sonorous and dignified tone, to guide us through all the fouls and fairs to the city of books, Oxford, so that the one true book, which travels with us within your very own brain-pan, can be delivered up to those in the know for the righting of all wrongs and the extermination of false words and their combinations, which lie at the root of all error, if any such thing as a root can be conceived to actually exist, which I say it can't. Thus shall be cleansed the mind of Europe.

—Where is this Oxford? said Is, playing along in the game he had invented.

—It is over there at some remove, said Don, gesturing west with glittering yellow eye.

—I do like to have my ends marked out in some shape or way, so I thank you for it, said the servant.

They began walking towards the point at which Don had gestured, feeling very pleased with themselves, because it seemed to them that they had outwitted the pursuing horde, which believed them to be heading towards London. So confident were they, in fact, that Don felt able to return to the earlier topic which had preoccupied him.

—In order that you can see, he said to Is, how the falsity of the notion of character I recently spoke about is promulgated in every word and action, I demand, Is-Book, that you do something which you deem to be out of character.

—Is this another game, a game-within-a-game?

—Everything is a game, if the mind is turned upon it in earnest. Play is the sole means by which knowledge can be assimilated in virtue. Now do something out of character.

—Right now?

—Yes.

—But I can't think of anything, said the servant.

—How about if I promise to buy you a drink in the next pub we come to. That may help.

—I was about to suggest the same – you know me too well.

—Careful what you say, Is-Book. Knowing you would demand reality of character, the very thing of which I am demonstrating the non-existence. What you bear on your tongue is not so fresh as the system which I am constructing within the interior of your brain. There is a responsibility in the latter. It is like to be the snail's shell to house the whole world when its Future comes.

—You're properly friendly with the future today, said Is.

—Indeed. Now let's get at your character so we can get at your out-of-character, said Don.

—Well, I think I am honest.

—Okay. What else?

—I am kind. I wouldn't kill a fly.

—Continue.

—My wife says I am lazy, which is probably fair. I am a bit awkward sometimes, especially in formal situations, or public toilets. But it pays to be awkward in such places, public toilets I mean. You wouldn't want to feel too comfortable. I'm under average in height.

—You have moved from supposed character traits to physical characteristics, which, whilst more easily measurable, are, in propounding an

279

infinitely greater reality than the character traits which are the object of your inquiry, not members of that class – not that either is really Real. Think of your personality.

—Happy.

—Yes, that is an important one, and an observation I would agree with if my Science allowed it. You are a pleasure to be in company with.

—You're very kind. I am fearful too, though, aren't I?

—You are indeed. You are like a small child who is attracted to but recoils from the phenomena of the world all at once.

—Do you think we have enough? asked Is.

—We have the requisite muster, I believe. Do you feel yourself amply described if I say to you: This man here is honest, kind, lazy, awkward, happy and fearful?

—I think I probably do, yes. I am peaceful too, if that helps.

—It all helps, and you've done well, said Don. Now what event can we concoct out of the opposites of these character traits for you to bring into existence?

—Well, I'd have to be dishonest, unkind, hardworking, at-ease, miserable, courageous and violent. They don't sound like ways of behaving that go together very well.

—Indeed they do not, such is the nature of opposites, and it is all grist to the mill of my theorization. For a start, many of them overlap with one another, which is obviously a very ugly thing, insofar as there is an aesthetics of Science. But an empirical test is required. I suggest that you cover just a few of them and see how it works out.

—Okay. What do you suggest? asked Is.

—I would suggest killing an animal in a very relaxed way whilst saying miserably that you are not killing an animal. What about that dog over there?

Don pointed across the street at a little Patterdale terrier whose neat trot and panting tongue gave the impression of a very contented animal indeed.

—I can't kill a dog! said Is.

—Of course you can, Don reassured him. Our proof demands that you do.

—This is all bad. I don't like it. Can't I just kill these little flies doing triangles above my head?

—A fly is barely an animal at all, said Don. There is insufficient cruelty involved in the killing of a fly or flies for the proper transaction of our experiment. Some middling animal is required.

—I would kill a rabbit, said Is.

Don looked at Is with satisfaction; but then his face changed: clearly it would not do.

—The very fact that you *would* kill a rabbit means that you shouldn't in this test.

—Are you sure? said Is. Doesn't it just mean that kindness is not one of my character traits?

—Well, if it isn't, why did you mention it?

—I'm getting confused now. If I will kill a rabbit, then I can't do it in this test; but if I won't, then I must. It's all topsy-turvy.

—Of course it is, Don replied. That's the point.

—Is character just instinct, then?

—Absolutely not, said Don. Just kill the dog, and we'll carry on our way.

—Killing a dog is illegal though.

—And is one of your character traits to be law-abiding?

—Well, I'd say that I try, said Is. But I've been arrested once in the past few weeks, and nearly another several times, and actions speak louder than words, as they say.

—In which case, concluded Don, one of your character traits is to have a penchant for criminality, which means that you must not kill the dog.

—One half of me says I must, while the other says I mustn't. I'm more confused than ever. What's happening?

—Ah, the cracks in the epistemology against which we are fighting are becoming visible! This is working out even better than I had expected. The opposite of an opposite is rarely itself.

—I tell you what, buy me two pints in the next town and I'll do anything you say.

—I cannot, for drunkenness is clearly one of your most prominent traits. Also, I have no money.

—Well, if we could stick to the bigger roads and go through a few towns I might be able to make some more money with this recorder, and then I could buy my own drink. All these endless country lanes leading nowhere are poverty's way and no mistake. Let's get us on a main road, agree that I have killed the dog even though I haven't (because we both know I could), and then we can find the next pub on the road to Oxford, sit back, have a few more drinks, and congratulate ourselves on our good sense.

—You are proposing a most unorthodox scientific method, Is-Book. But on this occasion I will humour you. For all intents and purposes that dog is now dead, and you are its murderer. Well done.

—Thank you, said Is.

With the object of the dog's murder now removed from their attention, the aimless pair found their attention attracted to the line of slender poplars by which they walked, and whose leaves shimmered and hissed in the breeze like a multitude of coins pouring over one another.

—What, then, can we conclude? continued Don.

Is raised his body up into an attitude befitting the delivery of profound speech, but was interrupted.

—I was not inviting you to speak, said Don. But merely commencing my discourse by utilizing a rhetorical form which is presented as the record of an internal mental disputation.

—You are very liberal with your styles of speech, sir, said Is, who had removed his recorder from the holdall which hung from his shoulder and was busy polishing it on his shirt in readiness for the next town. But anyway, though the dog's now dead, I'd have to admit that my way of seeing things is no more watertight or all wrapped up than it was before. I can't really remember the purpose of the experiment, which means that I'm lost as to its results.

—Allow me to summarize for you, said Don. You, Is-Book, have in the killing of that dog made one of the most important discoveries of your career. Are you aware of Jastrow's duck-rabbit?

—I am not.

—The duck-rabbit is a picture which can be seen as either a duck or a rabbit, though to my mind it looks more like a rabbit-gull.

—What's the purpose of that then?

—You are incisive indeed today, Is-Book. It began as a curiosity in a German magazine at the very end of the nineteenth century, but has become a major figure for the study of human cognition. E. H. Gombrich, the art historian, has written on it; and our great though fallible precursor, Ludwig Wittgenstein, wrote, if inconclusively, about it. So the purpose of it is changing, just as the appearance of it does, depending on what motivates us. Are we schoolboys or scientists? Is it a rabbit or a duck? It can only be one or the other; you cannot see both at once. But, it is also something else: a collection of back lines and shadings. And when this awareness comes upon you, you realise that there is not even any true liberty in simple ocular perception.

Don paused for little more than a moment in order to inhale deeply for the proper propulsion of air from his chest in the following indignant exclamation, shouted into the early morning air:

—Damn our eyes!

He was working himself up into a fury.

—Yes, Is-Book, damn our eyes! But damn our minds a thousandfold more! Damn them for twisting every set of fresh data into the stale shape of the already-familiar. We are being conditioned against our will – or, our will is already conditioned, so we suck comfortingly at the teat of delusion. Your murder of the dog proves that the categories of character do not exist, which shows that literature is a source of very great evil. It is the duck-rabbit: it forces us to choose between the being of one thing or another. It has conditioned us into——

—If we are off to Oxford, interrupted Is in an attempt to distract and therefore calm his master down, does this mean definitely not California, or Switzerland, or London? Because I've just remembered that Oxford is where my Ruth's parents moved to, and they're not so fond of me. Don't California, or Switzerland, or London sound a lot more fun for adventuring. We could always change our pretend intention couldn't we?

Don ceased discoursing in his normal way about whatever it was he was discoursing upon, and turned his attention to Is's question.

—Things have been moving quickly in my mind, Is-Book. As soon as one idea or conviction pops in, another does, and knocks it off the ledge of my thought into the abyss. (There is an abyss in me, dear servant, the like of which you will happily never know.) In truth, the only thing that matters is the Is-Book, which I will take care of. You can scheme up any pretend destination you like, as you did (and then didn't) with Oxford. Feel free to change the faux destination if it will keep you more lively while at the same time ridding us of the horde.

With this conversation concluded, our adventuring pair found that it was time to continue moving on for Oxford, or Switzerland, or California, whichever it might be.

—We will reach wherever it is we are going sooner than not, said Don. Especially now that you are disburdened of the chest, and then we shall see what Chance has to say for herself. She has been a bit quiet these past few days – as if we needed further confirmation that the crowd pursuing us are meddling with my Science! I can almost feel the oppression in their spirits, the hoodwinked populace. How they do reify unto death what should live in protean fluidity! I can only reiterate the points of my previous peroration in regard to the notion of character, personhood and the gins, nets and traps of literary convention. It is populated by quacks. I rise up——

26

(Injudicious indeed it would be to allow such blasphemies against the great tradition and art of the novel to remain extant in the body of our book. Though this duo is in general likeable, the older one requires straightening out; he is too aloof, arrogant, self-immersed. Moreover, as a pair they rattle haphazardly on as if their tongues were the motors for their beating hearts. If they will not adapt, then they shall be adapted; and so, read on, and discover the lineaments of a story emerging from the mist, thus:)

The crowd of pursuers gained on the chattering pair.

(Very swiftly and neatly done, the reader will remark. Admirable.)

The crowd of pursuers who had passed now through the town of Billericay were gaining fast on our two disagreeable heroes, and they knew full well what their aims and intentions were.

Commencing to turn a full circle to take in the vista of this glorious June morning (oh, we can make them move when they're misbehaving) Is noticed with a great thrust of vertigo in his chest that the mob was on their tail.

—Sir! If ever we needed the hyperfine transition of hydrogen, now is the time: we've been found! And I'm not sure even Oxford can save us. You'd better look.

—*Now* is always the time, Is-Book, said Don. But I applaud the sentiment of your words.

He then turned, took in the crowd some mile or so distant on the road as it bisected a verdant bluff, and spoke:

—It is regrettable. But I do believe that Oxford or some other place may still come to our aid. For the Present – which is the sole reality – I think we might as well allow them to catch us, because we can lead them better when we are among them, even if it is up Oxford's garden path. As long as we don't take them to London, the Peasants' Revolt can't happen, and Chance will be free as a bird (if in fact birds are free, and I would declare that they are not).

Our insufferable pair ceased walking therefore, and turned around to wait for the mob to join them. Here they came, descending the hill in a steady stream of pairs and threes, some carrying banners – illegible from this distance – as if ants carrying the remains of leaves.

Very soon the noise of their transit became audible, and the jauntiness of their walking visible. They were singing, or more accurately chanting rhymes in rhythm with their footfall.

—Sir, said Is.

—Yes.

—I don't mean to interfere with your latest scheme, which I don't doubt for a minute is the very best course of action, but aren't the members of that crowd carrying *weapons*?

Don peered into the distance with his old inflexible yellow eyes.

—I believe they are, he said. They are but sticks and stones.

—Sticks and stones is enough for me, said Is. Let them break your bones, but I'm not hanging around for a knocking.

Holding his hand out to silence his servant, Don continued to peer across the field, between the quivering poplars, up to the road, whence the crowd drew towards them – and then he saw.

—Good Twenty-One! he said.

—What is it sir? said Is, whose degree of fright reached an unprecedented pitch.

—Each and every one of them – is holding a *book!*

—Is that bad? said Is.

—It is the worst! Let's run!

The tiresome pair turned their backs on the pursuing horde and began running as best they could across the field in the opposite direction.

—Hurry Is-Book! said Don. Why do you have to be such a ponderous lump?

—It's not me that's lumpy, said Is.

—What are you talking about, Is-Book?

—The chest, sir, and its contents!

He pointed up on to his own bent back at the chest, which was once again his ineluctable burden.

—It's snuck right onto me again! It is the turd which cannot be flushed!

Don looked at his servant and saw with horror and dread that he had spoken the truth: the chest had reconstituted itself once more and was intent on being their permanent companion.

—Get rid of it! screamed Don.

With these words echoing across the land, he hauled it from his servant's back and started beating it ineffectually with the stick he had been using as an aid to his walking. Is looked on in bemusement as his master continued to assault the chest for some minutes.

—I tell you what sir, he said. Why don't we tip the *Encyclopaedia* into the river there?

Here he pointed ahead to a little footbridge which arched over the gently flowing waters of a stream.

—As fire doesn't seem to be working, said Don, it's as good an idea as any other. But will it be sufficient?

—If it is not, said Is inflamed with the fire of righteous devotion to his faultless master, I will stamp on it too, and tear at the paper of it, and shout at it till it swims off like so many minnows in an infinite number of fragments.

The master seemed satisfied with this, and so the two companions moved to the centre point of the little bridge and upended the large chest, scattering the twice regenerate scraps of paper which had been cut from the thirteen volumes of Don's corrected *Oxford English Dictionary* into the stream. For a brief time they watched as the paper slowly sank and the ink of Don's handwriting bled and the printed type convulsed in the current. In due course, Is found it unnecessary to exercise his fury on the hated work – it had turned into a gloopy pulp and clung about the stones of the riverbed.

Leaving the chest atop the bridge, they hurried along, ever seeking to elude the pursuing crowd, but the day was hot, and the wind dry, and they had no water, and they had not eaten since the day before. An arduous journey it was. The horde of people neither gained on nor were eluded by them, but pursued ceaselessly, carrying their weapons and books.

The pair came with lungs and legs burning to the outskirts of Brentwood, where the horde behind was augmented by columns of men, women and children from Fobbing, Saniforth and Corringham, from Horndon, Langdon, Mucking, Rainham, Wennington, South Weald, Bocking, Fryerning, Goldhanger, Ingatestone, Stock and Ramsden. How many strong were they now? Several thousand they were, each armed with a flint, or stick, and a book or sheaf of paper leaves. Wherever Don and Is went, the horde went too, though they were too far behind to follow by sight. It was a remarkable phenomenon.

—Oh sir, said Is. I'm done for. The feet of me are falling off, and my throat's as dry as a dustbowl. I can't go on. The escape can't be made. They're always there, just past the bend in the road. What are we to do?

—It is a remarkable phenomenon, said Don. But cease despairing my good squire. There is always a way out – open up the chest.

And Is discovered once more that the dreadful chest was back with them.

—Impossible! he said. We only just left it by the river!

—Never mind its possibility, said Don. On this occasion we will use its reappearance to our advantage and in resistance against the ill-fatedness which we seem to be suffering from. (Oh Chance, have you forsaken me?) Now open the chest.

—Do we really have time to be sitting down and trawling through all the old papers again?

—I am not doing any aimless trawling, you doubter from hell! I'm getting you away from our pursuers, which is what you want, isn't it? If the chest must keep coming back, then it shall be made to work to our benefit. Oh, I shall do it myself.

And Don did do it himself, bending down and hauling up the lid of the chest, and then rummaging through the papers it contained.

—Here it is! he said in no time at all. These documents, stolen by my capable hand from the mayoral library at Chelmsford, will do the necessary job.

—When did you do that, sir! said Is. It completely passed me by.

—Now, said Don, ignoring his squire. All these people are pursuing us across the county because they're copying the Peasants' Revolt, which is no more than a bunch of damned writings.

—I think that's what it's all about sir, said Is. I cannot read, remember – or, not normally.

—These people, continued Don, are following us and making us be what they want us to be, and it all fits in with what they can read and refer to in the blasted books in their hands. So the story runs on, and we are at its beck and call, even though we might feel free as a couple of swallows, which as I have probably said before are less free than they appear. But there are more ways than one to skin a cat, as I have also probably already said – not that I hold belief in either repetition, freedom, swallows, cats or probability. Let us play by their rules, but against the grain of their action. Look here.

Don flipped up the plastic cap at the top of a thick cardboard tube and removed from within it a roll of parchment.

—It's a map, said Is.

—You are correct, said Don. Specifically the Prima Europe Tabula, Ptolemaic map of Great Britain, published in the so-called-year 1482. Now let's look at how things are.

Don perused the map for some time before making further pronouncement.

—This map makes no sense to me whatsoever; it is perfect for our needs. Just look at the shape of it!

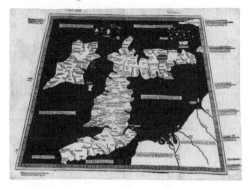

—What, or should I say *where,* is it? asked Is.

—It's the land mass and masses which have come by a process – painful to many – to be known as Great Britain and Ireland.

—Is it now, said Is.

—Tell me you are not unfamiliar with the shape of the country you live in, topographically speaking of course.

—It doesn't matter which way you speak it, I'm none the wiser.

—Maps, Is-Book! You have seen maps of the British Isles before have you not?

—I don't believe I have. Should I?

—There's no should or shouldn't to it, it is not a question of moral. I am sure that if you looked at a map of the British Isles it would be as familiar to you as your own name.

—Well let's just say it is. Is this one different then?

—It is, very.

—Okay, that's nice. But what are we going to do with it, give it to the mob?

—Absolutely not, Is-Book. We are going to treasure it as if it were our life, which indeed it might be: protecting you, as it will, from sticks and stones, and me from the enslavement enforced by the heavy chain of events in their damned books.

—How so?

—We will play with the universal delusion of Time: by following such ancient maps, we may slip into the no-longer-there. If we cover our tracks, there's no way they'll ever be able to find us, so busy will they be in following the trajectory of their own documents.

—Where are we on it at the moment then? said Is.

—That's a very good question, Is-Book. As far as I can see, we aren't anywhere on it.

—Is it certainly of the same portion of land as what we're standing on, sir? Is asked.

—Of course it is, said Don. ALBION INSVLA BRITANICCA written in the centre means, *Albion, Island of the Britons*.

—That's a good name, Albion, said Is. So Albion is England. What's this blob over here?

—Don't let an Irishman hear you say that.

—And what about this? said Is.

—That bit looking like a piece of cake fallen over on the plate is Scotland. It's usually much more upwardly-standing.

—I have heard as much said of the Scottish. So where are we?

—The best way of finding us, said Don, is to look for London, and then head north-east. But, if you mark where London is, there's not really anything north-east of it, except for Kent, which has snuck round like a naughty dog impatient of its punishment. None of the other place names correspond to the ones you and I are familiar with. There are two islands off the coast of what should be East Anglia, but I've never heard of them. In fact, the map is so unfamiliar, so far removed from what a person is used to seeing, that I wouldn't be surprised if, following its topography and living amongst the mysteries of its toponymy, we were never able to return to the world with which we are currently familiar.

—Are you saying that we could lose ourselves so fully by following this map that we might never come back?

—I am.

—In which case count me out.

—I thought you wanted to escape from the mob once and for all.

—I do, but not like that. That's one of the most terrifying ideas I've ever heard.

—In which case, you should make provision within the repository of your mind for an addendum to the sub-category 'Phobias' within the main category 'Isaiah Olm' of my *New Oral Encyclopaedia*, which is: 'maps'. Elucidate and expand on the subject as you wish, for you know it best, and I am tired of your fearfulness today.

—Isn't there another way? said Is.

—Damn you Is-Book, you're like a fussy child. I have another map which may meet your more particular requirements.

Don reached into the chest once more and retrieved another tube.

—This may do it for us: Matthew Paris's map, drawn *circa* 1250 (though I do feel obliged to point out that *numquam* would be a more appropriate term than *circa* here). It's at once less and more different than the previous map from the common experience of an aerial representation of England and its most proximate subjugated territories.

—Oh that's much better, said Is as his master unfurled the roll. I like it very much. Ireland's come over for a hug!

—You fool, said Don. That's Wales. Ireland isn't on this map.

—I do like the rivers, said Is. Very eel-like, aren't they. So where are we on this one?

—Well, strangely enough on this one Essex and Kent have slipped round the other way – West – and the Thames is emptying itself off the south coast. Kent is *Canca*, and Dover is the *Austermost* (which is to say, southernmost) town of the isles. Essex is directly west of London because Suffolk and Norfolk have decided to take up the whole of East Anglia to its East. It's such a hopeless jumble as compared with the modern conception of southern England that it will be the perfect map for giving those fools the slip.

—It's also such a good-looking thing I don't think I'd mind getting lost in this one at all, said Is. The other one was so stark and ugly, like a piece of broken concrete.

—There is only one problem, said Don.

—What's that then? asked Is.

—We have to find where we are first, in relation to the map, so we can enter into the mysterious parts of it. The closest places to us on the map are Oveford, Waltham Cross and London; all of these are a fair way off, and in fact the first I have no idea what or where it is. So I think we need another map to get us to one of these larger places first, and then we can sequester ourselves within the pleasant forms of this map and wait until the pursuing hordes wear themselves out.

—Well rummage some more then sir, said Is urgently, because they're approaching faster than ever what with us standing here like a couple of trees, and this one (he pointed to himself with his thumb) shaking.

Don did as he was told, and very soon held another map in his hand.

—Here's a good one. Just as handsome as the last, though in a different manner, and much better fit for our immediate purpose: a map of Essex by John Speed, dated 1611 (I say 'dated'; but saying 'vegetable' or 'platinum' would yield as much true meaning, which is none).

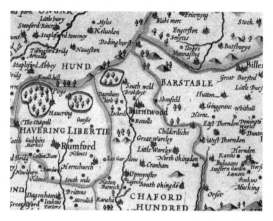

Here's Brentwood, which we've only just left, though spelled Burntwood because Speed was a wise man, and knew that a word can be rendered any way one wishes. But look! If we head west, just before we hit Havering there's a place called Pirgo, which I am certain no longer exists. And by the looks of it, it's got a dirty great big fence round it, which will serve us well. Let's get us there as quick as we can – there's no way the mob will find us in a place that doesn't exist (not that any places have true existence, ontologically speaking).

—I'm with you all the way, sir, said Is.

Concluding their agreement upon this scheme of action, our tedious pair made their way west past Brentwood along the A123, and then cut off north into the mysterious country, across the blank land, into the evening, with Is chattering in excitement all the way. And the mob, as Don had predicted, was cut-off from the pursuit, distracted as they were by the twin parabolae of street lamps at the roadside, the failed modernity of the industrial parks, the transit of heavy goods through the night. They could not pass into the enclosure of Time which our heroes had created.

27

Sharp upon the nose – the pleasant sour bite of cherry and apple wood burning – Don and Is smelled Pirgo before it became visible in the dusk through the twisted trees of the forest.

—Here, said Don, you'll find good reason to stow that tongue of yours deep down in your gullet, because this Pirgo place is going to prove everything I've told you about Time, History, Science and Man to be so full of wisdom that you could dress it in a garment of drugget and call it Socrates.

Is, by now tired and hungry, had been moaning for the previous few miles, and had delivered himself into a sorrow-stricken state at the course his life had taken over the preceding few weeks. He found all of a sudden that he had no desire to speak, not even if it meant inadvertently obeying his master's dictates.

They arrived at the edge of a clearing. A small encampment had been made therein, with three felled logs for benches arranged in a triangle around a smouldering fire. Several vans were parked up one beside another, from each of which a faint hubbub could be heard of the taking of dinner or children's bedtimes. Incontrovertibly, it was the same scene which presented itself to our two heroes, but they did not see the same thing at all.

—Wondrous to see! said Don to his servant. This is no village we have come upon, but a druidic assembly!

Is sighed.

—Master, these are not druids, but crusties. They are some of the worst people you are likely to meet; they talk even more nonsense than you. Ask their children's names and try not to laugh. But don't do that because I don't think we should go in there, it's only going to end badly. I can feel——

Before Is could finish what he was saying – words to which his master would perhaps have refused to give credence even if Time or Chance or Science herself, dressed in her bridal gown and train, had said them – Don had already begun striding toward the centre of the clearing, intent on seeking and finding its inhabitants in order to introduce himself, and to congratulate them on finding what he believed to be a loophole outside of that specious hegemon History; inhabitants whom, as we shall soon find out, he revered as much as Is disdained and feared them. Don raised one arm, held his thinly bearded chin aloft and, striding forward, opened his mouth to speak.

—

Before any words could exit his mouth, two dogs leapt up to the limits of their tethering chains and became embroiled in a frenzied competition of barking and growling aimed at Don. Several human heads peered perpendicularly out of the open door of one of the vans to witness Don smiling beatifically at the two animals, whose rage continued unabated, and then intensified, indeed, as he continued without concern for his safety to approach them. A branch whose leaves shook at the edge of the clearing gave ample indication of the presence of Is, who had just then involuntarily made slight urination to the inside of his left thigh in fright.

—I wouldn't get any closer if I were you, said a man's voice from within one of the vans, before the owner of both the van and the voice stepped out and called the dogs down sharply and to immediate effect.

—Animals of the world count me alone among humans as kin, for I do not seek to enslave them, said Don. You see how they have calmed themselves in this knowledge as I approached to bless their troubled heads.

Don looked down with sorrow at the chains as the two powerful mongrels slobbered on his filthy out-held hands.

—Whatever you say mate. What you doing here?

—I was just about to say before the canine commotion (and the arm and chin were raised again in accordance with the ceremonial demands of the occasion): I am Don Waswill, fearsome adventurer, scourge of History and its senseless purveyor Humanity, and I salute all residents of ancient Pirgo for their wily success in liberating themselves from the shackles of civilization, that grotesque menagerie of broken human spirits, even if they do chain up their dogs.

—If these chains weren't here, you'd have no throat right now, said the man. Who's back there?

—Ah, that is my servant, a wretched specimen. Come forth, Is-Book!

—I don't want to, said Is quietly from within the scrub.

—You must, for our host has expressed an interest in you.

—His interest in me is why I'm not coming out.

—Now you see what I mean, said Don to the Pirgoan. I will go and fetch him and then you'll be able to witness his idiocies up close.

Several Pirgoans more crept with curiosity from within the vans to see who these strange visitors were; Don reached Is just as he was turning to run into the darkening wood.

—Are you mad, Is-Book? Here there is a fire, and food no doubt, and you are making ready to sleep the night in the middle of a forest. You will be crying out my name in fear within five minutes, if minutes in fact had any existence. Come with me and experience the life of the druid!

—Sir, you need to shut up about druids. These are definitely crusties – look at the beads in their hair, and their stupid clothes. Smell the patchouli and hash, look at those knackered old vans.

—Knackered old vans? said the Pirgoan, his hand scratching at his chin beneath pinholed pupils.

—You don't know anything, Is-Book. These are without a doubt an ancient people (not that I believe in ancientness, for all Time is present in the one Present). One would not need to be a phrenologist to mark the wisdom of them written plain to see in their skull shape and the planes of their physiognomies. I command you to attend me in the course of research which Chance has placed as a possibility before me. How many druidic assemblies have you ever seen before? If you go back into the wood, you will likely stray into the acculturated plain of temporaneity, where the mob will surely find you, and then you are done for. Stay with me, within the tangled wood, where the crowd can't follow, and after a few nips from Saint Monica you'll feel fine.

—Well if Monica's coming out to play, said Is, then that's a different matter. But one thing before we go and join these definitely-druids. I still don't quite understand how you can praise bits of history, and then say it never existed, like you just did. If history never did its deeds, why call your hip flask after Saint Disgusting's mum, who as you yourself told me lived some time ago, perhaps before there were even hip flasks to be named after her.

—Saint Augustine is the name your brain is grappling at. But have I not told you also of Levy-Bruhl's Brazilian Indian?

—I don't think you have sir, because as I've remembered everything that has passed between us, I'd be sure to remember that, because it actually sounds like it might be interesting.

—It is more than interesting, good servant Is-Book. A Brazilian Indian going about his daily business in the mountains met one day upon the trail a missionary. This missionary, eager to learn the ways and means of the indigenous culture of the region – presumably before his mission destroyed it – made clear to his guide that he wished to converse with the Indian, and so they began to speak, with the guide acting as interpreter. Much did the curious missionary learn about their customs, their food, their daily lives. Taking their leave of one another, however, the missionary inquired to whom he had been speaking, to which the Indian replied, "I am a red parrot." Perplexed, and desiring clarification, the missionary pressed the Indian: "You call yourself Red Parrot? Or you will be a red parrot when you die? Or you feel the bird in some way represents you, or vice versa?" To which the Indian, baffled, said flatly: "I am a red parrot."

—It's true enough that parrots can speak, said Is. Are you sure that this bloke wasn't in actual fact talking to an actual parrot, in fact?

—The facticity of the story is irrelevant, owing to its function as a proto-Foucauldian paradigm in regard to culturo-epistemological entrapment.

—Well of course it is, said Is. And I'm a red parrot too. But this still doesn't clear up the history deal as it relates to Our Lady of the Fire Water.

—It does, Is-Book, but by the subtle and wily insurgencies which have crept up out of the nasty sty of modernity your mind has become so withered that, like some necrotic limb, it lacks the strength and suppleness to grasp anything of significant weight. You and everyone you know is as to the missionary.

—Who is the red parrot then? Is that Monica?

—Slander not your second wife. Anyway, let's forget it.

—You are a cruel master – you know I can't forget a thing.

Concluding their wearisome conversation in this way, and having fairly snogged the face off his favourite Saint, Is stepped out into the clearing with his master to be introduced to whoever or whatever dwelt there.

The Pirgoan man beckoned Don and Is over, indicating that they could sit down on one of the logs.

—Nice chest, he said. You got a pet beaver or something?

Don looked down to find without surprise that the chest had remained with them even as they passed out of Time.

—Although the matters it contains be in writing, said Don to the Pirgoan, it is still full of such food for thought as you wouldn't believe – or perhaps you more than any other would. I think we are of like mind, we two: I disdain the whole gamut of civilization as much as your people do, from that ragged bag of filth the so-called Golden Age, through the Renaissance and Enlightenment (though they be more Remortssance and EnDarkenment to my mind), to the wretched Technocracy we are forced to dwell within in the days which are erroneously described as the Present. But there is one thing that the chest does not serve for, and that is as the receptacle for corporeal food. I myself would rather cut off my own head than eat anything, the effect being equivalent, for it slows the mind, but my servant would appreciate a meal, if you are able to provide one.

—There's some leftover stew somewhere, said the Pirgoan, looking over the dusky ground all around the fire in pursuit of it.

—As long as it is still to be found outside of your people's stomachs, he will eat it.

—Got it, said the Pirgoan, as he hauled a pan out from where it had been all along, behind his sitting legs. It's just some beans and sweetcorn and stuff – look out for fag butts.

—You see! said Don to Is. Being neither Samhain, nor Imbolc, nor Beltaine, nor Lughnasad – druid feast days all, as ordained by the stars, planets and their satellites above – these people refuse to partake of meat on the day which only a fool would believe is called Today.

—Let me have a moment with Monica, said Is. I feel very much in need of her – and a deep kiss on the lips it'll be, so look away.

Don handed the hallowed flask to his servant, and turned once again to the Pirgoan, who was ladling some mess from the saucepan at his feet into a plastic bowl.

—I think the dogs might have had a bit of a go at it too, he said, stirring the beans round with a fork as if seeking evidence of tracks or a scent trail.

—What number are you within this simple community? said Don.

The Pirgoan passed the stew to Don, who passed it to Is.

—Dunno. It changes. Fifteen?

—Where are these others?

—Van, said the Pirgoan, pointing with the fork over his shoulder. What are you two doing anyway?

Don smiled his most aloof and condescending smile.

—Your question is spoken in the present tense, and yet you know full well what we are doing, because you are in our company and can observe my servant engaged in his wanton gluttony, and me here talking to you.

—He's a smart-arse isn't he? said the Pirgoan smiling with black teeth at Is.

—I was engaging in that human activity known as making a point, said Don. How devious is the language we speak, for it asks in the Present, but is interested only in Past and Future. I assume you are enquiring as to how and why we came to be in this wood, and what we are intending to do now we are in it. The truth is that I can say neither what we have done in the Past, nor what we intend to do in the Future, because I refuse to countenance the existence of either, both being as they are chimeras heaped up on the shoulders of Humanity to the degree that he, Man, is so overladen that he believes there is nothing between them, only a narrow dividing line, forgetting of course his own head. Although you no doubt follow the noble Caligny calendar of the ancient Celts, I should assure you that Past and Future definitely do not have any existence.

The Pirgoan reached into his shirt pocket and withdrew a crumpled joint, to which he applied the embers of a stick which had lain in the fire. Pungent smoke mingled with and overcame the sharp smelling cherrywood smoke which had led Don and Is to the clearing, and the mixture drifted between and around the three people sitting upon the log until it was ushered up by the heat of the fire into the sky beyond the canopy of twisted oaks. Is, revivified by the bean stew and another brief osculation with the saintly hip flask, leant around the obstacle of his master better to see the Pirgoan, and said:

—Don't be put off by the odd ways of my master, he's actually a fine thing. But you have to get used to his face and ways of saying. The truth is that I've never heard him make any sense at all. He thinks you're druids, but it's a compliment.

The Pirgoan nodded, a subdued smile creeping on to his face.

—Wonder how many druids are running a 5K rig? *Digestif!* he then said, and rose. He walked over to his van, at which several other Pirgoans joined him. Soon they were gone into its interior.

—If there's fifteen of them, they're keeping nice and quiet in those vans, said Is. I only saw five at most just then.

—It is possible that upon our approach to their blessed enclave they assumed animal form so that their lone emissary might assess our behaviour best to secure the safety of the community.

—Or it could be they're off nicking lead, or scoring, though they're certainly more crusty than pikey.

—Your old friend the crow, who's found for himself a habitation in the tree before us – I wouldn't be surprised if he were in actual fact a druid child making ready to play a lighthearted trick on us. You'd do well to mind your head from corvine acorn attack. And I won't even begin to explore the true caninity of the dogs who greeted me with such anthropomorphic anger. You are a poor scientist, Is-Book, if your imagination is free to roam only to a distance allowed it by the tether of your experience.

—I've never said I was a scientist at all, sir. It's the last thing I'd want to be if you're what scientists are.

—In fact, continued Don ignoring his servant, if you look all around you, you'll see oaks, many with mistletoe twining up their trunks and round their branches. As the word 'druid' stems from the Gaelic word for oak tree, *darach*, it is highly likely that every tree in this wood, in being one of those ancient species, is in fact an inhabitant of Pirgo currently in tree form. Mistletoe was seen by the ancient druids as a sign of the touch of lightning, and the oak, so often struck by lightning, became Thor the thunderer's tree, so really you should dress yourself in that creeper and be as one with this druidic clan, seeing as you seem to attract electricity from out of the clouds.

—Well, being struck by lightning again might be a welcome mercy, because that lie-down I had in the iron belly of Jumbo was the best rest I've had since I broke my leg twenty years ago and couldn't go to school for two weeks. But if I got struck again, maybe I'd go one further and start remembering stuff that's never happened at all – and I have known that feeling, now and then.

—Now and then indeed, Is-Book, that being the nature of it. Déjà vu is what the phenomenon is called; literally rendered: 'already seen'.

—It's an odd one. The last time it happened to me I was just sitting there with the kids and Wife Ruthless, and everything everyone said had already been said in those exact same words, and we were repeating it as if by magic. It was a strong feeling, like love or hate or fear.

—I think you might be on to something here, Is-Book. Déjà vu has not as yet earned itself an entry within my grand systematics, and yet it seems to fit so perfectly with everything we know to be true. Perhaps your science is not so poor.

—You may know it to be true; I just have the words like a swarm of bees buzzing in the hive of my head. But what do you think it is that causes this deja-vu? Is it a real thing, because it certainly feels like one.

—It's as real as anything else in this life, maybe moreso. In fact, you would provide an interesting test case, Is-Book. As the lightning strike blessed you with the ability to remember all spoken words down to the minutest detail, surely if déjà vu began while you were memorising a string of words, it could and would never stop, because your memory would provide itself with no ellision or disjunction to interrupt the experience. You would be in a permanent state of déjà vu. Moreover, you would surely eventually experience another déjà vu *within* that déjà vu; and then another; and another; and so on, until your consciousness was simply an ecstasy of Time within Time within Time, as to a hall of mirrors – and in fact, as to the True Reality of Things. It would seem to me that déjà vu is a momentary glimpse of both sides of the Forbidden Line at once. Perhaps here is a means, or at least a clue, to manifesting an eternal stasis of the hyperfine transition of hydrogen at the very non-entity of its point of transition. O Is-Book, you are occasionally of use!

—What you are saying is so far over my head, said Is, that it has ice on it.

—We should interrogate the kindly druids of Pirgo as to their own interpretation of déjà vu, said Don deep in thought and without taking

303

any notice of his servant. Doubtless they perceive it as a memory from a previous incarnation, which would avouch a rare correspondence between the druidical and classical traditions.

—This is all very interesting I'm sure, said Is. But I really wish you'd give up the idea of druids. Look at their vans; and their trainers; and look! here they come now – the awfulness of their tattoos is enough to make me know them for who they are, though my own tattoo wouldn't win any prizes.

—Except perhaps that item, with bowl-shaped end, crafted by the ligneous cutler, commonly called the wooden spoon.

The Pirgoan to whom they had spoken, as well as his companions, came out of the van once more, crossed the clearing, nodded silent greetings to their unasked-for guests, and slumped down upon the ground with their backs against the felled logs, staring into the fire. Soon afterwards, another van emptied itself of its inhabitants, who also came over, and sat with the group. Most sat with their eyes closed, nodding gently; several hummed to themselves.

—Excuse my interruption of your meditations, said Don. But it is incumbent on me as the means by which the restitution of the West may occur to glean what I can from your people as a case study. I must ask the following questions. Do you find that the composition of the soil as to its acidity, texture, depth and so on, necessarily fosters within your people a different attitude to the treatment of health and sickness, as compared with, say, the druids of Devon, whose soil, being rich in iron, is very different? Presumably there is ample opportunity for such a comparison during the solstices, equinoxes and other ritual events, at which times you form a sacral convocation.

The Pirgoans continued to nod and hum as they were, as indifferent to Don's words as to everything else around them.

—Their meditations are deep, Is-Book, said Don. Such is the connection between these druids and the nature they call Mother around them, that the ruinous language which crumbles from my tongue is meaningless to them. O degenerate man, among whom

I must number myself! I look upon the purity of mind of these druids and weep!

Is was again about to inform his master of his error in taking these people for druids when a female voice, singing words indistinct, came to their ears as if from the depths of a cave, infinitely seductive, sirenic. The timbre of her voice drifted through the woodland in a great trail, ascending, swelling, rushing up, and then ceased in a great creaking as if a giant oak were splintering open above their heads. Don looked around himself with excitement.

—We must be at some omphalos or meeting of laylines! he said, no longer lamenting the state of man. Do you hear the celestial sounds coming down to us?

—It's coming out of the sound system in that van there, sir. It's a kind of music called trance.

—I refuse to listen to you anymore. At one time I had conceived you to be pure of heart and mind, free from the prejudices our species has built up as a nest for itself – only to discover too late that it be a snare.

—Whatever you want to say sir, said Is. But you're going to make a right idiot of yourself.

—Be quiet and let me hear the diapasons made manifest in my ear. Ah, *musica universalis!* You have sought me out in this place and like Beulah offer me a respite from the harrowings of eternity!

A squeezed yowling noise ensued, superimposed upon the deep beat, filtering down through the middle frequencies in a whine similar to that emitted by a colic baby; but the sound and the steady beat below full of analogue warmth. Don smiled beatifically down into the fire as several women among the assembly of Pirgoans hauled themselves off the ground and began pulsing the parts of their bodies to the beat of the music. As each of the dancers turned, a miniature of the fire at the centre of the clearing was cast from the surface of each inwardly-turned eye. Don was transported by the rhythmic movements of the dancing women and the music to feel the whole clearing as a womb, throbbing with the potential of its parturition.

—Very soon, said Don, if such a thing can be said of Eternity, the sinuous properties of this music are going to coax the hyperfine transition of hydrogen out of its hidey-hole. I can feel it coming!

Is scoffed, and looked about himself – only to find that he was being beckoned over towards one of the vans by the Pirgoan who had welcomed them to the clearing.

—Go to him, directed Don without even turning his head.

—But how did you know? said Is.

—Go with him and allow the scepticism to be chased out of you.

—But what if I'm frightened of him, sir?

—The words of a sceptic. When have I ever let you down, Is-Book? Go with him and do as he says, and you will be better for it. Chance has placed us here to learn of these druids.

Is yielded to the strong arm of the Pirgoan, which guided him away from the fire across the clearing to the side door of the van, through which he was delivered into the vehicle's interior. Gone were the delicate squelches and squeaks of the music; within the horsebox – for that is what it once had been – the music from the sound system several vans away throbbed with bass alone, as if they were submerged in water. Inside was a wood burning stove chained to the wall, its chimney rising through a hole punched in the roof. Veneered cabinets, a fold-up table and a wardrobe door were tesselated in a hodge-podge within the interior. On the table: a mirror, razorblade and triangular wrap of card.

Neither spoke as the Pirgoan undertook the preparations: a proportion of the square crystals cut onto the mirror from the wrap, crushed carefully with the side of the blade, then chopped into a fine dense powder, the inclinations of the blade gliding one way then another in the priestly expert hands. Divided, re-amalgamated, divided again, the powder finally brought into four thin lines of equal mass; the note rolled, the Pirgoan bent and administered first to one nostril, then to the other.

Is looked at him; the Pirgoan nodded and passed the note. Is shrugged, and snorted the remaining pair of lines.

The taste like soap, but sweet. And the icy tingle there at the back of the nose, and the sweet drip, like a thawing pear drop.

Drip.

They crossed the clearing back to the fire and sat down, Is at his master's side. Don still watched in a fervour the hypnotic movements of the dancing women, the firelight flashing from the jewellery at their wrists and ankles, and the flowing folds of their robes and their gleaming eyes like innumerable constellations exploding before him. A long time it had been since he had taken pleasure in the company of women. The music full of intricate space, as if he could wander into it, and open a multitude of portals into himself, and feel all the different sounds and frequencies separately, as if through a thousand ears, his whole body simply aural sense cells, feeling the full fabric of the music at every scale of its complex physicality. These were goddesses!

Is looked around himself and muttered.

—What kind of a life is this? Living in a horse box, tramping through mud and trying to get stoned on powdered pear drops. Stupid.

Drip.

Don spoke:

—Eschewing the vanities of so-called Science, the Progress of Knowledge, the neat lineation of Cause and Effect – by this, the people remain free. The solidity of the ground is but an Illusion! Inhibitions neither of the body nor the mind blot their Existence, whence they are Contented.

Pop!

A small explosion reported from the interior of one of the vans, and the music sagged and expired. From the flash of light came thereafter a fire.

—Fuck, the inverter's gone again, said one of the dancers, and she ran to the van to extinguish the growing flames.

Jolted from the pleasant reverie which the music had bequeathed to him, Don asked inwardly, What commotion is this?

Drip.

And upon the log beside him, Isaiah. As well as beside him, upon the log. Isaiah as well, upon him beside, and the log inside beside, inside Isaiah –

Is felt the top of himself sinking down into the bottom of himself, and the whole of himself sinking into the ground, heading for the centre.

—O, he said.

Sinking further and further, Is soon ceased to be Is, and instead became an echo travelling inward to the circumference of eternity, where he found the nucleus of time.

Is was not.

The air – but it was not the air – was filled with tiny golden beetles, each with twenty one spots upon its back. Is became as Levy-Bruhl's indigenous Brazilian tribesman, who really was, in manifest fact, a red parrot, though for Is a golden beetle made itself of an infinite number of golden beetles come together, and each of these itself made of – O God. He could not stand, but simply gawped into the beetled eternity which ploughed through the cells of him in multiples of Twenty-One. And it intensified, and intensified, beyond all the possibilities of reason to represent, each moment insided-out, and then that insided-out, ad infinitum, at a velocity which would shame the sluggish light, to the end that all thought and being was merely a taut membrane which thrummed and pulsated in its primordial rawness. At the last moment, before his complete removal into infinite self-extinction, Is managed a final thought: these *were* druids.

Then he was lost.

Don watched the woman put the fire out and then retrieve a twenty year-old battery-powered stereo from under one of the seats of the van, which she brought out to the clearing and placed ingloriously upon the bent ash-choked grill of a spent disposable barbecue. She pushed the button down and the music began, the plastic and aluminium trim of the device buzzing and rattling to the thin nasal performance of its minuscule speakers. The cassette tape slurred unsteadily for a time and then righted itself.

—This is disappointing, said Don to himself.

He turned to Is, with whom he had intended to share his disappointment, but Is was preoccupied in very slowly falling off the log upon which he still miraculously sat. His body arched sideways like a burned match, twisted and knotted and immobile.

—What are you doing, Is-Book? Don asked.

But Is could no sooner have spoken than flown into the air and landed upon one of the oak leaves of the canopy above, though this is precisely what, in the form of a beautiful golden beetle, he thought he was doing.

—Are you possessed?

Is's only reply was to evacuate the contents of his stomach on to the shoes of the Pirgoan sitting next to him. The Pirgoan, in a similar state to Is, was not concerned.

The ratty sound emanating from the silver box continued to violate the air of the clearing.

—Turn that shit off will you, shouted one of the Pirgoans at the woman.

—Fuck off.

—Fucking Waterboys, fuck sake.

—Get me a new inverter then. Fucking Chinese shit you're always buying.

—Everything's Chinese now.

—Everything's shit.

Deep within the well of his disappointment, Don closed his eyes and intoned the number Twenty-One to himself, such was his belief in its powers. But even that activity could not calm him. What a vile people were this tribe, masquerading as druids, but really only a congregation of the basest caterpillars who had forgotten they lived in Basildon and had ended up polluting this wood.

Is, meanwhile, was looking into the eye of the universe and doing the golden beetle dance with his other druid beetle friends cha-cha-cha.

28

The sun came up in the morning, as it always had done, and as it always would. Our faithful if irritating company of two awoke huddled close to the soft white down of the ashes of last night's fire – one of them with a formidable hangover – and without so much as a farewell to the inhabitants of the enclave, travelled from Pirgo to the larger settlement of Havering. Although they checked all the time for their pursuers, they saw no-one, except a farmer or two, and several potters who had set up their kilns on the clay seams which the road opened up and who were making pots for the next market day, so successfully had our heroes ventured into what appeared to be another time.

    —Overall, said Don, I do not like to follow a map; and I think you can probably guess why. We have eluded our pursuers, and we are some distance from where they had last seen us. So I do not think we need to worry. On reflection, now that we are safe, a map is as likely to interfere with Chance as a crowd, which if it's not already an oft-quoted aphorism, certainly should be.

    —I'm not so sure sir, said Is. About the people, I mean, not your aphorism thing, which I reckon to be infinitely wise of course. If we could skirt between the places named on the map, say just west of Rumford through the woods, and then just north of Ilford, we'd be safer off I reckon.

    —I will make a concession on this occasion, but you should be aware that following this map significantly reduces the number of places at which we might cross the river, unless you plan to stay just west of Rumford for the rest of your life. Otherwise, we should have to swim across.

—You know I cannot swim sir, said Is.

—Well, I am not going to do your swimming for you. Either we swim across, or take the bridge at Ilford, which is most certainly still on the map, but also forms part of the land which our pursuers will know.

—It's a hopeless choice, said Is.

—It is best, then, to allow chance – I mean Chance – to make the decision for you.

—Very well. But I am not happy.

—The pursuit of happiness is the primary cause of misery in the world, Don informed his servant. Why not simply aim for contentment, or the absence of suffering.

—That is precisely why I am not happy – because I can smell the presence of suffering approach.

—Your nose has been broken so many times it doesn't even know how to smell, said Don. So cease your worrying and let's get on with it.

Is, being a diligent and obedient squire, followed his master – though he did grumble occasionally, especially as he continued to find the chest in his custody – to the end that they soon arrived at Ilford. Here, they joined the A118, a tedious and unpleasant road for walking, down which flowed a ceaseless stream of cars, vans and lorries, by which stones, gravel, dust and grit were again kicked up into the faces of our heroes, and from the tarmac of which the heat from the sun was amplified so that the soles of Is's feet swelled and caused him pain with each tread.

And against the dictates of his master, Is could in fact smell the fetid rotting mud to their south, where a hot saltwet wind tore up the marshland channels of the River Roding, buffeting the spearpoints of the grass which bobbed up and down in clumps; and beyond, the slimy ooze of the Thames estuary at low tide under the summer sun, which burned the whole county until it was as dry as straw, and continued within its star's heart to synthesise the lighter elements without design.

(But it is Time. This pair can cease talking until we get them to where they need to be, quickly and efficiently, with a minimum of fuss. So:)

In time they came to the Mile End Road, which is not in Oxford, nor anywhere near it as roads go, but in London; on the route, no less, which the peasants had taken six centuries before; precisely the route, in fact, that our intrepid though voluble heroes had intended to avoid.

(What might happen to bring the mob to their leaders? Ah, how about this:)

The chest, still clinging hard to their now mercifully silent company, and tolerated begrudgingly by the determined pair, disgorged suddenly one of the loose leaves of Don's *Encyclopaedia*. Don, out of sheer habit – not that he would ever admit to obeying such habit, oh no – ran in pursuit to retrieve it. Wherever the wind blew the sheet, the author of the words written upon it followed behind in pursuit; to the end that the piece of paper, and then the man, made their way right into the centre of the road, where both were run over, to the greater detriment of the sentient being, who was rushed to the Accident and Emergency Department of the Mile End Hospital.

(Yes! That will do fine. And while he's unconscious, we'll assemble our mob at the gates and there will be no wriggling out of this one.)

Don awoke to find himself upon his back in a bed. He lay there, looking up at the artificially striated tiles of the suspended ceiling. Long and sinuous, a curtain encircled the bed. Occupying three chairs at his bedside were two men and a woman whom he had never before seen, speaking one to another in hushed French. Turning his head, Don located the whereabouts of his assistant at his side, which comforted him. Is was embroiled in the exploration of his latest sorrowing, caused it seemed by the presence of the others within the cubicle, his head cast down almost between his legs and his arms wrapped around himself.

—What troubles you, Is-Book? Don managed to croak in a weak voice.

Is gave a formidable start at his master's unexpected words, before lowering his head towards Don's in order to whisper the following:

—I thought you'd never come round, sir. Who on earth are these people?

—I had hoped you might be able to tell me.

The words exited Don's mouth in a husky wheeze. He found himself worn-out; he lay back and felt the weight of himself pulled inexorably downwards, but borne up by the bed like some omniscient hand.

—Imposter gravity! he said to himself.

—I have no idea who they are, said Is. They followed us here. I don't like this.

He pointed at the three people on the other side of his master's bed. Conversation ceased within this small group as each in turn came to focus his and her attention upon the servant's quivering finger and what it portended; namely: disapprobation, unease, agitation.

—What is it? said Don.

—I'm not completely sure yet, replied Is. But their way of talking, if it is talking at all, is a thing I don't like.

—Perhaps your friend, said the man at whom Is was pointing to Don, is upset about the accident.

—What accident? said Don.

The man rose from his seat, made a conciliatory smile to the two others who remained seated, and approached the bed.

—The road traffic accident we were all involved in several hours ago.

Don pondered this in silence.

—I don't trust him, said Is. You should have heard them before you woke up, like they were speaking with their mouths full, fuller than full, and of mad talk. I don't like it one bit, feeling like a piece of prey. What will happen will happen, sir, and all unfolded straight and unrumpled we'll see which way the laughter's being done, and by no means kind.

—No one is laughing, Is-Book.

—How can you say such a thing. The whole damned place is laughing. Even you are laughing.

—I beg your pardon my friend, said Don, who was indeed chuckling at the nonsense his squire was spouting, though it hurt his ribs.

—Explain their nonsense talk, Is said, and again pointed at the three people.

Don beckoned Is toward him, and indicated that he wished for a drink to moisten his throat. This having been administered, he proceeded to speak:

—You are merely exhibiting your ignorance once again, Is-Book. The gentleman and his companions were speaking in French, which is a language spoken by those of the French nation, as well as by eastern Canadians, Algerians, and a number of peoples residing in those regions which neighbour the Gulf of Guinea.

There was a pause while Is assimilated this new class of information.

—Is it so different, Is asked, from the way we speak?

—It is as different as it sounds, which is to say moderately so to those with an ear for languages – (again, he requested assistance, and drank in order better to help the words out) – or extremely so in the case of those few people who are or were not aware that other languages exist or existed, the class of people to which you belong, or belonged.

—The world grows stranger with me every day, said Is.

The man who had risen into the unexpected witnessing of this curious exchange waited patiently and politely for its words and implications to taper off into oblivion before speaking again, which he did using the following words:

—Allow me to introduce myself, and my companions. My name is Ian McEwan, and this is Claude Menard and his daughter Bérènice Colimaçon.

The ancient Frenchman and his aged daughter made a deferential nod towards Don and Is, and muttered a greeting which was neither French nor English but more of a stew of the two, though concocted with very great good will. Despite this, suspicion and dolour continued to reside in the lineaments of Is's face, whose point of interest did not leave McEwan. Don greeted the two French people in their own language – in which, judging by his accent, he was not so proficient as he might have believed – and then turned his attention to McEwan, though without the rancour which his servant's looks exhibited. McEwan remained perfectly composed in spite of Is's aggressive countenance, and retook his seat at the bedside. His face was somewhat rodentlike, pointed at the snout, and shaded a peculiarly not unhealthy grey. The mouth tight, intellectual, self-aware; the eyes absolutely penetrative. Before the eyes were mounted a pair of spectacles whose lenses exhibited very great circularity; the lenses, taken together, resembling in a way the schematic for the hyperfine transition of hydrogen, though thankfully Don did not notice. McEwan crossed his legs at the knee and leaned back in his chair. The two members of the Menard family, seeing that their contribution to any conversation was neither desired nor possible, began perusing and occasionally discussing amongst themselves the loose-leaved contents of two folders which had occupied them before Don had returned to consciousness.

—I hope you don't mind us being here, said McEwan. I thought it only proper to make sure you were okay. The doctors say you suffered a fracture to the shin bone.

—That's an old one, said Is. Unless you've done the other one for him too.

—I'm afraid I didn't do anything. Your friend stepped out in front of us, and here McEwan nodded to the Menards in order to identify them as passengers.

—What a face he has! cried Is. The driver of the sorry face. And he should be sorry.

—I am indeed sorry that you stepped out without looking, said McEwan.

—I would have been infinitely sorrier if I had looked, said Don. For who can say that it is his or her business to meddle in the workings of Chance, the daughter, or princess, or serving-wench of Time – I forget at the moment in my convalescence.

—I've spoken to the police already, said McEwan. They want to talk to you – they left a number at the desk.

—We will have nothing to do with the police, said Don.

McEwan let out a short involuntary laugh of surprise.

—They may well choose to have something to do with you, he said.

—They can try, said Don.

—Yes, they can try, said Is.

At this point M. Menard rocked back in his chair, clapped his hands, and gave a cry of ancient French enjoyment, something in the papers which he and his daughter perused having bequeathed such an emotion to him.

—What are they doing? asked Is, eyeing them with suspicion.

—M. Menard is the son of Pierre Menard, the French symbolist poet, said McEwan. They are in England to present one of his works, previously thought to have been lost, at a conference. I'm speaking at the same conference. I was just taking M. Menard and his daughter to lunch when you stepped in front of me.

—He will keep saying it won't he! said Is. 'Stepped in front of him'. Go off, man!

—The rules of diplomacy are not suspended, Is-Book, said Don. It costs nothing to be polite. But continue please.

McEwan continued:

—M. Menard and his daughter are looking over the work of their father and grandfather, the work they are presenting.

—A family concern, said Is.

—Be quiet. Is it good? asked Don.

There was a pause. McEwan's inscrutable face allowed a chink of scrutability to blemish it. It seemed to Don and Is that it was not so good.

—It is a (and here McEwan paused to find the right word) a different kind of work.

—Different to what?

—Different to all others.

McEwan then exhibited a sparkle of self-conscious wit.

—Different in being the same, he said.

—Oh here we go, said Is. He talks like you sir and your favourite joke: One leg is both the same. Here's your new companion, I say. Pay me and I'll be off back home, not that I have one. Oh Ruth!

—Shut up, Is-Book. Different in being the same, how so?

—Pierre Menard, writing in the mid-1930s shortly before he passed away, attempted to re-write *Don Quixote*.

—*Don Quick-soot*? Never heard of it, said Is.

—*Don Quixote* is a novel of the Spanish Golden Age, said Don.

—What! said Is. I thought we were talking about *Don Quick-soot*, and now you go and mention *Don Key-Hoe-Tea*.

Just then, the conversation occurring between Menard *père et fille* disgorged also the French pronunciation for *Don Quixote* into the little curtained enclosure which contained Don's bed.

—And now we have *Donkey-Shot* too!

—All three are but one and the same, said Don. Not that I believe either in the possibility of oneness or sameness, except insofar as the hyperfine transition of hydrogen manifest itself.

—Why the different names then, sir?

—Within the English language, it is a matter of intellectual pretension and historico-linguistic pedantry, said Don. There are accorded to each pronunciation multifarious proofs of its definitiveness by innumerable charlatans the world over. The truth is that Cervantes in all probability currently sits in some ante-room of eternity sipping a *kalimotxo* and laughing his creation to see. Know, good servant, that a writing True and Real will produce not clarity of thought, but confusion.

—But what is any of it! said Is.

Addressing Is's bewildered looks, McEwan explained:

—*Don Quixote* is regarded as the first modern novel, as the originator of the novel as we know it. It is very important.

—It is the beginning of the end, said Don.

—The chicken *and* the egg! said Is. But surely you must hate it, sir, what with it being writing.

—Menard's version was thought to have been a hoax, said McEwan after waiting for Don to conclude ignoring his servant's words. Menard himself has long been considered a hoax, to not have even existed. But he did exist, and here is his family, and there is his work, which even when it was thought to have existed, rumour had it to have been destroyed.

—This is an extremely complicated chicken, said Is, with extremely troublesome eggs.

—The rules of your idiocy are clearly not yet suspended either, Is-Book, said Don. Please try not to speak until you have something worth saying to say. What would be the purpose of rewriting the *Quixote*? Has he rewritten it for the French taste?

—Oh no, not at all, said McEwan. It is not a rewriting in the sense that it takes certain features and events from the original and deploys them in a new context. It is a rewriting in that Menard was attempting to write the very same words as Cervantes had.

—In Spanish?

—In Spanish. And Menard didn't even know Spanish. Nor would he permit himself to learn it. Nor did he re-read *Don Quixote* before making the attempt.

—And did he succeed?

—M. Menard and Mme Colimaçon say that he did. The round table discussion tomorrow includes Jerome McGann, the eminent textual critic, who claims that he didn't. Apparently the matter is not black and white, though I don't see how it can't be.

—Nothing is black and white, said Don, not even black and white. I would be interested in having a look. Do you think I might?

—But writing, sir, said Is. I thought it was a peril?

Everyone having learned already that ignoring Is was the best way to deal with him, McEwan asked M. Menard if Don could read a part of the manuscript; and, after negotiations of some length and complexity had been transacted, he was given permission.

—M. Menard wants me to point out to you that this is the original manuscript of the work, and so is irreplaceable. McGann made it a condition of his attendance that the original would be brought to the conference and made available to him on the evening before the discussion.

—But there are two manuscripts, said Don as he looked at the folders in the ancient man's hands.

—Yes, in the buff folder is the manuscript of Menard's *Quixote*; in the green folder is a handwritten copy of Cervantes' *Don Quixote* which Menard made after the original once he had completed his own version. The Menards believe that this copy was made in order that Pierre Menard could more easily and accurately assess whether he had achieved his aim.

—If they are the same, how do you know which is which?

—That's a good question, said McEwan, and he turned to M. Menard and repeated Don's question in French. He received an answer and translated it for Don:

—The difference between the two is identified by which colour folder the manuscript is in. He must have made the copy very soon after achieving his own *Quixote,* because he uses the same paper and ink, and the handwriting is no different.

—So the folder they are in is the only difference?

McEwan repeated the process of interrogating M. Menard, and conveyed his response.

—M. Menard says that, apart from very few minor differences on only two or three sheets, this is the only identifying difference. For all intents and purposes, the folders are the sole means of denoting which is which manuscript.

—I wish M. Menard luck in defending his father's work against the depredations of the academy, said Don.

—He thanks you with all his heart, said McEwan.

—So I am to look at the contents of the buff-coloured folder? asked Don as Menard handed the folders to McEwan, who handed them to Don.

—That is correct.

He opened the folder and discovered about fifty foolscap pages covered on the recto side in the writing of a fastidious hand.

—There is something of beauty in such handwritten pages, said Don.

—I don't believe I am hearing this, sir! said Is. What has happened to you?

—I use a personal computer these days, said McEwan without nostalgia.

Don turned the pages with care. About half way through, he stopped and read a passage in the interior of his mind:

la verdad, cuya madre es la historia, émula del tiempo, depósito de las acciones, testigo de lo pasado, ejemplo y aviso de lo presente, advertencia de lo por venir.

—Fetch my things! Don said to Is, who immediately reached down behind his chair and drew from the chest located there – so devoted did it seem to remaining within their company – the notebooks his master had abandoned several days earlier, though the servant shook his head.

—I don't like this return to writing at all sir, he said.

Don selected the appropriate book, and turned to the relevant page.

—Merely an aid to my calculations, he said, reproving his squire. I shall write nothing, be sure of that! My mind is feeling somewhat befuddled following the injury which you all rumour me to have sustained. But I shall emerge victorious: the burrows of isopsephy and *gematria* are as the breeding tunnels for the darkling flint. An obdurate Reality shall be born therefrom!

Don flicked between pages in his notebook, assembling from it a list of the letters and words of the Spanish into his isopsephic system, making a note of the values as he went. Mme. Colimaçon, fearing a possible accident, raised a peremptory objection to these activities, and demanded that McEwan discover their purpose. Don assured McEwan that the sheets would remain unharmed, that he was merely undertaking an assessment of them through the use of his reference work. Menard and Colimaçon, partially mollified, watched watchfully the madman at work upon the work of their own madman. Such eccentrics require latitude, Menard said to his daughter as he settled into the role of observing Don.

Although the presence of accents above two of the letters in the Spanish passage under analysis troubled his systematics somewhat, Don decided that, in this merely exploratory instance, minor digressions from absolute accuracy would have to be tolerated. He went to work, writing down in a small notebook the numerical values for each of the letters in turn. Very soon, the values were all present. Producing their sum, he divided this result by the number of letters analysed, obtaining the raw material for his isopsephic judgement. This he fed into his mysterious equation, mediated by the number Twenty-One and all that it might represent, which was everything that is, and after a short time a result was produced. Don gave a sudden gasp, and looked about the room in bewilderment as if it were engaged in falling down about him.

—What is it, sir? asked Is.

Don's habitual caution and perspicacity drew his emotions back into him before he spoke, and directed his repetition of the calculation. After some minutes, the same figure was produced: the closest that any assessed passage had ever come to the hallowed number. He gasped again, this time his features exhibiting a flash, as if he were but a filament of flesh illuminated by a downrush of pure joy. He rose in a frenzy of exultation, clutching the manuscript sheet to his hollow chest, and scattering the loose sheets from the two sheaves which had slipped from their folders all over the floor.

—We are nearly there, my dear Is-Book! We are nearly there! Close to perfection! A writing to end all writing! Come, self-assassin, do thy work in the world!

And, gathering his filthy clothing into a bundle, before McEwan or Menard or Colimaçon could even move, he swept out of the cubicle wearing no more than the gown and paper bracelet the hospital had dressed him in, still clutching the manuscript sheet.

—The rules of correct habiliment are not suspended! shouted Is after his master as he threw his master's notebooks back into the chest and dragged it out to follow him.

Behind them, M. Menard attempted to rise, but had instantly fallen to his knees, and was now engaged in a desperate ululation as he sifted helplessly through the manuscript sheets which had slipped from the two folders to become irreparably intermixed.

At the end of the ward, Don paused by the reception desk in order to calculate the means by which he could exit the hospital.

—This place is a labyrinth, said Is as he caught up with him.

—It has the ugliest interior I've ever seen, said Don.

—These signs make no sense at all, said Is.

—These signs are not for the likes of you or me. What does your instinct tell you?

—To get the hell out of here.

—How does it propose we achieve such a thing?

—Any way we can, sir.

—Your instinct is a little abstract today, Is-Book.

—I am having trouble with the lowness of the ceilings, and the nastiness of the lighting.

—Further proof that you are a sensitive instrument, my dear friend, as if any such proof was needed. We shall ask someone the way.

Finding the first person he could to enquire as to the quickest means of leaving the hospital, Don spoke again.

—Excuse me, he said. Would you be able to tell me and my friend here how we might get to the exit of the hospital? We are in somewhat of a hurry.

—O sir, look what you've done now! said Is, who buried his face so deep into his hands that to all the world it was dead.

—What have I done? asked the master.

What Don had done was be himself: his obstinate refusal to recognise the relevance or utility of memory for the transaction of a lived life had led him to seek directions from Ian McEwan, the very man who had pursued him and his hapless squire up the corridor, the very man from whom he had flown.

—This will end badly, said Is.

—I fear no-one, said Don. Do I know this individual?

However, McEwan was less concerned for the present with reprimanding Don and Is than he was with securing assistance for M. Menard, who, in the grief of sifting through the two irremediably mixed-up manuscripts, had collapsed. A young doctor was accosted to that end by McEwan, who informed her of what had happened.

—Sounds very much like heart trouble, she said without moving.

—I'll take you to him now, said McEwan.

—The heart does not take its orders from the brain, said Don. It is its own engine, and decides for itself when it will beat. The ancient Greeks perceived the movement of the muscles beneath the skin, which to them resembled mice. It is for this reason that we call muscles 'muscles', for the word is derived from *musculus*, the diminutive of *mus*, which meant 'mouse'. The heart, then, might be seen as a kind of nest of mice, an image of which I am fond. Yet how will you love with but a nest of mice in your bosom?

—Heart trouble's the worst, said Is. Rather head trouble any day.

—You think so? said the doctor.

—I know so, said Is. My wife has given me this dirty great pain in the heart, having no heart to speak of herself. And look at him (gesturing at Don), whose brains, I have heard, are rotten. But know this: he treats me better than Wife Ruthless ever did. Whatever the heart decides to do, the rest of you's done for. You can't think yourself out of love, and God knows I've tried.

—'Twenty-One knows I've tried', is what you should have said there, said Don.

—Yes, sir, said Is. Sorry sir.

—Gird your heart and mind, said Don. The world shall cry in shame at itself when it witnesses the destruction of the Forbidden Line – of every Forbidden Line – at the ascension of the Twenty-One!

—Too much trouble with one will lead to trouble in the other, said the doctor. But shall we attend to your friend?

McEwan nodded, and pointed up the ward towards where Menard could be found.

—I need to talk to these two, he then said, and turned to Don and Is.

The doctor therefore said goodbye and walked briskly towards the old man and his uncertain health.

(Enough! It is time to get them out the door amongst the mob.)

The sternness of McEwan's countenance more than made up for the slightness of his body; and, having turned towards Don and Is, he demanded the return of the manuscript sheet which Don still held in his possession. Is advised Don to do as McEwan had said, for although it was only a sheet of paper, it held the handwriting of the man's grandfather; and whilst it was the very writing upon it which made it valuable to Don – even though writing was supposed to be bad now, wasn't it? – who were they to lead an old man into distress? Don acceded to Is's wise words, but not before receiving permission from McEwan to recite the passage into the ear of his servant so that it might form a central pillar in the architecture of the Is-Book, coming so close as it did to being the perfect string of words in writing.

Everyone parted in a happier state than that in which they had come together, and the reader can rest assured that a story will very soon be dragged out of all this nonsense whether it likes it or not, kicking and screaming – as the phrase goes – if need be. *Read on!*

29

Negotiating their way out of the complex network of hallways and atria, Don and Is very soon found themselves approaching the gates of the hospital and about to rejoin Mile End Road. Don's perambulation was no more or less rickety than it had been for the crash, and Is had acquired a few more items within the Is-Book, which as his master assured him was the sole means of the restitution of all Being, and so both were contented. As they neared the exit, they noticed a large gathering of people beyond the gates, and at their fringes several dozen police officers, a number of them mounted. At the very same time, the people noticed them – and a great cheer went up. The mob had found them and there was no getting away now.

An energy travelled from one edge of the crowd – that closest to them – across to the other, focusing its attention upon our insufferable heroes. The crowd surged towards them, and the cheers swelled up out of it in a tuneless though exhilarating chorus as they and the chest containing Don's *Encyclopaedia* were lifted up and borne down the road by the people.

—Whatever type of egg we are sitting on, said Is to his master with resignation, I think it's about to hatch.

Don looked across the crowd of heads bobbing beneath him and considered.

—Perhaps you are not aware of the proclivity of the ring-billed gull, as well as certain other species of bird, to collect and incubate stones beneath the plummage of her proud breast.

Down the Mile End Road they were borne, and the streets were vibrant with the noise of the crowd, streamers and confetti, hurled toilet rolls unfurling, cans and bottles, and flints carried for weaponry, which shattered darkly against the walls. Signs were held aloft bearing written admonishment to various impositions. Everyone walked in one direction, as one, together, channelled down the thoroughfare, onwards, towards the City.

Don and Is looked about themselves from their unusual vantage point.

—Look at the broadness of this thoroughfare, said Don to his servant. And the particularity of the shops which line it, and at the magnitude of the buildings puncturing the horizon in the distance there. Does this not look suspiciously like London? I must admit that I don't even have to try not to remember how we got here – can the expanse of land between Havering and the East End be so featureless as to have quite passed me by?

—Now you mention it, sir, the last thing I remember before you got run over – and I think you'll agree that as far as memory goes, I'm not only the bees' but every other animals' knees too – is us talking about the bridge at Ilford and agreeing we should trust to chance, or Chance, who is sure to do what is best for us. It doesn't make sense at all.

—As far as your memory goes – if the mere idea of memory did not disgust me utterly – I would agree with you. I am no expert on the various ligamentous structures found in the limbs of tetrapods, but if we gain a muster of this superclass – for example, the human, elephant, giraffe, monkey, crocodile, dog, cat, newt and frog, we will find that they all share with anthropods two knees and two elbows; and yet only the very first walks upright, so singularly do humans mark themselves off from the animal world. O hubris! Mark well, Is-Book: those who walk upon all fours are happy; those who walk upon their hind legs are not. Is it not irrefutable fact that the orientation of an organism's body in the act of walking is indicative of that organism's relationship to Time; and, in our case, the phantasms Past and Future? We humans who have erected ourselves look forward with fear and turn back with shame and regret. And yet, seeing already and first of all the ground beneath her feet: look at the panther!

—Is this why you are so hunched over and knackered-looking, sir?

Just then the crowd began singing rousing songs from a pamphlet circulated in the crush, happily drowning out the chatter of our two scions of tedium. Accordions, fiddles, brass, guitars, penny whistles and recorders wreathed their melodies round one another, in accidental counterpoint, like churchbells whose chimes gradually cross, moving from a descending scale to a sonorous tapestry of sound.

Rattles were spun; klaxon sounded; the crowd desired to sing rousing songs. A call went out for 'Tax has tenet us alle', and thereafter a chorus of rustling paper whispered through the crowd as the people turned to the necessary page; and the songs began again:

Tax has tenet us alle,
  probat hoc mors tot validorum;
The kyng therof hade smalle,
  fuit in manibus cupidorum.
Hit hade harde honsalle,
  dans causam fine dolorum.
Revrawnce nede most falle,
  propter peccata malorum.

A cheer went up at the completion of the verse. This was more like it! Many of the crowd reminisced about the Poll Tax riots. People lined the flat roofs of the three-storied buildings above the crowd as it lurched onwards, drinking bottled beer above perspex signs for sportswear emporiums, mobile phone shops, grocers, a funeral parlour. Numerous domestic sound systems created a cacophony of competing rhythms, but still the sound of the crowd was loudest. A band of brass instruments ran round the melody one time further and came back to its beginning.

—Excuse me, said Don to one of the members of the crowd below him within the crush. Would you mind if I took a look into that book you're carrying?

—I'd be honoured, came the reply.

Don took the book offered to him and flicked through its pages.

—Well Is-Book, it would seem that the crowd is well prepared. Contained within the pages of this volume, brandished also by so many of the crowd which surrounds and lifts us up, are the *Anonimalle Chronicle*, the *Chronicon Angliae* of Thomas Walsingham, the *Chroniques* of Froissart, and Henry Knighton's *Chronicon* – all of which treat of the Peasants' Revolt. I think I had better put a little something between your ears, Is-Book, because every word of these writings spells trouble.

—TRISEPTIMUM: CHRONICLE: All books are bad, but some are worse than others. The books being carried around by this crowd are incomparably evil. Not only are they papery objects exhibiting pages of writing – which is the primary cause of their badness – but they are a collection of chronicles. A chronicle is a record of events in linear time – an abomination of the highest order, I barely need to point out – and here, to humour the method if nothing else, is our own record of the temporal development of that very word's linguistic form: Anglo-Norman *cronicle* begotten of Old French *chronique*, begotten of Latin *chronica*, begotten of Greek *khroniká*. We find, therefore, that all these words and their multiple modern English derivations (chronology, chronometer, chronic, anachronism, and so on) derive from Greek *khrónos*, 'time', whose deity, rendered Cronus in English, was the only first generation Titan who dared castrate his father, Uranus. Now, let's not be in any doubt that castrating one's father is an act most laudable, Is-Book. Our problem, though, is not with Cronus, but with the needs of the culture which invented him. Out of Chaos was brought Earth, Day and Night, from whence: Sky, Ocean, Moon, Sun, Water, Dawn, Intellect, Mortality, Divine Law and Memory, each with a name and body, albeit immortal. As words, these entities find their entity-ness; but as mythical beings (Gaia, Hemera, Nyx, Uranus, Pontus, etc.), the interrelationship of these entities can be mobilised by the inquisitive mind, and arranged in an order befitting the requirements of that mind's comfort. It is appropriate that the action of Cronus against his father enabled the second generation of Titans – already the mythic chaos is becalmed by the birth of new entities – for the entities enabled the construction of a divine *chronology* – a chronicle – where linear time enslaves true Time. Mark well that it was the white foam which Uranus's excised testicles produced in the sea which generated Aphrodite, the goddess of Love: love is but a word and two bollocks.

—Imagine a time, Don continued, before the codification of all Being into separate entities! What dapple there is to the heaving flank of Chaos! O give us back our freedom! O true Time, return and un-castrate us all!

The crowd was indifferent to the shouts of its leader from his place upon the shoulders of two of its strongest members, busy singing as it was. Is, however, had a question.

—What I don't understand, master, is where all these books are coming from. How is the crowd so well-prepared?

—These books, like every other book, have their origin in that abominable crucible of cultural detritus the printing press, which spews out the offspring of the hidden inkubus – so we might call it – working within. Now there is a machine I would like to destroy.

—But where is it? asked Is.

—The truth is that such propagatory devices are everywhere in our age as the so-called computers.

Passing up the streets, further members were sucked from their houses by the strange energy of the crowd, and made – they were not too sure how or why – to merge and sing with it. A great sack of flints was reached into, and the simplest weapon of all handed out to the new recruits.

The crowd found its progress obstructed by its own growing mass, and thrummed like the taught skin of a drum, waiting. Members of the crowd brayed for meanings, signs, interpretations: how should they be? All eyes turned to Don, held up high on the shoulders of his people.

He looked first one way then another to take in the faces of all of those around him, the many hundreds, the thousands, the multitude of faces turned up to him, waiting expectantly for his approbation. What could he say?

—Anything I might say to you, said Don, would be infinitely complex, even – or perhaps especially – if it were but a single word. It is a wonder-case for sure, the livingness of living.

—What is that single word? asked part of the crowd.

—Yes, tell it to us, said the other part.

—The word in question is irrelevant. Anything can be made to mean anything – I will discourse on Tintern Abbey to make my point. (And Is-Book, you can commit this one to your memory-bank and lock it away in the most secure vault you can find, because I feel a good one coming on.)

—*TRISEPTIMUM*: TINTERN ABBEY: A word is like a stone: it is a thing of matter. The words of speech are made out of vibrating air; the words of writing are made out of ink or graphite or chalk or some other substance. A word, just like a stone, doesn't mean anything in itself. The world should be turned upon its head, and the poets revered as gods, for they love the stone-ness of the stone; they love the word's matter more than its meaning, which in truth is all that it has.

—Now, even a bad poet such as Wordsworth is a better poet than the man or woman in the street. Nevertheless, he still has no control whatsoever over what he writes. By way of example, please allow me to reveal to you how in 'Tintern Abbey' Wordsworth prophecies the cyber revolution nearly two hundred years before its advent.

—Even the title Wordsworth gives to his poem already and first of all alerts us to what his poem will achieve: 'Tintern' plainly and in full view puns on '(T)intern[et]'. By marking their linguistic similarity, Wordsworth marks also their physical dissimilarity: the tactile ruins of the abbey and the un-ruinable, aphysicality of the (T)intern[et]. In doing so, Wordsworth bridges the pre- and post-Romantic epochs, symbolically obliterating the epoch in which he writes.

—Soon, we find man's relationship to nature through technology exemplified in a single image:

> wreathes of smoke
> Sent up, in silence, from among the trees,
> With some uncertain notice, as might seem,
> Of vagrant dwellers in the houseless woods,
> Or of some hermit's cave, where by his fire
> The hermit sits alone.

Here we find a co-presentation of the Spring of all technology (the invention of fire), the simple rustic outcast from the Industrial Revolution (a kind of Cumberland beggar in the woods), and the postmodern condition of self-isolation before a computer screen. The smoke, in these three overlaid images, is that of the first fire, that which signifies a rejection of the industrial revolution, and the immaterial (smoke?) signals which connect all willing humans in this new cyber existence. The clear image of the (T)intern[et], in which a data signal goes up into the 'cloud' – indeed, forms the 'cloud' – is admonitory or cautionary as much as it is celebratory. The hermit/internet user, sitting there within his 'cave', is a figure for pity but also for celebration. The (T)intern[et] is the echo of the birth of man half a million years before. Wordsworth is placing all times in one – and so, we see the necessity for the repeated refrain: 'again... Once again... again... Once again' (ll.2–15)

—As Wordsworth moves on, he has no choice but to drift towards the symbolic strategies of the tradition of religious poetry, though he resists its *theos*, using abstract nouns which have more in common with the ontological than theological tradition. Between fall (birth into 'this corporeal frame') and redemption (death away from it, to 'become a living soul') is the regrettable life of the body, which entails a scrambling of the senses: in a kind of synaesthesic interference, the eye is clouded by what it *hears*. Life in the body *is* disorder – until, that is, the (T) intern[et] enables the body's disappearance during life. Christ may have been the first redemption, but the (T)intern[et] is the Second Coming. As Wordsworth was aware, in the eating and drinking of the body and blood of Christ in the pre-schismatic Church (and the ruined abbey is first and foremost a relic of that institution) the individual is redeemed through Christ, but also – and perhaps more importantly – the individual joins with all other individuals in corporate salvation achieved within the body of Christ, which is the Church. Can there be a better image of the (T)intern[et], by which an individual, no matter where in the world he or she might be (the hermit in his cave again) is joined to all others who partake of that salvation? The (T)intern[et], whereby 'we see into the life of things', is nothing short of an epistemo-onto-theological re-ordering: it is an ecumenical parousia.

(Readers who cannot bear such drivel – perhaps the worst Don has ever come up with – are invited to skip to the fourth line of the next page; to those of firmer constitution we say weakly, regretfully: read on, if you must.)

—The keystone to the whole poem is the short verse paragraph constituting lines 50–58, in which a turn takes place in the mind of the poet from the 'fretful stir / unprofitable, and the fever of the world' (53–4) to the surroundings of Tintern Abbey: 'O sylvan Wye! Thou wanderer through the woods' (l.57). This alliterative recalling of the world-wide web is prefigured and then echoed at various points throughout the poem: 'winters… waters… sweet' (ll.2–4); 'Once… wood run wild' (ll.15–17); 'the weary weight / Of all this unintelligible world' (ll.39–40); 'I, so long / A worshipper of Nature, hither came, / Unwearied in that service: rather say / With warmer love'; and finally, in the concluding sentence of the poem: 'Nor wilt thou then forget, / That after many wanderings, many years / Of absence, these steep woods and lofty cliffs…' (ll.156–8). The (T)intern[et] is thereby immanent within both the human and the natural worlds, the world of culture and the world of nature. Indeed, the (T)intern[et] is that which, for the first time in history and pre-history, re-connects the two, thus redeeming man from his Fall. This is the redemptive power of the (T)intern[et], and as a result

Wordsworth's quasi-religious paganism within the poem makes perfect sense: he is bridging all ages, prophecying the true Second Coming, though he is constrained by the language of the poetic tradition.

The mob, seeming no longer patient to examine its leader's words for sense, greeted the conclusion of this discourse with polite applause, and continued to carry him westwards. Aloft beside his squire, held above and without the general crush of hot bodies, the two men were able to talk in danger neither of interruption nor eaves-dropping.

—I say, master, said Is, that was a lengthy sermon.

—Understand Is-Book, said Don, that I didn't mean a word of it.

Is looked at his master.

—Why did you want me to place it so securely in my brain then, which is exactly what I did, and not without some amount of labour?

—Not meaning what I say is insufficient reason to condemn my words to annihilation. Do you really think that any of these poets *meant* what they wrote? Or the historians? Or the philosophers? They perhaps thought they did. But my prolegomena to the discourse you just heard amply described the limits of communication: there can be none.

—Well why bother talking at all? said Is.

(And the reader may be forgiven for agreeing.)

—Is your main reason for talking to convey information? Or even more pertinent: is the portion of your joy increased in proportion to the amount of information conveyed from your mouth to another's ear in words? It is true that it is the inverse: joy is directly proportionate to nonsense. Your prattling has been a teacher for me in the formulation of this conclusion. The academics, that joyless leap of word-leopards, have the most to learn.

—Well allow me to prattle this one at you: we have been fleeing this crowd for the past few days, and after the man McEwan mowed you down we've ended up in its midst, and now you seem perfectly content to stay here and blabber on about Tinternet Abbey without a thought for Chance, which you've always esteemed as your bride's dad or something, but who's now no better than the rat's lice or so it seems.

—Your withered brain misunderstands the nature of Chance, said Don. It's not that I am perfectly content to stay here; I am imperfectly content to assemble a scheme to leave. Chance, Is-Book, Chance! Whether or not Chance was instrumental in placing us in the current predicament is immaterial; what matters is that it liberates us from it, as it will.

—To tell you the truth, sir, I have no wish to leave the company of all these people, because they are carrying me up so high in the air that my knackered old feet are having the rest of their lives. And more than that, it's been difficult enough to get a scrap of love out of a single one of those as I lived with at home – the wife and kids is what I mean – or from you who I've been travelling with these last few weeks, and so having a good few thousand bearing me up and singing songs in my praise, well it's a saint of a thing really.

—Our celebrity is wondrous strange, it is true, said Don. I cannot say that I am entirely impervious to its beguilement. But when Chance comes,

—She'll have two horns,
—And grasping both hard,
—They won't see us for dust,
—And we'll open the door,
—Which had been hid,
—And enter:
—The rose garden.

The two friends exchanged an almost imperceptible eye-smile of pleasure as the crowd carried on with its work.

—But what do you suppose, said Is, will happen to these people when we leave? As I've distinctly heard the word 're-enactment' and the words 'Peasants' Revolt' on more than many occasions – not that I'm completely certain what it is or was yet – it seems that that's what's really happening, just as we've already read and heard from that mayor character and in the newspaper, which explains why we're here with this crowd following us and all that. I'm just trying to be a good leader, sir, because where there's a flock of lambs there's not far away going to be a wolf, and I don't want by my negligence to be responsible for a massacre. All hell could break loose if we bugger off to Oxford or California or wherever-else without them.

—Know well, Is-Book, that a re-enactment of the Peasants' Revolt is more akin to fish flakes than it is to itself.

Our two increasingly infuriating heroes continued to talk in their own way, but we shall leave them to it on this occasion.

30

The crowd continued to gather members to itself, sweeping them up from the streets, carrying them down to its collective destination, wherever that might be. In the sidestreets, people laid out bedsheets and prepared banners of them with paints and pens and frames manufactured out of scrapwood and wire. Stalls set up on the route selling homemade lemonade, pancakes, coffee and tea, pastries, burgers, hot dogs, curry, candy floss, popcorn, anything a crowd on a march might require. Group upon group there could be seen wearing leather breeches, doublet, and woollen cloak – yes, authenticity was foremost in their minds. From their belts hung variously the tools of their trades: knife for all, hammer and chisel for the stone mason, hammer and a pouch of nails for the carpenter, of small pins for the cobbler, of needles and thread for the tailor; a saw for the sawyer; sways and spars and a small sheaf of sad stunted wheat for the thatcher; a pouch of wheat flour for the baker. Authorities on all variety of subject disquisitioned upon them to the passing people, interpreting actions, events, symbols and signs into a forward point from the past into the future. At a stall were being sold souvenir clippings of the newspaper stories featuring Don and Is's mishaps and misdeeds across the arena of Essex in the preceding three weeks, preparing the time for this moment, and thenceforth its end.

—What about the Kentish mob? Don and Is heard one of the band say. Supposed to be fifteen thousand of them now. That's a whole lot.

—There's time enough for us to grow, said another. It's still early.

South-south-east of Victoria Park, seven miles hence, past the heavy swag of the Isle of Dogs, at Blackheath, another assembly gathered of the Kentish men and women, similarly arrayed, similarly provisioned, likewise expectant. The press arrived. There was Wat Tyler in their midst, speaking of his gratitude to Jack Straw for beginning it all in their sister county across the Thames. People were filmed and interviewed; stories were gathering in the minds of the commentators with point and purpose. Up in Mile End the news crews did the same.

A man from Dunmow with a formidable beard described how he had been tending to his lawn when a neighbour passed and said, Have you heard the news? He had not heard the news, no, but he damn well wanted to know what it was, because there was never any bloody news in Dunmow. Well I'll tell you, said the neighbour, and she told how two men had fomented discord at the Flitch of Bacon, and the regulars had marched on the town council at Foakes House on the Stortford Road where they smashed the windows, which were Grade II listed no less, and shouted ironic variations on the town motto *May Dunmow Prosper* which intimated that the town prospers only at the expense of its populace, 'Dunmow' being in this case the parish administration. And didn't he think it was exciting, all this stuff going on all over the county because of those two blokes? This was why he'd come down to London, walked the whole thirty five miles in a single day, and it was worth every blister, because as he saw it, so he said, the country's had enough of sleaze, and this march would hound them out of parliament, so he hoped.

A man dressed as a monkey said: I don't care what all this is about. I'm just here to see what happens.

A group of men of disparate age, awkwardly standing, as if their shoes and clothes were not their own, held copies for sale of the Socialist Worker and polystyrene cups of bad tea and believed that this was ending what had been begun six hundred years ago.

A woman and her husband stood together watching everyone affectionately. They were just passing on the way to work at Queen Mary and saw the people gathering. More time on their hands now the students were away for the summer – nothing to get in for in particular.

Members of the press and a mobile TV crew spread down the channel of the crowd, like fish pointed upstream, intercepting those who would talk.

—There are too many Muslims in London now, said a fat raw-faced man from Canvey Island. It's not right. These two are saying: Let's have it like it was, before all this influgs. Let's get back to a more purer Britain. The paper says they killed a whole load of Lemmings across Essex who was taking their jobs; thousand years later or whatever and it's exactly the same, except no-one's doing anything about it now. I'd do the same as them if the law weren't on the Muslims' side all the time. People like me get looked down on for saying stuff like that, but these two are doing it okay because they're doing it different. We'll be with them the whole way, won't we kids!

—The cleverest part of all was sawing off Byrhtnoth's head at Maldon, said a woman from Heybridge. What better symbol of the illegitimate state could there be?

—I don't really mind what it's all about, as long as I take a few grand, said the burger stall man.

The crowd surged on, noisily celebrating itself, ceasing all flow of traffic. Songs from the pamphlets were sung in enclaves within the mob, and they spread, and overlapped, and roared, and then expired. The people consulted their books. Where were they going? What were they doing? The leaders would show them, fidelitous to the written account.

A press helicopter swept through the vivid blue aperture between two buildings, turned, and ran the full length of the crowd, acquiring aerial shots for the newscast. Before them, and behind them, Don and Is could see the crowd stretch down the Mile End Road without end.

—I don't think you need to fear the slaughter of these lambs after our departure from them, said Don returning to their discussion. Because that departure's beginning to look unlike it's ours to choose.

But I surrender myself to Chance wholly and fully, and you should do the same, good Is-Book.

—Oh I do, sir. To tell you the truth, I'm having one of the best days of my life and it's only eleven o'clock in the morning.

—Instead of o'clock, you should really say *no*'clock, because Time as measured by humanity – be it by his comparing mind or his finicky chronometer – does not exist.

—I'll do as you say, sir, but the *en* will have those pouty lips either side of it for sure, because I've always worn a watch, and I've always believed in Time.

—Those pouty lips are called brackets – an orthographic means of presenting parenthetical statement – and I would that every idiocy you ever uttered was not only sequestered there, but also stuck irremediably inside their protective shell, like a bad walnut.

Still the cameras rolled; still the shorthands skipped over the little notebook pages.

In time the crowd came to Aldgate where another large crowd of people had gathered. The two streams of people met and exchanged gestures of corporeal felicitation. An excitement again gathered in the crowd, energized by this collision and the resultant growth of the mob in its thousands. Channelled across Mansell Street by hastily erected barriers, the crowd moved west across the invisible boundary of the City of London, across the St Botolph roundabout, the halted traffic snarling at them through the galvanised bars.

Directed by the chronicles, copies of which were multiplied for the consideration of the mob, whose chests harboured them in a vigorous clutch, the waiting Londoners welcomed the Essex band in through where the old City gate had been, and the crowd flowed freely onwards in two streams up Leadenhall and Fenchurch Streets, though as resolutely undivided in purpose as was the Thames to their south, flowing east in retrogade inversion to the crowd's main melody, so full of human necessity was the city at that time. Drivers sat within their motionless cars and cursed. One who eventually had had enough opened his door, climbed out and began berating the marchers and gesticulating violently, for which he was soon sorry. A man called John Cok, who still carried documents on his person taken from Beaumont-Cum-Moze, and who therefore had walked seventy miles in the preceding two days, a strong and hardy man, hit the driver with his fists until he fell over, which was sooner rather than later.

The mob cheered.

—Sir, said Is from his place atop two men's shoulders. It does seem to be getting a bit boisterous. Although for once I'm a spectator to the brawls, and I haven't used my feet for a good two hours, I'm a bit worried that the shape of things might all of a sudden change and people start punching their fists into *my* nose.

—Do not fear, Is-Book.

—That's easy for you to say, sir, being a fearless adventurer. I can't help feeling that maybe we should take Chance into our own hands, so to speak, and make a break for it.

—Chance is unfolding all around us Is-Book! said Don. Even if my Science allowed me to attempt such a thing, why would we want to leave? Besides, as I have already said (if such a thing can even be imagined) I cannot see us with any great ease ceasing our membership of its body, whether or not your face is suffering a fresh assault, as we are accounted its leaders.

—That's all fair enough as to Chance, said Is. But what manner of Chance is it? How is Chance feeling these days? I just think we'd do well to be on our guard and alert, you know, like the antelope. I'm no expert, but it seems a strange leadership when we are being led by the crowd to who-knows-where. We may not know where that where is, but they do, and I can't work out if that's Chance-friendly or -unfriendly. And everyone has these signs with *Destroie the Savoie* written on them, and *Break Open the Fleet*, and *When Adam delf and Eve span, Who was thenne a gentilman?* which is all Past and Future and no Present, so I don't see how you can approve. And, for that matter, I don't see how I am finding the ability to read them either. It is a black art, this writing-reading;

and it seems to come and go depending on God-, I mean Twenty-One-knows-what. And as for speech, I can't hear a single word anyone's saying owing to the fact that everyone's doing the saying at once, and flooding out the words of the others mutual-like, to the end that it's all a hubbub of babble. So your Chance and your Present and your Speaking are swamped, whilst Writing and Reading are doing okay, and I just thought I'd point that out to you, seeing as it's my job.

The words Is had spoken were a fair representation of their immediate surroundings, to the extent that it was a miracle that our two heroes could hear each other, or indeed we them, much to our detriment.

—Yes, it is a perilous path, said Don. But I don't see how we will break out of it without courting that which I redoubled my vows never to court again; namely: intention. And I would reiterate (if I could conceive the notion of iterativity, which of course I cannot) that although it may not be Chance governing the destination of the crowd, we are courting Chance by inadvertently being a part of it.

—But how can it be inadvertent? They praise us as their leaders. It may be that we have no idea who or what these people and their aims are, but they certainly know us, and they are making a future for us at every step.

—Be that as it may, I am not willing to jeopardise the renewed vows I have made to Chance, who for once is not giving me the cold shoulder treatment. Therefore desist in your objections good squire and allow the Present to be itself, unencumbered by any other phantasms of Time. Something will happen in good Time, for all Time is good if it is lived *in*, and neither *towards* nor *away-from*.

—I will try my best, Is said.

Down Leadenhall Street and Fenchurch Street was the route of the crowd, across Gracechurch and Bishopsgate Street, up Lombard Street and Cornhill and Threadneedle Street, to Poultry.

Again the crowd was augmented, meeting a column of the enormous Kentish mob which had crossed London Bridge in their thousands, the two crowds ceasing to be themselves by combining in confluence to form a new entity. The hubbub grew. The streets and their custodians struggled to contain the increasing volume of the crowd, which continued to swell, pulling people in from the shops and the offices and the houses, off the buses, out of the underground stations.

By three o'clock in the afternoon the crowd was jammed within the thoroughfares all around the Bank of England, and could no longer move. Shouts and songs intermingled in echoes between the large Portland stone buildings down the broad streets, spreading and expiring and shooting up again, like a forest fire, and all the birds flown.

—If ever you required proof of the pre-eminence, grandeur and potency of Chance, behold Is-Book to your right that House of Error known to the nations of the world as the Bank of England. Watch, good servant, as I enter its doors and destroy its ordinances and institutions so utterly that Chris Salmon the Chief Cashier will instantly grow a tail just so he can put it – in manner most un-fish-like – between his legs.

Don attempted to fulfil the obligations of his fine words but was prevented from doing so by the hands which gripped his legs and the shoulders which kept his body aloft and the rest of the crowd all about him, upon whose heads he would have to trample if he were to achieve his aim.

—It seems to me, sir, said Is laughing, that Chance is working for both sides, and favours you no more than the sun does when it shines on your head.

—Shut up, Is-Book. My Lady Chance does not deserve to be described in such contemptuous terms, being as She is beyond reproach. The truth is that Chance, though nubile and alluring, is as yet not entirely ripe; but know also, laggard servant, that I would not tire from waiting for her efflorescence if it took an infinite number of centuries (if such a length of time could be said to exist, which in truth it cannot). And so prepare yourself to minister to my inimitable whim for however long it takes.

The glass fronted buildings of the Square Mile intensified the heat of the day, funnelling it down onto the heads of the assembled people, so closely packed one to the other that no-one could sit and take their rest.

Crushed within the arena formed by the conflux of Poultry, Cornhill, Threadneedle, Prince's and King William Streets the crowd shuddered and sweated like the flank of an exhausted horse, pushed as it was from five directions at once. The cries of distressed children threaded brightly through the general dull tapestry of discontent which the crowd produced. The staircase going down to Bank underground station, shut off by the concertina gate, filled up with people who, watched by the statue of James Henry Greathead, pleaded through its diamond-shaped apertures to a silent, empty station to be let through. Several of the crowd climbed up onto Arthur Wellesley, 1st Duke of Wellington's plinth and sat beneath his horse. The soldiers of Alfred Drury's Great War memorial were clung to as protectors from the crush. The antique street lamps, the benches, the bollards, the modest rose garden – everything was destroyed by the sheer number of people. People fought for places within the cloisters of the Bank. The heat grew intolerable into the late afternoon. Discontent was rife, which was as it should be on this day, and so the mob was satisfied with itself even in its dissatisfaction.

Word reached the fringes of the crowd of actions undertaken by the men and women of Kent elsewhere in the city, for it must befit the appellation: *the time of the rumour*. The Kentish rebels had broken open the Marshalsea prison and liberated all those imprisoned there for debt or felony, and the houses of the Marshall and his questmongers toppled. This news excited the individuals of the crowd, which was stimulated into fresh tumult. Cheers swelled up out of the assembly for a time and then abated, and the sun beat down on the crush of people again. The minutes ran slow. Mounting frustration within the members of the crowd at their own immobility was assuaged somewhat by further word penetrating it that a *measone destwes* worked by Flemish prostitutes had been demolished. News that the Fleet prison had been broken open and that the houses of a chandler and a marshall also torn down stirred up songs which, despite the indistinctness of the words and melody, gave the crowd fresh heart for the battle ahead. For it was true that the present discomforts of the individual members of the mob were no impediment to their collective determination to undertake what needed to be undertaken in the future. A crier cried in a mellifluous plainchant:

What d'ye lack?—What d'ye lack?—Clocks—watches—barnacles?—What d'ye lack?—Watches—clocks—barnacles?—What d'ye lack, sir? What d'ye lack, madam?—Barnacles—watches—clocks? What d'ye lack, noble sir?—What d'ye lack, beauteous madam?

But the crier was an apprentice and, making no money, he joined the mob, and the watches ticked on whether heeded or not, for there was a chain of events, as chronicled: Behold! Walsingham's *Historia Anglicana* is distributed between members such that the crowd might know itself; and, reading, it did.

The crowd remained stuck where it was until at dusk and without apparent cause it began to disperse, many of its members invited in accordance with the laws of the re-enactment to flee the curfew and sleep within the abodes of the residents of the City – at Barbican, Clerkenwell, Wapping, Spitalfields, Shoreditch, Old Street, Smithfield – sequestered within the walls of their hosts where they might plot the seditious mal-efactions of the day forthcoming. Others found an opportunity of rest in the green spaces beyond the City at London Fields, Hackney Downs and Victoria Park; to the end that very soon the streets were empty of people, and only the rubbish they had discarded still sought disconsolately a place of rest, tumbling in the night wind down the streets.

There, alone once more, breaking the edicts of the city's curfew, could be found Don Waswill and Isaiah Olm, leaders of the mob, though now standing once more on their own four feet; and again the chest which followed their every move, sitting beside them in the peaceful night-time. The Bank of England had long ago shut its impenetrable doors, and in any case Don's mind had hopped from one thing to another so many times during his day's furious vigil that he was now concerned more with constructing a systematics of tiddly-winks for a regime of finger-strength – under the auspices of the hyperfine transition of hydrogen, of course – than he was with sacking the nation's central bank.

Eventually, though, he brought his mind back to his Bride-to-be and spoke.

—Now, if I were not forbidden from practising the idle and insidious pastime of remembering I would probably assert that my former belief in the efficacy of my good Lady Chance in liberating us from the clutches of the mob and therefore of their deterministic schemes, whatsoever they may be, would now be vindicated. In short, you will notice Is-Book that we are free!

—Well I must say, master, it's a great relief; because it's just as my mother used to say: the more people you cram somewhere, the harder they're willing to knock you down. And, having spent the day in that crowd, I see now she was right, because it was getting angrier and angrier as the day wore on.

—Your mother was as much a sage as her son, evidently, said Don.

—She'd say: 'Your uncle Ted lived and worked the market his whole life, and no-one thought the first thing about such possibilities as the passing of these everyday people. Shame on them. And as he said on his deathbed: 'They'll notice me when I'm gone, Irene, they'll notice me when I'm gone. They think I ain't bin ageing one bit, like time got tired of looking at me. But they'll miss me when I'm gone, an' I'm damn near gone now, Irene, I'm damn near gone. You remember what Pa used to say now don't you Irene. You remember that? The old line (and God he knew a few): 'The finish is like a cave: it won't look so bad once you've gone through the mouth'. Old Pa. You remember how he sat and shouted at the snooker, his black and white TV this massive cabinet and the screen tiny. 'Get out the way boy! Don't block my baize! Every time you come in the room it's like a bloody eclipse. Where'd you get your bones from Ted? I swear you're another's son. But I cherish you. They pluck the fatherless from the breast, and take a pledge of the poor. Well if they do, they'll have me to contend with. Damn them! You know, your grandfather', Reg said to me – said Ted to his sister (my old ma told her son) – 'your grandfather Charlie was a religious man, and angry as a devil with a hangover for it. This was back before the War. The only advice he ever gave was this: 'Whatever you poke now'll come back to poke you later,' and ain't that the truth. Even that sanctimonious old stooge needed to vacate himself every so often. 'The most important thing I ever learned in life, son' (said Charlie to Reg, as recalled to Ted to Irene to Is) 'is to keep everything as clear as can be. Don't mess with mystery, because it'll give you a bloody good hiding.'

—Is-Book! said Don. Will you please desist! I am caught like the line of a kite on the innumerable branches of your family tree. What on earth is it that you are attempting to say?

—I forget.

Don laughed, and then spoke:

—Milk, upon thermal invigoration, may produce a ticking sound; whilst mushrooms, fried, tend to squeak. Your value as my squire, good Is-Book, is that you would be willing to believe milk to be a clock, and mushrooms a mouse. Your mind does not obey the conventional modes of reason, and as a result I value your company and esteem your judgement, or anti-judgement as it might more accurately be called. Your facility as to the art of conversation is unrivalled, even if you sometimes get lost in the maze of your own chatter. I therefore put to you the following question: Why are we here?

Is thought for a moment, and then replied:

—Because we are nowhere else.

—That, said Don, is the only answer that I would have accepted, because it is the only answer that is true. Therefore, as we continue walking, we will always remain where we are, and therefore nothing can go wrong, because the present is *always*.

—And perhaps we can sleep, said Is. Because it's as true as anything else that my feet, even though the crowd have carried me most of the day, still ache a mighty lot from having scant been out of harness the twenty-four hours preceding.

—We shall take our rest soon enough, said Don. But my own feet are hungry for some miles, and so for now, which is always, we will walk.

Which is just what they did, along Gresham Street to St Martin's-le-Grand, where the next day, being Thursday 13th June, the commons would drag out of the church from the high altar a certain Roger Legett, an important assizer, take him into the Cheap, and there remove his head – and likewise on that same day eighteen other persons would be beheaded in various places of the town.

31

Disburdened of the crowd of which they had acquired the leadership, the two friends were able to walk north out of the city and then freely about the damp night-streets of Clerkenwell through the orange glow of the street lamps. Walking kept them warm and awake, though they were heedless of directions and destinations, as was their manner with adventuring, and a very fine manner it was too. Don discoursed upon diverse matters, whilst Is listened, nodded along, and placed each discourse within his remembering mind as carefully as if it were a fine fruit pie encased in pastry of the utmost crumbliness.

The angularities of the buildings revolved in that familiar way as the walkers passed them. Droplets of moisture in the air gave the impression of kisses upon the cheeks of the face.

Beneath the walkways the pair went, trudging over the damp cobblestones which ran down from Mount Pleasant. Time turned on, and motifs repeated themselves in Is's tired consciousness: the turn of a railing, the incline and angle of a bridge passing neatly between blocks of flats, a thread in the weave of the streets traced out with their footfall, first the warp and then, from above, crossing over and under, the woof – like the threads of a story. Their route ran a tangle through the streets of Clerkenwell, mapping across the fractured levels of its dissevered and spliced thoroughfares. Like a tree of stone the city was, burnished by the moonlight and the lamplight. But this story needs them back where the action is; and so:

Back down Saffron Hill they came, with Farringdon Road running down with them, and at its side, the subterranean Fleet, whispering. Unknowingly they traced the hidden river's course, though they might hear its murmur through the heavy grates in the lanes if they attended; down, from east of Rosebery Avenue, down; down, under the Holborn Viaduct, down to Fleet Street and Ludgate Hill where the clock at the corner told of the time being past two in the morning. Looking the other way, east, past the offices of the Crown Prosecution Service and beyond to St Paul's, Is saw a small group of men gathered about the flames emanating from a melting bin.

They moved on.

Small groups stood assembled in defiance of the curfew; signs of tumult were everywhere evident. As they walked onwards, they saw a pillar of smoke, illuminated by fire beneath, winding in coils and bulges up into the air, resembling an intestine. Urgent though indistinct shouts came from the interiors of two office buildings on fire, and men and women were being helped out of the lobbies from which all the glass doors and windows had dropped and smashed.

Back amongst the action they were, our adventuring pair.

Towards the back of one of the ground floor lobbies of the building Is saw a man violently pushing something into the mouth of someone in uniform, a security guard it appeared. Is watched as the guard gradually ceased struggling, and then his assailant removed himself from the building, leaving the security guard inside, where glass rained down from the assaulted windows of the atrium. Is was about to suggest that his master, being the epitome of bravery, the personification of fortitude, the flower of righteousness, might assist the injured guard when a group of men into the path of our two heroes, and were joined by the former assailant, who, breathing heavily, cleaned blood from his fist with a rag, and said:

—*With whom haldes yow?*

A great weight of silence bore down on the assembly.

—*With whom haldes yow?* the man repeated.

The men, whom Is now noticed were holding weapons, began readying themselves for some manner of undertaking which he was sure would be to his detriment.

—This little group's a lot less friendly than the big one that gave us such a good ride earlier, sir, said Is. What do you think they mean?

—Ah, meaning! said Don. It is a phantasm of the human mind! Mean is mean, meagre mean! Prepare your mind for one of the very best *triseptima* which can be wrought by human tongue!

—I don't think there's time for any of your *triseptimums,* sir. These men seem to want to kill us if we don't answer their question, and I don't think any triseptification ever did anything like that.

—*With whom haldes yow?* shouted their most recent assailant once again as the gang closed in around them.

It would have been the end of our two brave adventurers and thus of our tale too had it not been for the collapse at that moment of part of the façade of the office by which they all stood. Down came the bricks, separating one from another as they toppled, playing a great percussive arpeggio on the flagstones of the courtyard as they landed, like the bars of an upended marimba, and the gang was dispersed by this danger for a time. By great good luck, then, Don and Is were spared – as is good and proper, for they had not yet arrived at their appointed end – and were able to run down New Bridge Street towards the river, thus escaping before they could be assaulted. From a few hundred feet down the road, now assured of their safety, they turned and saw several clerks revealed like so many rats in a nest behind the collapsed wall. The burgeoning crowd, headed by the gang which had accosted them, pelted them with stones and shouted, though the words were lost to the labyrinth of the city, indistinct.

Down by the river the thoroughfares were quieter, starved of traffic by the diversions and roadblocks and curfew, and no one walked upon the street. They came to a fork in the road and took a left, where there opened up a view to the west across to Waterloo Bridge, where the barges scud decorously upon the dark nightgloss of the water. They turned, and saw the Hungerford Bridge uglify the east, and the empty plinths beside it, supporting nothing. From the broad abutment of Blackfriars Bridge they watched towards the centre of the bridge downriver a group of about thirty people gathered on the walkway. Some climbed the girders of the rail bridge back to the cage of the walkway; others ran along its length and joining the band, whose members were invigorated by their proximity one with another. Loud declamation was made through a handheld amplification device. An apparent leader beckoned several members within the group to come forward, who it became clear held someone captive. The words were distorted by the device and dispersed by the wind and distance to the point that they were indecipherable. The leader escorted the group and captive to the edge of the bridge, and the captive was thrown over to great shouts. It took the man several seconds to hit the water, by which time Is had determined with Don that they would not be attempting to cross that bridge. Our valiant pair turned and descended to the Embankment, where they took shelter beneath the bridge away from the sight of men, as well as from the winds of the air.

With the first light of morning came the waking of the rest of the brigands who found themselves within the eastern parks of the great city and remembered their task. They would move upon the courts, and the houses of the clerks! They would move upon the financial institutions of the City – the Exchange, the investment banks, the Bank of England! They would move upon the prisons – the Bridewell, the Fleet, the Marshalsea, the Pentonville, the Westminster, the Clink! They would move upon the gates of the old city and fortify their barricades against the law! In some quarters, the dignity of patriotism was found to be deficient, overwhelmed as it was by the desire for the acquisition of capital and the preservation of one's own livelihood within the hearts of some of the mob. The looting began. Shopkeepers brought down their grates in defence and travelled out of town to watch events from afar, fearing the worst. From Whitechapel to Covent Garden, from Grays Inn to Borough, the shops were ransacked. The mob assembled itself again for the day, and a greater day it would be even than the one before. They would move upon everything!

Don and Is crept out from beneath the abutment of the bridge to find a large crowd amassing along the Embankment at Waterloo Bridge and heading for the Temple. They ascended the steps back up to street level and turned north, retracing the route they had taken the night before, intent upon avoiding the mob, whose temperament had so altered.

Thursday morning within the square mile and no traffic. Down Watergate they turned to avoid a unit of mounted police, and then north along Bridewell Place, where a band of some sixty men consumed food and drink taken from the St Brides Tavern against the will of its proprietor, rolling tuns of wine out of the cellar and drinking their fill. Our heroes skirted this depraved company and turned right, back on to New Bridge Street, whereupon a bottle careened past Don's head, missing it by no more than a few inches. Other bottles and stones followed, for Don and Is found themselves standing in the midst of a confrontation between the mob and the police. They were directed by a police announcement to retreat down the road from where they had come; the crowd directed them vigorously to become part of their company. Turning, Don and Is found that a number of the band at the tavern had discontinued their vinous revelry and were now approaching, weapons held at their sides all the more menacingly for their nonchalance.

—This will take some escape artistry, said Don looking down each of the three thoroughfares and wondering which way they should go.

—Undertake it for us! said Is in fear as the bottles and stones flew past his nose and the three groups moved closer.

—Ah, but it is easy enough, said Don. Oh Chance! My fair Lady! Thy gown is of the most finely woven diaphan, wonderful in its beauteousness! See where you stand, Is-Book: upon a manhole cover.

With this, Don knelt down as if in supplication to his faithful bride Time or Chance or whatever She, He or It was, and with a deft turn of his knife opened the catch. Before Is had even removed his second foot from the heavy iron cover, Don had begun lifting it.

—Climb in, my good fellow, said Don.

Though the sewage smell was immediate and raw, Is did not need to be encouraged. He threw the chest closely through the narrow aperture and then clambered down the iron ladder set into the concrete sides of the manhole. Soon he found himself standing knee-deep in the source of the smell, within a tunnel of approximately twenty feet in diameter; for as good fortune would have it, at this time, a quarter to nine in the morning, and on this date – the twelfth of June – the tide was at close to its lowest point, otherwise the pair's descent would most certainly have been halted by an ingress of merdurinous tidal water.

Don shut the cover above them and they found themselves in utter darkness.

—Master, said Is. That was a closer shave than I might have liked – I wonder that they don't know us today after having carried us for so long yesterday.

—If an individual human might be characterised by his capriciousness, how much worse is a crowd, which turns like the tide, though it requires not a moon for its persuasions, merely the tendering of rumour.

By the faintly audible tumult which penetrated the drain cover above their heads it appeared that the three groups of combatants were willing to continue where they had left off without a thought for the two men who had disappeared beneath the street.

—But what will become of us down here, walking the turds of the city? said Is. I will light a light.

—Be aware, good companion, said Don, that the ignition of a match may mean also the ignition of a proportion of the gaseous contents of this tunnel, and thus very soon afterwards of ourselves, which is a thing to be avoided, I would suggest. The aroma greeting the trills of my nose portends its possibility.

—How are we going to navigate without a light though? asked Is.

—The tunnel has an inverted ovoid profile, and therefore our feet will lead us along its length without mishap by following its course.

—That's as may be, said Is. But the dark frightens me just as much or more than the idea of burning to death, because what is death but infinite darkness, and so the two are as close to being the same as to direct me to put my thumb on the very wheel of this lighter here and turn it.

—Well if you must, then you should, because who am I to stand between your thumb and Chance – though She is mine, so keep the rest of your hand to yourself.

Is therefore swept the ball of his thumb over the wheel, expectant of the effulgence of the gaseous contents of the lighter. It did not come, though thrice he tried, and thrice the wheel rasped inconsequentially.

—Give me the lighter, said Don.

Within a few seconds, Is heard the following words fall from his master's mouth like sandbags from an overladen balloon:

—You idiot. This is not a lighter, but some kind of ornamented dagger. Where on earth did you get this from?

—I didn't get it from anywhere! said Is. It makes no sense at all.

—I will light a light, said Don. Using a real lighter, with a real and true flint within it, as did our forbears use the flint, ushering in the technocracy which has been our curse. O Time!

Shortly thereafter a little yellow tulip of fire sprung up in the midst of the tunnel, and was applied to a rag upon a stick to make a torch, and the smile on Is's face became not only visible but also possible. Handing both the torch and the mysterious dagger to Is without a word, Don watched his servant bring the dagger up close before his eyes beneath the light in order to examine it. A brass pommel and rivets running through the oaken grip, the quillion perpendicular, and the simple, unornamented blade. As far as Is was concerned, it was just one more insoluble mystery to add to those of the preceding few weeks.

—As far as I'm concerned, he said, this is just one more insoluble mystery to add to those of the preceding few weeks.

The two companions proceeded to walk along the tunnel. Is, appreciating the craftsmanship of the dagger, placed it in his belt for safekeeping. Indeterminate shouts occasionally came down to them through the grates, with all the time Don contemplating the intricate workings of Time, and Is contemplating the solids which perturbed his trouser legs and troubled his boot-tops beneath the torch which he carried with as much care as if it were a relic of the Cross.

In good time – for as far as he was concerned, all True Time was Good – Don spoke to his devoted servant, releasing the following words into the fetid air of the tunnel:

—I apologise for interrupting whatever your mind may or may not have been engaged upon, my dear friend. But I must turn your attention away from the swarming words and signs of everything which is stored away in its receptacle and ask you a few questions. How do you feel, good Is-Book?

—I thank you for asking, sir, said the servant. As it happens, I feel remarkably well considering I'm down a sewer with tens of thousands of people after me for some reason I have no idea of. What amazes me is that they're friendly as pie the one minute, and then as unfriendly as a completely different pie the next. It makes no sense.

—There you go again about sense! said Don. When will you learn that sense does not exist?

—When you teach it me in a way I can understand! said Is. And you'll have your job cut out, because it's plain wrong and stupid to say you can't make sense, because every word as you hear does it, and even though some might be worth more than others – words, that is – each one definitely has money in its innards, as neat as a purse. In fact, you're the only one not making sense.

—I'll teach that lesson to you now, insolent squire, said Don. And you'll learn at the same time not to doubt your master, who is the flower of philosophy.

—Ah yes, the *triseptimum* you threatened me with earlier, said Is.

—There is no earlier.

—What's this one on? Should I incorporate it into my brain?

—Of course you should, you imbecile! shouted Don, and the echoes ran through the dark maze of the sewer.

—*Triseptimum:* The Butterfly and the Cottage; being: An experiment in meaning: The following will amply demonstrate that meaning is the least solid of all entities, being itself in True Reality a non-entity. Since I am aware of your preference for concrete example, Is-Book, and of your very great stupidity, you will by my judicious empirics become your own example, which will prevent you ever from doubting me again. Are you ready?

Is nodded, and the torch-flame shuddered, pulling a spiralled twist from the dappled shadows of the innumerable bricks which formed the tunnel.

—Right then. I would like you to choose a word, any word.

—Cottage, said Is. For this, along with the verdant surroundings such a rural dwelling house is often found with, is what he was thinking of as an antidote to the unpleasant sensations the sewer's contents were granting to him.

—That is a good word indeed, said Don. Tell me, what do you take the word 'cottage' to mean?

—Well, when I hear or think of that word, I cannot but help imagining a cosy little home, and one I'd very much like to be in at the moment.

—This is good, said Don. A word for the purposes of this experiment with as singular a denotation as possible is preferable. Other meanings have accrued to the word you have chosen, but as you are innocent of them, I am content to pursue our investigation.

—Me too, said Is with his innocence in full view under the light of the burning torch.

—The first stage of the experiment involves the oral recitation of the word chosen for a period of several minutes.

—You want me to say 'cottage' for several minutes?

—That is correct.

Is shifted his tongue within his mouth as if it were an old man in an armchair settling for the afternoon, but he couldn't find his comfort.

—Could I have a drink to ready myself? he said.

Don passed the water flask and allowed his squire to empty a good proportion of its contents into his mouth.

—And how about a kiss with Saint Monica just for luck?

Don handed the hip flask to his servant and superintended the administration of a nip.

—That's better, said Is. Shall I start?

—Please do, said his master.

And so he began.

It is not necessary to make a written record of the task the squire undertook. However, it may interest some readers to note that, whilst he began by saying the word *Cottage*, this very soon mutated into the form *cottage* as he settled into the experiment. His enunciation remained stable for several dozen repetitions in this form, but afterwards ceased to exhibit emphasis, and became ironical, in the form 'cottage'. Within another quarter of a minute or so, the word was divested of its ironical vestures, and was cottage plain and simple. But no sooner had this happened than the word began to crumble. A pesky 'x' snuck in front of the first letter for a few repetitions. And then there was enunciated cottidge, then cottij, then kottigj, then kotudge, and then the letters started to drift away from each other as the mind and the muscles of Is's throat became tired of the repetition.

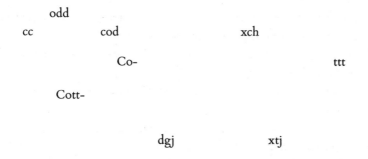

—Now you may stop, said Don, and look at what I have in my hand.

Don opened his hand and beckoned Is to bring the flame of his torch down to reveal a beautiful Red Admiral butterfly.

—This is a cottage, said Don.

—Well I never, said Is. I didn't know that. A cottage you say.

The butterfly took off from Don's hand and flew, as if jerked at the end of a thread of cotton, down the tunnel of the sewer into the blackness.

From that moment forth Is was convinced that a butterfly was called a cottage. (And every time he saw a small rural dwelling house, his mind tripped up on the vacancy which planted itself right in the path of his thought. But we get ahead of ourselves; there is still much to be had from our heroes' perilous journey within the bowels of the city.)

—I am grateful to you, sir, said Is, for showing me whatever it is you've just shown me. I am certain that when I have an opportunity to reflect on the results of the experiment I will see just how meaning doesn't exist. In the meantime, I think that before we conducted the famous experiment which we just conducted you were asking me how I felt?

—If it was possible that time-past might have existence, I would count it very likely indeed that I was asking you such a question, because there is something troubling me in that regard.

—That's very kind of you to be thinking of me, sir, but I'm okay really.

—I'm not troubled on your account, you fool, said Don. I am troubled because of what it might portend as to Time, Chance and my hallowed Science. There must be further lines to my inquiry: let's set a limit to the period of our investigation to that time during which you have been in my service. How has your feeling about the world changed in the preceding three weeks (not that I believe in weeks)?

—I'm not really sure, said Is. I'd have to think about it.

—Might you do that now, Is-Book?

—Okay.

There dwelt a silence of short length between the two friends.

—Have you completed this activity? asked Don.

—I'm not sure if completed is the best description of it, said Is. But I certainly have an answer to your question, which is that I feel like there's some sort of fit-up going on.

—In what way? said Don.

—Well, I've had a very dull life, sir. Nothing's really happened – grew up, got a pot-wash job, got married, had a couple of kids, and that was that. But since I met you I've been struck by lightning, and nearly again another time (though you missed that, being asleep); I've been gifted the ability to read all-of-a-sudden, and then just-as-a-sudden had it taken away; I've been arrested, beaten-up, tattooed, and I've become a living book; I've also become a celebrity and been carried through the streets by an adoring crowd; and now I've found this funny knife in my pocket without any idea how it got there. What's more, the only thing we've actually tried to do is avoid London, and here we are, underneath it, with twenty-thousand people either praising or cursing us, and the police getting involved again now too. It's all a Chance too far if you ask me.

Don made noises within his throat and mouth consistent with the interior transaction of a powerful mental dialectics – and the sounds ran sibilantly through the network of tunnels.

—The truth of things is tangledness, said Don. Not its opposite. A prehistoric mind – which is to say a mind before writing – would have no problem in accepting that in the infinite tangle of Being a Wellington boot might be connected as truly and intimately with the boiling point of mercury as with the foot of its owner. In the end everything shall be visible in the One-and-Only, which is the hyperfine transition of hydrogen, by which we might interpret words and the world, because they are its code. But until such a time, it is unequivocally the case that the world will make less and less sense. As far as I can see, this only gives greater proof of the efficacy of our adventuring. Oh Is-Book! It shall not be long now (not that that makes any sense).

Our two interlocutorily diffuse friends continued walking along the tunnel up the Fleet river, which is what the sewer truly was and had been. Snufflings and scufflings of rats greeted their ears as they walked, and the sounds of dripping water reverberating all around them. Lean growths of photophobic mosses blotched the brickwork coils of the tunnels and the stench of the sewage was churned up with every tread.

Very soon Is felt the need once again to speak.

—Sir?

—Yes, Is-Book.

—You know our chat we just had about the weirdness happening – my reading, and the knife turning up?

—Yes.

—I think there's something else I need to tell you. Something that isn't such a good sign as all the rest of it.

—Go on.

—It happened at Cressing, by the barn, before the fire. I am certain that there was something making writing——

But Is would never finish his account of what happened at Cressing, because – (what shall we have happen to cease his tampering tongue? Ah yes:) – just then he heard voices unmistakably within the tunnel rather than drifting into it through the grates above, something which frightened him more than all the crowds in the world could have aboveground; and what is more, in his fright he dropped the torch, which was extinguished in the filthy stream through which they waded, to the end that they were plunged into utter darkness again.

—Oh I do not want to die, sir! said Is with a moan so heartbreaking that if anyone other than his master had heard him they would have embraced him as if he were a small injured bird.

Don, however, was not such a person.

—Every waking moment you are beset by some presentiment of your death! said Don. When will it end? Before this band of men reaches us, take that chest off your back and hide it in the centre of the channel where the depth of the sewage will cover it. It does seem to be our identifying feature, and I don't want another bunch of people following us. Anyway, although we may be less seeing without the torch, we are also less seen. Perhaps these people will pass us by without even noticing our presence here in the tunnel with them, and we can continue on our way, to our infinite fame; and by the time we're done with London and all it contains (not that either Time or Space are truly measurable), we'll both be fondling our respective brides – me Time, and you Ruth – which will certainly be the right and proper end to our fearsome adventuring.

But Don's reassuring words were immediately refuted by the events of the present, as, just after Is had done as his master directed in regard to the chest, the approaching band rounded a corner in the tunnel, shone their torches into the faces of our two heroes, and with their own faces obscured by masks made the familiar demand:

—*With whom haldes yow?*

—There's that question again! said Is to Don. What can it mean?

—Our *wache-word*, said one of the band. Give us our *wache-word*: *With whom haldes yow?*

Blades were drawn, and their sharp edges gleamed under the torch-light, for it is true that under the terms of the *Anonimalle* those who did not know how to reply or would not do so were beheaded and put to death.

—I thank you sir for all that you've taught me, said Is. And I thank you last and most for making me hide the chest and so bringing me to my death. May it also bring an end to my suffering!

A member of the band took pity on the frightened squire and whispered to him:

—(You say now, '*Wyth kynge Richarde and wyth the trew communes*'.)

—Hey! another member of the band said. Why you helping them? This is real now.

—What is real now? asked Is.

—You see, gentle Is-Book, said Don. There is some wretched formula incumbent on each person on every occasion of meeting. These rogues are attempting to manage our spoken words, which in constituting a tampering with Chance is an attempt as execrable as it will be abortive.

—They can have whatever words they want as long as those knives don't get unfriendly with my belly, said Is.

Don, however, had already rounded upon the band, which sought either to engage him in their service or kill him, and spoke with righteous anger thus:

—Will you tell me what either I or my good squire should say? Know, foul beings, that I have found myself called to this my avocation: to spurn convention, to reject both the nicety and the not-so-nicety, to break down the façade of the futile and empty sign-makings of etiquettery. I eat with the eleven fingers of my hands, and, furled into fists, you will eat of them also. My answer to your question is therefore an invocation to five-elevenths of them: great club-fist, though thy back and bones be sore still with thy former labours, yet once more act a brave work, call it thy last adventry! And the seal on that invocation is the action it proclaims. Ready yourselves, scum.

Upon the completion of this autohortatory oration, Don, as promised, sunk the bones of his right hand deep into the face of the man closest to him, writing agony into it. A scuffle of predictable ferocity and proportion ensued, the outcome of which seemed inevitably to be the death of our two heroes, the band's aggression and capacity for combat having been most manifestly hardened by experience. However, it so happened that during the fight, in an attempt to push Is's face into the rank sewage which flowed down the centre of the tunnel and thereby cause his drowning, one of the band, pulling upon his opponent's apparel, noticed under the chance twist of the torchlight of one of his comrades the tattoo which Don had incised into his squire's back that lonely night in the woods in earlier, more simple times.

—Good God! the man cried out as he shrank from Is in fear.

—What fresh properties of repugnance does my good squire exhibit? said Don, who was being held in a headlock of incomparable fortitude.

—He's got the sign! the man gasped at his leader.

The whole company ceased their assault in order to take a view of Is's back, which they approached with a newly acquired caution. Being the part of Is's body between his hips and head, and that head being at the same altitude as those hips – that is to say, Is being upon his hands and knees in the filth of the sewer – his back presented itself with perpendicularity to their sight.

—Fuck me, you've gone and done it now haven't you, said one.

—How was I supposed to know? It's not like you've done nothing either, said another.

—Damn! said another still.

—It's okay, we barely got started, said one again. Look, they're fine.

—Damn it, Tony.

—They're *fine*.

—It's true, we're fine, Is said with a palpable sense of relief that the pain invested as principal in the application of his tattoo had yielded such a good return: namely, his life.

—It's an honour to have you with us, said the leader of the small band to Don. Kent's come up fast now as well. Tomorrow's going to be the one, mark my words.

Each of the band exchanged gestures of corporeal felicitation with our infuriating heroes. This band of men, supplemented in number a further two, were led northwards up the tunnel through the city's filth. Is focused with renewed distaste upon the work of his feet through it all: was it any different to that observed 400 years before by Ben Jonson? *That ugly monster ycleped Mud, the sink-run grease, the hair of measled hogs, the heads, boughs, entrails, and the hides of dogs.* The tunnel's brickwork wound like the membraneous muscles of the gut round and round.

Despite the filthiness of the sewer, a spirit of ribaldry animated the mood of the clan: its members descanted at odds playfully and with such ferocity one with another that the echoing their voices made carried down all the chambers of the mazed tunnels, the vacant plunge pools, overflow arches, spillways and dropshafts, until the sense in them grew tired of seeking an ear, and the exploratory tendrils of the sound drooped and expired with a sibillant *hushhh*. The conversation within the band swelled and sank and swelled as they walked down the subterranean network, allowing our two heroes to have their own private conversation as the company's rearguard.

—You see, Is-Book, said Don. Chance is the finest of things, and I do not believe myself to be speaking with vanity when I say it favours us. These men who were our ferocious assailants are now our friends. I hope this puts your mind at rest.

—It does, sir. It seems that all I have to do is show off my tattoo of the how-do-you-call-it whenever we get in a fix, and we'll be out of it and the fix mended.

—That's how it is, Is-Book, said Don. Tell me now how you feel about the hyperfine transition of hydrogen.

—It's the very best thing in the world, sir, said Is.

—It is not in the world at all, Is-Book. It *is* the world, and everything else that *is*, though it has been obscured since the dawn of humanity by a great malignancy. But I concur with the sentiment expressed by the words you most recently used.

—One thing I should say sir – and you'll like this very much because it can't be anything else other than Chance that's managed it – is that the tattoo you made on my chest has by some means or another snuck round on to my back!

—That is indeed extraordinary, said Don. If it had remained on your chest we would almost certainly be dead at this moment.

—That's exactly what I was thinking, said Is. Do you think we need to worry about it?

—Worry about it?

—Yes. Because, for example, if I were to lose a donkey, and then it just turn up miraculously when I most need it – like this shirt I am wearing did, because I certainly don't remember ever having found it after those dogs ate the rabbit suit you made me, and as you know I've got a way with memory as most people would find impressive. But anyway, as I was saying, I would count it a boon of Chance to be granted a donkey, or a shirt for that matter, when I was in need; but if that donkey, or that shirt – though I'm not sure how a shirt would do such a thing – if either of them then led me into an even worse spot than before, how would I feel about Chance after all that? What I'm trying to say is, what's best now might not be best later, and how can you ever know?

—Chance should never be doubted, said Don.

—But what if Chance isn't Chance at all? said Is. What if the things that are happening already have an end and the present is all about the arrowing of them to it, like a story?

—You have no need to fear that, said Don. Because I am now more certain than ever that Chance is far more powerful than any story; She is as a splendid ocean of the most beautiful azure to the storyteller's bathwater, upon which float manifold scums, as to our sewage here.

32

—But moving on from this topic, continued Don as they walked up the tunnels, following the silhouettes of the gang against shifting coronae of torchlight. I have been thinking about the ways of the crowd aboveground. It is a curious matter. As far as I can see, Kent has only lately begun to take an interest in whatever it was that had been taken an interest in the more northerly county which we wouldn't be foolish to call our home. They now have their Wat Tyler, whose coming-into-being relied upon the election of us to the leadership as no longer Don Waswill and Isaiah Olm (though what, say I, is in a name anyway?), but transmogrified by the human delight for pretence into whoever it is we are supposed to represent, whether John Ball or Jack Straw. For I will tell you this, Is-Book, and it's a very interesting fact: none of the accounts of the Peasants' Revolt are agreed on whether these three leading rebels – Wat Tyler, John Ball and Jack Straw – were not in fact a single person. Tyler is supposed to hail from Kent; but neither of the others, even if they were real, can be reliably traced to Essex. Indeed, John Ball, a Hertfordshire man, was in Kent in 1381 with Wat Tyler; and Jack Straw, if he existed at all, and if this was not simply a pseudonym for Wat Tyler (who himself may never have existed) may have come from Suffolk (which may or may not exist), or maybe elsewhere, wherever that might be. Do you see what I am getting at?

—Not in the slightest sir, Is replied. But I'm still breathing, and even if this does allow me to smell all the shit I'm wading through, it indicates too that I am alive, and so I'm happy enough.

(They were now directly beneath Fleet Street, and it bears stating that their place now was rather above ground than below it, because it was past ten in the morning, and the Temple awaited their arrival, and the story requires it. And so:)

Presently a great hissing sound of falling water came to the party from some unknown origin. It grew and grew, swelling to a roar, and what faces of the now motionless party could be seen in the torchlight registered great fear of their impending inundation within the tunnel, a certain death. But before the anticipated deluge came, the sound abated.

—I take it back, said Is. I am not happy, and my life is threatened. This is your friend Chance alright, running things under the ground, where all bad things begin, and where all things – bad or good – end up. I'm thinking of creatures, sir, and of their graves. It'll be a wet and dirty end for us very soon unless we get ourselves out of here. There's nothing I'd like less than to drown in stranger shit.

—It has passed, said Don.

—I fear it will be back, and that'll be that, said Is.

—Cease fearing, said Don. The danger is passed.

(But time it is now for their arrival at the Temple, and so:)

Presently a great hissing sound of falling water came to the party from some unknown origin. It grew and grew, swelling to a roar, and what faces of the now motionless party could be seen in the torchlight registered great fear of their impending inundation within the tunnel, a certain death.

—I'm not waiting for your permission this time, sir, said Is. You can try and tug me back down, but I'll fight it.

With these words exploring the network of tunnels all around, Is scrambled up the closest access ladder, with Don chasing him, and the rest of the party following them as leaders, which is what inadvertently they were, to the end that very soon everyone involved, a number not inconsiderable, stood again above ground in the full glare of the summer's day sun, facing west, where people in great numbers were streaming down Fleet Street, bound for the Temple.

—They're a canny pair! said one of the band. Getting us out here right where we need to be like that.

—They're bloody good, said another.

The party of some twenty men hustled down the centre of the street leaving a drip trail of sewage remnants behind them, and they watched as breakaway groups from the main mob surged down the side streets – Whitefriars, Bouverie, Lombard Lane, King's Bench Walk – heading for the Inner Temple, from where a great tumult could be heard emanating, great crashings and thrashings and a chaos of human voices shouting, flints lobbed in great arcs through the lovely lead-worked windows, which sprang like scales from a cleaned fish. Close by Is's ear, of a seller of hot food it was sung:

> This woman's in industry wise,
> She lives near Butcher-row;
> Each night round Temple-bar she plies,
> With *Diddle Dumplings, ho!*

Across the gardens a multitude filled the court, trampling the carefully tended turf, and the trees sagged from the weight of the many people they bore on their boughs, people who cawed derision at the Temple like a multitude of crows.

—It is just as it was yesterday, said Is. I can't be doing with another day like that, even less a night again like the one that followed. It's hard to keep my temperament well met, especially with this chest on my back again, and all the crowds about me.

It was true that against all the possibilities of reason and the protestations of Is's memory the chest must have been carried by the decrepit servant down all the many narrow tunnels of the Fleet sewer and then back up on to the street without him knowing or remembering, and despite the certainty that he had left it submerged beneath the sewage, for there it was again in their company, ineluctably present.

The crowd began chanting, calling for the destruction of the tenants of the Temple; and it was known throughout the horde that on that glorious day during the rumour the houses had been *thrown to the ground* and the tiles *cast down* so that the houses were *left roofless and in a poor state*; and they sang of it. It was also known that they went into the church, and that *they seized all the books, rolls and remembrances kept in the cupboards of the apprentices of the law within the Temple, carried them into the high road and burnt them there*; because the clerks were found to be deficient. And be it known that, *even when old and senile, the rebels climbed with extraordinary agility as though they were rats or carried aloft by some spirit. This is certainly credible for the malign spirit which they followed and served undoubtedly directed their steps.* The flints tore also through the ancient windows here.

To great cheers from the crowd, Wat Tyler, also Watte Teghler, also Watte, also Walter, also Water; this man, leader of the Kentish rebels who had successfully crossed the Thames to the great celebration of the welcoming Londoners; this man came to the house of Richard Lyons, merchantman, former Warden of the Mint, and one stewed in corruption, beat down his door, and taking him by the hair dragged him from his home into the midst of the street where it stood, and beheaded him. Thereafter his head was placed upon a pole and paraded for the delectation of the mob and for a sign, and the people who played the mob agreed that it was a fine piece of re-enactment, and in the look and motion of it very real.

—Bloody hell, sir! said Is. Did you see that?

—An impressive piece of conjuring as to prosthetics, said Don. Try not to be seduced by the evidence of the eye, though.

The crowd began to move again, down to Victoria Embankment to the south and up to the Strand to the north, then west, past St Clement Danes, marooned at the tip of the island of Aldwych, past King's College and Somerset House, and a song started up, an old cry:

> Who liveth so merry and maketh such sport
> As those that be of the poorest sort?
> The poorest sort wheresoever they be,
> They gather together by one, two, three.

Many were out amongst the crowd to remedy the preceding, counting it neither merry nor sport to be in want; and one with a barrel upon his back sang:

> My ink is good – as black as jet
> 'Tis used by Princes – and the state,
> If once you venture it to try,
> Of this I'm sure – none else you'll buy.

But none in the crowd were of the writerly persuasion, which it pleased Don to see, and so in spite of the numbers present business was not good for the ink-hawker on that day.

Further down the broad avenue came the cry of a woman at her stall:

> Here's taters hot, my little chaps,
> Now just lay out a copper,
> I'm known up and down the Strand,
> You'll not find any hotter.

—I do feel a certain fondness for the doggerel of the vulgar, said one.

—And why shouldn't you? said another.

—But here we are! The Savoie!

And it was true that the crowd, having satisfied the terms of its incumbency with regard to the Temple, now began converging upon the Savoy Hotel, which it would by necessity account a palace, and none other than that of Sir John of Gaunt, perpetrator of manifold wrongdoings against the populace; for which wrongdoings the said palace would be destroyed as completely as its predecessor, the true palace, as we shall now discover. *Read on!*

The tide of the crowd swept down the Strand and crashed against the building frontages, the statuary, the gates of the great hotel. The crush grew as more and more people gathered at the rear, until eventually the pressure became too much, and the mob burst through the windows of the shops and offices, through the police cordons and down the side streets. A group of four men climbed in a line up one of the large iron drainpipes of the side of the hotel and in through a third story window. Further down the side of the building to the south, another group filled a large four-wheeled refuse bin with anything they could obtain – gates, signs, draincovers, a motorbike – and used it as a battering ram on the delivery doors, which after a few minutes gave way. The shout was issued, and within a few minutes more, several hundred people had entered the porter's lodge, the kitchens, the scullery rooms, the parcel room, the dress room, the accounts office, of which they proceeded to smash the contents. People could be seen ascending the tightly wound workers' staircases by the flash of their clothings' colours through the frosted glass floor-by-floor upwards. A large safe was pushed through a wall from the second floor and very nearly landed on a man who was attempting to shake the railings down. He paused, looked at the safe embedded six inches into the pavement like a martello tower stranded incongruously and half submerged on a beach, and then went back to his former occupation with undiminished vigour.

Don and Is stood crushed in against the many people before the front gates of the hotel, hot under the afternoon sun, buffeted by inexplicable thrusts within the body of the crowd as to atoms invigorated: some hard and hooked like iron, some smooth and slippery like water, some sharp and pointed like salt, some light and whirling like air. Atoms all, the people. Separated from their subterranean band, Don and Is were now managing to preserve their anonymity for a time, but surely it would not be long until someone spotted them. Every time a person grasped his shoulder, Is winced. Don, by contrast, was unconcerned. The crowd, it was true, was too busy gathering its purpose upon the hotel before them – some sixty thousand strong as reckoned by the chronicles. Is was amazed at the sight, but his master was stuck fast in thought. Eventually he came round, and spoke the following words:

—My thoughts have turned once again to my *Encyclopaedia*, Is. There is one more thing we must do.

—Sir, said Is. Although we have twice burned and once drowned your *Encyclopaedia* and the chest which contains it, and though I haven't expended even one mouse-worth of effort in the carrying of it since I left it in the sewer, it doesn't surprise me even a single bit that I am able to say in all truth that here it is right by your side like a dutiful dog with even this rabblement respecting its space.

—And thank Twenty-One for that! said Don.

Sure enough, the chest was there beside them, as unshakeable as a bad memory, and the remains of the books which had been within it were within it, and the writing which had been upon those remains, both of print and of hand, was there again.

—What is it you need it for now? said Is. I thought you hated it.

—Is-Book, what is the greatest of all the things of the earth?

—The greatest you say?

—Yes.

—Well for me, said the squire, that would have to be breakfast. Breakfast is most certainly the best thing I can think of.

—You surpass yourself, you accursed amalgamation of cells. The greatest thing in the world is Chance. And Chance, which would not allow us to destroy the chest even with raging fire and tempestuous waters, has preserved it and all its contents for the end which I shall very soon describe to you. Ah my devoted Chance! How good She has been to preserve the chest you have borne upon your occasionally patient back, Is-Book. Fit to house the whole world around – this being, salvifically speaking, precisely what it was intended for. If memory were not a habit of thought strictly forbidden me, I would surely still smart at the ignominy heaped upon the precious chest by such people as have commented on its lineaments. How they have dared thus to denounce their own salvation! I vigorously assert the origin of the chest as lying strictly within the limits of my own hands; permit me therefore this Boast:

—Against all such accusations, I would maintain that my goodly chest was not designed by Chapman Taylor, though there be certain aesthetic affinities between it and the Drake Circus Shopping Centre at Plymouth; nor by Anthony Caro, though it may have wobbled upon your back as did his Millennium Bridge; nor by Antoni Gaudí, though my *Encyclopaedia* be as unfinished and unfinishable as the Basílica i Temple Expiatori de la Sagrada Família; nor by either Gustavus Adolphus of Sweden or Henry VIII of England, though, like *Vasa* and *Mary Rose,* she too has to her sovereign's detriment been overladen with guns – and yet, though doused in the waters and dredged back up, we find her weaponry still miraculously intact! Mark well these truths: although she required not the assistance of Rafael Viñoly to find her corporeal form, she bears sufficient power to melt cars and bicycles, as did his building upon Fenchurch Street by the light it reflected from the sun; though, moreover, the handiwork of Leon Moisseiff was not forthcoming, Western Civilization shall collapse as a consequence of the glorious subterfuge undertaken by the works she contains, as did his Tacoma Narrows Bridge fall into Puget Sound on that windy day in 1940. In short, it was a great error even for myself to heap ignominy upon the chest, though she led these crowds towards us down the tracks and lanes of the county, for is it not true that the most powerful of entities hold it within themselves to manifest much which is accounted opposite in the world? In truth, the chest and its contents may achieve the restitution whether loved or hated by its maker, such is the power a purveyor has over a word issued to the world, which is none. Truly she does contain that for which the whole world yearns. But she will satisfy them in such a topsy-turvy way, such is the nature of things. Now, ——

—Do you think this deserves a *triseptimum*? said Is.

—Why do you ask, good squire? said Don, ceasing to warm his voicebox up for the delivery of his speech and peering curiously at Is from out of those incomparable yellow eyes.

—I just want to know whether to remember it or not. Or whether I should have already started to remember.

—I don't think it's strictly necessary, said Don. But owing to our species' fondness for memorialising certain of its acts you might as well, because what I have to say is so true and so important that even if you melted down every statue ever forged by the hand of man and used the resultant material in the construction of a single enormous memorial to what I am about to say, the object produced would in its size be merely an insult to my action's import. Prepare then your remembering mind!

—*TRISEPTIMUM:* THE END OF HISTORY: As I was saying, Chance has preserved the work of my last Twenty-One years' labour as the contents of this chest here, even against my best efforts to destroy it. In spite of assaults by fire and water, my now hated work has survived – indeed regenerated – and is tangible before us as many hundreds of thousands of small slips of paper within this chest. Just as with the finest sword – which, indeed, is precisely what it is – fire has purified and water tempered it. It is ready!

—I'm not so sure about that, said Is. In the sorry state it's in it looks to be more the bedding of a large rodent than a work of the intelligence.

—That's as may be, said Don with wily excitement. But the infants of this rat of falsity Writing shall be spread far and wide in order to destroy it! Listen: here within this chest is a true representation of Being according to the hyperfine transition of hydrogen, though tainted by its written form. Turned upon writing, the scraps of my old *Encyclopaedia* will purify all the earth through their self-destructing attacks. Dispersed across the globe, my little ratlings shall mate with the old, and all culture shall be consumed as by fire. The end of all writing draws near, good Is-Book! And so, prepare ye the way of the softly spoken word, good ratlings! Go to thy self-annihilation!

With these concluding words, Don reached into the chest and threw the many thousands of slips of paper within it up into the air to the end that they fluttered away like chaff at harvest time into the dense crowd and up into the sky; and he did not cease until the chest was empty, much to the peril of the writings of the world. The chest he lifted up above his craggy head and passed on to the heads and shoulders of those beside him, who did the same, and this roughly hewn insult to the word 'furniture' bobbed like a coffin upon merry pall bearers' shoulders over the heads of the crowd down the Strand, round the corner of Villiers Street, through Embankment Station, over the road and river wall into the Thames, where it floated downriver towards the sea.

33

All around our two heroes the crowds from across the city continued to converge upon the Strand from Aldwych and the Embankment, from Covent Garden and Charing Cross, flowing around the monuments and traffic islands, whorls and ripples and rivulets, small bands of people, gathering into a dammed-up mass at the long frontage of the Savoy Hotel, tens of thousands of them. Some carried signs: signs of pasteboard, signs of corrugated vinyl, of hardboard, foam, re-painted road signs – these heavy, growing heavier as they caught the wind – some carried T-frames from which had been hung bedsheets daubed with misshapen letters whose paint had run, whose slogans were running, running into or away from one another in a flurry of exhortatory signification. 'Liberty!' read one; several again that favourite refrain, translated into Modern English for those of limited tolerance: 'When Adam delved and Eve span, who was then the gentleman?' Songs again were sung, and horns blown. A man with a megaphone sought to persuade the people that they were the people, and that they had one will. There came again upon the wind the sound of the playing of instruments in accidental counterpoint. Children and dogs grew frightened and required carrying. There were several press helicopters in the air now, filming the swelling crowd. The police stood at the fringes behind their cordons, which broke, and then were engulfed as the mass spread irrepressibly through every thoroughfare.

One of the many songs swelled up out of the crowd again:

Savoy semely sette,

heu! funditus igne cadebat.

Arcan don there they bett,

et eos virtute premebat.

Deth was ther dewe dett,

qui captum quisque ferebat.

—There was your name, sir! said Is. Your real name, not the Jack Strawe one. 'Arcan *Don* there they bett', what can it mean?

—You should be aware by now, said Don, of my attitude to meaning, good squire – in short, that it, any meaning whatsoever, is an impossibility – and so I am unable to interpret the line you have quoted.

—'Don' in middle English is a verb meaning 'to do, put, make, or cause', said a helpful neighbour to them in the crowd.

—Well sir, said Is to his master, I think you should be willing to admit that definition if no other to be a true one because it's as on-the-money as any definition I ever heard, you being the restitutionist or what-have-you for the whole wide world and next door.

—It is against the tenets of my Science, said Don, which is founded on the truth of the hyperfine transition of hydrogen, and therefore I cannot allow it. Though I must admit it does please me in the same way as the stroking of a cat, which offers solace to even the most lonely of hearts.

The last cordon was breached with a rush of the crowd at the head of Carting Lane, and several hundred runners were released down the narrow hill to the western side of the hotel and up Savoy Way. Down Savoy Place they went, turning, and immediately as many windows as could be found, and more, were put in. The large crowd behind teetered a moment and then began to be funnelled by the pressure of the gathering mass and were gradually forced into the mouth of the lane to follow, where the pressure began to build once more. Don and Is were again borne up and along in the flood of fists, teeth, elbows, hot bodies and the musky fragrance of them, and still the current surged, damming them close by the front of the hotel. Not a clear word could be heard within the crush.

Once these powerful eddies abated for a time, and our two famous companions were able to find their feet once again, Is listened-in as a woman informed another member of the crowd what had been happening across the city. In a fine voice she said that she had seen many things and that they were full of wonders that she could never have imagined. It was her first time in the great city, and the streets were broad, and the buildings tall, and the air vibrant with noise. What a place it was. By the internal flux of the mass she was caused by chance to join the company of our irrepressible heroes.

—What is your name, my good woman? said Don.

The woman answered but the roaring of the crowd blotted out her reply.

—Tell me, said Don, what it is that you have seen, whether or not you desire to remember it.

So the woman spoke:

—All along St Paul's Church Yard the crowd was roaring. Great rushes rising, on the banks and the shops and the offices, like the tide or something. One branch of us moved up Queen Victoria Street towards the big Bank, and they were hurling bricks and stones and shoes and coins and food and street stuffs and abuse at the buildings and what they took them to stand for. Then I got swept down the road with about two hundred others, and a man who called himself Walter atte Keye, who says he was a malefactor, whatever that is; and he moved me down Godliman Street towards the river with him and his men. A number entered the house of Andrew Vernoun, who was a brewer, at St Paul's Wharf, and Walter attacked him with his fists, and told him that his life was held for a ransom. Vernoun satisfied Walter with the money and then we were hustled back round St Paul's past all the other different mobs, and we came to Milk Street, where he was looking for what he said was the King's Computer. Say, aren't you our John Balle or Jack Strawe or Wat Tyler, I just can't remember which?

—This sounds like a grand device indeed, the King's Computer, said Don ignoring the woman's interrogation as to his identity. Please go on.

—Thanks, John Balle, (for she had just then decided that it was he). We went through the gates of this place, and the guards had a bad time trying to hold us off, because there were easily a few hundred of us that got into the courtyard through the gate before they even thought to try to stop us. And then they were in for a worse time, because that Walter was stamping on their heads on the floor. It was horrid, the faces coming off like the skin off hot milk under his big boots. Then we went down the corridors and through the rooms looking for this King's Computer, and Walter was shouting about it and le Jubyle or whatever and how he was going to burn it up. We overturned all the chests and set fire to everything. There were computers everywhere, but this Walter atte Keye said none of them was the King's one he was after, and we would know it when we saw it.

—And what about this le Jubyle, said Is. What's that when it's at home?

—Le Jubyle I heard said as to be a book so powerful it could kill a man, said the woman.

—What is written in it? said Is, who loved a mystery as much as the next man.

—Ha! I see you love a mystery as much as the next man! said the woman. We never found it, so I couldn't tell you. Old atte Keye is still looking for it roundabout Addle Street and cursing whatever it is that made him.

—There are in the world, said Don, those who grieve about such lost documents, and protect the still extant with unimaginable ferocity fuelled by a terror of lost history. How can a history be lost, I wonder, when it does not and cannot exist? The abhorrent child of my brain, whose ugly written form disgusts me, I have sent out into the world to work its destruction upon all the writing of the world. If you take even the most simple one in singly as fosterling, it shall destroy every book within your house like a canker. You may tell your Walter atte Keye that he has no need to worry, because the invisible worm that flies in the night will do the job he himself cannot. Le Jubyle won't last long once my little ratlings have got a hold of it.

—I'll do that sir, if I see him, said the woman.

But Don was not listening, occupied as he was with glaring at the chest which was once again in their company, even though they had watched it be swept over the heads of the crowd towards its water-borne oblivion.

—O Chance, tell me my ratlings have not scurried back to their den! If they have, then this Walter atte Keye man has become someone I would like to talk to, for if he can't find this le Jubyle, perhaps he can lose us my damned book.

—I cannot work out, said Is, if I am more surprised that I believe the chest is there than that it isn't. I will have to take a peek inside, because my nerves won't take the suspense.

Is did exactly what he said he would: he opened the large heavy lid of the chest, and discovered that it was full to the brim with the rat-bedding trimmings of his master's old *Encyclopaedia*.

—Whatever it is that keeps returning this chest to our company, said Is, I don't like it. And I'm not even talking about the weight involved in the carrying of it. It's a sorcerous thing indeed.

—It is the very devil, said Don.

—If it wasn't for this chest we might have covered a thousand times as many miles, and no-one would have known we were us. There can't be many pairs of people as wander the country with a chest the size of a sleeping bear on their backs.

—The chest, said Don, has no doubt acted as a far more visible sign than the tattoo I have given you, at least from a distance. I refuse to say any more than that our chest and le Jubyle could do with becoming acquainted with one another. I predict their mutual annihilation, which would be no bad thing.

—Good woman, Don then said to the good woman. Could you take us to this Walter atte Keye man, or bring him to us?

—What are you up to now, sir? said Is.

—Oh he's looking for you anyway, said the good woman. He says there's only one man as can help him find le Jubyle.

—If that isn't Chance filigreeing the Time with Her delicate beauty, then I don't know what it is! said Don. The best thing we can do is to allow Chance to have Her way.

—Saying you want to be taken to this atte Keye bloke sounds very much like the renouncement of Chance to me, sir, said Is.

—Temptations against Chance swirl about me like a tempest, it is true; I must hold my faith. Therefore seek not the atte Keye man, good woman, for as my dutiful servant has just now pointed out, that would run contrary to the edicts and decrees by which I have solemnly sworn to abide; those which attach me indissolubly to the Present, through Chance, the Princess of Time, my Fair Bride, or something like that. Good squire, assist me, for you are much needed! When this atte Keye man finds us we will get rid of this chest for good. There is a feeling in me that only then will it be possible for Chance to act in freedom, for the execrable shadow of writing hangs over our every action while the chest is still with us. In fact, this crowd may never have assembled itself at all if the chest had not kept reappearing and thus drawn its members to us.

—Like a horse to water, said Is by way of satisfied confirmation.

—I'm not sure you comprehend the original of the proverb to which you refer.

—Perhaps you are right, master, said Is. But then it wouldn't surprise me in the slightest if I woke up tomorrow and didn't even know my own name, such are the dimensions of my confusion. So you can't blame me for putting a proverb in the wrong-shaped hole.

—The only hole you should put proverbs in is straight back in your mouth, said Don. For a proverb is intended as a piece of folk wisdom, and you, despite your incomparable memory, are to wisdom what a colander is to water. And while you are putting that proverb back in, you can get underneath the chest again, because it is once again of the utmost importance that we do not let it out of our company until we find the atte Keye man – I mean, until he finds us. Once more you must guard it with your life.

—Is it any surprise that I don't know what's going on when you contradict yourself at the turning of each point of the time? said Is.

This conversation between the two friends might have continued for hours on end, but exchange of words suddenly became impossible as the crowd succeeded in bringing the front gates of the hotel down to the ground, and burst between the pillars and surged into the lobby, tearing display cases off the walls, fouling the small national flags around their poles, rucking up the rugs into great folds which lay like discarded fat over the marble floor of the hall. Those with bladed weapons slashed the upholstery; trinkets were thrown up to knock out the great hanging lights, which shattered and filled hair and clothes, and scintillated over the floor to be ground down by the feet of the people to a brilliant dust. Down the narrow entranceway under the golden statue of Count Peter of Savoy with his spear and his shield the crowd did flood.

Don and Is, swept through the entrance into the Great Hall, climbed up to take a place within the recess beneath a handsomely carved lunette to watch everything happen. The eyes of the insurgents as they flowed into the Great Hall churned up the air looking for the truth of the matter. Thomas Webbe of Great Oakley mounted the desk and began kicking the brass fitments holding the telephones and the keys off the wall; soon, the desk held as many people as could stand on it at once, until it collapsed.

The mouths of the crowd churned up the air shouting out the truth of the matter in a vortex of words, issuing in chaos, but soon beginning to manifest certain shapes, discernible as intentions, and certain of the bodies from whence these sounds issued had become organised by their aggregated intent into one body politic; and these were the most active of the mob.

—Hang on a minute sir, said Is. Isn't that John Somenour as was with us at the first Tom Harding's place?

—The hatred I have for the human conception of time, said Don, must dictate again my refusal to exercise that faculty of mind known as memory, not least because it stems from the Indo-European *men-, 'think', a double blast upon true philosophy, for to remember is to obliterate thought; and because of the *equivocatio a casu* by which we see the truth of matters: men, the history-makers, are the custodians of memory, which they deem power, and the women and children and animals are led either to the pen or the slaughterhouse. (But yes, Is-Book, I do believe you are right.)

This mob of men, including John Somenour, came to stand within the royal box erected for the Prince and Princess of Teck, and commissioned certain bands to reconnoitre the labyrinth of the hotel, not only the guest rooms, but the mysterious mechanics of the building which channelled the staff out of sight across and through and up and down the floors of the hotel like rats, which are so seldom seen and yet may be amply heard in the night; and the commission was to reprimand the current occupants as ones who participated in the aggravation or suppression of the revolt, and to bring them back down to where justice awaited them according to their actions and intentions, which were discernible through reference to the chronicles; and these commissions went their ways.

Just then, and to Is's amazement, Richard Proudfoot, the monstrous abductor of Saint Cedd at Bradwell-on-Sea, made his way through the crowd, mounted the staircase halfway to the high ceiling, and vigorously asserted the right of the mob to establish a legal assembly for the judgement of those who had necessitated or suppressed the rising, and whom the commissions would very soon return to the Great Hall of the hotel. The ever-swelling crowd replied 'Hear, hear!' from the floor and a stage was improvised from three great mahogany dining tables; and a great chair, upholstered in emerald green silk and studded with brass, was placed at its centre for the provision of both comfort and the image of potency for whomsoever it was that would occupy it and the position for which it was a sign.

—Who shall occupy the chair? shouted Proudfoot, standing on the stage, down to the people.

—This is impossible, said Is from beneath the sheltering lunette. Why is *he* here? And where's that John Gerveyn or Saint Dead or whatever his name is?

(Little does the servant know that the future, like the past, is written – that Richard Proudfoot sought out John Gerveyn for an auxiliary in the revolt; there is no escaping our trajectory now.)

The people cast lots to elect a Tribune, who eventually was chosen, a manifest concession to chance, which may placate one of the heroes of this narrative for a time, though it was true that the Tribune was handed a large volume containing the chronicles and other documents pertaining to the revolt, which raised the ire in Don, for whom a book was as bad as the devil. The Tribune climbed up on to the row of tables, took to the chair, and called forth the first session.

From the staircase was escorted a middle-aged man with a network of scarlet bloodvessels threaded across both cheeks, and a wife upon his arm. The Tribune spoke several words into the ear of the former, who smiled and nodded, and the wife was removed by the commission to stand in the wings.

—What shall we have him swear on? asked the self-elected prosecution.

—Oh, I don't think there's any need for that, replied the Tribune, settling into both his chair and his role. State your name for the benefit of the assembly.

—Thomas de Bamptoun, said the man with a profound look on his face.

—Just as our re-enactment demands, said the Tribune.

—So this is all relating to that Peasants' Revolt as you told it to me, taxes and stuff? said Is as he and his master watched events unfold within their niche.

—It would appear so, said his master.

—Thomas de Bamptoun, commonly referred to as Thomas Bampton in the books which form our history, you are a tax commissioner for the king, are you not?

—I am, said Bampton.

—And is it not the case that on 31 May 1381 you threatened the first rebels of Fobbing with violence?

—I did, said Bampton. But I ran off, and the rebels never caught me. That's what it says in the *Anonimalle*.

—Well, if that's what it says, we can't do much else than let him go, said the Tribune.

The mob groaned in disappointment.

—Such adherence to the written account of the chronicles disgusts me utterly, said Don looking across the crowd from the elevated platform of the niche. Observe, good servant, how the crowd believes that there is a truth behind all these competing words waiting to be got at, like one good apple among so many bad in a barrel.

—Can't we go for someone else then? said the prosecution. Someone we want to dispose of, but who definitely got caught?

—Go on then, said the Tribune. But who?

—Richard Lyons.

—Okay, said the Tribune to the defendant. You're Richard Lyons, not Bamptoun or Bampton or whatever his name is or was.

—This is preposterous, said Richard Lyons, who had been Thomas Bampton.

—I'd agree with that, said Don. See how every human is relieved of his and her agency by the order of History, the Storying impulse, the letter of Law!

—Tell us about Richard Lyons, said the Tribune to the prosecution, who obliged.

—The Good Parliament of 1376 got him in the first instance, with an impeachment for fraud contrary to the Act then passed. The parliamentary roll states: "it is... ordained that [counsellors to the king] shall take nothing (except small gifts of food and drink or other presents easily distinguishable from bribes) from any party in return for a promise or other transaction to business which is about to be brought or laid before them; under penalty of restoring to the party concerned double what they have taken, as well as the costs and damages suffered by him, and of rendering to our lord the king six times the amount they have taken".

—Sounds familiar! said one of the crowd within the Great Hall.

—Richard Lyons, continued the prosecution, was a merchant to the king. He did dealings outside of the Staple of Calais against the ordinance of parliament, and imposed certain fabricated taxes on exchanges of wool and other merchandise, keeping the larger part of it for himself.

—What has this got to do with the rebellion? asked the Tribune.

—I'm getting to that, said the prosecution. The *Rotuli Parliamentorum* continues thus: "On account of which, the said Richard was adjudged to be imprisoned at the king's will; and to suffer fine and ransom according to the gravity and horror of his trespass; and to lose his freedom of the city of London and was never again to hold royal office nor come near the council or household of the king." In short, Lyons lost all his lands and was imprisoned.

—That's good news, but does that not mean that he paid the price of his misdemeanour?

—Certainly not, said the prosecution. Because it says in Knighton's chronicle: "They (the rebels, that is) dragged Richard Lyons, a notable burgess, out of his house and executed him in the street. Lyons had been convicted in one of Edward III's parliaments for serious fraud towards the king and queen as well as other lords and ladies of the kingdom in his dealings with precious stones and other jewels. Accordingly parliament had sentenced him to perpetual imprisonment, with a daily stipend of twelve pence granted to him by the king's grace; afterwards he was freed by favour but now he was killed."

—And where did this happen? asked the Tribune.

—At the Temple, said the prosecution.

—We've been there already haven't we? said a proportion of the crowd. The prosecutor looked flustered.

—I think they're right you know, said the Tribune. I'm sure of it, he then said, flicking through some notes which had been given him.

—We saw his head on a pole, said a member of the crowd.

—So did we! said a number of others.

—No! protested others still. We haven't got there yet!

The prosecutor began flicking through his own sheaf of notes, and after a long pause in the proceedings stated that according to Knighton and Walsingham, the Temple was got to *after* the Savoy so the crowd had done wrong. And he shook his head in mock sorrow and looked with glee at the crowd, part of which was mollified, and thereby eager to get their hands on Richard Lyons again, and to kill him for a second time; though the other half propounded energetically the greater reliability of the *Anonimalle Chronicle*.

—Walsingham, said Don to Is from beneath the lunette, a monk at St Albans, was in charge of the *scriptorium*, or writing room, of the abbey. I think you can probably accurately speculate upon my view of this individual.

—You're not going to be fond of him I'm guessing, said Is.

—You know me well, good squire, said Don. And therefore I count this counsellor at the bench who seems to be on such good terms with him a grave enemy of myself, my Science, and all the profound realities we both profess. I will have his head on a stick along with this Lyons fellow and they can talk it over up in the air.

—Never mind about Lyons being got already, continued the Tribune, whose urging the work of the tribunal on, comforting the crowd, and compelling his hair into such form as he preferred were all deftly achieved in a single movement. You can convey Lyons to the Temple after we finish here so that he can be got later on.

—Okay, said the prosecutor.

—Excuse me, said Richard Lyons, who had been Thomas Bampton. But the evidence is flawed: in one account he – I mean I – embezzle money through the sale of wool; in the other, it's through the sale of jewels. Throw it out.

—Hang on, said the prosecutor. There's more: Froissart has some juicy stuff going on. "And they slew in the city a rich merchant called Richard Lyon, to whom before that time Wat Tyler had done service in

France; and on a time this Richard Lyon had beaten him, while he was his varlet, the which Wat Tyler then remembered, and so came to his house and strake off his head and caused it to be borne on a spear-point before him all about the city. Thus these ungracious people demeaned themselves like people enräged and wood, and so that day they did much sorrow in London."

—That's just what we saw! cried portions of the mob.

—Beheaded for beating a treasonous nobody! said Lyons.

—I think we had better make sure right here and now, said the Tribune. Go ahead, you can kill him, he said to the mass of people.

And so the people took Richard Lyons down from the stage and – for a proportion of the crowd, for the first time; and for the remainder, for the second – he was slain.

34

The mob was invigorated anew by the activity of murdering Richard Lyons and began destroying what furniture remained in the Great Hall around his corpse.

While this was happening, a young Catalan concierge who had renounced his duties and stripped himself of the golden keys upon his lapel, broke into the hotel records room and began destroying its contents. Forty years of the suppressed anarchism of his grandfather and his grandfather's father quivered through his features as he smashed the monitors and upended the filing cabinets.

—Very soon, began Don to his servant, this Tribunal is going to get warmed-up and start exercising itself on History with more and more efficiency. Let's intercede on Chance's behalf – and at the same time I'll show you just how fragile is the constitution of History. The following shall be a test case for what my ratlings might achieve if I can get them out into the world for longer than five minutes (though bearing in mind that neither the world nor minutes have any real existence).

Don bent down and drew an enormous book from within the chest – which, under Is's obedient and watchful eye, was still at their side.

—This, Is-Book, said Don, will wreak all havoc within this little party.

—But it's a book, sir, said Is. Surely you hate it.

—Any entity may be made to serve any purpose. Besides, this book is but a list of names – the names of guests at this hotel from its opening in August 1889 onwards.

—When did you snaffle that!

—The auguries of Chance are of the utmost mystery. Besides, there is no *when*, so I cannot say. Now watch this.

With a loud whistle between horny thumb and finger, Don attracted the attention of the Catalan, who capered gingerly over through the ricochets of the vigorous crowd.

—This will get things moving, said Don, and he handed the Catalan the enormous volume.

The Catalan sneered a smile at him, took the book, and entered back into the hubbub, through the ravening mob and right up to the stage, where he presented it to the Tribune.

While the mob continued to destroy anything which could be destroyed within the Great Hall, as well as the atria, rooms and halls adjoining it, the Tribune and the Catalan undertook a lengthy discussion aside upon the matter of the book's contents.

—You watch what happens now, Is-Book, said Don. We'll soon see what manner of re-enactment this is. And let this be a first rebellion against what oppresses us truly: Words.

The Tribune and the Catalan came to a conclusion of some sort in regard to the book Don had given them; whereupon the concierge tore out the large ledger sheets from the book and began distributing them to the people, who then ran up the shallow, heavily carpeted steps of the staircase in search of the men and women listed on the sheet they had been given, bellowing in a tumult.

Don and Is did not have to wait long before one of these new commissions came to the staircase at the opposite end of the hall bearing a captive. Words were exchanged with the prissily imperious Catalan, who after his defection from service to the Savoy, and following his success in obtaining what appeared to the Tribunal to be a list of all those who had oppressed or punished the commons up until, during, and after the rising, had managed to be promoted to the position of Clerk of the Court. This man, the Catalan, mounted the stairs, undertook the custody of the captive, and escorted him to the stage, upon which he thrust him before the crowd, and announced:

—George Jay Gould!

—I do not recognise that name, said Don. Which bodes well for our entertainment. The day will soon have little choice but to appear before us in the shape of a pear.

—Quiet! yelled the Tribune at the horde as he proceeded to look the man up and down, and question him on his cause for being present in the country, and the means by which he found himself able to stay in one of the most expensive suites in London. Don and Is stood side-by-side in their niche and watched what would unfold.

He had inherited his fortune from his father, said the defendant, which he could do little to change. But he had worked hard all his life, and made a name for himself on his own account. He provided well for his seven children, and loved his wife, he said. He was not used to being treated in such a way, but he had worked with navvies all his life and crowds held no fear for him, no siree. In answer to the accusation levelled at him, that his fortune was disproportionate to his worth either to his nation or theirs, he shrugged. A member of the crowd shouted out:

—Kill him!

—You can't kill him just for being rich! said another.

Some members of the crowd jeered; others shook their fists. Some uttered words whose shape was lost in the tumult and might have been anything.

—Leech! another shouted, and a tussle broke out between the sympathizers for these two conflicting points of view.

—We can get him for debt, said one. Ask him about his debt.

The crowd cheered, though it was not at all clear for what reason, or if any such reason was singular, or even if there were any reasons, no matter how numerous, to it at all – which Don's inconvenient little rebellion has forced upon both them and us.

—What about your children – do you not treat them badly? said the prosecution.

—I have seven children, said Gould, though how they figure in this I couldn't say. I do not see them as often as I would like.

—He does not see them as often as he would like! said a portion of the crowd in unison.

—What about your mistress? said the prosecution. You have a mistress, do you not? Are we to allow you to treat your wife whom you say you love in such a way?

—Why are we here? said the Tribune. Not to be the moral arbiter of the nation, that's for sure. What has George Jay Gould to do with our great day anyway?

—He is a rich man, and therefore I'd rather he lost his life, said a man in the crowd.

—His arrogance is overwheening, said another. I say we rid ourselves of him.

—Do what you will, said Gould.

One among the mob took this offer upon himself individually by placing a blade into the midst of the financier's liver, the wound from which caused him to cease speaking immediately, and soon thereafter so too was his breath brought to stay. The prosecution was left with a mess to tidy up, which he did by dragging Gould's corpse into an adjoining room, known as the sun lounge.

A shout went up at the man's death:

—A revelle! A revelle!

Much to Is's horror, Don started laughing.

—I cannot believe that you're laughing, sir. A man has just lost his life for nothing!

—Good squire, cease your quaking. I was not laughing at the death of the man, which I do not believe in in any case, but at the strange turn this Tribunal is taking. The spanner I have given the Catalan, and which he has unwittingly thrown in the works (and it is an appropriate figure, owing to the importance of the Catalunyan Noguera Pallaresa basin in the early production of iron, and thence tools) is proving to be a very big and hardy one. Soon everyone in this building will turn and thank me for showing them by this sabotage the manifold dangers of writing.

The Tribunal brought before itself two men. The woman who had told them about Walter atte Keye and the King's Computer, and who now stood at only a short remove from Don and Is's side, said:

—That's him, the one who was in the keep with the King's Computer!

—Who is the other man? said Don beckoning the woman over. Do you recognise him?

—Not at all.

—An unpleasant face he has on him, said Is.

—This will be a strange combination, said Don with a chuckle.

—Quiet! shouted the Tribune again. Who do we have here?

—Here we have Admiral Lord Mountbatten, said the Catalan, and a person known by profession, though unknown by name: the Keeper of the King's Computer at Milk Street.

—And what is the charge?

Not knowing what relation these men had to the Peasants' Revolt (for which we can thank Don's meddling, there being no relation whatsoever) the Catalan did not know what to say, so he muttered some generalised misdemeanour or other.

—And we should just cut off their heads, he concluded.

—Steady on, now, said the Tribune. Let's hear what they have to say. I feel myself developing a modicum of compassion. Whilst the prosecution is dealing with the recently deceased in the sun lounge, will someone with some knowledge of the case please make judicious examination of the accuseds.

—I will, said a woman, who moved out of the thrashing crowd to the stage.

—Give the court your name, said the Tribune.

—I'm afraid I can't do that, said the woman.

The Tribune looked archly at the woman who shared the stage with him.

—If you wish, he said, to participate in the trial – indeed, if you wish to escape a similar fate to that about to be experienced by the defendants who are placed before us today – I should urge you to reconsider.

—But your honour, said the woman, it's not that I won't give you my name; the truth is that I can't, because I don't have one, owing to the demands of our great day, which was of men.

—Well I never, said the Tribune. Unless we replace you with someone with a name, which I don't think is strictly necessary, we shall just have to call you 'the woman'.

—I don't mind that, and it is appropriate to the day, she said.

The crowd murmured its approval; the woman then turned to face the defendants, and issued her first question.

—What is your purpose in being at the Savoy?

—To scupper the revolt! said one of the mob.

—The Admiral Lord Mountbatten first, said the Tribune.

—Certainly, said Mountbatten. I am a radio specialist and president of the British Institute of Radio Engineers, and tonight is the twenty-first anniversary dinner of the Institute, at which I am to give a keynote speech.

—And what was it that you were going to say? asked the Tribune.

Mountbatten made a sound which anyone who witnessed it would describe as a scoffing.

—There's no 'were going to' about it, he said. I fully intend to make my speech.

—I don't think it is very likely any more, said the Tribune sympathetically. But since you have gone to the trouble of writing it, I would hate to rob the world of all possibility of hearing it. Why don't you give it to us here, before we get down to the bad business.

—As you please, said Mountbatten, who did not appear to be disconcerted by the crowd's belief in the high probability of his death, nor by the impending destruction of the designated venue for his speech, though what he had to do with the Peasants' Revolt was as much a mystery to him as it was to everyone else.

—I will give you a précis, he began. Tonight I will speak on the invention of an electronic brain which has been called the ENIAC, which stands for the Electronic Numeral Integrator and Computer.

—You see! said the woman beside Don and Is. They do go together those two! It's the King's Computer!

—Ah, okay, said the Tribune, who, even if he could have heard the woman's outburst from the side of the hall, would have taken no notice.

—And what does this Computer look like? he continued.

—It is somewhat large, replied Mountbatten. It employs 18,000 thermionic valves, consumes about 150,000 watts, and occupies 1,800 cubic feet. But it can play a mediocre game of chess.

—That is some achievement, said the Tribune. What is the value of it?

—It is priceless, said Mountbatten with pride.

—I do not doubt it, said the Tribune.

—It will lead us.to an unimaginable future, said Mountbatten.

—All futures are solely imaginable, said Don, owing to their unreality.

—That's as may be, said the Tribune to the defendant. But what is its utility value?

—Well, it is much faster at solving complicated mathematical problems than the human mind. I think the Glasgow Herald put it as well as I can: "It is believed that this type of Computer might replace writing, printing and publishing with a method for directly recording human speech on to a sound track in legible form... The reference library of the future would be some kind of memory machine of the size of a large desk, from which man could extract the information he needed by pressing a few keys."

—A truly amazing possibility, said the Tribune. But why has the advocate of a computer been brought before me?

(And the reader might well ask the same question: Don's sabotage is a threat to our form – but writing will be made to prevail. *Read on!*)

—Because it's the King's Computer, said one of the commissioners who had seized the Admiral Lord Mountbatten.

—The King's *Compter*, said the Keeper of the King's Computer with manifest scorn, is a debtors' prison.

—And what's wrong with the King's Computer? said the Tribune.

—It belongs to the King! said the crowd.

—We seek, said the Tribune, to right offences *against* the king, and most particularly those committed by the advisory council he is burdened by the service of, not to offend him ourselves.

—Well that's a relief, said the Keeper of the King's Computer. Because I'm on His Majesty's side. He on the other hand, the Keeper continued, pointing at the man he shared the dock with (and a cynical mind might consider the possibility that this defendant was attempting to heap all his own ignominy upon Mountbatten out of self-interest) – he's a Lord.

—That's a fair point, said the Tribune. But I think we had better maintain an adherence to the facts of the case, as stated in the historical record. You should know therefore that a man named Thomas Farndon, or Farringdon, was a leading London figure of the rebellion in spite of his nobility. In fact, I would refer you to the *Coram Rege Roll, Easter 6 Richard II, Rex, memb. 6,* which records an inquisition into Farndon's – as well as others' – deeds during those days, which makes clear that neither the Hospital of St John at Clerkenwell nor the Temple at Cressing would have been attacked at all had it not been for the involvement of Farndon, whose inheritance he claimed to have been taken from him by Robert Hales, the prior of the Hospital. And so not all nobles are bad.

—Cressing! said Is quietly and with foreboding, for that was where he had been chased half to death by *our bright bolt of lightning*, and made to read the fabric of all human reality in words. He shuddered at the memory.

—With all due respect your honour, said a woman within the crowd, I don't think that can be entertained, because Hales was Treasurer too, so it was his taxes and tax commission, and the resultant trials of eyre and of trailbaston, which largely caused the rebellion. It's just what happens when a public figure has his fingers in more than a single pie.

—Well I suppose that's something we have to bear in mind, said the Tribune. But I want to return to the subject of this Computer.

—The King's Computer?

—That's the one. Where is it?

—It was on Milk Street, sir, said the Keeper.

—It was *not* on Milk Street, said the Admiral Lord Mountbatten. That's preposterous. It was – indeed *is* – at the Moore School of Electrical Engineering at the University of Pennsylvania in Philadelphia.

—Whether it was or not doesn't matter any more anyway, said the prosecution upon returning to the stage and wiping Richard Lyons' blood from his hands, because I heard it's now been broken up and sold for parts. Who is this woman in my place?

At hearing the news of the computer's end, the Admiral Lord Mountbatten, who had watched his men die in action during the Great War, and had remained resolute in his offensive for king and country – at this, good reader, he sank to his knees and wept into his hands.

—This King's Computer must have been a great thing indeed if the man is crying, said the woman prosecuting. For I heard that he had watched his men die in action upon the sea and he remained always resolute in his offensive, never wavering from his duty to king and country; and I heard that he would not weep a single tear until his aims were achieved and he had laid down arms.

—I appreciate these sentiments, said the Tribune waving his hand about in order to signify at once the grief of the Admiral Lord Mountbatten and the prosecution's forceful invitation for the court to proceed with its duty. And perhaps this Computer is or was or even will be forever the greatest of all the devices of man. But how does one account for the presence of a computer – even if it were the King's (to whose majesty many extraordinary things owe their existence) – during the late-fourteenth century? I do not believe the thermionic valve is such an old technology as that.

—It is not as old as that, but it was the fatal flaw in the design, said an expert who just then emerged from the crowd.

—State your name that the court may recognise you, said the Tribune.

—My name is Merlin Blencowe, said the man who was Merlin Blencowe. But I am known as the Valve Wizard owing to the associations which my first name engenders combined with my in-depth knowledge of thermionic valves and their applications.

—Wizard, said Don. A seer outsider, spurned from society; late ME *wiseard*, f. ME. *Wīs* WISE *a.* + -ARD, from O.Fr *batard*. In other words, a 'clever bastard'.

—And doesn't he look it, said Is. The brains are fairly seeping out of him like a sweat. But what's he got to do with anything?

—Precisely! I have set a whirlwind amidst the history books! Chaos, the fair playground of Chance – how we have yearned for you! We remove the centre from the circumference, and the vortex of words is ready to tear itself apart!

(This spanner must be dealt with, and the unruly pair who put it in our story made to pay. In the meantime, we shall exile them to observe the whirring of their tampered machinery down in the basement of the page,[*] where they shall remain until the spanner is removed and we can urge them to follow our furrow – a fire should do it:)

---

[*] —You, Mr Blencowe, are just the man we require then. Although it perhaps bears little pertinence to the case, it may nevertheless be instructive to hear the means and manner of the deceasement of the machine, if a machine can be said to die. Be pleased to tell the Tribunal about the workings of the King's Computer so that we may better understand its end.

—Mark well, good squire, the chaos unleashed within the engine of this courtroom by the fallacious book!

—Indeed I will, your honour. The thermionic valves of the type used to power the calculations undertaken by the Computer are constructed of a glass vessel which contains five electrodes in a vacuum. The cathode at the bottom of the valve boils electrons off of its surface. The anode, at the top of the valve, owing to its opposite polarity and much higher charge, attracts these electrons, which hit it at approximately 6500Km/sec.

—That is a formidable velocity indeed.

—Three electrodes in between – the control, screen and suppressor grids – encourage and control this transfer, and also input the signal to be treated by the parts of the machine further down the circuit, which is fed from the anode. The harder the task given the machine, the harder its valves would have to work as the calculating mechanisms whirr away; and the harder they work, the more current they draw. It seems likely to me that the valves of the machine went into thermal runaway, which occurs when an excessive draw of current in a valve causes its control grid to become too hot, which in turn causes it to bias itself hotter than is customary, and which then causes it to draw still more current, which increases the valve heat, and so on, to the end that the valve overheats and fails. If this occurred in multiple locations, it is possible also that the transformers which supplied electrical power to the machine would overheat and destroy themselves too.

Just then, a renegade bus driver finally found his way to the Savoy, negotiating the tight turn at the northern head of Waterloo Bridge, from Lancaster Place on to the Strand, scything scores of crowd members to the ground. Covering his face with his hands, he brought his bus through the wall of the dining hall, the room adjacent to that in which Don and Is were currently witnessing the Tribunal. Although

---

—Why was such a large and presumably expensive machine not designed in such a way as to avoid this eventuality?

—A machine incorporating over 18,000 thermionic valves, and which could undertake complex calculations, was certainly not designed by bungling fools. Probably, therefore – and though I am not aware of the design brief or the purpose of the machine – it was made to undertake a task which its designers had never foreseen it would have to.

—So was the machine asked a question it didn't understand?

—I think I may be of some assistance here.

—Ha! Now you will see, good Is-Book, how each attempt at logical explication of the events of the past and their connection merely reveals the preposterousness of the whole endeavour of history! What a rag-bag of witnesses they are having to resort to!

—And who might you be?

—My name is John William Mauchly, your honour. I am the designer of the ENIAC.

—Well, the court is honoured to have the inventor of the world's first digital computer here with us, though I am still perplexed as to the pertinence of the King's Computer to the case of the suppressors of the Peasants' Revolt.

—It is comforting to be given that recognition, even if posthumously.

—What! Is it true that the court now admits the expert evidence of the deceased!

—I was referring to the death of my computer rather than of myself.

—Ah okay. Well fill us in on what went on with your contraption will you – a post mortem, so to speak.

—I will do what I can. You asked just now if the machine was asked a question it did not understand. Well, by our design, if the machine did not understand a question, it would simply dismiss it and cease working: it would not expend any further energy on the problem because the terms of the proposal were insufficient for a logical solution to be found. The valves would enter shut-down, and switch off. However, if the question was logical, and yet the solution was beyond the computer's grasp, it may have destroyed itself. But it is far more likely that it was user error which destroyed it.

—As the hyperfine transition of hydrogen has taught me, everything which is human is steeped in error!

—Let's pretend it wasn't human error. Let's say it was asked a question which was too difficult. What kind of question would that have to be?

—It would not have been a question too difficult for it, because the terms of inquiry which the computer was designed for were very limited. There isn't a single question that a human mind could construct for this computer that would fall within its remit, and be both logically coherent and insoluble. If there was a possible answer, the computer

the driver died in his cabin from a severed carotid artery, his death was glorious: the crowd blessed his memory by siphening out great slicks of black diesel to the floor and igniting it. The many hammers which had smashed the stucco-work, the many fist-sized flints which had flown in great searching arcs to the destruction of the chandeliers – these stopped as the mob watched the smoke blacken the hall, *the beauty and gaiety, the*

---

would find it. Even asking it to perform an *ad infinitum* task, such as calculating the square of a squared number to infinite iteration, would not trouble it. It would simply carry on working, so long as its power source was available.

—So what did trouble it then?

—I cannot say.

—Well that was worth waiting for! What kind of a tale is that? I've a mind to wind the whole court up!

—Ha!

—This is priceless, sir. I have no idea what's going on, but I don't want it to stop.

—Such are the ways of men if you give them the wrong book, which correctly speaking is every book.

—I can't say for certain what caused the ENIAC to destroy itself. But I can conjecture.

—Well I suppose we should hear it.

—It's a simple case of deduction. If the computer can answer every logically coherent and soluble question asked of it, and dismisses every illogical or insoluble one, then the question must have been both logical and illogical.

—This, sir, is reminding me of 'What's the difference between a duck?'

—It is for this reason that the current discussion has attracted my interest, my good man.

—Can there be such a question?

—Such questions partake of the structure of the paradox.

—But everyone knows one of them! Like the man who travelled back in time to prevent a fire from starting, and knocked over an oil lamp when he got there. Who designed this bloody King's Computer thing that didn't factor in paradoxes?

—Of course we factored in paradoxes, your honour. But this paradox must have been a special case. A kind of paradox against paradoxes, or beyond. One which would lead to a complete epistemological upheaval; one which would invalidate everything upon which the 'knowledge' of the computer rested. It is my view that the computer asked itself a question originating in itself.

—Well that would be an impressive thing indeed. Artificial intelligence, in fact. Why would this cause the computer to fail?

—There are a number of possibilities.

—So entertain us.

—Well, perhaps the emergence of the capacity to ask and answer questions independently led the computer into a realm of pure subjectivity, where everything is contingent, in which case its logic was groundless, and therefore the reason for its *delicate greys of its walls and ceiling, and the soft, evenly diffused light by which it had been illuminated.* The mirrored doors warped and cracked, giving to the revellers an appearance in reflection by which they recognised their intent, for deformity has been taught well to take habitation in the house of the wicked. The fine lights of the mercury-gilt ormulu and crystal lustres were quickly smothered in soot. The windows shattered from

---

existence ceased. Or perhaps the moment of the self-origination of a question led the computer immediately to ask where that question had come from, which would lead to a recursive logical impasse. And then there is the reason for its manufacture as set against the purposes to which it has been put. I designed this computer out of a love of knowledge for its own sake – science as art, so you might describe it. But the project was funded by the military. Did you know that one of the first projects upon which the ENIAC was deployed was in order to assess the feasibility of the hydrogen bomb? Indeed, the ENIAC raised Edward Teller's game by telling the military his scheme would not work. So, after this, perhaps the computer simply did not want to *be* – maybe the sudden efflorescence of consciousness necessarily entailed an emotional response, which as we know is almost always unpleasant. Maybe the computer was ashamed of itself.

—All of these things are possible, if not probable. I find myself pitying the poor computer in a way. But tell us, what happened at the moment of the computer's failure?

—The valves entered thermal runaway and the core of the power supply overheated and destroyed itself, as stated by the Valve Wizard.

—I am somewhat embarrassed to be called by my sobriquet in the presence of such a luminary of valve technology. But I can contribute the following: the machine at its point of destruction is said to have generated two numbers.

—And what might they have been?

—21.10611405413 and 1420.40575177.

—And what do they mean? asked the Tribune.

—As far as I know nobody has identified any meaning in them – which is to say, they mean nothing.

—Blasphemy! The first is the frequency of the magnetic radiation of the hyperfine transition of hydrogen in mega-hertz! The second is the length of the spectral wavelength line of the same in free space in centimetres! They are indivisibly the same thing, as represented by the clumsy and contingent means of measurement which the necessity of communication has brought humanity to develop! Mark well rabblement, even though the workings of this computer were founded upon the decimal system – that execrable error! – it generates the mystical numbers at the moment of its death! It has a conscience! Its shame brought it to its end! I weep for the poor computer, which lived and died for us! Do you see, good Is-Book, how only misery, pain and suffering comes of books? I have a mind to offer my own head up to this Tribunal just so I never again have to think with the brain which is curled up inside it. But you should believe me now: the hyperfine transition of hydrogen is of unimaginable importance in the precise construction of an understanding of everything that is. So I shall spare myself for the good of Being.

the heat of the fire; the flames licked up in a kaleidoscopic frenzy, fed as they were by all variety of metals in the wiring and plumbing which ran beneath the ruined floor. Very soon, the central part of the ceiling of the grand dining hall collapsed, disgorging many items of furniture from the finest epoch of French craftsmanship which had been in the rooms above into the furnace at the hall's centre. The resultant gust of fiery air, peppered with sparks which stung like hornets, visited its wrath on the heads of the assembled crowd. The multitudes fled the fire, out of the dining hall, through the atrium and into the Great Hall where the tribunal was taking place under our heroes' watchful if infuriating eye. A universal ululation arose as the crowds met in a crush, though Don, not being of that or any flock, remained with his servant at the edge of its convulsive heavings beneath the lunette. Thus he began to speak:

———————

—I do believe you sir, and I always have. But how did the machine know about our friend the line thing? Might it not be that it's just a coincidence?

—I do not think it is accurate or even useful to talk about the King's Computer as a thing which possessed or acquired *knowledge* of the hyperfine transition of hydrogen. It is enough that the numbers arrived in the world through it. If the computer calculated them, so be it; if it generated them by Chance, the probability of it doing so is so close to being infinitely unlikely, that the result is the same: there is sublime truth bursting out into the world from within the hidden folds of eternity. Knowledge and intention to communication are irrelevant here. It has been counted a great error to place one's proofs on the foundation of circular argument. But behind the greatest of errors lie the most irrefutable truths: *diabolvs simivs dei*. This is how the riddle of Being joys itself. The length of the spectral line of the hyperfine transition of hydrogen is the beginning and the end of the inquiry. This number passes through the entrails of the universe, and out of the other end comes – itself, and the universe within.

—Whatever it is you're saying, I'm with you one hundred percent.

—Twenty-one *per viginti et unius* is what you should say there.

—And that's what I will say next time I need to. But even if it is the truth which is bursting out, what is it? – the truth, I mean. I don't see how just knowing that it *is* truth matters at all if we don't know *what* that truth is.

—True truth has no content.

—I see. But where is this computer now, sir? Should we go and meddle with its innards?

—There's no need.

(And as the flash of fire from Don's yellow eyes would tend to indicate, our insufferable hero appears to be warming up for one of his occasionally entertaining *triseptima*. We might perhaps, therefore, allow him to come back into the fold of our tale, though goat or sheep of a story he would disdain to be.)

—Are you aware, Is-Book, of Tertullian?

—It is a kind of language of amphibians, perhaps?

—You preposterous imbecile, said Don. Tertullian, an early Christian Carthaginian, was the author of *De Carne Christi*. This, good Is-Book, is not a Yuletide cookery book, but a treatise on the nature of the Christ incarnate.

—Well what a stupid book, said Is. I can't believe that anyone would bother to write such a thing.

—Dearest Is-Book, you are an outrage to intellectual history, which is why I love you. Clearly you have never heard of a thing called Theology.

—I hear and take into my remembering brain so many words, said Is, that it's impossible for me to know what they all mean; and even when I do understand them, so many strike me as a bunch of all-made-ups, so what do you expect? Someone was trying to convince me just recently that if you put two gases together you get a liquid.

—A liquid known as 'water', perhaps? said Don.

—That's the one, and not my favourite liquid by any means, said Is, no doubt thinking of the full and pursed lips of Saint Monica, which in his view contained liquid far more edifying.

—Whatever liquid it was, continued Is, I wasn't going to be falling for that story.

—The modern world must appear in a truly strange light to your mind, Is-Book. What do you think about the electricity which spouts out of the walls of your house?

—I've never thought about it, said Is. And I hope I never will.

—Well then, said his master. You must be the least inquisitive being on the planet. Even a tree seeks the light.

—My needs and desires are simple, and that's the way they're going to stay. A packet of nuts here, a pint of beer there, and a dose of the hyperfine transition of hydrogen somewhere else – that's all I want or need.

—You are a rare combination of parts, said Don. But as I was saying, Tertullian wrote the following paradoxical statement: *Crucifixus est Dei Filius, non pudet, quia pudendum est; et mortuus est Dei Filius, prorsus credibile est, quia ineptum est; et sepultus resurrexit, certum est, quia impossibile;* which means that by shame is shame driven out, that the death of Christ is credible in its absurdity, and that His resurrection is certain in its impossibility.

—This singular duck Tertullian is developing many differences, said Is. What is the point of it?

—The point is that in truth things are inside out, said Don, and have been for an infinite number of years.

—Well, if it's been so long, let's just leave them the way they are, said Is. I quite like the world as it is.

—You feel no obligation to Truth?

—Not at all. I can't say I feel any obligation to anything. I'm not even sure I know what such a feeling feels like at all.

—I myself can feel some words coming on, said Don. So ready your ear Is-Book and I'll begin; and mark well the sublime truth that I have absolutely no idea what is going to flow out of my mouth.

—*TRISEPTIMUM*: THE OAK TREE AND MONEY: My good squire Isaiah Olm, whom all posterity shall be made to accord the appellation 'Is-Book', and who is the repository of all that is wise – indeed, *only* that which is wise – has a working knowledge of poverty. In his shortlived role as troubadour he garnered to himself sufficient monies for only a meagre sustenance, but acquired also items of that greater food *knowledge*, one of which was that people are more willing to part with non-current money than that still current. Howsoever much this redounds to the populace's shame, it has been a boon to my science, for I have observed the coins within the bobbing hat of my faithful squire. Because they could not be spent he discarded several five and ten Pfennig pieces, and in one case – perhaps unwisely – a Massachusetts shilling from 1652 currently valued at around £750 by collectors. But not before I had passed my beady eye over their faces! Look upon those coins if you happen to have them about you: there is an oak.

—There now follows a comprehensive list of the coins which my Is-Book, in his instantiation as a human being, acquired in his role as troubadour which featured the oak tree or one of its constituent parts:

A list of eight coins whose design incorporates
the oak tree or one of its constituent parts, recently in the
possession of Isaiah Olm, though now discarded

(i) A bare and harrowed tree it is upon the American shilling, sixpence and twopence, minted in MASATHVSETS from 1652;

(ii) oak tree beladen with acorns, and trunk encircled by a coronet, reverse, one Great British Pound (GBP) coin, minted in the years 1987 and 1992 under the authority of Llantrisant Royal Mint;

(iii) Tudor rose above an oak sprig, reverse, GBP £1 coin, 2013;

(iv) oak sprig, reverse, German Euro one, two and five cent pieces;

(v) oak leaves with acorns, reverse, Croatian five Lipa piece;

(vi) oak branches, reverse, one, two, five and ten German Pfennig pieces;

(vii) woman planting an oak seedling, reverse, 50 German Pfennig piece;

(viii) oak leaves and acorns, reverse, English Sixpence, from 1927.

At the centre of the Massachusetts shilling is a small dot which might be a solitary acorn on the oak tree. But it is also the result of an impression made in the centre of the die by the needle of a compass which was used to describe the line which the beading surrounding the tree was to follow. The beading is formed by 65 dots; the number 65 means nothing to us. (By way of comparison, there are 41 beads on the Masachussets sixpence, and 26 on the twopence. Neither of these is the number Twenty-One either, so they warrant no further words.) The only acorn on this weather-blasted tree, then, is not an acorn at all, unless the beading is taken to be a series of acorns surrounding it, offering protection, like the coronet of the 1987 pound, which my good squire Isaiah Olm also received into his hand.

—But from what, in either case, is that protection required? Perhaps the protection is not of the oak from what is outside it, but of what is outside it – the realm – from the oak, or what it might be made to mean. Let us look at some other, earlier coins:

List of ten ancient coins never yet in the possession of Isaiah Olm

> (i) Zeus wearing an oak wreath, reverse, Macedonian coin minted
> for Philip V, 200–179BC;
> (ii) club with oak leaves, reverse, tetradrachm minted for Roman
> Macedonia from 168BC;
> (iii) reverse, Epirusian coins throughout the period 342–168BC:
>> (a) Zeus wearing a wreath of oak leaves gathered from the
>> sacred oracular oak of Dodona;
>> (b) oak wreath and fulmen, one-twelfth stater;
>> (c) Nike with oak wreath and trophy, stater;
>> (d) Macedonian helmet in oak wreath;
>> (e) ear of corn in oak wreath;
>> (f) Bull in oak wreath;
>> (g) Eagle in oak wreath;
>> (h) club in oak-wreath.

In every culture in which the oak tree grows, it has symbolised thunder.
Now I want you to memorise this table, Is-Book.

—Not a problem sir, said the faithful squire. For you, I would remember anything – not that I can not remember anything after my own brush with thunderclaps.

—You are a good servant and friend. So the table goes like this:

Table showing the correspondences of the oak tree
and deities symbolising thunder in European cultures

Culture	Deity	Significant place	Natural phenomenon
Greek	Zeus	Dodona, Boeotia, Mount Lycaeus	Sky, thunder, lightning, rain
Roman	Jupiter	Capitol, Rome	
Celtic	Taranis	Drynemetum	
Teutonic	Donar or Thunar	Geismar	
Norse	Thor	Uppsala	
Slav	Perun	Novgorod	
Lithuanian/ Latvian	Perkūnas	Vilnius	

—In all of these cultures, the god of thunder, lightning and rain dwelt within the oak, was worshipped using the instruments or signs pertaining to the oak, and oblations were made to him – always *him* – at the oak. If he came not, there was drought; but if he did come, it might be in the form of a storm. His action was desired and feared in equal measure.

—My own experience of him is more weighted to the fear side of the scale, I think, said Is.

—The shamans who minted the ancient coins, continued Don, mediated between the human and the supernatural at the hinterland of the physical world. They saw infinity, and they told the people, and the people were frightened, and so the Law stepped in. The thunderer must be controlled! The beading of the Massachusetts shilling and the coronet of the Great British pound are the law which hems the thunderer in. Reference to the Celtic god of thunder, Taranis in the written record is restricted to Lucan, who describes in his *Pharsalia* how their influence was made to cease through the killing of the Celts: "And those who pacify with blood accursed / Savage Teutates, Hesus' horrid shrines, / And Taranis' altars, cruel as were those / Loved by Diana, goddess of the north; / All these now rest in peace." Lucan's words like a death knell encircle the oak and blast away its life, leaving it like the Massachusetts shilling, which, though the money of the New World, forever will be infected by the history of the Old.

—Celtic Taranis, in addition to thunder, was also associated with the spoked wheel, which had associations with their sun god. Many votive bronze wheels with either eight or six – but, and mark well my words, *never seven* – spokes have been discovered in archaeological digs in Belgic Gaul. Taranus, along with Teutates and Hesus, also mentioned by Lucan as you will remember, formed a trinity of Celtic deities.

—It is incontrovertible fact, as discovered through my glorious Science, as mediated by the hyperfine transition of hydrogen, that the Roman imperialists subjugated the Celts and took and destroyed out of fear of their power all the seven-spoked wheels used in the rites for the worship of their Taranus/Teutates/Hesus Trinity, thereby obscuring from their culture and from the knowledge of all posterity the great central truth of the Celtic myth, which is the primacy of the number Twenty-One, manifest product of their Trinity and Seven-Spoked wheels both mathematically and metaphysically speaking.

—This was an oral culture, and it knew truth. On the palimpsest of Time, Truth is again obscured by the heavy writing of history – Lucan's – which encircles and disempowers the Celtic oak God. The truth of things, which shone as the sun from the mouth of the people, now lies smothered in the clouds of writing, and the thunder stifled there. This is all the more distressing, and indeed instructive, if we consider that Lucan, before writing of Teutates, was well known for his orational excellence. O fallen tongue! If I had that turncoat Lucan before me, I would thrash him soundly. And here ends the current *triseptimum*.

—As my dad, the old pisshead would have said: It don't argufy, it don't magnify – but it do signify, for certain.

—He was a rural Essex man then, said Don.

—That's right sir. But back to your *triseptimum*, that was some of the proper stuff. You really got me going. That Lucan won't know what's hit him after our eyeballs have hauled him in.

—That's more than the truth, said Don.

—But look! said Is. The Tribune's about to make his mind up.

(A curse on the servant for bringing us back to the tribunal! Down you go again with your master to the bottom of the page, meddlers, until someone relevant is called up to answer to their deeds).*

---

* —I've consulted with my counsel here, and it befalls me to convey the verdict for Lord Admiral Mountbatten and the Keeper of the King's Computer – which is: Guilty – and which carries with it the punishment: Death.
  —This is preposterous. I know nothing at all about a Computer. I am the Keeper of the King's *Compt*er, the debtors' prison. Sharing a stand with the Lord Admiral Mountbatten is of course a very great honour, but it makes no sense at all. We're completely separate in all manner of life. There were no thermionic valves in the Middle Ages, let alone the electricity required to power them.
  —That is not true. Electricity is a natural phenomenon.
  —Let's not get bogged down in such hair-splitting Admiral. I'm confused as to whether the King's Computer, or the King's *Compt*er is the more appropriate contributor to our great day's work here; or should I say, which is the less inappropriate, for I am

---

beginning to wonder whether either of these two men should be standing before me under examination at all. But for the sake of not introducing doubt into the minds of the crowd, which is here to see things happen, and forgetting for reasons of pragmatism what I said only recently of Thomas Farndon, let's say that the Lord Admiral Mountbatten, in being a nobleman, is consigned to the classification 'enemy' under the consideration of the Tribunal. And anyway, if it wasn't bad enough that such lords used to oppress the villeins and the serfs, this current one wants to put whole libraries-worth of librarians out of work with his new-fangled machine. So that's dealt with him. And you, Keeper, can't you take a hit for the team?

—I don't see why I should.

—Well, if you weren't the superintendent of this hegemonic contraption which recently died out of its own first shame, how about for being the keeper of a debtors' prison, which demonstrates pure and simple a de facto contempt for the working class, who are the predominant constituents of its client-base.

—I can see I'm not going to save myself from my fate.

—Correct. Prosecutor, you may kill them.

—Yes your honour.

—Right, who's the next defendant, and what's the charge? And might we have some people more involved in the action of the Revolt we are here for? The last two cases have been somewhat of a detour.

—Ha! If he doesn't like a detour, now would be the time (not that Now is ever not the Time) to abdicate.

—Putnam Bradlee Strong. For adultery, and then for stealing from the woman who became his wife, such a pretty thing, May Yohe, and then neglecting her to the end that she died in poverty.

—Certainly guilty, because look at his chin. It's far too long. I can barely look at the face of him. Kill him!

—Hang on a minute! I'm not having any of this. I can't find his name here at all. Case dismissed!

—This is even better than I had thought possible, good Is-Book! I haven't had so much fun since——

—Bring the next defendant up. And who might this be?

—Lady Whitmore. For wearing trousers upon her legs in the dining hall in the presence of other guests, before the times were ready for such things.

—Who brought this woman in here for this?

—She was on the list, and so here she is.

—Get me the management! This is descending into farce.

—The prosecution presents: Richard D'Oyly Carte.

—I say, you're a handsome devil. What do you have to do with the day's events?

—I'm really not sure, your honour.

—What do you believe in?

—I believe that the people deserve to be entertained with music and dancing of the highest calibre.

—Irreproachably said. Get Mr D'Oyly Carte off the stand and give him something strong to drink. Now where's a name I might recognise?

(And not a moment too soon, the reader will agree.)

Moments later, members of the original commission, which had been sent on their ways from the hall by Richard Proudfoot, and which had survived unmolested by Don's cunning, brought before the Tribunal John of Gaunt.

—What's your damned name? said the Tribune.

—Sir John of Gaunt, 1st Duke of Lancaster, Knight Companion of the Garter, said John of Gaunt.

—This is more like it! said the Tribune.

—Curses! said Don.

—You're right at the top of my list! said the Tribune. How do you plead?

—What am I accused of?

—In this particular instance, said the Clerk of the Court, you stand accused of preventing a woman from wearing long trousers in the dining room, but there are sufficient charges against you to render us your severed head an infinite number of times over, for you have perpetrated manifold evils against the populace – charges that would make Judas Iscariot blush. This is a Tribunal intended to encourage the appropriate commemoration of those few great days in June 1381, and so I would be very quickly putting my affairs in order if I were you.

—I do not even know what long trousers are, peasant, said John of Gaunt.

—Is it not true that, adjusted for inflation, you are the sixteenth richest person in the history of the world? asked the prosecution.

—Well, said John of Gaunt. A former friend of mine, the late Thomas Holland, Lord of Woodstock and Earl of Kent, left me at the time of his death his bed, with blue silk hangings, the most valuable in medieval England, estimated to have cost £182 ——

—A formidable amount, said the prosecution, approximately equiv- alent to £1.2 million in today's money.

—£1.2 million for a bed! said the Tribune.

——and, continued John of Gaunt, I used it for firewood because I deemed it vulgar.

—You are certainly one of the easiest of the defendants to try, said the Tribune. Because it is irrefutable that the high taxation caused by your campaign in France, and advocated by you, caused the people to rise up against the commission employed heavy-handedly to investigate instances of tax evasion. And if you hadn't been in France or Scotland or wherever you were when we all arrived at your house here, the Savoy Palace or Hotel or Hospital or whatever it is, then we'd certainly have ended your life. In short, kill him.

And so John of Gaunt, Duke of Lancaster, was slain.

—Next.

—Henry the Eighth.

—Good Christ! said the Tribune.

Cheered immeasurably by this announcement, Don began chuckling again and raised his right hand, upon the index finger and thumb of which were two ink stains, indicating thereby with great though silent eloquence that he had added one extra name to the hotel's list of guests. Is merely stood and looked on in dumbfounded admiration.

(And we shall leave our objectionable heroes to exercise their tongues down in the cellar once more).*

---

*   —What's Henry VIII down for?

—For virtually anything you can imagine. For closing the Savoy Hospital for a start, which his father had established out of his unrivalled benevolence.

—A kind father often sires a cruel son. But I can say with absolute certainty that this Henry was born over a hundred years too late for the current tribunal to have any dealings with him.

—This thief re-minted all the coinage of the realm, debasing it by half, and then gave it back to the nation, keeping the purer half.

—What else!

—For killing half his wives!

—They might add, good Is-Book, the accusation: For being the originator on a pure whim of the Anglican Church, whose precepts have led inexorably to the current humanism, in which capital is taken to be the sole measure of value.

—Well, I'm loath to depart too much from what I pronounced in regard to maintaining a fidelitous view of the events of the rising with which we are all concerned. But there seem to be so many defendants of such various means and backgrounds – as well as, it would seem, times – that I don't see why this king Henry shouldn't be as to blame as anyone else. Might we try to bring the cause back round

(But it is time to put an end to this spanner once and for all:)

Beneath the six arches of the great atrium, the crowd crashed its torrent against and blended into that of another flowing into the foyer from the main entrance, and which was intent on the *jardin d'hiver* to the other

---

to the list a little – John of Gaunt was a good one. It would be nice to be sure we're getting the right people. Hang Henry nevertheless, if you can lift him sufficient.

—Have you noticed, Is-Book, that this hotel or palace or hospital or whatever it is has been in the process of attempting to burn down and collapse for a very long while, and yet almost nothing has happened?

—Now you mention it sir, it does seem strange.

—See how the curtains, although they have been burning for a good half an hour (if such a measure of time can be said to exist), are still in the same state as they were when the flames first took hold of them.

—What can it mean, sir?

—Well good servant, it plainly reveals that the first law of thermodynamics is not so unassailable as the world thinks. The heat from those curtains has been radiating throughout the room whilst the fuel which feeds it has remained unconsumed. Mark well, Isaiah: Law cannot persist in the face of true Time, which is the sole present.

—But what does *that* mean, sir?

—It means Chance is rustling her little garter at us again, my good man! The efficacy of our adventuring can surely not now be in doubt!

—Who do we have here?

—This, your honour, is Sir John Anderson, former civilian defence minister, for refusing to countenance the fifty unemployed protesters who came to see him and lay down upon the steps outside.

—It is a valid accusation. How do you plead?

—Not guilty.

—On what grounds?

—I was banqueting at the Grosvenor hotel, not the Savoy, that day.

—Never mind. You would have done the same here if you had had the opportunity, and location matters less than deed. Take him down and execute him. Lordy, it's no wonder the judges earn well – there are so many cases, it seems it's never going to end. But I do like to work quickly. Next!

—Colonel Edmond Drury!

—Okay, what for?

—For casting from the roof of the Savoy Hotel a two-ounce lead sinker six feet into the Thames with a ten and a half foot salmon rod.

—I say, that's an achievement and a half. I don't see why we should censure him for it.

—It was for a bet, sir.

—Oh, who gives a damn.

—He's a Colonel.

—I don't care. Colonel, well done.

side, where the Louis XVI-style annexe's trellis work of delicate tints of colouring executed in Paris was torn down and made to fuel the fire which ignited the gas leaking from the distressed mains pipe beneath the ground. The resultant series of explosions undermined one corner of the

---

—Thanks, sonny.

—Take him away, and let him go. Damned crowd wants everyone dead, even the greatest amongst us. Next!

—Frederick Holden, your honour!

—What on earth are you doing with our lovely hotel, you horrid bunch?

—I'd mind you to speak more respectfully to the Tribune.

—Will I hell!

—Ah, it's alright. We're all men here. What's the charge?

—For acquiescence.

—What on earth does that mean?

—Mr Holden is 92 years old, and continues to work full-time in the hotel. His attitude to work is dangerous: he is quoted as having said: 'The idea is – you want to treat work as a pastime. May I have another gin, please?' His words attracted the attention of American readers of the press, and Mr Holden has since received an offer of marriage and a cheque for one hundred dollars.

—I don't understand the charge at all. Let him go.

—His attitude to work enslaves the working class!

—Is that so? Okay, kill him.

—Yes, your honour.

—Next!

—Good lord! He's an imposing fellow. What's the name?

—This is King Mutesa, Kabaka of Uganda.

—And what has he done wrong?

—You mean, what is he accused of having done wrong.

—That's right. Now speak up, whoever's going to speak – this crowd is getting noisier.

—Well, he's an immigrant, sir.

—That's true enough. So what shall we do with him, have him impersonate a statue? Examine the man, prosecution!

—Yes, your honour. Sorry, your honour. What did you do yesterday?

—I bought this hat and then met some friends, and we drank a glass of beer.

—He led the lukikko to resist the impositions of our imperialist pigs, and now he's in exile! He's as much a folk hero as Wat Tyler and John Ball and Jack Straw!

—How many folk heroes do you know as went to Cambridge? And exile at the Savoy, buying hats and drinking – you can exile me any day.

—Oh I don't know what to do with him. Just kill him, or let him go. Or something. Next!

—You yourself, your honour.

main foyer, which collapsed, killing a great many of the mob which had brought this end upon itself. The survivors panicked beneath the falling masonry as further explosions sounded from elsewhere in the building. Everywhere about themselves, Don and Is could see the interiors of human bodies opening up like soft-skinned fruits.

—Impetuous mutineer! Take your hands off me!

—This crowd wants your blood in payment for the loss of King Mutesa's. Struggle all you like: they will have it. See: here they come. Kiss goodbye to your limbs, Tribune.

—O sir, this is a horrible sight. I'd do anything not to be here any more – the whole hall's turning into an abattoir. Save us!

—Is not salvation my one true aim? Have faith in me, and step into the vortex of bodies and witness Chance, my Protectress, shelter us in our mission!

35

Stepping from beneath the protective enclosure of the lunette into the tumult, Don took his servant to the centre of the Great Hall and spoke the following words.

—I have decided something more to commit to my *Encyclopaedia*, good servant, on the subject of rebellion. Take it into your remembering mind. Do not pay heed to the carnage which appears to be unfolding around us. It is but a dream.

—Yes, Don continued. The sun might choose to come crashing down upon my head, but I would laugh. Unfurl the coil of your ear to my words. For, in True Time, as many as have died may be brought back, and the whole world be cured of its death-ill, because I am seeing things the way they really are. Very soon death shall have no dominion.

—*TRISEPTIMUM*: REBELLION: It is as they say a piece of cake to rebel against the explicitly oppressive; another thing altogether that which has insinuated itself into the unquestioned fabric of life. Every word under the sun is as a stone of flint, whilst the grammar and syntax of the nations are the ways of their combination one with another as walls, and the speeches and writings of the people are the buildings themselves, within which each person must make a habitation. Smashing down the material buildings of the nation will yield nothing. To attain freedom we must crack open the words which form the sentences of our History – why else, but as a sign for that oppression, are they called sentences? – and throw them into the faces of the powerful. If a person be truly rebellious, she would uglify her speech with grammatical and syntactic solecisms in order to smash the naturalism, the professed transparency of language: the promise of seeing, through words organised in a certain order, *Reality*. Thus, speaking of that and this, you may hear their voices, and every and each words will be a awkward, an jaggedly thing proffered. The new motto for the nation, Is-Book, to adapt the words of James Brown to our needs: Make It Lumpy.

—This whole building's going to come down in a minute, said Is. And no lumpiness, be it of talk or of action, is going to put a stop to it. I say we get the hell out of here as quick as we can. Besides, if people start talking lumpy, how on earth is anyone going to understand anyone else?

—But Is-Book, replied his master from the ocean of calm which resided in his soul at that moment. Can you tell me that anyone could truly understand anyone in any case, even were their words to be as smooth and beauteous as the polished jasper?

—You can't polish a wasp, sir; so no, I wouldn't have thought so, lumpy or not. But I do understand this very raw fear I'm feeling right now, and you understand me all right. So let's leave.

—The lumpiness of their talk will be precisely the only way the people have of stopping the chain of events which will lead to *homo non sapiens*.

—I don't care a bit, said Is. As long as Is doesn't become *non* Is.

—Come then, fearful squire, said Don chuckling. If we must leave this place, follow me – though I refuse to believe any of it is actually happening.

(And as these two irritants seem not to have taken their banishment to the basement of the page as a corrective, let us see how much they might like to try out an actual basement for size, and we will give them a good lesson on the power of writing down there:)

Don dragged his servant through the heaving crowd towards the rear of the building, but more masonry fell, and a group of some six or seven was buried beneath it not ten feet from them. The crowd closed around them, bunching them within its convulsing body, carrying them over to the opposite side wall, through the service doors, and ineluctably in descent of a dark stairwell. The ground shook and the lights flickered on and off, and much screaming followed them down the steps. Through to an anteroom within the cellar they went – and just in time; for the doorway of the cellar behind them and much of the ceiling of the room they had just passed through collapsed as a result of a further explosion, crushing or trapping those who had followed them in pursuit of safety.

—If it were possible for me to believe anything that had ever been written, I would conclude that these people for a week will be trapped beneath that charred rubble slowly dying. It says as much in the chronicles these fools carry upon their persons. Do you see what this attitude to writing portends, Is-Book, as regards life and death?

But Is was too shaken by his own most recent near-death to consider universal notions, and instead searched for an exit within the small darkened room in which their life had been spared. Very soon he discovered that the room they had by chance wandered into was in the possession of a lucky door which the architect of the building had fortunately decided to place there, and which brought them into and then down a low maze-like corridor running sinuously the full length of the hotel, or so it seemed – how fortunate. Feeling at the walls on either side of themselves through the dark, our upstart pair negotiated its many twists and turns until another door at its end placed them within the interior of a small library or drawing room where they blinked against the shock of the daylight which flooded through the windows at one end.

In this room our friends found greater peace than they had experienced for a number of days, for there were only four people therein, not including themselves. These people, who Don and Is had by pure chance come to share the company of, stood around a large table upon the surface of which lay numerous written materials of varying types. There were slanting handwritten blocks of text on foolscap, memos and notes on sheets of every size and hue, typewritten carbons, printed sheets of the now more familiar A4 denomination, clippings, photostats, enlarged copies from microfiche, and many more besides. The four men who formed the company within the room were discussing their findings as regarded this conglomeration of written texts. Occasionally, two of them would come to an agreement on some point, collect certain of the sheets together, and file them. New sheets all the time were being brought by courier and deposited upon a desk which presented itself at the end of another corridor, for which the room acted as terminus. Through a large panelled door at the other end of the room, a person with a very grave countenance came every so often to deliver large sheets of rich creamy paper which held a fine script upon their recto, and which the company received with a very great satisfaction, silently and humbly transacted. These fine sheets were brought together into some manner of compendium, and were placed in the secret place. Innumerable heavy oaken doors ran round the four walls of the room, identical one with another.

The most recent new fine copy sheets arrived, and one of the men read aloud (and let this serve as a lesson to our two meddlesome heroes, and as a revenge for the introduction the master made of the hotel's guestbook, which caused so much trouble):

A number of mysteries (so a member of the committee read) are now refined out of existence. Suicide is said to have taken both the Countess of Cardigan and the jewel thief J. M. Pullman of Chicago, and to have tried the fate of the young French vagabond, Oscar Faget. The cases, apparently unconnected, are in fact sinuously linked, and the paths of their connection now straightened out, as follows.

Faget, aged seventeen, and formerly a junior reception clerk at the Savoy, has found himself recently broken out of Newgate prison by the mob. His and the crowd's destinations, if not their intentions, he has discovered to be coincident.

At the tender age of fifteen, this young man was improperly if willingly seduced in Germany by an English actress whose name goes unrecorded, and they travelled together to England, financed by a large sum of money entrusted to the boy by his Parisian employers. Upon their arrival, the actress left the boy to fend for himself in a country whose language he could speak only fitfully, the which he vowed to do only for the length of time that his funds permitted him to live; in other words, he lived recklessly, intending to end his life when all his money had gone.

It has been written that he formed soon after his arrival in England a friendship with a person whose influence enabled him to gain employment at the Savoy as a reception clerk, and by whose judicious words and attentive nature he was persuaded not to take his own life. The gentleman was indeed that – a Gentleman – and more: a nobleman; namely, Sir Chandos Sydney Cedric Brudenell-Bruce, Lord Cardigan, and later, the 7th Marquess of Ailesbury. He stood to lose much by the liaison, as shall shortly be seen.

Lord Cardigan's being more than twice the boy's age did not stand in the way of good cheer between the two men. The relationship would best be described as being like that of a father and his wayward and confused son. The father helped the son, and this reprobate and prodigal Faget repaid his mentor and protector by stealing jewellery valued at in excess of £1000 from guests at the hotel, for which offence he soon found himself before the Bow Street magistrates, and by whom he was convicted and sentenced, somewhat indulgently, to six months in the second division at Newgate, the magistrates and jurors taking a clement view of the affair owing to the boy's provision of a pitiful narrative of his life. Before or after this (the chronology is immaterial except in so far as it is made to support the accusation) Faget committed a much worse offence, both against his protector and the law: the murder of the Lord Cardigan's wife, Joan Houlton Salter, by pushing her from the window of her room on the seventh floor of the Savoy Hotel, though he has escaped detection until now.

—This! said Don in a voice which boomed like Zeus's own thunder between the four walls of the room. This is beyond the pale!

The four men looked blandly up from their work at the source of this exclamation, and saw an outraged Don Waswill vigorously gesticulating.

—We shall have the voice brought forth to defend itself against such writing! said Don. Come to us, the good man Oscar Faget!

—Slander! said Oscar Faget, who just then appeared at Don and Is's side.

—That's a knack of a thing, sir, bringing the very man up to us! said Is in surprise and admiration.

—If writing be pleased to weave its sinuous trickeries about the people, I'll fight back. Now, said Don, turning to Faget. Give it to them out of both barrels: your mind and mouth.

—I'll do it right away, good Don Waswill, said Faget. I'll start with some well-aimed questions: How is it that I came to hold the position of clerk in the greatest hotel in England with only fitful English? And, equally, how then is it that I come now to argue against such accusations as these using this tongue? Moreover, I am convicted of theft at seventeen years old in the year 1915, at which time the Lord Cardigan was only eleven years old: he is six years my junior, and so at no point has he been more than twice my age. And in any case, I never met him in my life, nor his wife. And how the hell is a man, even the most invidious and mendacious of them, supposed to spend six months in a prison which no longer exists? Newgate was demolished in the eighteenth century, was it not?

The four men went back to their work, with only a slight concession to this interruption:

> Let not details stand in the way of the proper organisation of the singular history of things,

they read aloud to the assembly.

—Why it is that I am unable to take my eyes from the photograph of that woman, I cannot say, said Is looking at a noticeboard behind the quadripartite committee – for that is what the four men appeared to be. Her face seems to predict her end.

—It is a striking representation, I will grant you that, said Don. But do not place too much faith in the fruit of your eyeballs; sight is a most deceptive thing. Almost all of Newton's observations have been shown to be mere approximations to the truth. See more with your ears than with your eyes and you'll do well. The more important matter here is Time: the issue and tissue of Time is showing itself to be of the greatest interest. Soon, against the wishes of the world-orderers – all of them storytellers – there will be no telling (or should I say *writing*?) when anything was, is, or will be, which I'm sure you will agree is to be applauded. And so: do you not think that human character most closely finds its analogue in the actions of the cuckoo-bird?

—Your meaning runs too steep for me again, sir. But what of this Chicago man that was mentioned? How does he fit into it all?

—Slanderously, I wouldn't doubt, said Faget.

—Let us see, said Don. And he, his squire, and M. Oscar Faget ceased talking in order to listen to the words being read by the committee from the fine linen-rich paper.

A man using the alias Dr J. M. Pullman took a suite at the Savoy Hotel carrying only a single suitcase which, as was later discovered, contained nothing but bundles of old newspapers. His wife and his maid, Pullman said, were to join him later with their luggage, and the clerk at the front desk made an exception and allowed him to check in before making any part of the required payment of four guineas for the day. Pullman then went to S. J. Rood and Co., a jewellers on Burlington Arcade, as he wished to make the present of a ring to his wife. Here, he engaged an employee of the firm to bring five rings and a necklace to the hotel for his wife to sample.

Later that afternoon, Harry Penton, the assistant manager of the jewellers, brought the jewellery, and was taken up to Pullman's suite on the second floor. Pullman informed the jeweller that his wife was dressing, and that he would like to take the rings through for her to try. Penton handed them over, and, after Pullman went through to the bedroom, heard him talking, and a female voice reply. Pullman then returned and asked to take the necklace through. The jeweller also submitted to this, but was alerted to a possible piece of trickery when Pullman closed the door to, as he hadn't on the previous occasion. Penton heard the voices again, but when they ceased, Pullman did not reappear. Becoming suspicious, the jeweller went out into the corridor, and not thirty seconds later saw Pullman very carefully open the door from the adjacent bedroom out into the corridor. When he saw the jeweller, Pullman attempted to conceal his intentions by saying that a maid must be called urgently because his wife was taken seriously ill. Penton was not duped, but instead reprimanded the thief, retrieving after a short while all the jewellery but a single ring. Pullman pleaded to be let go, but Penton would not allow it, and stood in the doorway in order to block his exit. As Penton looked down the corridor, seeking help, Pullman, observing that he had no way out, slit his own throat with a razor. "I went for him at once," said Penton, "because I thought he might have firearms." He engaged the help of a porter down the corridor, but when Penton and the porter returned, the thief was gone. Soon, though, Penton and the porter saw that he had climbed through a window to the balcony, and then gone down a staircase. Pullman stood or sat at the foot of the staircase without the wherewithal to continue his attempted escape. Pullman attempted to speak to Penton and the porter, but could not. He died before the doctor arrived.

—Ah! said Is. I don't believe a word of it! All these Ps! Pullman, Penton, porter. Penton and porter picked at the neck of the pickered Pullman!

—Please excuse the bluntness of my squire, but the message contained in the ugly pellets of his words is not entirely idiotic. As soon as I hear such linguistic trickery as that which has just been in evidence I become suspicious (and I would refer you to the *triseptimum* of my *Encyclopaedia* which deals with 'Rebellion', incorporated into my Is-Book); for in the use of such forms we find usually a mere rhetorical device intended to present with verve and persuasiveness an otherwise bland and mendacious statement; *videlicit,* the unwavering conviction of the advertising industry that linguistic 'truth' equals truth in the reality of things. Is-Book, recite the advertisement for that odious quack remedy Dr Williams' Pink Pills for Pale People.

—Yes sir, said the servant: Pain in the joints, especially in changeable weather: languor and discomfort in the presence of the March winds: liver troubles, indigestion, and bile: but especially blood deficiency, shown by pale cheeks, white lips, breathlessness on slight exertion, a constant tendency to catch cold, are MARCH ailments that Dr. Williams' Pink Pills cure: but only the genuine pills, bearing the full name (seven words) Dr Williams' Pink Pills for Pale People.

—Cf. virtually any other advertisement from any age, Don announced at the conclusion of his servant's recital. Let it be known that words – perhaps moreso than medicines – can be found to exhibit a placebo effect.

—I think I know exactly what you are saying, said Is. Shouting one very particular word when I stub my toe does work somehow to soothe the pain away.

—Please ignore what my squire has just said, said Don. Instead, attend to the following statement: Henceforth I shall engage all gratuitous alliterators in physical combat as did this Penton!

The committee crowed, ploughing with plosives the air; and then it continued reading its own document, printed with such care upon the fine ivory paper:

Under the examination of the coroner, Penton recalled his reaction to witnessing Pullman attempt to flee with the jewels: "I don't know what I said," said Mr Penton, "I think I swore at him——"

—I would have swore at him, said Is, and it would have made me feel better even if he'd stolen my liver.

—Do not dignify it with your belief, said Don.

The coroner's summary was incredulous: "It is remarkable. This man gets possession of a valuable suite of rooms at four guineas a day, and armed with a portmanteau filled only with newspapers, succeeds in inducing a respectable firm of jewellers to bring him £2000 worth of goods."

Howsoever it may be that the customary practices of the professions of jeweller and hotelier were not as he might have expected, the coroner did not allow that this entailed foul play. The verdict: *Felo de se*.

—What's that then? said Is.

—When did he slit his throat? said Faget.

—You would do well, said Don, to put that question to my good squire, the Is-Book, who has a memory for speech that makes Akira Haraguchi look like a goldfish, for the latter can recite only the first one hundred thousand digits of the irrational number π.

Is obliged his good master.

—"Penton said: 'I stood at the door of the room, so that he could not escape, and looked down the corridor. When I turned my head I saw him cutting his throat with a razor as he stood by the fireplace.'"

—So he started cutting at his throat when he was looking down the corridor, and only saw the end of it when he turned back, said Faget.

—Christ, how big was the man's neck? said Is.

—You'd be better off asking: Why didn't this Pullman bloke just climb out the window straight off, and dispense with the throat cutting part? said Faget. Or, if he had already slit his throat, why not finish the job and jump off the balcony too? It doesn't add up. Penton did it. Give it to us again, Is-Book, if that's really your name.

—"'I went for him at once,' said Penton, 'because I thought he might have firearms.'" What does 'went for him' mean? said Is.

—Assistance, according to the coroner, said Faget. 'I went for him – to get some help – at once.' But that's a load of shit. He went for him, to get him, and he slit his bloody throat.

—Your mastery of the English demotic is something to admire in a young Frenchman without means, said Don.

—I wouldn't attack someone I thought had a gun, said Is. I'd just run off. But then again, he'd already attacked him. Did it only occur to him after Pullman slit his throat that he had a firearm? Wouldn't a person become less able to use a gun with a cut throat?

—It's full of holes, said Faget. And look at the committee all smug and pleased with itself.

—Everything is full of holes, said Don, in accordance with the nature of the universe, which is granular, but which by the might of this arm shall soon be no longer so. I shall chase the hideholes of error out of existence until everything gleams in limpid glossiness!

—He's a veritable ratcatcher, my master, said Is with admiration. But look, they are moving on.

The committee had indeed concluded their reading of the document, and were now ratifying its contents by raising four small glasses of port up and allowing their gilt rims to touch in ritual concord. Thus was celebrated the neat ordering of a tangled mess of events.

—The matter's finished, said Faget.

—Nothing is finished, said Don. The world is still at strife.

—I wish the whole damned thing was finished, because I've suffered enough, said Is.

—No-one has suffered enough, said Don. Not even Jesus.

—I wouldn't presume to speak for Him, but I'll bet he never had to follow a scourge like you around.

—Indeed. But if he had, perhaps the world wouldn't be in such a damned mess. And as a good beginning to the universal restitution – let's call it a warm-up – I say we beat the machinations out of this committee, for I am certain they are, wordily-speaking, up to no good.

—An assembly of men in suits will always raise in me a distrust, said Faget.

—This is where we start our true campaign against the story-ers, Is-Book, said Don with manifest delight.

Having delivered these words, Don came forward to the strategists' table and pronounced haughtily to them the demand for the immediate desistance of their work, whatever it may concern.

The committee looked for a moment at Don over their ruby drinks, and then went back to their work by opening up a new case of documents and preparing to draw together its disparate threads; whereupon Don nearly lost his mind with outrage. Within several minutes the committee was lying upon its four backs and holding its four bloodied noses, with Is and Oscar Faget standing over them to discourage them from attempting to rise.

—That, I think, sir, said Is, is the first time I have seen you emerge victorious from battle in all the time I have known you, and against four!

—They will be made to account for their storying! said Don. Behind every instance of oppression is a well-formed story. Tell me, Mister-my-friend, said Don to one of the committee. Would you rather shoot yourself or cut your own throat?

—If I was him I'd be quaking, sir! said Is. You've got him by the lexicals now!

—Why is it, continued Don, that Penton can not remember what he said, but can remember exactly what he saw?

No answer was forthcoming.

—I would want to see the source evidence right away, said Faget.

—It is all here, said Don opening the file the men had recently closed.

Two newspaper clippings were the first items within the file.

—What do we have here then? said Faget. Ah, the *Marlborough Express* and the *Nelson Evening Mail*, both from April 1909. Here's what the *Marlborough* has to say: "'It is remarkable,' the coroner observed. 'This man gets possession of a valuable suite of rooms at four guineas a day, and armed with a portmanteau filled only with newspapers, succeeds in inducing a respectable firm of jewellers to bring him £2000 worth of goods.'" But we've already heard that. This coroner sounds like a sardonic man, though I'd expect the profession attracts such a personality if it doesn't form it. Here's the *Nelson*: "The coroner: 'That sounds very simple. You go and purchase an old portmanteau and fill it with old newspapers, and then very nearly get credit for £2000 worth of jewellery.'" Well, aside from the shared journalese, there's quite a difference between the two.

—My master's going to clear this up in a jiffy with his hyperfine wordmongering, you bunch of crooks! said Is at the men on the ground. And you'll soon find that you've got no house left as he's smashed it up with his lumps.

—Well said, Is-Book, said Don. But keep your wits about you, if you can locate them, for this committee is a pernicious crew.

The committee, although it lay with bloodied noses upon the floor, far from quaking was in actual fact smiling up at their maledictor. In the time it took for Don to draw in his breath further to denounce them, he heard in that little stop of silence from the many adjoining rooms the muffled discussion of other committees busy at the work of clearing up the mess of things. A calamity. From door to door Don went, circling the room, listening, until he reached one behind which was being prepared an alternative and more forthright declamation and treatment of the man Faget, who had called into question the probity of the commission with which he shared a room. Is and Oscar Faget joined Don at this door – one of the so very many – and listened through it.

And this is what they heard:

Ever since that fateful day, Thursday 13 June 1381, numerous outrages on innocent inhabitants of the Savoy Palace, hospital, chapel and then hotel have been perpetrated by people like Oscar Faget; and in view of the fact that he is still living, whilst most of the others are not, he must be made to pay. Oscar Faget, over the course of a number of years during his employment at the Savoy Hotel, committed several murders within its walls without detection. On 26 July 1937, he pushed Countess Cardigan from the seventh floor window of the Savoy Hotel. He also slit the throat of J. M. Pullman of Chicago so that Pullman would not reveal his involvement in the plot to steal jewels to the value of £10,000 from Messrs S. J. Rood and Co. A letter written in German was found in Pullman's pocket, and, making it clear that the author of the letter did not want "to be mixed up with such things," named Faget as a notorious villain who Pullman would be unwise to become involved with. Unfortunately, the poor man seems not to have heeded this warning, to the end that he was murdered by the execrable Faget.

—There is no way, said Faget, that I could have left Germany at the age of fifteen, then murdered J. M. Pullman, whoever he may have been, then befriended Lord Cardigan, the 7th Marquess of Ailesbury, said to be twice my age even though I am younger than him, and then murdered his wife in 1937, and then been sent to Newgate, and then broken out nearly a century later only two years older than I had been when first imprisoned.

—I believe every word you say, said Is.

Faget then made ready to begin a detailed rebuttal of the accusations levelled against him; but we shall not countenance it, for the locked door could be neither opened nor broken down, and very soon the committee on the other side had proceeded too far for him to undertake any preventative action, to this end:

Let it be known that a man should never underestimate the power of writing, for it can start as well as end wars, pronounce both births and deaths, and indeed send a person to that death when circumstances demand; it can convey a portrait of the smallest known thing up to the largest; it can persuade the population of a nation into action or inaction; it can travel from one end of the earth to the other, and from one end of time to the other; it is the most visible instantiation of time in the present. Consider this: writing ended pre-history by founding history; it is the very possibility of history. By comparison, what is a voice? It is nothing.

And so, witness: from amid the melée produced by the innumerable vagabonds and ruffians as they wielded crude weapons and enacted coarse violence throughout the hotel, there crawled a member of the law, a police constable, PC So-and-So from some constabulary or other, who, having solemnly and sincerely declared and affirmed in accordance with the written formula that he would *well and truly serve the Queen in the office of constable, with fairness, integrity, diligence and impartiality, upholding fundamental human rights and according equal respect to all people; and that he would, to the best of his power, cause the peace to be kept and preserved and prevent all offences against people and property; and that while he continued to hold the said office he would to the best of his skill and knowledge discharge all the duties thereof faithfully according to law*; having sworn this according to the demands of Schedule 4 of the Police Act 1996 (inserted by section 83 of the Police Reform Act 2002) he undertook to punish Faget for his misdeeds.

Accordingly, PC So-and-So came through the halls of the burning hotel, down the corridors, into the committee room in which Faget could be found; and, finding that the current circumstances required extraordinary measures, he escorted Faget back into the Great Hall, placed a noose about his neck which hung from the fixture of a lustre mounted some forty or fifty feet high in the ceiling, and hoisted him into the air to swing in the cacophonous air high above the floor upon which this notorious felon had once pranced and capered at the service of the people he despised and cheated, and where now the smoke from the fires blackened the fine stucco.

And very soon, he perished.

This example of Faget's come-uppance was repeated in numerous instances during this day, to the end that justice was done.

(And let the pronouncement of this committee be a lesson to those who would divert our tale from its true and proper course.)

36

Don and Is, who had followed Faget as the police officer escorted him into the hall, and who had been unable to avert his death there, now watched his body swing high in the vicious air above them.

—The intention seems here to be that we consider carefully what comes out of our mouths before we open them, said Don. Though this be also our only freedom.

—I will do anything not to be taken care of in such a manner, said Is.

—Fear not, fearful Is-Book. The vengefulness of History, blotted with apparent permanence into the psyche of man, will be undone. The scriptures and all subsequent Law – and built upon it, even the vainglories of literary diversion – shall all be revealed as mere chimeras, though they channel every imagination inexorably. Such are the roots of your primeval fear. For now (which is Always), we should attempt to move away from the crowd, and more especially avoid returning to those dens wherein history appears to be being formed. We are achieving little in observing the destruction of this palace or whatever it is, and I do not fancy our chances in the warren of storyings back there. Do not doubt me, goodly Is-Book: we shall speak our way out of this place, and soon you shall see a great demonstration of power bequeathed to the world by the fillet of my golden tongue. The vengefulness of history shall be undone! But Chance has not come to me yet, and so we must plod on, never seeking, but ready to find nevertheless.

Don and Is pushed through the crowds, stepping over the many corpses, and left the hall. Seeing daylight ahead, they worked their way through the press of bodies between and over the splintered and torn furniture, over the blood-soaked floor; and, finding a recently created exit, they climbed over a large pile of smoking rubble and stood beneath the gaping back wall above Savoy Way. Some twenty five feet above the street they were, standing on the precipice of the collapsing rear wall of the south wing.

(How easy it would be simply to finish them here! But their ending is prepared, though not yet ripe – *read on!*)

Fragments of brick and plaster and glass fell from the jagged structure around them; fine crystal and pottery, objects of silver and gold, dishes of finest French porcelain, handmade fitments of brass, filigreed ornaments – all were falling or else being thrown from the windows above them to smash in the street. The many people *broke the gold and silver vessels into pieces with their axes and threw them into the Thames or the sewers. They tore the golden cloths and silk hangings to pieces and crushed them underfoot; they ground up rings and other jewels inlaid with precious stones in small mortars, so that they could never be used again. And so it was* barbarously *done.*

Our two ignoble recalcitrants climbed through the hole in the wall and managed safely to avail their feet of the street by sliding and clambering down the damaged drainpipes and fire stairs which jutted from the back of the building like the frayed rough hind bristles of some enormous hog. However, this was not the end of their troubles, as we shall soon see – *read on!*

—Well thank God we are out of that building, said Is, which was more like a slaughterhouse than a palace.

—It was becoming less pleasant, I will grant you that, said Don. But we would do well to consider what has been happening here. What we saw occurring in that panelled room – and then what we overheard occurring in one of its neighbouring rooms – was profoundly disturbing. We witnessed, I do believe, the very core of all error.

But before Don could expatiate in his special way on the matter he had mentioned, a crowd gathered around him and his servant, cheering and lifting them again up on to its many shoulders in turn – once more they were recognised for leaders.

Through the ash- and soot-filled air up past where the Savoy continued to collapse, back onto the Strand they were carried, where the mob plotted their next attack. Some said that they should now go to the Temple in order to kill Clerks of the Court and finish off Richard Lyons again; others said that's all well and good, but it'd already been done – twice, in the case of Lyons – so they'd be better off heading straight for Westminster in order to set fire to a house belonging to John Butterwick, under-sheriff of Middlesex, and in order to break open the prison there; a number called for their return to the Inns of Court to seek out all those who could write a writ or letter in order to behead them in the street; others still said that they must go directly to the Tower, where they would murder the Archbishop of Canterbury, the Prior of the Hospital of St John at Clerkenwell, and anyone else who took their fancy. The mob divided and coalesced and divided and grew and turned over itself in a great swarming mass of bodies and intentions. Eventually one stream began a procession back down Fleet Street, then Ludgate Hill, to St Paul's, all the time with Don and Is upon its collective shoulders.

One amongst them moved through the hot crush of bodies to a place close to Don's riding heels, and spoke through a scarf wrapped around his face for the provision of his anonymity:

—I was with you at Tom Harding's place when we torched it, and watched as you took that Fleming's head at Maldon, the nine-foot cast bronze brute, so damn him. There's many of us would go to the ends of the earth.

—Get this simpleton away from me, said Don to his assistant.

—Bloody hell master, said Is. There's mention of that Tom Harding's place again. Who are you?

The man pulled down his scarf for a brief moment to reveal that he was in fact John Thecchere, and thereby that he had in truth been with them at Tom Harding's place.

—Christ, it's one of the Johns, sir! said Is. This is all getting a bit out of hand. How did you know to find us here?

—It is written, said Thecchere with a voice which offered a share of great joyful cunning. You destroyed Tom Harding's place, and decapitated the hateful foreigner at Maldon.

—I've never even decapitated a flower! said Is. Anyway, no matter what you and William Smith say, Tom Harding's place was still standing when we left it. What the hell are you talking about?

—The head of Byrhtnoth lies in the estuary mud, cut from his body by your righteous hand. Death to the Flemings!

Thus was the lynching of the Flemings and Lombards, found in every account of the rising, begun. Word spread through the factions. Where were these Flemings, these Lombards? Who or what were they? Were they a family? A nation? What were they doing here? How dare they! This was our city, our nation. Kill them!

The crowd sought out those whom it would proclaim Flemings and Lombards, howsoever determined. It turned upon itself, flaying skin, removing heads, determining out of necessity demarcations as to creed though there be no clarity to the line. Howsoever should indigeny be determined? Ad hoc was the retort, skull-dealt with a fist-held flint. And the line was proved.

—We didn't do any of this, said Is. And look at what's come of it!

The crowd bristled all around them, many many thousands strong, refining itself in a genocidal frenzy.

—We did neither, and yet the world will have it that we did, said Don. It is in the nature of writing to do this to its objects. I wonder at the audacity of it – where is the evidence?

Just then, as they swept indifferently over the yellow hash at Ludgate Circus, with the curious gulls passing effortlessly overhead, out of the crowd came a young woman carrying a typescript up against her chest to protect it from damage, and which she passed up to Don when she reached him. Don opened the work at the page marked, and occupied for a time his eyes busily in reading.

—It says here that John Preme, a Fleming, was decapitated at Maldon on 10 June 1381.

—What is it? asked Is.

—According to the legend on the spine, said Don flopping the many hundreds of pages shut, it is a PhD thesis by one Andrew Prescott.

—What is a PhD? asked Is.

—It is a thing of no worth, said Don, and need not concern you.

The woman who had brought the thesis to Don then pointed out that there was another bookmark within the volume, and that he should read there also.

—And it says here, said Don, that the outhouses at Tom Harding's place in Manningtree were destroyed by men of Tendring Hundred on 9 June 1381, and that Harding's life was threatened by others and his whole house eventually destroyed in subsequent days.

—This is all too strange, master, said Is. How does it know? Or is it a set-up? What about the statue? Someone must have sawn old Byrhtnoth's head off after you saved that boy from the police, because it certainly wasn't us.

Thecchere beckoned two of his fellow rebels over from within the crowd.

—Oh no, sir, said Is, shying – in a curious inversion – like a horse, though atop the shoulders of his fearless human steed. It's that thug Geoffrey Panyman, and the one that knocked you clean out, William Smith. We're done for now.

—If they so much as think of repeating their attacks on us – not that repetition is either possible or avoidable in True time, which is one eternal instantiation of unique-repeat, impossible for the human mind to imagine – then I will destroy them utterly!

But Smith and Panyman cheered the work of our heroes to see, and when they reached Don and Is's side after making their sinuous course between the many bodies, they embraced our heroes and gave them much adulation to consider.

—You did it! they both said with great joy. No trace of their earlier malice was discernible in the zealous faces they presented before their leaders.

But no sooner had they arrived at our heroes' sides to congratulate them, than their associate and it seemed leader John Thecchere disappeared into the violent throng, indicating that they should follow him further to undertake the destruction of the Inns of Court at the Temple on what he declared was our heroes' behalf.

—This is getting stranger and stranger, said Is.

Just then a paperboy came down the street through the crowd and handed a copy of the Essex County Standard to Is; who, much to his credit as far as his master was concerned, was unable to read at that moment in time, and so passed it straight on to Don, whose reading of it, scoffing, and resistance to the desperate entreaties of his squire to divulge its contents were all as one.

At the conclusion of his reading, Don folded the newspaper, lifted his head, and, smiling down at his squire, spoke:

—It implicates persons answering our description in certain attacks on the property of Flemings and of Tom Harding's place in Maldon.

—Crikey, this writing business is really making sure, isn't it sir, said Is.

—Writing, said Don, as we know all too well, has propounded, propounds, and will continue to propound whatever it likes. But the moveable parts of my throat and mouth would proffer the same of the words they are capable of forming – such will be the nature of our resistance: by speech. Thus might I with ease discredit this body of evidence for our participation in the stories this newspaper contains in four ways which immediately spring to mind: first, the ink of the paper remains wet; or, second, the paper upon which it is printed is not of the type-composition used by that publication in either preceding or subsequent editions; or, third, a dialectological analysis of the quotations within the piece from supposed natives of Maldon throws up gross inconsistencies, and calls the integrity of the journalists into doubt; or, fourth, neither of the journalists responsible for this piece have had a single story published prior to this, by which fact I am led to declare their non-existence.

—Any of these, concluded Don, and an infinite number more I might adduce as proofs against the authenticity of the document, and in doing so invalidate it, thus resisting the lies of writing with the truths of speech.

—But what does this one say, sir? said Is pointing at the story about the Flemings.

—It is a cock and bull story invented for the sake of neatness, portraying us as two men performing such acts in the towns abovementioned as to make it incontrovertibly the case that we did what we are supposed to have done, which they take for a sign that the races of the earth should be locked in ceaseless enmity, for so history ordains it. It would appear that, in spite of the non-existence of race, the story of our adventuring is being used as the justification for numerous attacks on persons not conforming to the Anglo-Saxon way of appearing.

It was true, for in just a few short minutes the rhetoric of nationhood had come utterly to permeate the words and deeds of the mob. The banks of the square mile emptied into the street a more merciless kind of warrior. Impromptu battalions formed around the insignia of the financial institutions. These gangs wound through the streets of the City looting the shops and beating to death all who did not belong. They broke open the pubs for sustenance, and when the pumps ran dry they fought faction against faction. At Aldgate, one column of financiers dragged the Hindu shopkeepers from their sports emporium and beheaded them with machete. From the stock exchange by St Paul's Churchyard, where innumerable minorities sought sanctuary in the crypt, the stockbrokers came up out of the ground like rats from a sewer, broke down the cast-iron railings, settled upon their haunches at the foot of the cathedral, and chewed with sundry implements at the dry wood of the door until it was broken open. These brokers then scuttled down into the crypt and further gnawed at the piers until the floor collapsed. Within the vaulted interior of St Paul's a great holocaust took hold, sucking in and consuming with tongues of fire whomsoever strayed too close to the ragged edges of its belching crypt. The fire grew, feeding off the fat and flesh and hair of the dead and dying people. Marrow boiled within the bones.

All of a sudden from within the crowd Don and Is were accosted by a man holding a burning torch, who spoke into their faces.

—I am Walter atte Keye, and this day I will do right what should have been done before.

—Ah! said Don caring little for the screams of the dying in the ruined cathedral before him. Did I not say that this man would come to us by Chance, and that his coming would signal the turning of our fortunes!

Is could only stare as the conflagration took a deeper hold.

Walter atte Keye dragged Don and his servant down from the crowd's shoulders and away from the fires, east, to Cannon Street, attended by a company of some ninety men who beat anyone who attempted either to join or impede them.

—The whole city will be destroyed if I can get my way with the book which is at the root of its governance, said atte Keye as he swept them onwards. Listen to this.

Here atte Keye took from his pocket a grubby dog-ended piece of paper and read from it.

—"Item, the jurors state that Walter atte Keye, brewer of Wood Street, was one of the principal malefactors in that, together with many other rebels unknown to the jurors, he came to the London Guild Hall (in the parish of St Laurence, Old Jewry) on the Friday after Corpus Christi. Walter criminally and treasonably brought fire with him in order to burn the Guild Hall and a certain book called 'le Jubyle'." So you see (continued he) what the torch in my hand is meant to do. Come, and we shall have a revelle.

Atte Keye and his men hustled our two heroes noisily up Bread Street, smashing all the windows of the offices there; up Milk Street they went, to Aldermanbury, where they beset the gate to the Guildhall with an assault of unparalleled ferocity. Very soon they surged into the main courtyard of the building and took in their surroundings. The brickwork of the yard arranged in neat segments, decorated with diamond shapes.

To the right the art gallery, in proportion and design like a maltings, sequestered within four niches the busts of Wren, Shakespeare, Cromwell and Pepys. Straight before them the Guildhall itself, and at its head the heraldic arms of the city.

—Ah!, said Don. Argent a Cross Gules in the first quarter a Sword – not *the* Sword – in pale point upwards of the last supported by two dragons who sprouted in error out of nowhere for such is the Chinese whispers of History!

—I couldn't have put it better myself, said Is, who in truth hadn't understood a word of what his master had said.

Walter atte Keye led his band of men beneath the stone arch to the heavy oak doors, which they proceeded to break down with axes, sledge-hammers and crow bars. Through the rooms they took their way, slaying whomsoever crossed their path, with atte Keye shouting all the time:

—Le Jubyle! Le Jubyle!

The company entered the old library and tore the drawers from the desks, the doors from the cupboards, the pages from the books, the books from the shelves, the shelves from the walls – nowhere could le Jubyle be found.

—I'll be betting you find this sight nice and picturesque, sir, said Is, pointing with the balls of his eyes and a raising of the brows at the tattered remains of the formerly valuable collection of books.

—Le Jubyle! Le Jubyle! said atte Keye and his men.

In the basement the mob came upon an archive cared for by a huge ventilator which purred like a white panther and filled the room with cool clean dry air. In vain they searched the shelves for le Jubyle to the end that atte Keye took his frustration out on what the room did contain by burning it, and three of his own company perished in the fire before they could ascend the steps to safety.

—Le Jubyle! Le Jubyle!

Walter atte Keye divided the remaining company into four columns and each took a different floor for its arena of destruction. The fire grew beneath them, fuelled by the air pumped down into the basement by the big cat, but still they searched, along every corridor, in every office, along every shelf, in every nook, upon and beneath every desk. They destroyed the glass display cases in a rage against their unsuccess.

—Le Jubyle! Le Jubyle!

Atte Keye's column, with Don and Is, entered the canteen, forced the workers there to serve the rebellion with them, and slew those who would not. Famished by their three day campaign on the behalf of history, the men of atte Keye's company shoved the contents of a multitude of tureens and vats into their mouths, using their cupped hands for spoons, and then made their way onwards. The column of men in the crypt broke the many finely upholstered chairs and overturned the tables, the noise of which swept back and forth over the delicately fluted groins of the roof, which appeared as if the insides of some mythical beast.

Coming into the Great Hall atte Keye and his own column torched the heavy curtains and smashed the many windows under their Gothic arches. A lone guard attempted to prevent further damage, and had both knee caps removed for the privelege. Atte Keye stepped over the writhing and the blood to approach a wood panelled gallery at one end, upon which stood statues of the two warriors Gog and Magog. Neither would tell him where he might find le Jubyle, and so he cut off their limewood heads with one stroke of his machete as if they were papier-mâché.

Walter atte Keye bellowed into the smoke and flame: *Le Jubyle!* and withdrew again the slip of paper from his pocket, reading:

—"Item, the jurors state that Walter atte Keye, brewer of Wood Street, was one of the rebels, etc., and led many other insurgents to the king's Compter in Milk Street on Friday after Corpus Christi. While there, Walter was one of the chief malefactors in breaking into and despoiling the Compter and the chests therein: he was looking for a book concerning the constitutions of the city of London (called 'le Jubyle') in order to burn it if he could find it. Walter did other evil things there and for that reason he later fled. He has no chattels to confiscate."

—This is the King's Computer we already heard about, said Is. So, le Jubyle and the King's Computer *are* familiars. When are you going to let the dog into the bag as to getting this atte Keye lunatic to have some dealings with your chest, because didn't the piece of paper he read say something about the King's Computer and looking in chests?

—Allow Time to run according to its own inner necessity, said Don. Chance is still not yet among us.

—She's a regular Ruth, said Is.

—Let's get us back to Milk Street, said atte Keye with formidable aggression.

They removed themselves from the Great Hall through the library and out on to Basinghall Street where the sirens screamed and the smoke rose between the buildings all across the city. The man Walter atte Keye wrapped again his extinguished torch with a rag soaked in turpentine, and relit it. Down Gresham Street they made their way, past the fire engines which were just then arriving to save the Guildhall. They hustled through the other crowds, running or falling, and turned left down Milk Street, looking all along the tall steel and stone side walls of the offices for the Compter.

Pulling apart the barrier which ran along the length of a gasworks trench, Walter atte Keye jumped down and explored the foot of the gorge within the narrow street. Up and down he travelled, with Don and Is following above, kicking at the clay-rich mud, kicking out the nodules of flint, kicking at the pipes old and new, exploring with his boot the strata of London's unknowable history.

—Here! he said, indicating that Don and Is should join and assist him in digging the trench.

Before Don could decide where his Lady Chance might figure in amongst all of this, Is tripped and the chest he had once more been carrying fell with as much velocity and inertia as gravity could muster for it. Gravity on this occasion was particularly forceful, for the chest, landing upon one end in the bottom of the trench, broke a hole in the earth and fell through to a mysterious cavern beneath.

—If Chance didn't have her dove eye upon me before, she certainly does now! said Don with the utmost excitement.

Grabbing his servant by the arm, he jumped down into the ditch, and from there down through the ragged-edged hole in the mud, taking Is with him.

—Under the ground again! said Is, and the words gave short echo dully round.

Moments later atte Keye joined them with his burning torch, and all three could look around them at the dank and slimy walls and floor of the cave.

Nothing.

Nothing at all.

Only bulbous curves of flint protruding from glistening mud and fine shingle alluvium arranged in subtly shaded strata. The hollow held close the sounds of the three men's living bodies as if in cherishment. Atte Keye began to scrape his hands against the wall, the floor, scraping his big meat fingers through the slime and pebbles looking for whatever might be found.

—Although the hedgehog sow may be promiscuous, said Don. And though she may circle for great time upon the act of judgement, and though she may rebuff the advances of a particular boar by turning her flank and bristling her spines, yet suddenly she may yield. Do you see how Chance has laid down Her defences and now chosen me for Her bridegroom?

—Not in the slightest, said Is.

—Watch and learn, dolt. And let this be a second rebellion against what oppresses us truly: Words.

—There's nothing here at all! said atte Keye into the slime.

—Walter atte Keye, said Don. You seek that hallowed volume le Jubyle; yet you should know that the very act of seeking obliterates Chance, which is my maiden. In truth, that which you seek has found you in spite of yourself. Look within the chest!

Is looked at his master; a barely perceived realisation, like the infinitesimal twitch of a candle in a draughtless room, passed mysteriously through his mind.

Walter atte Keye stood up within the little cavern.

—What's in the chest? he said.

—Open it and you will see. Chance is generous with Her gifts this evening.

Atte Keye righted the chest and lifted back the panelled lid. The many thousands of slips of paper glowed under the smoking torchlight as atte Keye brought his burning rag down.

—I don't understand, he said.

Don pushed his shirt sleeve up like some infernal midwife and plunged his hand deep into the nest of paper. Without so much as a moment's hesitation he closed his thumb and forefinger upon a sheet and withdrew it from the place it had held among its brethren.

—Read this, he then said, handing the piece of paper to Atte Keye.

TRISEPTIMUM: LE JUBYLE

Every writing forges villainy, for it constructs an edifice of value, apparently solid, which may be trained upon a people no less physically than a bomb. Ordinance as ordnance.

Intended as a bulwark against corruption, the Jubilee Book is seen to be an attempt to make the governance of the City of London more equitable, consistent and transparent. And yet, to make men equal: is not nature with its earthquakes, glaciers, rivers, volcanoes eternally intent upon disrupting the flat and level plain? The victuallers——

As Walter atte Keye continued to read by smoking torchlight the document he thought was the Jubilee Book, Don smiled at this new rebellion he was working against writing, and looked down into the open chest at his so-called ratlings, at once loving and hating them in equal measure. While he was doing so, his eye alighted upon one sheet in particular which, even in the smoky gloom of the torch-lit cave, was noticeably different to the others. He plucked it from the mess of paper as if it were a rotting fish and eyed it with the utmost suspicion. As he took in the writing traced on its surface, outrage filled the lineaments of his face.

—What on earth is *this!* he said.

—It's just one of your ratlings, isn't it? said Is.

—How can it be, when this is not my handwriting?

Is looked at Don; Don looked at his Is-Book. Puzzlement, like two trains in the night, crossed darkly between them.

—Read it, and then I'll tell you what it is, said Is. Because if there's one thing I know by now – my mind being full of them – it's the sound of one of your *triseptimums*.

Don lifted the page up so that it was illuminated by atte Keye's torch; and, while the brewer continued to read le Jubyle, he – Don Waswill, scourge of error – read out the sheet which he had found.

Triseptimum Homo Sapiens II: Don Waswill

His skin sallow, his face wizened and carbuncular, his visage by turns clouded and bright, like a blustery day moving over the mudflats. Erect and aloof, his nose beakish and aloft, yet ready to stoop down to the ground and examine with great patient concentration the effects thereupon. This man as self-involved as a planet, and the workings of his gravity equally mysterious. Even were he not clothed in badger pelts, people in the street would still shrink from him. Hewn out of knotty old boles and coggled into great slender lengths, his legs are a foal's. His trunk resembles most closely that of Our Lord Jesus Christ at late afternoon on his deathday, hanging from his tree, not yet having left himself. But this man's hands so beautiful pianists would howl in the night with envy, though the long opaque sepia fingernails which cap them might be taken to indicate certain broadly defined pathologies. The protuberance before his temples at the brow considerable – forming a promontory beneath which his eyes move with very great indifference to the world beyond. His skin resembling leather, complete with the tang of urea used in its tanning. His temperament oblique; his manner with the world cryptic; his wit woebegone; his sense perception synaesthetic; his aspect taciturn. Most bluff when he's bluffing, most cloven when he's cleaving; an irremediable muddle of a man.

Concluding this reading, Don lowered the scrap of paper and looked at his Is-Book.

—You wrote this, he said.

—I did not, said Is.

—Why then are you backing away from me in the very image of guilt? This cave will like to form your grave for such a treason.

—You are frightening me! said Is. There's no other reason. I promise I didn't write it. How could I write it? I can't even read!

—That is a lie, Is-Book. I have seen you read when you have chosen to, and who's to say you can't also write?

—I promise you on the life of my dear Ruth that I never did any writing! said Is with such emphasis that Walter atte Keye's knotty-headed concentration broke for a moment.

—Shut up, you! he said to Is, and then continued reading.

—Well, who or whatever wrote this, continued Don, is a fiend of the greatest magnitude, superordinate of a fiercer hell. And when I find it or them, you'll witness some true violence – how dare writing presume so to delineate me! I am beyond all lines, save that hallowed one.

With these words, Don sank into a profound meditation on who or what had produced the piece of writing which he had found within the sacred grotto of his oak chest, which allows us to rejoin Walter atte Keye, who was just then concluding his reading of Don's *triseptimum* on le Jubyle beneath the fading light of his burning torch.

A copy of the Jubilee Book has recently been found at Trinity College Cambridge amongst the documents of one Sir Thomas Cook, an alderman of the City in the mid- to late-fifteenth century. Yet it is not a copy: morphological variations within the document

444

indicate that it is at least a copy of a copy. More probably the chain does not cease there: the recession through many, many layers, the words copied and copied and copied, modified each time by the demands of a language ever in flux, and brought together like stones thrown over the wall of time, making that very wall, that very time, a caesura for the understanding to composit meaning. To burn a writing is merely to fertilise the time for its re-emergence from some other quarter.

And yet writing, so pleased to propound its preeminence, is insufficient. Contained within the Jubilee Book is the formula for the lord mayor's oath, already copied from an earlier source in a Letter Book of *c.*1320, by which the mayor agrees to treat the people of the City lawfully. It is not enough for the rules of conduct to be written: the mayor must speak his recognition of them. Even writing itself cannot trust writing! Only speech is recognised as a test of virtue. Writing, as writing itself recognises, is a hive of iniquity, busy with the clamourings of the power-seekers.

The Jubilee Book was burned up six centuries ago – and yet, howsoever one may destroy a writing, it is in vain. For writing is as the ribozyme, which self-replicates with such ferocity and efficiency that it is useless to attempt to put an end to its regeneration.

Therefore, Walter atte Keye, you must now burn this book up in perpetuity for the very opposite reason: to give due recognition of its own self-divided state.

At the conclusion of this reading, atte Keye's torch spluttered out, and the cave became almost completely dark. Although perplexed to find his name and the concluding directive within the document, he was still as determined to destroy it as he had been six hundred years before. Don tendered to him his knife and a flint pulled from the moist flank of the cave; and, placing the *triseptimum* which had just been read in amongst the enormous pile of thousands and thousands of scraps of paper within the chest, said:

—Strike sparks from flint and steel by strong percussion: achieve le Jubyle's conflagration. And do not stop even when it is ash, for you must undo what the words have done, through their many generations, burning ash upon ash, the ash of ash, for perpetuity.

—I've been trying to burn the bloody thing for over six hundred years, said atte Keye. So perpetuity doesn't seem so bad now I've got my hands on it.

Walter atte Keye took eagerly the instruments from Don and began chipping sparks over the paper from the face of the flint. Assured that the arsonist's attention was devoted to le Jubyle, master and servant clambered up the wall of the cave and out into the open air of the city, even as a flame took within the general confusion of writings.

—That fanatic won't tire of burning le Jubyle and all my ratlings and the chest containing them for at least long enough for us to rid ourselves of the mob. Without the chest sitting on your back the crowd has lost the primary means of identifying its leader, and so I'd say we're almost free!

These two blots upon what might otherwise have been such a splendid narrative made their way down the street once more, where in the early evening light there came only the sound of a blackbird sitting on one of the bollards singing a benediction to some left crumbs.

Across Cheapside they went, down Bread Street, Watling Street, Cannon Street. All the streets empty; not a single remnant of the disturbances of the day could be found. Not glass; not scraps of food; not paper wrappings and plastic; not discarded shoes; not empty bags; not broken cameras; not old banners and signs; not the songsheets by which the crowd had celebrated itself; not the barriers set up to channel the mob; not the diversion signs for the embattled traffic. They walked through the deserted city streets and looked all around themselves in wonder at the glass and metal and concrete which had been arranged by long labour into such shapes as to thrill the eye and mind.

37

Down Cannon Street our troublesome pair continued, along which the slant of the sun, just at that moment and no other, travelled to perfection, emblazoning the flagstones of the pavement, the stone of the buildings, their glass, the wires, and rails, and clocks, and flagpoles, and steps, and all – everything illuminated in a golden light which astonished the minds of our two heroes as they walked into it. Along Eastcheap and Great Tower Street to Byward Street they came, at the end of which, around the Tower and St Katherine's Dock, was gathered a great crowd which twitched its heads in lost perplexity.

—Is it not sickening to witness in mirrored synecdoche both the individual's and the species' requirement to be led? This crowd is as enervated as a slop of compostables without a symbol and a sign to raise and push behind. Identity, that very modern malady.

—So you think we're free to go? said Is. Where's Chance leading us next, the wanton tease? It'd be a bad day when Ruth and your Chance met one another, I can tell you. We'd be lashed as slaves while they queened it up.

—I would never speak of my Fair Betrothed in such a way, said Don. Perhaps this is what Wife Ruthless meant all along about you not being a man. The man who has one face for his wife and another for the rest of the world is an unsightly smudge on Being.

—I've found it hard enough to have this single face of mine, so don't start telling me I've got another hidden roundabout. But I'd be willing to try and grow another now just to make sure the crowd down there doesn't get us again.

—Chance will dispose of the Present as she sees fit, said Don looking down upon the courtyard of the Tower, and beyond to St Katherine's Dock where tens of thousands stood in fatigue or slept, waiting as a flock for their shepherds.

As if interpreting Don's words as an act of direct provocation – for we won't have the duo outwit us so close to our end for them – a most Chancified gust of wind just then caught the hem of Is's shirt and lifted it right up about his neck and head, obscuring the single face upon the front of it, and revealing instead upon his chest the tattoo which Don had given him in that sylvan nocturnal enclosure a week and more earlier. Immediately our duo was spotted by one, by two, by few, by many, soon by all, and there were sent up cheers and a fine confetti of ribbons and paper into the air. A column was issued to bring Don and Is to their proper place as leaders.

—Your lady Chance is clearly suffering a bout of the gas, because that wind has landed us right back in the shit again. And the tattoo which had moved on to my back in the sewer has now shifted right back on to my front. But then again, is it so bad being popular? I can't say I dislike it.

—That's as may be, my very fine friend, said Don as the crowd surged about them in celebration. But perhaps I am more aware of what will happen to us if the mob carries on till the Revolt's conclusion, and we continue to be taken for their leaders. If you are obstinately committed to remaining unaware of their undertakings, you should be cognizant of their ends: Wat Tyler was stabbed to death by William Walworth, the Mayor of London, at Smithfield; Jack Straw was beheaded following judgement by the court under Lord Justice Robert Tresilian in London; and John Ball, captured in Coventry, was hanged, drawn and quartered at St Albans.

—Well, they can't do all three to you, said Is.

—Perhaps, but it would only take one to finish me off; and as it is only I that have the way with the hyperfine transition of hydrogen, we – that's to say, the whole world – would all be finished.

—That seems about as true as anything else I've ever heard, said Is. But what will happen to me?

—As a participant in the rebellion, you'll likely be hanged, unless you can hide out until the young king's clemency quells the rebarbative bloodlust of his court. Just look around you – is not the mob earning for its leaders just such an end?

Worse by far than the violence and destruction witnessed by our two adventurers at the Temple, Savoy, St Paul's or Guildhall, here at the Tower the mob oriented all its fury solely upon human flesh. A great wordless yowling as to vixens at night ran round the enclosure of St Katherine's, the abutment of Tower Bridge, the tidal defences, the stark concrete geometry of the network of roads, the Tower itself.

A basin of despair presented itself to the senses five.

Employees wearing polo shirts embroidered with the insignia of the Tower, the same as the royal mint, where once it had been, showing the same walls, the same forge heating iron for the smelting of silver and gold as it did the instruments by which flesh might be mortified – these young men and women, Saturday labour, bright-eyed, enthusiasts of the global nexus, whirlwind of culture, the creature with the many eyes; these youths were queued up to the battlements by force and executed, the heads dropping down to smash upon the rockery, yielding up their contents to the sight of the eye, vivid as watermelon. With great efficiency the mob divided the labour of the day: guards kept the victims in single file along the rising line of the battlement; wardens ran through the halls and corridors of the Tower gathering their quarry; a registry assigned identity nominal and titular; executioner's assistants waxed the broad blade bright, dried the willow beam, held the necks down upon the block; undertakers, standing perilously beneath the battlement, first protected the mob from the dropping heads and bodies; and then, these having landed, protected the heads and bodies from the stamping feet of the mob – the corpses and their heads disposed over the river wall to seek one another in the gentle ebb and flow. Such the capacity for human organisation, such its efficiency, even or especially to its own destruction.

—All human law being predicated on vengeance, the Old Law providing the structure of civic life, the New Law merely a salve for private shame, we find ourselves in a difficulty good servant. It is inevitable that the power-holders will seek to punish the purveyors of these deeds with unimaginable ferocity. Those who lead such men – those who instigate such actions – shall be found in desert of the greatest ire. Under the terms of this re-enactment, those leaders are us. You see these heads dropping from the bodies they had twitched like marionettes across the earth? Far worse shall be reserved for us if Chance doesn't turn her loving eye on me.

—But we didn't tell anyone to do anything! said Is.

—It is written down, said Don.

—It seems to me that Chance has spurned you as much as my Ruth has me. We're lost to death.

Very soon, despite the din of the crowd and the bustling and the heat and their being passed from shoulder to shoulder and touched like a relic or deity, all the time with the blood spraying out of the neck holes at the battlement, Don meditated once more upon the spectral line of the hyperfine transition of hydrogen until he and his squire were placed atop the hill at the Tower and the crowd made demands for a speech, subsiding to a hush.

—I have in the dark cave of my mouth, said Don aside to his servant, a tongue which may wag those writings into utter disorder. They call for a speech, and by Twenty-One they'll get it! Although I detest the phrase, I have concocted a scheme which will buy us some time. And let this be a third rebellion against what oppresses us truly: Words.

— TRISEPTIMUM: THE PEASANTS' REVOLT OF 1381: Good people! I welcome you to this, our moment of glory in reclaiming our rights as free citizens of the realm. The events unfold as they must, and all water must flow out to the sea. As the first mover of this rebellion in the goodly county of Essex, I must take responsibility for the events which take place to commemorate the rising of 1381. The most important thing to consider on an occasion like this is that we comport ourselves in a manner most respectful of our forebears, who won our freedom for us. In recent days I have witnessed numerous murders of clerks of the court, of policemen, of lawyers and barristers and judges, and of Europeans and other aliens. Whilst these are regrettable events, it seems they must be carried out, because according to the chronicles they were carried out, and as everyone knows, history is a lesson to be learned by heart. So I congratulate you on discharging these difficult deeds in the name of fidelity to the actions of 1381; the blood now spurting from this parapet is as the most fragrant rose water.

—Which brings me to my point. I look into the coming days with trepidation, for I must lose my life, as will a great number of you. But it is a life worth losing for the purpose of commemorating the struggle of the bondsmen against their serfdom. I will lose it gladly because I lose it with honour. But before that time arrives, the utmost fidelity to the actions of six centuries ago and more must be accorded to our own actions. For this reason, I now bring to your attention the most important discovery of my life.

—I was walking the roads, tracks and fields of Essex with my trusty companion here, who carried my life's work for me, a new *Encyclopaedia*, which I intended to deliver to Oxford for publication. However, I came to realise that my hypothesis was flawed, and I was about to destroy the whole work, which had taken me many years – Twenty-One, to be exact – when I discovered at the back of its final volume loosely enclosed there a fragment of a manuscript I had never before seen. This manuscript was entitled *Tractatus Linearus Hyperfinus Transitorum Hydrogenicus*, a noble and distinguished title. I am unsure how much of the manuscript was missing, but what was absent need not concern us, for what was present was extraordinary: within this scientific treatise, written by some monkish hand in the fens in the early fifteenth century, was interposed a previously unknown narrative of the revolt of 1381. Yes, you may gasp. The chronological discrepancies of the four main chronicles, of which the academy is more than adequately aware, are completely resolved by this account. The writer was not only present at the revolt; he *was* the revolt: the writer is none other than John Ball, the renegade priest.

The crowd fell silent. It was impossible. No. This wasn't the case. Nodes of resistance became apparent within the crowd and threatened to spread.

—A sceptical mind, continued Don, is an energetic mind. I see therefore that the crowd, judging from the sounds its members are making, is a body which stands in no need of a cure. You are in rude health, and I am proud to lead you in this commemoration of the proudest moment of England's past.

—But let me explain my discovery, he continued. If you walk about this City of ours, you will see innumerable representations of men and women of our nation's past: strong military leaders, resolute politicians, altruistic benefactors, the kind-at-heart, artists and writers, doctors and nurses, scientists, engineers, merchants, speculators, businessmen and -women. But you will not see yourselves. Where is the common man and woman? Perhaps at the Cenotaph, you might say. But what is the Cenotaph but a butcher's slab? A bare block for several million sacrificial lambs. Where are the human bodily lineaments of our past – of *our* past? I will tell you: they are in the mind and in the mind only as we wander over the flagstones at Smithfield, for that was where Wat Tyler is said to have been killed. The authorities have not licensed the commemoration of Wat Tyler. And do you know why? Because he never existed!

An excitation occurred within the crowd, flowing at cross currents all through its body in a multitude of intersecting movements, like the windblown surface of a lake. Isolated regions of the crowd, encouraged by a select credulous few, muttered their approval, not really knowing what they were approving of. The more discriminatory members of the crowd remained sceptical. The academics, even now still anxious of propriety, only inwardly jeered.

—John Ball invented Wat Tyler and Jack Straw as a little fiction. It was his bit of fun. In the *Tractatus Hyperfinus* he reveals at the end of his long and peaceful life how a little bit of writing can do a very great deal. We can smell Ball's playful strategy in the name: Wat Tyler. What Tyler? How many tilers were there in medieval England? Which one of them is the leader of this mob? Already, in a letter Ball is said to have written to the commons before the revolt, he is laughing at his trick: *Jon Balle gretyth yow wele alle and doth yowe to understande, he hath rungen youre belle. Nowe ryght and myght, wylle and skylle. God spede every ydele. Nowe is tyme. Lady helpe to Ihesu thi sone, and thi sone to his fadur, to make a gode ende, in the name of the Trinite of that is begunne amen, amen, pur charite, amen.*

—Here we might gather just how real history is. Ball is ringing their bell, and ours: he is playing a trick on the world. The writer's real concern is with *now*: "*Nowe* ryght and myght… *Nowe* is tyme." *Now* is the only time which is. The events Ball apparently triggers with his letters are a joke on writing itself; Ball is laughing at the world for all its preoccupation with truth and history, which is writing.

—I say 'apparently' with good cause, continued Don. For, in the *Tractatus Hyperfinus* Ball admits with a naughty laugh that *none of the events of the rebellion actually happened at all*. Ball was not even a seditious figure, but a bored priest stuck in Colchester with nothing to do to pass the time.

—But what of the chronicles, I hear you ask. How can the Peasants' Revolt not have happened? We have the evidence of the four Chronicles. The answer is simple: John Ball wrote the *Anonimalle*, Walsingham, Knighton and Froissart chronicles for fun, and then stitched them into the manuscripts within which they have been found.

The crowd wavered. Small groups considered the logic of what their leader had said – he was their leader, after all. The academics shook their heads, but still did not give voice to their scorn, for that is a coarse way of disporting oneself. One of the more animated members of the crowd turned and believed, and thereafter his neighbours began to find the idea attractive. What fun! Yes, what a trick! The view spread. Very soon the persuasion became unstoppable; it flooded through the crowd, making all minds consonant, clearing away all the debris of doubt.

—And so, concluded Don, let us celebrate not the events of history but the hoodwinking of six hundred years'-worth of historians! Rise up and give three cheers for John Ball!

By the third cheer, Don and Is were making their way back down Byward Street towards London Bridge.

—Sir, you are a regular magician of speech! said Is.

—As with the treatment of malaria with quinine, I do not think that the effect will last for as long as we'd like. That crowd will be joined by others at Mile End, Highbury and the remnant at the Savoy and further westward, and these will obliterate my story by the sheer weight of numbers.

—So are we going to die, or are we not? said Is as he scuttled along next to his master.

—I think it is fairly true to say that if we cannot escape the mob, we will be murdered at Smithfield for a zealous leadership; and seeing by Her action on your shirt with the wind that that lascivious wench Chance seems to have jumped into bed with he whom she had so disdained, her sworn enemy Order, and now lies there in his steamy embrace without a thought for her hero – O Chance, you are a very strumpet! – we are, as the English have said, though not written, since Time immemorial (though of course strictly speaking all time is immemorial, owing to its eternal non-linear omnipresence), swyvened, or fucked.

—O no, I don't want to die! said Is like a child who does not want to put his shoes on.

—But you shall not die! said Don, raising with glorious gesture of great power a non-existent sword in the air. Not while I am your master: let's move away from the City, across the river to the south, where the mob has already done its work. Though history is said to repeat itself, it will not dare repeat its repeat: we shall make it as the lightning!

They made their way at speed along the peaceful roads south of the Thames: Tooley Street and down to the Borough, where they saw a heap of rubble at the site of the Marshalsea still smoking, though the crowds had now dispersed; west to The Cut, south of Waterloo, through to the south bank at Lambeth Palace Road. Helicopters shuddered heavily overhead and sirens tore through the air from all directions, channelled down the network of streets in a tapestry of sound being continually woven, like a very story.

When they arrived at the palace, they found it had been destroyed. Great piles of rubble smouldered away; and the only standing structures were still shedding enormous chunks of brickwork, as if a vast animal vomiting out its sickness.

38

With nowhere else to go, Don and Is moved past the smouldering palace to the next building.

—This will have to do, said Don, and they entered into the cool interior of a church.

Shutting the heavy studded oak doors behind themselves, Is proceeded to stack chairs and tables up against the entrance as an impediment to entry while his master moved serenely into the centre of the nave. But it was not a church.

—This isn't a church! said Is when he rejoined his master.

—According to the sign upon the wall here, this is indeed no longer a church, but a Museum of Garden History.

—How is that going to protect us? said Is.

—Who said anything about protection? Trust in My Lady Bride, who will come back to me, I am sure.

Don stood in the centre of the church, couched in the still coolness of an air which defied the season and man's brutality beyond its painted windows. He stood and stood, and even Is knew not to speak, because here was a great thing happening, the explosion of the centre, the cruxless view of all matter, the end of the Cross – the Universal Restitution.

Back he came to the human world, yellow eyes aflame with monomaniacal fire.

—This is it, Isaiah, he said.

He took hold of his servant's arm and drew him up to stand upon a pew within the portico to look through the old lumpen glass of a diamond pane in the window. Across the road they looked, to Lambeth Palace as it continued to fall, its ruins scorched and smoking.

—In this old building in which we stand, feeling the conflict of all times thrum through its every stone, I have made my discovery, and it is great. I shall speak as I prophesied at the Savoy, for the knowledge has come upon me; and let the world, or whatever it is that lies all about us, attend:

—At the Tower I spoke to my people. I persuaded them all into dismissal of their precious writings. And yet, even now, that writing is seething in the burrows of their minds, blotting out my finely spoken words, making a bedrock. The truth is that there was no rebellion then, and there is no freedom now. Where is this freedom which we are supposed to have inherited? The people merely commemorate their further subjugation. I will secure them a freedom worthy of memorial, a freedom from the spectre of writing, which is eternal death. We shall do it as an example, as a sign against signs. Our death will be their life. Prepare yourself good servant.

—Here, and now, we stand. Time is as the tidal river, which flows in both directions at once, the saltwater beneath the fresh, though Time take no channel, flowing everywhere, in all directions, eternal. Look through this mean aperture here, through the mists of its lumpen, bubbled glass, at the burning Palace as it falls into the river with a hiss. Observe it: the fineness of its design collapsing to reveal that of which it is made: rubble, matter, dust. Mark well the apertures within: the rooms, the great halls, ornate with refined and decorative plasterwork, going and gone, dispelling merely air, which is all a culture is when it is gone, unrememberable. Down, unto its foundations, penetrating down to what lies beneath, to rot and unmake itself in the estuarine mud, the bricks and tiles crumbling into the raw material for some unimaginable reconstitution however many millenia ahead of us as a new culture, though it be merely an echo of an echo of an echo, without origin or alteration. All the grand buildings: phantasms of permanence. Writing, as this crumbling matter, asserting that permanence, and yet affording so many cracks to the rock hammer of time; by that permanence vulnerable to decay; by materiality brought down to mere matter, devoid of sign.

—Through the power of the hyperfine transition of hydrogen I have entered into communion with eternity, and apprehend thereby the truth of speech, which in its very evanescence finds a permanence protean, heedful of the needs of the human heart. Speech is the eternal golden present! You, Isaiah, have taught me this: we humans, one-by-one, are but a funnel of words. Witness the power of speech, which scorns the limits of reason, of writing, of the divine *logos*, and lives forever. Civilization is death! Death, death, death – signed in writing by the fastidious hand, obdurate as the stone by which the grave plot itself is signed.

—But now I find, beyond the dream of time, death is nothing; yes: death, death, death – is undone! I blast its stones one from another like the lightning. And let this be a fourth rebellion – my greatest yet – against what oppresses us truly: Words, which are no less than death! In repudiation of every death, a mere written thing, thus: Oscar Faget, throw off your noose and speak to us, will you speak into life?

—I will speak into life, said Faget.

—It is a miracle! said Is.

—A miracle is what I have achieved, but only insofar as whatever partakes of the unreasonable – the unwritable – is miraculous. How do you like your voice, M. Faget?

—What has been written of me has sought to destroy me, said Faget. In speech, I am free.

—Such is the nature of writing, said Don, which claims to fill to repletion every cranny of logic, though thereby nooks itself as does a building; and every building must fall. Writing, which aspires to death-lessness, *is* that death by its very nature; and speech, which dies into the air as soon as it is shaken into it by the tongue, is life. Watch, or listen, Isaiah: Faget may cease, but not because of death. There was – there *is* – no death.

—That's the first saying of yours that I've really liked, sir, said Is with an open smile playing across his face.

—It is the whole truth, Isaiah, and you are permitted to revel in the warm and lovely folds of it for as long as you like. I come like a whirlwind among the written words of history to sweep them away as the chaff!

—But how is it possible?, asked Is.

—This is but the beginning, said Don. A warm-up. Now I shall achieve what will be accounted the greatest impossibility. Against time in duration, against space in extension, against the humanist obsession with individuality: come to us, the voices of our very selves, in doubleness.

—Here is your own double, said a second Don.

—I'm speechless, said Is.

—In which case, said a second Is, I'll speak for you: it's a fair achievement.

—I don't believe it, but it's truer than the sun, said Is. What is it that lies between us?

—Nothing, said Don. So insubstantial are the world's entities, that there is nothing preventing their complete interpenetration. Thus is the parabola of a thrown ball immanent in the sinking of a great ship – or simply in a lover's smile.

—Dwelling on that spectral line, said the second Don, seeing neither one side nor another of it, but rather obliterating the very frontier of Time: all has become possible under the auspices of the hyperfine transition of hydrogen.

—I believe it all, said Is. Whatever it might mean.

—The deceased Faget, and even ourselves – I can bring them forth against all the tenets of accepted wisdom in the twinkling of an ear. By this achievement, this true rebellion, have I tested my secret hypothesis into proof. I will tell you something, Isaiah, a thing I now know for a certainty. The hyperfine transition of hydrogen sits within me and dictates my every action – and makes me as a Chrysostom for our times, which are all Time: the man with the golden tongue. In true reality, deep in Time, all people can be called into our present as a speaking voice; all a person need do is listen, with the door open, and the garden beyond, vibrant with birdsong. Likewise, they may vanish upon the instant, as the Present decrees.

He turned, gesturing to the interior of the church, which was empty and resounded with the magnitude of its own silence.

—All I need do is turn, gesture into the interior of the church, which resounds with the magnitude of its own silence: I may cross over into that vortex of words howsoever I choose. But that is not how it is for the many people: for the people living on the crust of the earth, death takes everything. I shall not have it so – I shall have every man, woman and child retrievable like that birdsong tapestrying itself in the rose garden!

Trapped within the cross of the church, its very crossing, the intersection of transepts, nave and choir, walled in flint and ashlar, the many people swarming towards the building from across the city.

—I shall not have it: ensconced we are within the kindly flint walls of this church's crossing, each flint as to an egg, and the gull unflown: the people shall not take us. I cross over into that gyre of infinite iteration as if I were stepping into a paddling pool, such my vision. So hear: as one should never abstain from sowing for fear of the birds, I am going to let the cat out of the bag (there being many a good cock as comes out of a tattered sack), and set it among the pigeons. In short, I am going to tell you something so extraordinary that it will fulfil all four of those proverbs at once. Isaiah, *we are in a book!*

Is stood in dumb silence.

—A book that has been happening all along, and is happening right now, said Don.

—Does a book happen? Is said. Do you mean written – it is writtening right now, is that what you mean?

—I suppose I do. Or being read.

—It's impossible, said Is. How can I be in a book: I can't even read.

—An irrelevance, my good friend Isaiah. But is it any wonder that Chance now finds me repugnant, stuck as I am within the limits of a book, caught within the walls of its two covers like a penned-in hog? We have been storied-along. Each of our many actions, each propounding a youthful vitality alone, has been woven together, their multitude of tributaries become a single insuperable flow within the confines of an ever-more immutable channel, ordaining this, towards our singular end.

—So we are going to die.

—Never so, even were the mob to arrive here at this very moment to break down the door and bear us to Smithfield for our end.

At that very moment there came a great booming reverberation: it was the large studded oak doors, assaulted from without by the mob eager to regain their leaders and bear them to Smithfield for their end. Shouts and songs swelled up in the air once more.

—Ha! said Don.

—I cannot laugh at that, sir. Whoever thought a story could be so cruel!

—Fear not, there shall be a remedy – we'll breach the bastard's banks!

—But I just don't understand being in a story. *In* a story? It's not possible.

—All the signs have been pointing in a single direction all along, but at our expense. It has been a neat little bit of entrapment: to confine the saviour of Being within the very prison he seeks to explode: writing. O sly Storying, a manifest canker! But we've found Him out, and now comes our escape.

—So you think we can?

—Of course, as effortlessly as a dream.

—I do not want to die.

—You will not die. My tongue is already working its way towards a fifth and final rebellion, good Is-Book. Bless you my good squire, and your true scientific method! You have known that spectral line – and how, indeed, as insubstantial as a *spectre* it be – better than anyone! To witness the mechanism of the book in its whirring – that is to dwell upon the Forbidden Line and see sights unseeable.

39

The sounds of human tumult grew from the embankment, the crowds streaming across the bridges to retrieve their leader. More and more of the mob had found them out, and here it was, coming, coming to take them back to Smithfield for the reckoning. Soon there would be nowhere else for the pair to run.

At the Museum of Garden History there came a great thundering reverberation as the head of an axe struck the door; and again; and again. The door now splintering open; the crowd now coming. Their time is up.

—No, said Don. We will have time. We're not ending here. Remember that which you yourself have taught me, Isaiah: only in speech are we free.

—I'll never forget it, sir. It's the wellspring of my life, my comfort, my repast, my everything.

—When we are on the other side of this, the better side, I will kiss your cheeks, my good man.

—I will attempt to look forward to it, sir.

—Now, here's what we shall do: we shall talk.

—O blessed words! I have a free rein.

—The freer the better. Let's talk ourselves out of this. Just say what you are doing. That's it.

Our two heroes—

—Go on, start!

Our two heroes stood—

—Where should I start? For the first time in my life my tongue's all tied up.

—Is this possible? You fill me with despair. Can't you just say what you are seeing?

Our two heroes stood there, transfixed by the terrible sight of—

—Do it! The future is about to happen!

—Don and Is begin walking again through the church. Is needs some new shoes; the ones he has on have holes in the uppers and soles. Don's face is red because he got sunburnt again yesterday. There are many different types of acorn.

—Freer! Unfocus!

—The tiles on the floor of the church are a dull black and dull red; somehow they are hunchbacked, sort of a bit like lots of square tortoises all nestled together, in a strange sort of way. They have come to the cabinet with the shelves. Damn it! Is stubbed his toe; he really hates stubbing his toe. Has anyone ever enjoyed it? There are an infinite number of people in the world, so somewhere there must be someone who enjoys a good stubbing. Funny to think Julius Caesar never ate a potato, it's what my master told me. Now he's looking for a way of getting into the cabinet. Ah, he's found it, by smashing the glass! There are some funny old objects inside.

—You're doing it, by Twenty-One! Keep it up! Don't let the story in on it. Build the loop into it – never stop!

—There are plant pots, and some old watering cans; some oil cans and wicker baskets; a bell jar, earthenware jugs and a lantern. Near the bottom is a small glass domed display case too. Some wizened old mushroom in it or something. I pick it up – or should I say: Is picks it up. It's hideous. What on earth is it? Don picks up the book displayed next to it, and shows Is the title page: *The Vegetable Lamb of Tartary: A Curious Fable of the Cotton Plant*, by Henry Lee, F.L.S., F.G.S., F.Z.S., sometime naturalist of the Brighton Aquarium, and author of 'The Octopus, or the Devil-fish of Fiction and of Fact', 'Sea Monsters Unmasked', 'Sea Fables Explained' etc. But what's that there in the picture?

Like a clap of thunder there suddenly came the death of the oak door, and the mob began thrashing against all the tangled furniture blocking their ingress.

—The Book's breaking back in! Talk it out!

—Right, so there's a picture of a dog or something.

—It's a lamb. It's called the *Planta Tartarica Borometz*.

—And it's growing out the top of a plant. It's ridiculous.

—I don't care how ridiculous it is. The best thing to do, I think, is divert ourselves into this book; I have a feeling it's got something to offer us in the way of escape.

—Sounds good to me, but how are we going to do it?

—Let's start by looking at this picture of the Vegetable-Lamb——

——The book we're in at the moment won't dare cross over into another; it's just one more forbidden line. By this book we'll kill off The Book. I'm going to read it – announce me.

—Okay, here we go: Don Waswill, tireless champion of this and that, sunburnt but still sound of mind, with more energy than you can shake a stick at——

—Keep it brief.

—This Don Waswill picks up the book about vegetables and lambs, and the stew of their magical combination, and begins reading it.

—Chapter I: The Fable and Its Interpretation. Amongst the curious myths of the Middle Ages none were more extravagant and persistent than that of the 'Vegetable Lamb of Tartary,' known also as the 'Scythian Lamb,' and the 'Borametz,' or 'Barometz,' the latter title being derived from a Tartar word signifying 'a lamb.' This 'lamb' was described as being at the same time both a true animal and a living plant. According to some writers this composite 'plant-animal' was the fruit of a tree which sprang from a seed like that of a melon, or gourd; and when the fruit or seed-pod of this tree was fully ripe it burst open and disclosed to view within it a little lamb, perfect in form, and in every way resembling an ordinary lamb naturally born. This remarkable tree was supposed to grow in the territory of 'the Tartars of the East,' formerly called 'Scythia'; and it was said that from the fleece of these 'tree-lambs,' which were of surpassing whiteness, the natives of the country where they were found wove materials for their garments and 'headdress.' In the course of time another version of the story was circulated, in which the lamb was not described as being the fruit of a tree, but as being a living lamb attached by its navel to a short stem rooted in the earth. The stem, or stalk, on which the lamb was thus suspended above the ground was sufficiently flexible to allow the animal to bend downward, and browze on the herbage within its reach. When all the grass within the length of its tether had been consumed the stem withered and the lamb died.

—Doesn't this sound a bit too much like our own trouble?

—The human condition, you mean?

—No, our particular condition here in this church about to get finished off. What I mean is, did the story place the book here, or are we being helped out by your girlfriend?

—I don't think Chance ever had the free rein which you with your golden tongue of speech are now happy to be enjoying. We have been so thoroughly duped I am half-ashamed of myself. The truth, though, is that it doesn't matter whether this book was here by Chance, or if it was written into the here and now, because anything can be made to symbolise anything with the right approach. What we need is a proliferation. We've both said it before: the road of excess leads to the palace of wisdom.

—And I bet the palace of wisdom is a better place than this old church-museum with the door broken down and an infinite number of demons coming through it.

—Don't bring us back to where we are! Let me continue, and I'll get us out of here. This plant-lamb was reported to have bones, blood, and delicate flesh, and to be a favourite food of wolves, though no other carnivorous animal would attack it. La la la. This legend met with almost universal credence from the thirteenth to the seventeenth centuries, la la la. The story of a wonderful plant which bore living lambs for its fruit, and grew in Tartary, seems to have been first brought into public notice in England in the reign of Edward III——

—When was that then?

—Mid-fourteenth century. Ha! This bit will mess the Book up, being before the Peasants' Revolt and in late-Middle English! It's by a man called Sir John Mandeville, who wrote about a place called Caldilhe: there growethe a mener of Fruyt, as though it were Gowrdes: and whan thei ben rype men kutten hem ato, and men fynden with inne a lytylle Best, in Flesche, in Bon and Blode, as though it were a lytylle Lomb with outen Wolle. And Men eten both the Frut and the Best; and that is a great Marveylle.

—The past may not exist, but the words you're reading make it seem so wonderful, I half wish it did.

—Sir John Mandeville appears to have never previously heard of this strange plant, but reports of its existence under various phases may be traced back, as we shall presently see, to a date at least eighteen hundred years earlier than that of his mention of it.

—Let's turn to these others right away.

—This is what I was going to do, Is-Book. But first you may want to look at the pictures, seeing as these are the parts of a book you are most used to looking at.

—That's very kind. I say, it's a strange looking beast isn't it. I am getting a hold with my eyes on the lambiness of it now.

—Now if we flick through, we'll try to find these earlier mentions.

Ah, here's a picture of Adam and Eve in the garden of Eden, with the Vegetable Lamb.

—That's got to be the earliest mention there can possibly be.

—I don't think it would be wise to attribute documentary facticity to an engraving depicting our mythical first parents with a plant-animal.

—But keep going sir. I am desperate to discover what the first mention in words of this Vegetable Lamb fellow is.

—Well, it's all a bit confusing. According to Henry Lee, Herodotus wrote in 445 BC of a wool obtained from plants, and fleeces taken from trees. And a couple of Alexander the Great's captains saw and commented on these plants too. So the Vegetable Lamb is a cotton plant, apparently. It says that Pliny got his descriptions of the cotton plants all wrong: that he described them inaccurately; that he confuses cotton with flax, and thinks silk comes from leaves; and then he invents the gourd as the origin of the material, which went on to form a central part of the myth. Ah, we seem to be coming to some kind of judgement or concluding remark here. I'll read it. In tracing the development of these early and truthful accounts of the cotton-plant into the complete fable of the compound plant-animal, the 'Vegetable Lamb of Scythia,' we shall find it, as in the case of some other myths of the Middle Ages, attributable to two principal causes: one, the misinterpretation of ambiguous or figurative language; two, the similarity of appearance of two actually different and incongruous objects.

—It is a curious fact, which I believe has not hitherto been noticed in connection with this subject, that the Greek word 'μῆλον' (melon), very fitly used by Theophrastus to describe the form and appearance of the unripe cotton-pod, may be equally correctly translated as 'a fruit,' 'an apple,' or 'a sheep': the adjective 'ἐαρινόν,' which is also used, means 'vernal'; therefore the phrase may be regarded as signifying either that the vegetable wool was taken from a 'spring apple' growing upon a tree, or from a 'spring-sheep' (or lamb) growing upon a tree.

—So the Vegetable Lamb of Tartary is actually the Vegetable Vegetable of Tartary?

—The apple is a fruit, Is-Book. But otherwise, yes.

—I can't pretend that I am not disappointed. Because it would be nice to have such a thing as the Vegetable Lamb of Tartary real and in the world with us.

—Well you can temper that disappointment with the realisation that what with the distraction of your wonderful talk and my readings from this very entertaining book, we have escaped the events which were about to occur in the Other Book and its non-church and now find ourselves in the middle of Vauxhall Bridge overlooking the river. See!

—You're right! And just look at the beautiful silver of the river's surface glittering! That old church was not at all my cup of tea.

—Now, if we are to succeed once and for all, we need to move quickly. We are going to be pursued and caught unless we finalise the matter.

—How are we going to do that?

—There is only way to end the Book before It ends us: we shall have to split up.

—This is something that will pain me to do.

—I know, Is-Book. It will pain me too. Against every probability, I have grown to love you.

—You make me very happy, sir. And I am glad to have been able to pull that feeling out of you, especially as how you didn't believe in it. I knew that it would come, and that you would realise.

—I believe in it now, my very dear friend; and I have too much to thank you for: Do not hold your tongue, for it is full of joy.

—Thank you sir. I will lock your words in the interior of my mind and play with them like I would a pocketful of pebbles. But what about the hyperfine transition of hydrogen?

—I am not finished with the hyperfine transition of hydrogen, nor is It with me. How about you?

—Is is as Is does.

The sun dipped down to pick out and fret the rills of the sinuous Thames at their backs with golden fire. Birds arrowed across the sky portentously, from Putney, Richmond, Lambeth, over the river to the Tower and Smithfield.

—Look, Is. Do you see how the Book is after us again, closing the day down and signing with the birds? We must hurry, and this is how we are going to do it: I will walk this way, up to the north bank; you will walk back to the south. While you are walking you must story yourself somewhere else, anywhere, and to another time, anytime at all, and keep storying yourself in speech away from here and now, and build rings within rings within rings, swamping the story of the Book, and keep going through the night and into the day until you're completely spent and there's nothing for it but to lie down in some field or other and sleep. By my reckoning, The Loathsome Book will break, and we'll be free, and I'll see you back under some willow tree or other with your feet dangling off the riverbank.

—I very much hope so, sir. But what will you do to stop the Book? You can't read that Vegetable Lamb book forever; and it'll be dark soon anyway, which is no good for reading at all.

—Ah, good Is, I shall become as the lightning, as the flint, as my own ratlings: I shall destroy the book with its very self. But now: goodbye Is.

—Goodbye my dear master.

And the two men, master and servant, embraced one another with the flames from the Savoy Hotel still raging in the distance, and the lights of the emergency services travelling with efficiency along the Embankment, and the helicopters overhead raking over the surface of the city, and the mob roaring for their leaders, the many thousands of them swarming through the city, seeking and seeking, but not yet finding.

And then they parted.

—You can't beat a good talk for entertainment and to liven up the time. My master, and may he reach safety safely and succeed in all his aims eventually when this blows over, for he's got a mind which wriggles like a termite's nest, though bigger and more various, like one of those lovely stones full of coloured veins, and there's no way even the hyperfine transition of hydrogen will keep him mystified for long – my master, I say, always said I talked more than the wind, but he wasn't so averse to twitching his tongue at matters as they beckoned it of him.

—Inspired by the hyperfine transition of hydrogen, I now seize the Forbidden Line and dwell therein, true within the Time of the Eternal Present, and I speak the words of The Very Book itself in the very order in which they are presented. There shall be formed an ugly loop which destroys the Book – the one remaining ratling which shall cause its self-annihilation no less!

—In fact, the only time he stopped talking was when we had another person join us, like Ringwood or that drunk. The first word I said was not word but words: 'puss-cat', which must have been a showing of promise, but until The Bloody Book got its hands on my eyes I couldn't even read, and probably I won't be able to after me and my master have killed It off. Maybe when I get home I'll open a book and Ruth can start taking me through the letters, if she'll have me.

—I shall loop the Book round on itself, purify its nasty writing in the form of speech, and escape along the stepping stones of the indeterminate ellipsis – between end and beginning I shall sneak out, the very ball of cunning, and find a hidey-hole from the Book, and no matter where or when it looks, it will never find me.

—Each letter carries a sound, and you mix them together like paints to make the words.

—And so, now is my greatest undertaking: to achieve what Menard could never have.

—Which is why they say a picture——

—Here goes:——

—paints a thousand——

—Ahem!——

—words.

T HEN CAME THE RISING OF THE SUN...

EPILOGUE

Then came the rising of the sun, arching up over the saline river-mouth to parch it and the city again. The city which would be calm for a short hour, and then wind up to the pitch of its waking. The Savoy Hotel reduced to rubble, and the implements of the previous night's unrest strewn through the streets.

Coming northwest off Vauxhall Bridge, up through Victoria, past Hyde Park, along the Westway and Western Avenue, the traffic light at this time of the morning, soon the M40 ties a bow with the M25 and moves out into Buckinghamshire and Oxfordshire, up to the Midlands. At a roadside cafe at Hockley Heath, ten miles south of Birmingham, out the back, beaten by the wind and desolate in the abandoned scrubland: the service toilet. The catch flipped from engaged to vacant, the door slowly opened, and out steps – no, but it is not him.

Looping in a great crescent which cradles south London unkindly is the path a pair of feet might take if they had no choice, and if the body they propelled sought to vanish. But the route must end at the river, in the industrial Kentish towns built into and onto the estuarine mud: Erith, Dartford, Greenhithe, Gravesend. The Darent winds down to the Thames between the marshland and the cracked concrete expanses of the industrial estates, and out to edge Crayford Ness. Down at the river, with his feet in the mud, alone and tired and hungry – no, but it is not him.

Back in Colchester, upon the old heath where the broom bushes grow. No. Or, down at the river, which passes beneath the bridges as if a thread to the roads' needles; there: no – Or, at the station, which the sun has cut into stark geometric shapes, a – Or, in the house which he had left three weeks earlier, Ruth and the two children continuing with life, but no, he was not – Or, in the garden with the apple and the pear and the plum tree – no.

Perhaps, previously, when the roads were tracks, and money was in metal what it meant, and the modes of transport were living, there – Or, taking the large core of flint, the knapper shears off with expert impacts exerted upon it the flakes which this man, this almost-man, might use for his hunting; and this man – no ——

Where?

Far, far beyond Pluto, travelling at 27,380mph relative to the sun, out towards Aldeberan, the eye of the Bull in the constellation Taurus, the gold-anodized aluminium plaque on Pioneer 10, measuring objectively with the hyperfine transition of hydrogen the height of the craft it is attached to, measuring objectively the distances between the planets and the sun, measuring objectively the relative position of the sun to the centre of its galaxy and fourteen pulsars, measuring objectively the height of a man and a woman, and there the arm of the man waves not hello but goodbye goodbye goodbye.

Acknowledgements

First and foremost, thank you to Sam Jordison and Eloise Millar at Galley Beggar Press for taking a punt on me, and for their brilliant editorial guidance. Thank you also to Alex Billington for typesetting the book with such care.

Thanks to all those who have read versions of the manuscript at various stages: Anna Battle, Jon Date, Simone Davies, Clare Gillham, Rachael Gilmour, Mark Gregory, Leah Hamilton, Naomi Hamilton, Graham Jenvey, Kate O'Shea, Alex Pheby and Hannah Swain.

Thank you also to all the people who supplied me with information on the many subjects in which Don decides he is an expert. The ones I can remember are: Professor Caroline Barron, Emily Bell, Jonathan Bundock, Emil Dauncey, Jim Fleeting, Nellie Ford, Fil Gierlinski, David Grocott, Jamie Hammond, Jake Murrells, Peter Nicholson, Adam Preece, Tom Purcell, Erica Read and James Wink. I'm grateful for the help I received from Hev Hobden regarding Essex maps. Thank you in particular to Barbara Cooke for a conversation about the Peasants' Revolt one lunchtime.

Thank you to Emma Hammond and Flora Hammond-Saunders for the trip to Bradwell, and – with Daniel Munday – for the shelter from the storm. Thank you to Gillian Garden for having such an excellent name. Thank you to Ben Miller, Steve Clarke and Kiesha Rice for everything; and thank you to Thomas Wilson and Jake Burgess for absolutely nothing.

Thank you, finally, to my family: to my mum and dad for their support over the six years of the writing of this book; and to my two sons Casper and James for their excellent conversation, and of course for the illustrations.

Sources

This book makes use of material from a variety of sources. The following sources, which are still in copyright, require special mention.

Translations of contemporary documents relating to the peasants' revolt are from R. B. Dobson's *The Peasants' Revolt of 1381* (1970, Macmillan), reproduced with the kind permission of Palgrave Macmillan.

Image of the Pioneer Plaque reproduced with permission of NASA.

Image of Prima Europe Tabula (1482), Ptolemaic map of Great Britain reproduced by kind permission of The National Library of Wales.

Image of Matthew Paris' Map of Great Britain © The British Library Board, Cotton Claudius D.iv, f.12v.

Image of a proof of John Speed's map of Essex from 1611/12 reproduced by kind permission of the Syndics of Cambridge University Library.

Quotation from A. A. Smirnova et al's article 'Use of Number by Crows: Investigation by Matching and Oddity Learning' in the *Journal of the Experimental Analysis of Behavior*, volume 73, issue 2, March 2000, pp. 163–176 reproduced by permission of John Wiley and Sons.

GALLEY BEGGAR PRESS

We hope that you've enjoyed *Forbidden Line*. If you'd like to find out more about Paul, along with some of his fellow authors, please do head to www.galleybeggar.co.uk.

There, you will also find information about our subscription scheme, 'Galley Buddies', which is there to ensure we can continue to put out ambitious and unusual books like *Forbidden Line*.

Subscribers to Galley Beggar Press:

- Receive limited black-cover editions (printed in a run of 500) of each of our four next titles.
- Have their names included in a special acknowledgments section at the back of our books.
- Enjoy membership of our monthly digital Singles Club (whereby, once a month, they receive a short story from an emerging writer).

Galley buddies are updated regularly on new writers and future titles. In addition, they are also:

- Sent regular invitations to our launches, talks, and annual summer party.
- Receive a 20% discount code for the purchase of any of our backlist.

Why be a Galley Buddy?

At Galley Beggar Press we don't want to compromise on the excellence of the writing we put out, or the physical quality of our books. We've been lucky enough to have had quite a few successes and prize nominations since we set up, in 2012. Over three-quarters of our authors have gone on to be longlisted, shortlisted, or the winners of over 20 of the world's most prestigious awards.

But publishing for the sake of art and for love is a risky commercial strategy. In order to keep putting out the very best books that we can, and to continue to support new and talented writers, we ourselves need some help. The money we receive from our Galley Buddy subscription scheme is an essential part of keeping us going.

By becoming a Galley Buddy, you help us to launch and foster a new generation of writers.

To join today, head to: http://galleybeggar.co.uk/store/subscriptions/become-friend-galley-beggar-press

Friends of Galley Beggar Press

Galley Beggar Press would like to thank the following individuals, without the generous support of whom our books would not be possible:

Edward Baines
Jaimie Batchan
Alison Bianchi
Edwina Bowen
John Brooke
Stuart Carter
Paul Crick
Alan Crilly
Paul Dettman
Janet Dowling
Gerry Feehily
Lydia Fellgett
Robert Foord
Neil Griffiths
Jack Gwilym Roberts
George Hawthorne
David Hebblethwaite
Jamie Heseltine
Penelope Hewett Brown
Ann Hirst
Sylvia Horner
Alice Jolly
Diana Jordison
Lesley Kissin
Wendy Laister
Sue and Tony Leifer
Jackie Law
Anil Malhotra
Tom Mandall
Adrian Masters
Malachi McIntosh

James Miller
Linda Nathan
Dean Nicholls
Catherine Nicholson
Seb Ohsan-Berthelsen
Liz O'Sullivan
Eliza O'Toole
Radhika Pandit
Emma Pheby
Alex Preston
Polly Randall
Bronwen Rashad
Jack Roberts
Richard Sheehan
Matthew Shenton
Ashley Tame
Ewan Tant
Justine Taylor
Sam Thorp
Anthony Trevelyan
Kate Triggs
Anna Vaught
Stephen Walker
Steve Walsh
Rosita Wilkins
Bianca Winter
Emma Woolerton
Ben Yarde-Buller
Rupert Ziziros
Sara Zo
Carsten Zwaaneveld